CW01655116

BLOODY MARY

After the long anguish of disappointment to bear a child my people did not want! How might I endure that?

I buried my face in my hands; and, in the darkness of my own making, saw my sister's face, the hard eyes, the thin mouth, all a smiling triumph.

Also in Arrow by Hilda Lewis

A Mortal Malice

I Am Mary Tudor

Mary the Queen

BLOODY MARY

Hilda Lewis

Arrow Books

Arrow Books Ltd
3 Fitzroy Square, London W1

An imprint of the Hutchinson Publishing Group

London Melbourne Sydney Auckland
Wellington Johannesburg Cape Town
and agencies throughout the world

First published by Hutchinson & Co (Publishers) Ltd 1974
Arrow edition 1975

© Hilda Lewis 1974

This book is published at a net price and
supplied subject to the Publishers Association
Standard Condition of Sale registered under
the Restrictive Trade Practices Act 1956

Made and printed in Great Britain by
The Anchor Press Ltd and bound by
Wm Brendon & Son Ltd, both of Tiptree, Essex

ISBN 0 09 910830 5

As always, for M.

My grateful thanks, as always, to Alice Clarke of the Nottingham University Library whose specialised knowledge and kindness in obtaining books for me have been of the greatest possible help. My thanks, also, to the librarians of the Nottingham City Library who have shown me so much kindness.

It is strange that with so great a personal reputation for clemency in the midst of a ferocious age, Mary should have come to be regarded as an example of unparalleled cruelty by all subsequent generations. When we remember that, during nearly the whole of Elizabeth's reign, the rack, the thumbscrew and the terrible instrument known as the *Scavenger's Daughter* were never at rest, and that under Mary, contrary to the custom of every court of justice in Europe, torture was seldom applied to an accused person, the unfairness with which she has been treated by historians is unmistakably apparent. Contemporaneous historians such as Holinshed and Stow are guiltless of this injustice.

J. M. Stone *Mary the First*

The root and ground of Mary's character, flawed though it was with faults that her past suffering largely excused, was indeed of a plain and simple goodness. She was a woman to whom God and the world of souls was the reality, to which everything in the life of the visible world must be referred for judgment.

H. F. M. Prescott *Mary Tudor*

Foreword

Looking back over my life, remembering its many sorrows and its few joys, I put down my pen in such happiness as I think no woman ever had before; a happiness that should pay for all. It was Christmas Day in the year of grace fifteen hundred and fifty-five. And grace, to me, indeed! I was wed to my love and looked to bear his child. I think, now, it is all the joy I shall ever know. I am a sick woman with, I think, not long to live. So, if before I have written with extremest care that I depart not from the truth, now I must weigh every word at the particle of a hair's breadth that I go not to Hell-fire.

I came to this throne in the love of my people; so few the years ago! Now there are all too many that execrate my name. Yet I swear before God, there was never a punishment, greatest to least, that I permitted out of spite or hardness of heart. I say *permitted;* but what must a true believer do when the Church commands?

And still I ask myself *What is mercy?* It is a question I have asked myself all my life and am still no nearer my answer. Mercy is not an act; it is not a thing one *does*. It is an attribute of the heart. If I have not spared those my church has told me must be punished for their soul's salvation, still less have I spared myself. I have, as God hears me, sought to guard the soul of this people entrusted into my hand. What I was—the bloody Mary of some, or the merciful Queen of others—men will judge more truly when, all angers spent, I, myself, am but a handful of dust. For myself, I am content that God shall speak His last judgment.

Chapter One

I came, God knows, to this throne, with a heart set upon freedom of worship for all. I had seen enough of martyrdom in my father's time, in my brother's time—tattered rags of flesh hanging from the gallows for no better reason than it was Catholic flesh. I have seen the clean sky black with human burning in the name of heresy, to stink in the nostrils of God.

I desired with all my heart and soul, as always I must desire it, to win my country to salvation. But I wanted no burning of heretics, nor any punishment; only to lead them gently back to God; to save living souls from the everlasting fire. Ever since my hallowing I have kept mercy like a light before me. I put down Jane Grey's rising; under the clear proof of treason I might have rid myself of every heretic that followed her. Yet I was merciful; too merciful my Council said and not with admiration, neither. I broke Wyatt's great rebellion; hatred of my faith and fear of my Spanish marriage had driven him to spill the country's blood in civil war. Again, under that same cloak of treason, I might have rid the land of heretics—and not a voice lifted to blame me. Yet here, also, I was merciful. In those first eighteen months of my hallowing, I bore the name of a merciful prince. Jane Grey's father, pardoned once for treason, raising revolt against me a second time, and even in his own eyes no longer to be pardoned, proclaimed me from the scaffold *the most merciful prince in Christendom*. It is a name, God knows, I have striven to deserve. How few went to their death for treason, heretics all; and how many I might, with justice, have sent, the records also show. For still I thought that, with patience, we should cast out heresy, being assured that God, in His good time, would bring all safe within the fold.

All these months since my crowning, Parliament had been considering how we might bring this people back to God's church; the true church my father and my brother had tried to destroy, punishing the faithful with death, and making of this good country a heretic land. Good Catholics in both Houses had long wanted to bring back the old laws against heretics that we might lead the people back into the Faith; but heretic members, had, naturally enough, opposed it. There had been long argument, long discussion. Now, early in the year of grace fifteen hundred and fifty-five, and I, all gentle with joy at the thought of my coming child, Gardiner my lord bishop of Winchester, my Chancellor and good friend, came to me in some triumph, fierce eyes aglitter above fierce nose.

'Madam, the bill against heretics has been passed at last; the old laws brought back.'

'God be praised!' I cried out. 'Such laws are a fence to keep straying feet upon the right path. This people shall truly be brought back to God.'

'Madam, you understand that the old laws revived must bring with them the old punishments?'

'Why else, my lord, do we make laws?'

He said, and now he was very grave, 'For the obstinate heretic this means death in the fire.'

'No!' I cried out. 'This I have not bargained for. This I do not want. There are other punishments . . .'

'For the obstinate heretic, no other punishment. It follows, a natural consequence. Let the Queen consider how nearly the heretic revolts cost the Queen her crown and her life; how nearly they plunged the country into a bloody civil war; a war that has left behind it bitterness and unrest. And worst of all; had the heretics won, this country and with it many innocent souls had been lost to God!'

I said nothing to that and he went on, 'It is wise to hold the whip, even though one may never use it!'

I looked into that grim face of his and I cried out, 'Who shall hold the whip and never use it?'

'Madam the Queen knew this was to be done and had to be done!' was all he said.

'I did not think it would come as far as this! I thought, given time, the people will, of themselves, come to God.'

'We cannot wait for that! The safety of the Queen's at stake.'

'By God, my lord Chancellor, I am not such a coward!'

'If you do not fear for yourself, Madam, then fear for the country. Nor is it revolt, alone, you must fear. All crimes great and small shelter beneath the heretic faith.'

'There are no bad Catholics?'

'Alas, Madam, only too many! But they do not call God to witness that their crimes are done in His Name. Robbery, murder, rape—all these the Protestants do in the name of their faith. And Protestants they are rightly called; for they protest against everything—they protest against foreigners and especially Spaniards; they protest against the Queen's marriage; and some of them pray for her death!' And he crossed himself. 'If the Queen does not make an end of such men, then she encourages treason and sedition; there will be more innocent lives lost than ever by heretics burning!'

'My lord,' I told him, 'any man that is justly found guilty of treason shall die for treason; and he shall die as the law prescribes—on the scaffold or upon the block. But not in the fire. Never in the fire. Be careful, my lord, lest you entangle heresy with treason!'

He said nothing to that; he bowed very deep and took himself away.

And now I found myself continually reproached by those I esteemed most. Philip my beloved husband, and Renard my good friend, nor, in season and out, did Gardiner spare me word or advice.

'Madam,' Philip reproached me, 'you do not do your duty by God. You countenance heretics. Not only would you spare them the rightful punishment; you keep more than one in your own service.'

'Good men that shall yet come into the Faith!'

'Never deceive yourself! You have that heretic Underhill; he's so bold in his heresy they call him *the hot gospeller*!'

'He showed courage and loyalty in that last rebellion of Wyatt's. He defended Whitehall Palace; he stayed by his post when things were at their worst!'

'*The safest place for heretics is under the Queen's skirts!* he says and proclaims it everywhere. And, by God, he is right! I tell you again, Madam, you scant your duty to God!'

Did Philip truly mean me to burn this brave good fellow?

And Renard. 'Madam, heresy and rebellion go hand-in-hand. Where you find one, you find the other!'

And him I answered as I had answered Gardiner. 'Renard, it will not do! Heretics we punish for heresy—a sin against God; traitors we punish for treason—a crime against the state. Let us not confuse one with the other!'

'This is no time for leniency. It is the time for firmness, for severity, even. The iron heart of the country is melting; strike hard upon the anvil while it is hot. Let not the softened heart harden—or God knows where we shall stand!'

And again Gardiner; again and again. 'Since we have restored the old laws against heresy, you must restore the old punishments also. I have said it before and I shall say it again until the Queen see reason! For heresy and treason go hand-in-hand. Where you find one, you will find the other.

'One wrong-doing does not excuse another! Oh Gardiner, Gardiner. I am weary of this talk! I'll not make heresy a means to punish crime. I, too, have said this before, and shall say it as many times as is needful. We have laws for such things.'

'Madam, must you be so nice in your distinctions?' He shot me a glance beneath his shaggy brows. 'To drag a man's entrails from his still-living body—is that pleasanter than death in the fire; the cleansing fire that may save his soul?'

'The law is the law; it is not for me to judge. But justice I promised to all men at my crowning, and that I shall give. And mercy, also, if I may!'

'Mercy is not justice. It could be . . . injustice.'

'Blessed are the merciful, so we are taught.'

'Then Madam, you shall be blessed in heaven; and sooner, God forbid, than you may wish!'

'Meaning, my lord?'

'It is no riddle. Your Grace is forever pardoning; in those that are pardoned, mercy is apt to turn sour, to breed poison.'

'Traitors have received their due punishment. Northumberland came to his death and Wyatt; Suffolk and Jane Grey—'

He smiled that thin smile of his. 'Even you, Madam, would not avoid that! But Wyatt's lands that should be confiscate, lands you could ill afford to lose, you confirmed to his wife that his son might inherit. . . *because it is a child and blameless,* you said. But will that child grow up to love the Queen? No, Madam, human nature is not so; he will grow up to hate you! And Suffolk. You pardoned him once, leaving him free to work yet further treason, he and his brothers and his sons! Yet those sons you pardoned *because they are young*! And Jane Grey herself, arch-traitor you would have pardoned, save that your Council refused you. Do you think your mercy will satisfy those you pardoned for their father's death, for their sister's death?

'And, Madam, there are countless others. What of Crofts? Of Vaughan? Of Harper? Leaders all in treason, their guilt found; and all walking about free men! They rebelled from hatred of you, your marriage and your faith. Will they love you the more that they have spent some time in prison? Never think it, Madam! The only safe place for such gentry is the gallows!'

He paused. He said, very careful, 'And there is the lady, your sister, Madam Elizabeth. Her guilt is clear. You had her in the Tower and there she should have stayed. But no! Out she must come! Oh yes, you keep her now in custody; a custody so light she feels no pinch, save in her pride. Will she love you the more that you spared her life? Will she not forever remember the Tower and her present restraint? Will she not forget its lightness remembering only the restraint and her pinched pride? Yet even to save the country bloodshed you'd not make an end of her! I tell you, Madam, this mercy of yours will work more ill than ever justice!'

'When justice speaks clear then justice shall be served. Meanwhile, my lord bishop, have a care! For before God, I'll not endure that punishment for crime spill over into punishment for sin—even if the crime be treason. Treason shall not be equated with heresy. Do I make myself clear?'

'Alas, Madam; only too clear! I beg that you talk over this matter with the lord Cardinal, Pole.

My cousin, the Cardinal, had writ me often enough from Rome—where he had fled to escape my father's persecution—to urge the punishment of heretics. Since his return, however, save for an impassioned speech in Parliament to bring the country back to its true faith, he had said little. Being so new-returned, he decided, in his wisdom, to wait yet a little. I had offered him a seat in my Council but this, being a most subtle man, he had refused. 'For, Madam, the people might take it amiss. But though I have no voice in the Council, yet there are ears to listen; and into those ears I shall speak. Though my own tongue be silent, yet my voice shall be heard.'

Now that I sent for him he spoke his mind.

'The Queen is right; and the lord bishop of Winchester is right.' Always he stressed in Gardiner the bishop rather than the Chancellor. 'Burning of the flesh is a hateful thing. But eternal burning of the soul yet more hateful. If by burning the body we save the soul, then it is well-done. But we should assure ourselves that, in our own flesh we, ourselves, should suffer at need.'

'I pray God should give me that strength,' I said.

'Then pray for me, also,' he said, very earnest.

'Gardiner would not have me distinguish between sin and crime; between heresy and treason. And it is not always easy! Could Wyatt? Could Suffolk? Could Jane Grey? Can my sister? Treason and heresy—how often they are entangled! And, if my judges cannot see the issue clear, then there is nothing for it but mercy!'

'You would corrupt the whole tree for one sick branch?'

'The decision does not rest with me. And for that I thank my Saviour. For let those that judge be sure of heresy in a man, and burning must follow—and never a word from me!'

'And for every such burning we must pray for the sinner's salvation!' His thin face wore a look of exaltation; he had the look of a saint. He would, at need, unhesitating, offer his body to the flames; he needed no prayer of mine! But the flame within his soul would, I thought, burn out that frail body without other fire.

We were come into the first days of February; winter was still sharp in the air when the first fire was lit. And he that came to it was John Rogers, Canon of St. Paul's.

Within three days of my accession he had preached against what he called *popery*—a direct attack on me, his Queen. Loyal hands had dragged him from his pulpit and cast him into prison. And there, I had hoped, was an end. The old laws against heresy being at the time in abeyance, I could forgive him his treason. If he made no more mischief I would set him free. But no! Even from prison he must make himself heard. And, the laws against heresy having been brought back, this was a burning matter. Yet the man himself was good, honest and upright. But such good men make more mischief than your bad! Yet, 'Must he burn?' I asked Gardiner. 'For, this is the first to suffer; and, after him, the fires being lit, God knows how many to follow!'

'Had he held his tongue he had saved himself and spared us all much trouble. I like burning no more than yourself, Madam. But no! He must make himself a champion to challenge God from prison!'

'Must not a man testify to his God; and especially if he be a priest?'

'Then he must be prepared to suffer for it! Madam, I see you all-but torn between the strength of your faith and your weakness for mercy. You must not now falter. The man is inspired not of God but of the devil!'

The day Rogers suffered I stayed within doors praying that, at the very last moment of his human time, he might save his soul.

He died very brave, obstinate in his heresy. For he stood washing his hands in the fire as though it were cool water. It was that last, I think, shook me to the heart. I tried to comfort myself that this strength came of the devil; but all I could see was a man welcoming the torments of the fire. That day I shook as with an ague; my hands and my feet dead cold. Nor did it comfort me that his punishment was ordained by the Church; that in every Catholic country heretics must burn. No; nor that in Protestant lands Catholics must go to a cruel death ... *But not here in England! Pitiful Christ, not here, not here!*

Where one leads, others follow. That same month two others went to the fire, simple country priests; had they not spoken aloud there had no fault been found in them. I sent no spies to see the things they did nor yet to listen at the door. But, as my husband forever reminded me, through such priests men lost their souls.

I bowed my head, I said nothing; it was true enough. Yet I wanted no part in such burnings. I was carrying my dearest hope and I was open to tenderness for all. My child was to be born not in April but in May; like many another woman ignorant in this business, I was a little out in my reckoning. In me it was the more excusable since my rhythms have always been irregular. So now there was a whole month more to wait; it was not easy. For this birth all England waited, Spain and her empire waited, my husband and I waited. As a Queen I waited and as a woman I waited, knowing that for this thing alone, my husband had come into England. And if I was open to tenderness, I was also open to fear; for I could not but remember the thing he had hinted, but never yet said. If I were lax about God's business, why should he prosper me in mine?

That same February, Hooper, bishop of Gloucester, went to the stake. That he should suffer overthrew my very soul, leaving me rudderless in the storm of my distress. Conscience tore at me from opposing sides. The punishment was just and right; yet this Hooper was a good, old man that had never failed in loyalty to me. When I stood in danger of both crown and life, he had not waited to see which way the cat jumped. No! But when things were at the worst, he had ridden his see—town and countryside—to bring men in to my cause.

For him I had pleaded with Gardiner, with Bonner my good bishop of London, and with my cousin the Cardinal himself.

'At my most need he stood by my side. Could so good a man corrupt the community?'

One and all made the same answer, brows raised at my ignorance. 'Madam,' the Cardinal spoke for them all. 'You astonish us! The more virtuous a man shall appear, the more gentle, the more loyal, the more, when he turns his face against God, he corrupts the community! For the sake of the community such a man must burn!'

It was a philosophy to which I could make no answer. It was a truth I must recognise. Nor could I presume to argue with him that spoke for the Pope who is the voice of God. But still I could not put from my mind that good old man.

They had taken Hooper to Gloucester that all his flock might see the end of heretics. No-one told me the whole story, lest it disturb my pregnancy; but for all that I heard enough of his courage, his gentle obedience and the courtesy with which he suffered. Enough ... enough! The day he suffered so dire was my vomiting I retched blood so that my physician feared it must cost me my child and my life with it.

They say he went to the stake joyous as a groom to his bride; joyous he may have been, but he limped by reason of age and the chains they had put about him. Even when he knelt to make his last prayer, pardon was laid before him; I, myself, had sent it, very secret to Kingston who had him charge, that, even at the stake, the old man might save himself and so ease me, heart and soul. Yet, even as he knelt in the place of his death, he waved his life away. 'If you love my soul, away with it!' he cried out.

With his own hands he undressed himself and put the bags of gunpowder about his person; but the wind blew it all away; and the wood was green ... and it was a long, slow, bitter death. Yet all the time he prayed in a clear voice *Jesus have mercy upon me*. For nigh on an hour he patiently endured his agony, praying the while. Those that saw him, those that heard him wept ... and not heretics, alone.

'I think this man's faith will light others to their death!' I told the Cardinal. 'I fear that by such deaths we raise up enemies to ourselves.'

'If men are obstinate to die—then they must die!' But for all that his face was grey. 'As for raising up enemies, it is better that every man's hand be against us than that we make an enemy of God.'

The death of this man kept my soul uneasy. I must forever question my secret heart. Did God truly mean this way for His mercy? My church said Yes; and to that voice I must listen. So all through that dreadful month men went to the fire. When I could no longer endure the anguish of my spirit, I sought the Cardinal once more. Once more he put the matter plain.

"I would not dare cause any man such agony save for the saving of his soul. We have no choice in the matter; we do it in the name of God. It is the given death; and all heretics know it. Shall the Queen set herself above God's church?'

'Can we be sure we save a man's soul when we burn his body?'

'We are not sure. If he repent, though it be on his dying breath then his soul is saved. If not, it is good he should burn; he is the infected rag that destroys the community. As for your godly-seeming man, he is the devil's best tool. Especially so if the man be a priest; for he catches his flock in the snare of his very goodness. He is the most subtle, the most deadly of snares. Madam, forgive me; in such matters you are too-little learned. You speak with the voice of your heart—a woman's gentle heart; and that is another snare of the devil. Madam, you must obey the Catholic conscience that speaks with the voice of his Holiness that is the voice of Christ himself. Madam, I warn you. If you do not hearken to that voice then your own soul stands in danger.'

That last I knew well! Catholic conscience speaks with the voice of the Pope; and though my soul fainted, that voice I must obey. But for all that I wept still.

My husband caught me at my tears and was not best-pleased.

'Why do you weep—and with such a passion?' he asked. 'Do you seek to injure our child?'

'God forbid!' And I crossed myself.

'Then *why?*"

I think he knew without my telling. For there was that tightening of the mouth so that the Hapsburg chin stood out large and hard.

'I weep for all men that die a cruel death . . . and some, maybe, in mortal sin."

'A goodly spectacle! The Queen of England weeping for heretics! I tell you, Madam,' and he blazed with sudden fury, 'I came into this heretic country to win it for God and for no other purpose. He has shown His will in the matter by giving us a child. Take care, Madam, you do not offend Him. Take care He does not punish us both for what to me seems much like heresy!'

Heresy! I? He could be cruel this man I held so dear. That God should punish him as well as me; that I might lose my child for speaking—all unknowing—heresy, weakened me so that I caught at his arm lest I fall.

'Forgive me!' I said. 'You are wise and I am foolish. In all things I submit myself to my husband!'

Philip's face did not soften.

'Pray God's forgiveness; submit yourself to your priests and to your church! You have shocked me beyond measure! Had an angel from heaven told me you were capable of such heretical nonsense, I had not believed it. Madam, carry yourself with care and watch your words! For let me warn you! When the Queen slacks in her faith, then her judges, her bishops, even, will slack, also. Though the Queen say no word, yet her face is clear mirror to her mind; her thought is plain to be seen. I tell you, Madam, unless you whip on your own conscience in the matter, the wheels, already running too slow, will grind to a halt. Do you want that? And how shall you answer for it to God? I advise you, Madam, to stay your tears and to pray forgiveness.' And removing my hand from his sleeve he left me without further words.

When he was gone I knelt to Christ's sweet mother, begging intercession for my weakness. 'If such weakness be, indeed, sin, then I sinned unknowing. Let the punishment fall upon me, upon me, alone. Let not its shadow fall upon my husband, upon England; and least of all, upon our child. If I should die in childbirth, so the child live I will accept that punishment with my heart's thanks.' Thereafter I prayed that Philip should return with some word of comfort.

I knelt while the fire in the braziers burnt themselves out, and I rose cold and trembling. But for all my prayers and all my tears, I knew the justice of Philip's reproaches and my soul could find no rest. As for the comfortable word, I did not see him again that day—nor at night, neither.

Chapter Two

All through March the burnings; the terrible burnings. Buds were green, the sky clear and blue, birds sang. But in our towns, and especially in London, buds were blackened, the sky fouled, and the cries of men's agony frightened all the birds save the raven and the crow that waited, hopeful. I sickened at the stink of human flesh; yet I could do nothing, dared do nothing. When my cousin Pole, the Legate-Cardinal, spoke with the voice of the Pope, when my beloved husband commanded and my wise Chancellor directed, what could an ignorant woman do? I was weak in body, troubled in mind, grieved in my soul for the human pain I dared not end.

You may think, perhaps, I make excuses for myself; my only excuse lies in obedience to my church—and that needs no excuses. Lest you think I deceive myself, let me set down what the Venetian ambassador, that loved me not at all, wrote home.

> Her Majesty's face indicates great benignance and clemency which are not denied by her conduct. For although she has many enemies and though so many are by law condemned to death, yet did the executions depend solely on her Majesty's will, not one of them, perhaps, would have been enforced. But deferring to her Council in everything, she, in this matter, has complied with the wishes of others rather than with her own . . .

Did the executions depend solely on her Majesty's will not one of them, perhaps, would have been enforced. That is the plain truth; yet it brings no comfort to my heart.

As my pregnancy advanced the question of my sister became more pressing. I grew yet more unwell. Had I complained of migraines and nausea? Now I must contend with swelling in my limbs so that I must lean upon two sticks, and then not for long, since my crippled hands could not hold them; I could scarcely hold a cup nor even my pen. And all this time the child lay quiet within me so that, at times, I trembled with terror that it lay dead. Then I would feel a movement within me and thank God. Yet so weak I was, so troubled, flesh and spirit, so fearful lest my presumptuous pity had turned God from me, that I forever asked myself the question, *Shall I die in childbirth?* And the yet more terrrible question, *Shall the child die with me?*

Towards the end of March when I could endure my fears no longer I took them to Philip.

'If I should die . . . or if our child should die?'

'Do your duty by God and neither of you shall die!' He said it smiling, but he said it with meaning.

'Why so I do! But if . . . *if*, sweet Christ forfend, what must I do? To declare my sister next in succession would put the country back into heresy. Then the tables would, indeed, be turned, and all true believers come to a traitor's death!'

'Never declare her right. Give her no place at all; there are others with a better right! But never trouble your head in the matter. You'll not die; do not think it! You shall live to bear me many sons!'

'God grant it!'

'Nevertheless, send for her. Madam, I think you should! Parliament forever asks its questions concerning her, and your Council, also. Some there would make much of her, others make an end of her!'

'And if she start again with her mischief?'

'Then she is best under our eyes!' and he smiled as though the thought gave him some pleasure. 'My father warns me through our ambassador—though certainly you need no warning, Madam—that the lady Elizabeth is fixed upon the crown. I doubt, if she have her way, she'll wait much longer!'

'Madam two-face plays it both ways!' I said. 'She attends Mass to please my good Catholics, so I hear from Bedingfield that has her in charge; but her secret words go out to the heretics to protest otherwise.'

'Aye, Madam; all that and more! Our ambassador tells me she withdraws every day for several hours on the pretence of praying. But praying! Plotting's the word! Certainly she is better beneath our eyes. And I, myself,' and he smiled again, 'am curious to set eyes upon this bewitching person.'

It was then I felt again the sharp prick of jealousy. My face is forever a tell-tale, for he laughed aloud. 'Be easy, my good wife, she'll not bewitch me!'

We were still talking when that same ambassador, Renard, craved audience, and in he came with a letter he was even then sending to the Emperor. There was, it seemed, a new plot to make an end of me, to drive away the King, and to set Courtenay—last sprig of the Plantagenet and proven traitor—with my sister in our place.

'Sir and Madam, may I read my letter?' And we being all agog to hear, he read aloud,

> . . . Courtenay is to be King under the name of Edward. The plan is to set the lady Elizabeth free and to marry her to Courtenay. Also to publish that the Queen is not with child but that there is a plan, instead, to pass off another child as her own. The purpose is to stir revolt among the people, arms in hand . . .

The Queen is not with child. My heart went sick. She had an uncanny knack of being right, this terrible sister of mine. But—*to pass off another child as her own!* That was a piece of wickedness she alone was capable of devising.

'Madam Elizabeth is not as clever as she thinks!' Renard said. 'Does she pretend to know more than the physicians? And even if what she says prove true—that, God forfend, there be no child—no-one would believe such crookedness of the Queen! Never a woman more honest in word and deed; and that all Christendom knows full well! If she be not careful, Madam Elizabeth will catch herself on the hook of her own crookedness.'

'That the Queen carries her child, all England knows; that she shall, by God's grace, carry the matter to a good end, we believe,' Philip said. Nor does the linking of those two names trouble me; Courtenay lies in a safe place, beneath lock and key. No! But I am concerned and much concerned with the threat of revolt in arms!'

He paced the room brows knit.

'Madam Elizabeth shall come to court at once!' he said. 'And she shall stay for the birth of the child; that is her duty! So she shall herself prove the lie to her own mischief. Then we shall marry her off to my good friend Philibert; and so out of the country with her!'

'It will not do, and so I have said before!' I told him. 'She will never consent. Besides—bring her to London! What wisdom is that? Londoners long for the sight of her. It could be tinder to revolt!'

He laughed at that. 'Have her here and marry her off; it is the clearest wisdom. Her obedience you may leave to me. As for the Londoners—' he snapped his fingers.

'On this matter,' I said, 'I speak once and for all. My sister shall come for the birth; that is custom and her right; but I will not have her before that time. If she work treason, wherever she may be, she shall die. But—' and now I spoke surprising myself as much as them, 'force her into marriage, I will not. I know now what marriage may mean; how it may be either sacrilege, or sacrament. I chose my own lord—' and I took him by the hand; he let my hand lie in his and gave no sign of pleasure, nor even that he knew it was there.

'*She* is not free to choose,' he said. 'Suppose she choose . . . Courtenay?'

'Then she cannot have him; nor any other, save by our leave. But this freedom she shall have—to reject where she cannot love.'

April had come in; and, following the custom of the Queens of England, I must go into retirement for a month before giving birth. So down the river to Hampton Court we went, all of us very cheerful, though etiquette allowed me to see little of the sweet of the year, save what might be glimpsed through the closed curtains of the awning.

As the barge took its slow way I clasped both hands upon my belly to protect my child from any sudden movement of the boat; and all the time I thought, *When I return I shall hold him in my arms. He shall see, for the first time, this noble river, its ships and its wharves, its palaces and its Bridge, and my great fortress the Tower. He will not know what it is he sees but it will be sealed forever upon his heart.*

With me in the barge and in those following, were my own ladies and women, together with a host of noble dames come from every part of the country to bear me company and to be present—as many as the chamber would hold—at the birth. I had done better without these strangers that were noisy, and must prove an expense I could ill-afford. But this, too, was ancient privilege and Philip would have me offend against no old custom. For myself, I needed none but my own ladies, and especially old Clarencieux with her woman's wisdom and Jane Dormer with her young kindliness. With me, also, went my good physicians, my midwives and those that should rock the cradle.

My first few days at Hampton Court were pleasant enough. I would walk abroad in the early morning hours when mist from the river obscured the sharp shape of everything—including my own. Later in the day I would look from my window upon the water and the people; they would wave their greetings and I would wave back. The imminence of my labour seemed to bring me once more close to them; and that soon I should give them the longed-for prince was a great sweetener, all sourness was for the time forgotten.

There in that pleasant place I would try to forget that, in places less pleasant, men came to their fearful death. But forget I could not; the stench of burning seemed to pollute the sweet air, to follow me wheresoever I might go.

'It is but the fancy of a lady near her time,' old Clarencieux, governess of my ladies, said; and to her I must listen for she was wise in such matters. And so said the little Dormer, youngest of my ladies, that could have no such wisdom. So I would walk, arms clasped about my child exorcising black thoughts with sweet ones. *This is my child; mine and Philip's. And it is England's child. But most of all it is God's child to keep firm the Faith in the land.* And I thought, *This is the most important child in Christendom.* That grace to bear this child should be given to me, Mary Tudor, once despised, rejected and threatened, filled me with awe.Hands upon my belly, I thanked God that had vouched this blessing upon me and upon us all.

In my own apartments and in the child's, all was ready. There stood the cradle, delicately carved and inlaid with silver, that had been my own; there stood the chest holding the swaddling-bands and folded above them the christening-shawl my mother had brought from Spain. It had been used once only, for the little son that had breathed but a few days and died. It had not been allowed me, at my own christening. I was a girl-child; the shawl was for the boy only—the King's son. Anne Bullen, brought to bed of Elizabeth, determined to proclaim her child equal to any prince—and better than myself—had demanded it for the christening of her child. My mother had refused. It had not been allowed to me, my father's true-born child, it should not be allowed the new-born bastard.

Now my child, boy or girl, should wear it. *My child.* And, so thinking, I remembered myself, an unhappy girl of seventeen, heart-broken for a dear mother set aside, forced by old custom, as heir-apparent, to witness the birth of the child that should take from me the crown. And I remembered how I had prayed, Anne Bullen the while in labour, that they might die, mother and child, both. I did not want my sister ill-wishing me now as I had ill-wished her mother. I could not endure those black eyes upon me in my pains; eyes that could be so spiteful and so hard.

I would not send for her.

My Chancellor came to me where I sat secluded in my closet. 'Madam, it is time to send for Madam Elizabeth.'

'No!' I told him, 'I'll not have her!'

'Madam you have no choice. She is the heir-apparent—It is her right!'

'It is not her right. She is not heir-apparent; she has not been named.'

'It will not do, Madam. All England looks to her at present.'

'Soon it will look in another direction!'

And seeing me still obdurate, he said, 'It is for the Queen's own protection. Your sister, or her friends, have been busy! They say—Madam forgive me, that I repeat so vile a nonsense—that the Queen is . . . barren. They have spread the tale far and wide that a new-born babe shall be smuggled into the Queen's lying-in chamber and proclaimed the royal heir!'

'So I have heard.' I spoke quiet enough; but anger caused the child to leap within me. I calmed it, hands upon my belly.

'Is my sister, then, fit person to be with me at such a time? And since, already, she lies so wickedly, shall she keep her tongue from further lying? I will not have her!'

Philip followed him with what was less a request than a command. 'I will have every English custom observed when my son is born!'

He was right and I was wrong; and I obeyed him. But I wonder now, whether even then, he was weighing the chance that I might die and how he might stand then with my sister. This thought comes to me now; but then my trust in him was deep as my love.

Towards the end of April, my lying-in set for May, I dared hesitate no longer. I sent for my sister. She came under strong guard, commanded by Bedingfield. Once beneath my roof I neither sent for her nor enquired of her; but I had constant news concerning her. *Madam, she looks pale . . . she looks sad but proud . . . wherever she passed, on her way folk stood to bless her, to hasten with gifts . . . Madam, she smiled upon the people as she came hither, and they wept to see her pale and sad; and most of all they wept to see her close-guarded.* They blamed me, it seemed, that I showed myself unkind; but of her unkindness, her treason, they did not know.

For a full fortnight I would not see her. Once she had scratched upon a window in the Tower, defying us all,

Much suspected of me,
Little proved can be,
Quoth Elizabeth, prisoner.

And it was true; true. She sent humbly asking that I would receive her. I refused, lest I fall into one of my father's rages and thus endanger my child. Anne Bullen's rages had cost her her son; did my sister know that? Did she hope for a like result with me? And as much as I feared my rages, so I feared my mildness. I have a see-sawing in my nature that lifts me now high, in the next moment to cast me down. I feared that, let me see her again and I would take her, if not into my heart once more, then into my trust.

During this time my Chancellor had waited upon her, together with others of my Council, all, all urging her to submit, to make confession of her fault. They went away, a flea in their ear and always the same answer.

'Submit? To what? I am firm in the true faith. Confess? To what? I have done no ill. Would you have me admit guilt that am innocent? That I'll never do! If you believe my guilt, why did you not charge me? I was in the Tower long enough! If you still believe it, why not charge me now? If I am tried and my guilt found, I'll ask no mercy nor yet accept none. Why have I not been tried? Because, sirs, if you could find aught against me, it would have been found. No, you cannot do it; and not for want of trying.'

'Nor, Madam,' Gardiner reported, 'can she be, any way moved. No! Not though her own cousin the Lord William Howard himself besought her. On the contrary! Madam, she had us all on our knees asking pardon for the wrong we do her.'

'*You*, Gardiner?'

He bowed his head. 'To my shame! There, in her presence, I knelt with the others; it was as though she cast a spell. As soon as I left the room my wits returned. I knew, always, she was a danger; but how great a danger I did not know. Well, I see it now! Though she stand alone with neither friend nor any man's arms to her defence—and that is far from the case—she carries that within her to set the whole land afire.'

Proud; defying them alone. What had she, this girl, that made Gardiner, himself, that deeply distrusted her, that had so often urged her death, kneel to ask her pardon *for the wrong you have suffered and your long imprisonment*. That spirit within her was less a fire than a crystalline rock against which lesser spirits broke.

And now came my husband to trouble me again on her account. He spoke no word in her favour, calling her a sly piece that should be whipped—or slipped—out of the country. But, I noted, he spoke no more of his friend Philibert for whom he had destined her that she might be shipped out of the country. Nor did he stint to comment on my own behaviour. 'Madam, you sent for your sister and owe her some courtesy on that account. Yet you make no move towards her; it is manners unfitting in a Queen. But, more than that—it is a danger! The whole court talks; and what the court says today, London says tomorrow, and thereafter all England. Such treatment turns hearts from you; from you to her. Madam, you must mend your behaviour!' And I, refusing, he said, 'Then with your permission I will myself repair your discourtesy.'

'You are the King!' I said; that and no more. His interest was I thought more curiosity than courtesy and I could not blame him. Already my sister was becoming a living legend.

It was Renard who pointed out to me that it was less curiosity on Philip's part than expediency.

'For, Madam, should the untoward happen to the Queen,' and I knew he meant my death in childbed, 'then the King's death might follow!'

And, while I stared, he said, 'He is a stranger in this country where no stranger is loved. Many of his followers have returned home. How should he stand then? An accident? A mistake by a rabble? Some false charge of treason . . .'

'Treason! But he is the *King*!'

'He would be King no longer. Upon your sister's goodwill his very life could depend. Is he not right to cultivate that goodwill?'

'To make hay while the sun shines! That is a saying of ours, Mr. Ambassador. Well, since you put it so; there's nothing for it but consent. I'd not risk to have a hair of his head hurt.'

My husband and sister must meet. I fixed time and place; and sent to command my sister to attire herself fittingly to do him honour. For she was one to seize upon a moment to make the most of it. She would, if she chose, meet him in a shabby gown to show the cruelty of her situation; equally she might dress as for a state occasion to flatter him and startle him with her magnificence. But—fool that I was to warn her of his coming!—she did neither. For she appeared all virginal in green-and-white—our Tudor colours—reminding him without any word that she was the daughter of my father's house; and the flame of her hair, free-flowing as is proper to a maid, spoke yet more clear of untouched virginity. If women might act upon the stage what an actor is lost there!

It was then, I think, the mischief was done. If ever he had thought to use her for his own ends, he had taken too little account of her person. Now the fire of her youth against my fading looks confirmed my deepest fear, although I did not know it then. Looking back, making my addition of this word and that, I see how strongly he was attracted; what she thought of him, or does think, I know not. She is one to keep her own counsel.

My husband declared my sister a commonplace piece; it was a defence in him. Her spell was upon him, upon him too; my wise Philip is but a man! Now he gave me no peace. I must, myself, see her; for my own sake stop the tongues that spoke of her innocence and my unkindness. *I will not see her, I will not!* So I tormented myself, walking my closet, big with child; knowing full well that, let me refuse her now, see her I must when my pains began.

In the first week of May I looked from my window upon a world of green-and-white—colours of hope, my own Tudor colours. Today I would see her; on this day of hope, I would delay no longer. But the early summer day wore my sister's colours, also; for her, too, it might signify hope. So from hour to hour I put off the evil moment. It was ten of the clock, and the dark fallen, when I sent for her. Awaiting her coming I felt my own heart sicken as though I were the prisoner at fault and she, the Queen. Yet, receiving my summons she had shown herself much afraid. Clarencieux that had taken my message told me so.

'The summons was so unexpected and so late; Madam, she feared it was for her death; no doubt she knows what she deserves! *The Tower!*

The Tower! And this time my death! she cried out and would have fallen but that one of her women caught her, each side. She took her Farewell of those about her as though for the last time; then she held out her hand to Bedingfield saying *Gentle gaoler I am ready!* But even then she stood in the doorway looking about her as if she would never see this place again. And *Pray for me!* weeping she besought them; and again, *Pray for me!*

She came, torches flaring about her in the dark night. Bedingfield holding her by the arm lest she fall; at her back, and before her, went men-at-arms. She passed through the dew-wet gardens and stood for a moment, Clarencieux said, as though she looked her last upon the world.

I was in my bedchamber when she came in. For nigh on two years we two had not set eyes upon each other. She had ripened, showing a sweet bosom where before she had been flat as a boy. Her face had sharpened a little; she looked less handsome, but she had lost none of her splendour. Whatever she thought, whatever she felt, there was no sign of fear in her. The black eyes were inscrutable, the red hair a flame upon her shoulders.

She came, with that fine grace of hers, to kneel where I stood thickset in pregnancy and obstinate in anger.

She said, 'Madam, I beseech God's Grace to preserve the Queen's life!'

'Do you, indeed? You show a fine way to preserve it!'

'Before God,' she said, 'I am innocent of all offence against the Queen. I beseech you, believe it! My truth, my loyalty, my love are to the Queen's Majesty. So they have ever been and so shall they ever. I am your most obedient, humble, loving sister and servant.'

'So still you do not confess your guilt!' My voice came out harsh and rough as when I am moved and must not show it.

'How shall I confess? And what? I have committed no fault against the Queen's grace. I have nothing to confess but a loyal heart.'

'Pray God you speak true!'

'If I do not, I look neither for favour nor pardon at your hands; no, nor at God's hand, neither!'

There was innocence in her lifted face, there was a pride about her, too, kneeling there, and both pricked me with anger knowing what I did; knowing about those letters in de Noailles' post-bag, those letters written in cypher. Knowing; but not proving! Knowing, too, the danger her very living held for me and that, save for my own foolishness, she'd not be here to trouble me more.

'You stand very strait upon your innocence,' I said. 'No doubt you think yourself wrongfully punished.'

'I must not say so!' And I noticed the quickness with which she answered, and the cleverness, neither acknowledging guilt nor accusing me of injustice.

'But no doubt you will tell others so!' And already I had lost the battle, my slow wits against hers.

'No!' she said. 'I would never complain against the Queen's Majesty. I have borne the burden and, so long as it please the Queen, will bear it, humbly. Yet I do, most humbly, beseech your good opinion that am forever—as I have been and shall forever be while life is in me—the Queen's most loyal, loving subject.'

Innocent she might look kneeling there, white face lifted but the eyes! Anne Bullen's eyes. Yet, for all that, she was the child I had loved, once, with all a mother's care. The child that had gone lacking caps and kerchiefs, petticoats and shifts—a lack I had made good from my own scant store. I remembered how we had cut and sewed, her nurse and I, she standing lifting her thin child's arm to be fitted, the little red head tossed backwards, impatient to be gone.

It was a memory to overcome me; a child is the surest way to my heart. My breath came out on a sigh, knowing my own foolishness, 'Innocent or guilty—it is forgiven. You are my sister and we have been too long apart; not only in place but in our hearts. Here is your ring again.' I took it from my finger and held it out. 'It is a token between you and me. Once you sent it to me in vain; it shall not be so again. Whatever the fault I shall stand by you. It is a promise. Now let us be loving, one to the other, as sisters should.'

Still kneeling she took the ring; she put it to her lips and then upon her finger. 'God reward you, sister,' she said, and even in that solemn moment I caught the gleam of triumph in her eyes; clever she was but not clever enough to hide that. She kissed my hand and curtseyed herself to the door, leaving me to wonder whether I were a fool or no.

There was a rustle of curtains about my bed. Philip stood in the ruelle.

'Excellent, well done!' He rewarded me with a smile, unconcerned that he had come, uninvited, to listen, by my secret stairway; it was the Spanish way and natural to him as breathing. 'There goes a clever piece! We'll marry her off as soon as may be. Till then she's worth the watching!'

She's worth the watching. What did he mean by that? His careful, foreign English could, I thought, admit of no double meaning. He meant exactly what he said. But did he? He was subtle enough to pick upon an innuendo. I was not re-assured; he stood there smiling. My sister, it was clear, had pleased him well.

Chapter Three

My husband thought that, forgiving my sister, I had done well; he praised my wise and generous spirit. My Chancellor thought otherwise.

'Madam!' And the fierce eyes set too close aside that great beak of his, flashed. 'How long will you put your crown and your person in danger? Madam Elizabeth must stay to wait upon the birth of the Prince; but you should never have taken her hand much less given her a token of good faith. For the faith is all on your side. Madam, how shall I make you believe it?' And he cracked his bony hands together. 'Madam, read this!' He drew a paper from his pouch and thrust it before my eyes. 'It is from the post-bag of Michiel!'

'You rifle the post-bags of our friends?'

'The Venetian Ambassador is scarce a friend! At best a neutral; and even that I doubt! But, Madam, I rifle the post-bags of friend, enemy or neutral to serve the Queen!' He spoke quick and angry. He had a frail look these days, anger seemed to burn him to a shell.

I took the letter over to the window holding it close to my eyes that I might see it better. It was a long letter; and, while I peered upon the words, 'Here, Madam, here!' He came over to me and tapped with his forefinger upon the paper. 'See what he says! And, what he says is no news to me—nor to many another, neither!'

> . . . the lady Elizabeth will certainly be at the court with their majesties. She will not depart until after the Queen's delivery . . .

'For that reason she is come!' I said. 'There's no news in this!'

'Read on, Madam!'

> . . . it being supposed that, in case of the Queen's death the King's safety would depend more upon her than upon any other person . . .

'This is mere supposition!' I told him. 'I do not intend to die; but if God choose otherwise, then the King's safety is assured not through her but by Parliament. He is to have protection and honour so long as it pleases him to stay. Parliament has appointed him guardian of the child and Regent of this land. Do you forget, my lord Chancellor?'

'I forget nothing. But, Madam, forgive me! Those that cherish you most, must consider every possibility however unlikely. Women . . .' he spoke slow and careful, 'have been known to die in childbirth and the child with them. Madam, read on.'

I read on. It was very clear. My husband, it declared, had more in mind than friendship with my sister; he meant to put her in his bed. And with high hopes, too,

> . . . of being able, with the favour of the great men here, whom he has already won with rewards, to succeed to the Kingdom by making a second marriage with her. It is not impossible that she herself may incline that way . . .

A second marriage with her.... Jealousy bit deep. *She herself might incline that way!* I felt jealousy like a poison course through all my blood. Of course she would incline! Let her protest never so loud she'd no mind for marriage, she'd change that mind soon enough, given the chance of Philip. Not only the man, himself—and she had an eye for a pretty man; but a man gilded with all Philip's wealth, hung about with all his honours and titles. I had never trusted her; and how rightly! How rightly! But Philip. Philip whose child I carried? Him I did trust. He'd have no thought of any other woman so long as I lived; he was virtuous, he was chaste. And if I died, which God forfend, he'd not take my sister to wife though she came bearing the crown in both hands. Let the arguments be never so subtle; let the Emperor command and the Pope himself, consent, still Philip would have none of it. It was against God's law and God would stay him. How should he forget they had accused my mother of incestuous marriage; for though she had come to my father a virgin, she had first been wed to his dead brother. What then would they say of Philip that had got me with child and then lay with my sister! Though she show herself willing enough he would not consent; not he, ever!

All these thoughts came battering upon me, head and heart, while I stood sick with jealousy and fear; yes, in spite of my own reasoning—fear.

'No!' I told Gardiner. 'No!' But my voice came out in a whisper as though I did not believe my own protest.

'Yes, Madam!' he cried out. 'Yes! She's a schemer. Rid yourself of her! I have said it before and I'll say it again and yet again! I'll not cease till she or I be dead! But, before God, I have not much time to speak!'

He looked so frail standing there, all shaken with his anger; he looked so *old*! And he had served me if not with love—for who can talk of love in such a man?—then with utmost faithfulness. My heart went out to him in pity.

'You shall live to plague us all this long while yet!' and I smiled, making a jest of the matter. 'As for my sister, you may spare yourself distress on her account. The King means she shall marry Savoy; he means to send her from this country.'

'And if she refuse? Shall you force her?'

'No. Forced marriage is abomination to me; we shall find some other groom and so be rid of her. As for the King—were I to die, which is, God willing, not likely—he would never have her. He respects God's law. And, besides, he does not like her. She carries herself too forward for a woman, he says; forward and froward. He'd not take her though she knelt to offer the crown!' And I sought to reassure not him alone but myself, myself, also.

He said nothing. He gave me one of his long, fierce looks; and yet I thought there was pity in it ... or maybe my own fears imagined it.

I said, to keep a stout heart in us both, 'Well it is all a fantasy and not worth repeating. I am with child and I am well! So let us talk no more of dying! I am not so young as some women, nor yet so old as others; I shall do well enough! There was a woman older than myself by some years, brought me this last week, she and her babes with her! Three at a birth. And all of them in good health and merry! Well, one prince at a time will satisfy me. And with God's good help I mean to go about that business for many a year!'

'God grant it!' He knelt and set his old, dry lips to my hand.

But for all my brave words I was troubled. Who could trust my sister with any comely man? Seven years ago rumour had gone about that she was with child by Seymour—and she but fifteen; and the man himself wed to our stepmother, her friend and benefactor. The rumour had not been true; but what does the scandal imply? Philip might dislike her, but in women's ways he was innocent; or so

I believed. His wits were excellent; but when it came to love-play between men and women he could not match her.

Troubled I was; yet I could do nothing in the matter lest I lay myself open to charges of unreason common to women in my condition. For some days I kept her by me, abating none of her dignities, giving her always first place after the King and myself. But I watched them both. To me he appeared no more courteous than should be; nor, for all my watching, could I call her behaviour forward. She was all innocence, all quick obedience, all goodwill . . . and still Philip talked no more of sending her from the country; nor was the name of Philibert even mentioned. I did not want her by me; yet have her I must until my child was born. As soon as I might, I should send her away.

And now seeing her enlarged and nothing proved against her, Gardiner besought me for his beloved *son*, Courtenay that had played equal part with her in treason. And since justice is justice, what could I do but enlarge the young man also? Courtenay came to see me, all pale from his prison and swore—with never a word from me—to betake himself abroad never to return. 'I would no longer be a cause of further trouble to my gracious Queen,' he said. I was glad to let him go; young wings should not bruise themselves against prison walls. And seeing him there so earnest, and so chastened, I said, '*Never* is a long time! Conduct yourself to our honour abroad, and, maybe, we shall change *never* to *sometime*!' For I remembered his kinswoman that had governed my young days with kindliness and wisdom, and for her sake, resolved to bring him home again one day. So he took his departure; and so oddly we are made, that for all his treasons and his fickleness I was sad to see him go. Flawed, he had still been an ornament to my court.

Early in the second week of May, I was seized by a cramp in the belly; and the midwives, having consulted together, and my belly being somewhat declined, they declared my labour to be at hand. The child would be born by morning. Before this miracle so long promised, and now to be fulfilled, I could find no word. *Mary blessed among women.* I repeated it to myself over and over. Every pain that wrenched me apart, I received with rapture, thanking God. Throughout that night every lamp and candle burned in the palace, every cresset flared. In my bedchamber there was a constant coming and going; in the chapel priests never ceased from prayer, and to these I was constant to add my own.

Daylight brought the truth. Hope had been false.

But, if not today, tomorrow; and if not tomorrow, the day after—so the women said, trying to comfort me that had been better left alone to weep. *No mischief done!* They said that, too. But mischief there was; and great mischief.

At the first pains, news had gone forth to my lord Mayor of London. Even while I lay prostrate beneath my most cruel disappointment, London's joybells were ringing, to be followed by joybells throughout the country. Every shop, every booth was closed; people danced in the streets as though this were a second mayday, they crowded into the taverns to drink, stranger with stranger. And every moment tales grew about the child. A boy; a boy of course, and bigger and more beautiful than any child yet born. But later in the day messengers went riding with the truth and the dancing stopped; and though men drank still, it was in gloom.

And Philip? Hearing of the birth as imminent, he had come on the instant; but learning the truth, had on that same instant, turned the barge and gone back to Westminster, making no movement to see me. He had his duties, so the message went. Well, that was true enough ... but had he no duty to me, his stricken wife?

The news has spread to Antwerp; there had been no means of recalling it. Before it could be denied, it had been received with joy in Portugal and Spain. The dowager Princess of Portugal, Philip's aunt, wrote to him,

> I have just heard that God has been pleased to deliver my sister the Queen of England of a boy and that both Her Highness and the child are well. I am very happy about this. May God give you both long lives that you may rejoice over this child and others. . . .

It came, this letter, in a bitter moment; Philip had sent it on to me. He could be cruel as a cat, they said. I did not believe it ... then.

My physicians did their best to keep me in good heart. Dr. Buttes said, 'Madam, it was always my opinion that you were mistaken in your dates; the Queen's cycle has never been regular. Madam, you carry yourself so well, I think it cannot be until the end of this month; and my colleague thinks not until early June. Madam, it would be good for you to walk in the air; the gardens are beautiful just now, and the exercise would help on your affair. Meanwhile we promise you all shall be well! Already the country has shown great joy at the birth of its prince; and that is the main thing! And if it has rejoiced too soon—what matter? Men may rejoice more than once at the same thing, and the second time more even than before.'

Well that was true enough of good Catholics; but the heretics went about openly rejoicing *Believe that the Queen will bring forth a human child? Who is such a fool as to believe it? If she bring forth anything it will be a dog or a monkey!* When I heard this last I vomited. You may wonder that in my seclusion I heard such tales; but in a royal household, even the deaf hear and the dumb speak. News travels from the market-place, from strangers in the kitchens; servants are not slow to gossip, the very pages are all ears and the air grows sick with foul talk.

The month of May dragged on. I walked in the gardens in the early morning before it was well light; and in the dark of the night. I was afraid to look upon the daylight world, where the green darkened and the white dropped; where my colours of hope, my Tudor colours, were fading. My belly had gone down, though still it was high; but there were no more labour pains and I walked easy, as though I carried no child at all.

And so we came to the last days of that sad month; and, all sick with my fears, I remembered Philip's words, remembered the Cardinal's words, remembered Gardiner's words. *You put false pity before the true Christian spirit. You are content to save the flesh some short agony that souls may burn to all eternity. You would save the corrupted branch at the price of the country's corruption. You have been a laggard in putting an end to God's enemies.*

I heard the voice, inexorable, of my own soul. 'They are right!' I cried out in the empty room. Never with a whole heart did I consent to the burning of heretics; I pitied Rogers. I wept over Hooper. I thought myself merciful and was puffed up with pride, because of all virtues, mercy is the greatest. But that is not true mercy which brings more grief, more pain, more bitterness. Until this wrong be put right my child can never be born.

I sent, on the instant, for Gardiner. I was frantic lest he waste a moment and the child die in the womb. Together we drew up a letter to be sent at once to all my bishops. I thought then, working quiet with my Chancellor that I was a reasonable being; I see now, that I was crazed with fear. Too long, we wrote, had my bishops been lax; now they must gird up their loins and be about God's work. They were to

> have especial regard to such disordered persons as lean to erroneous and heretical opinions, refusing to show themselves conformable to the Catholic religion of Christ's church. . . . They must not be suffered to continue in their errors to the dishonour of Almighty God and the dangerous example of others.
>
> We admonish you, therefore forthwith, that, when any such offenders shall be brought to you, you shall use your good wisdom and discretion to remove them from their errors, if it may be done. But, if they continue in such errors, proceed against them according to the law, so that God's glory be better advanced and the commonwealth more quietly governed.
>
> Given under our hands at Hampton Court, 24th May.

And surely this was the true mercy; to try by good means to save a man's soul; and, if he himself prove obstinate, to proceed against him according to law that his soul might be saved and the community be uncorrupted. I must lose no moment in this matter, leave no stone unturned. When God saw that I worked unflinching to save souls for Him and burn corruption from the land, he would relent and I hold my son in my arms. And it never occurred to me that I was bargaining with God; doing the right thing for the wrong reason.

Philip came from Westminster to seal the letter with his approval. 'In every place in England God's fires must burn!' he said, 'and you must make yourself strong to endure it; for you are inclined to weakness, being hurt by the pain of others. This thing you must teach yourself to bear. To Oxford and Cambridge—your seats of learning, we must pay especial attention. For London I have no fear; its own good bishop shall see to it! Already the heretics call him *bloody Bonner*!' And he was smiling.

'And will they not call me bloody, also?'

'Those that listen to God pay no heed to the words of heretics.' He laughed; but he had not answered my question.

God saw me strong about His work and smiled upon me once more. Burning flesh no longer stank in my nostrils; for it was corruption that burned, leaving the soul purified and free.

June was sweet in the land; and in my heart hope was strong. My belly was risen again; when the midwife laid her hand upon it, she could feel the child move. When she examined my breasts—squeezing them gently between thumb and finger—the miracle! Like a pearl, yet more precious than any pearl, a droplet of milk.

That day, such time as we did not spend on our knees in thanks, we were merry together my women and I; for God likes us to be merry, it is, to my mind, another way of prayer. When the pains took me, we rejoiced, not knowing that the pain presaged not birth but death; nor that a pearl of milk may come from a barren woman that ardently desires a child.

June wore itself away and still I hoped; I dared not otherwise. Letters were going backwards and forwards between England and the Netherlands, between England and Rome. They were hopeful enough. in mid-June Renard was writing to his master,

> It is thought she'll not be delivered until ten days from now.

And as the days wore on there was anxiety and not in my heart alone; again I quote from Renard's letter to the Emperor.

> If God gives her a child all will turn for the best. If not, I foresee such trouble on so great a scale that pen can scarce set it down. If Elizabeth come to the throne, true religion will be overthrown; persecution and vengeance will walk the land. I doubt even the King will be safe. Rumours go about that the Queen is not with child at all; that another child is to be put into his place. People go about with closed faces. . . .

But not, it seemed, with closed mouths! Again the lying mischief-making tale! And so we came to the end of yet another wretched month, in which hope and fear had alternated—the fear greater than hope. Yet still I held on to what scraps of comfort were offered. Towards the end of June, when I was sick with despair, Renard showed me yet another letter he had written home.

> The Queen is as well as ever she has been; in such health one cannot doubt she is with child. There are certain signs. . . .

All the old signs mentioned, including the droplet of milk. And from my physicians and midwives, the same old comfort; my uncertain rhythms had caused the trouble; we had miscalculated by two months.

'The Queen's pregnancy is certain. Within seven days or so she shall hold her prince in her arms!' The women—those strangers that, from old custom had come to be with me during my waiting-time—crowded about me with congratulation, fouling the air with the stale smell of their skirts. My own ladies stood apart and said nothing.

'Do none of you give me joy?' I called to them. 'Have you never the good word for me?'

'The Queen's true friends will speak when it is time!' old Clarencieux said.

'*It is the time!* Have you not heard?' I cried out, thrusting down my fear; for my heart knew better.

The days dragged on. Among my friends there was dismay unspoken. Renard wrote to the King of the Romans—and this time did not show me his letter. But within a palace there are spies upon spies and the copy lies under my hand.

> ... It is now doubted whether she be truly with child; the outward signs are good....

For days I would not receive him. But, after all, he wrote what all men said, what my own heart whispered; and he had, at least, added that the signs were good. So back again he came into favour.

And all the time the holy fires burned. Throughout the country doubt that I was with child grew ever stronger; Catholics heard it all dismayed, heretics in good hope and laughter. In France laughter grew ever louder, ever more cruel. The French King could not restrain his mirth. *Ce n'est pas le ventre c'est le vent.* And his cruel jest crossed the sea to add to the dismay of the faithful and to swell heretic laughter.

Even in my own court at Westminster, where Philip stood deputy for me, laughter could not be quenched. The Polish ambassador newcome into this country offered Philip in full court, congratulations upon the birth of his son. Carelessness in not altering his prepared speech? Ignorance? Or the desire to add still more to my humiliation? Who can say?

Gardiner told me about it; but only after I had questioned him close; at first he would not speak.

'Madam, the whole court heard with surprise and concern. Then de Noailles was seen to smile.'

The French ambassador. He would! He would! I dug my fingers into my palm.

'And the King?'

'Black with anger, Madam; I know him, I can read his mind. But of that anger—never a sign! The King is wise. To show anger is to give the matter importance. The man was a barbarian from Poland! The King made himself to smile; to make nothing of the matter!'

'And was that all? I have heard a different ending!'

'When the King smiles, others must follow. It is as the Queen knows, proper!'

'No more than that?'

'There was a fellow, some lickspittle of France, that laughed. . . .'

'And then?'

'Madam, when one laughs, others follow.'

'Everyone?'

He was silent; but, my eyes holding his, he nodded.

'The King?'

'Madam, he laughed, too; what else might he do? But with him—as with us—it was not laughter from the heart!'

But it had been laughter. The King had joined in the laughter.

That night I prayed God for a dead child rather than no child. For who may find laughter in a dead child?

Chapter Four

June dragged itself out and still the womb remained locked; my physicians bade me be of good cheer; I should be delivered, they promised, early in this new month. I kept my rooms and prayed; my own ladies I had about me; the strangers I would no longer endure, they had come uninvited. I wished with all my heart they would return home and trouble me no longer with the expense of keeping them.

In my long waiting all England waited; but now, whispering no longer, the people cried their doubts aloud. In every true church prayers were offered for my safe delivery. In Brussels, my father-in-law, the Emperor, dared not close his eyes at night lest my news find him sleeping. In Rome, the Pope himself prayed for the birth of the child that should bind all our countries into one Christian brotherhood. But France, and that friend of France, my sister, declared it useless to pray. I carried no child; I never had, nor never would.

With so many doubting my pregnancy and with my sister's friends dropping that same poison into his ears, Philip came from London to speak his mind.

'Madam, you must be quick about this business. If God gives us a child, all will be well. If not, I foresee trouble so great I can find no words!' But all the same he found them. 'Bloody revolution; the true religion overthrown. Yourself cast down; and your sister raised up. Heretics cannot wait to see the heretic throned! Then, Madam, not you nor I nor any of the true faith—man, woman or child—shall be safe from slaughter!'

Fine words to cast at a woman in my wretched state and helpless in the matter. He felt the need to justify himself for he said, 'Renard's words, not mine! He wrote them to my father—Renard your good friend!'

I said, 'My sister is foremost in this mischief. And still she spreads the old nonsense about a smuggled child to be passed off as our own.

And why should she not? She hopes to gain all from it. I must send her away; I cannot have her about me at such a time!'

'Here she must stay until you are delivered. When that time comes—*if*, Madam, that time comes—she must be here to speak the truth and give the lie to all rumour!'

So my sister stayed; but I would not see her. She carried herself very humble, so it was told me; but still, as was also reported, she did not stint to spread her mischief.

A bad summer that summer of 'fifty-five. I suppose the rain must have stopped sometime, but it seemed without pause. Corn was already mildewed, the promise of harvest was poor. And everywhere, bickering, quarrelling—my Council at the old game of dissension. And everywhere the people, too, were at their old game—the game of baiting foreigners, and especially Spaniards. For myself, I was in poor health and sunk into a melancholy; Philip showed himself displeased thereat. And still my babe was unborn. I longed with all the passion of thwarted motherhood to see the face of my child; I longed still more to make an end of my sister's pretensions, to establish the Faith with the heir of my body.

July went by; August came in.

And still my physicians and still my women sought to comfort me *No one in his senses would deny the Queen is with child; the signs are certain—the breasts, the belly. And, above all, the child moves. . . .*

With a most desperate heart I longed to believe them, agonised to believe them. But now it was not only breasts and belly that had grown; arms and legs, alike, were swollen. And these were shot through with pain so intense that I must bite upon my lips lest I cry out. And I remembered my father biting upon his lips in just such a way; and I remembered his swollen arms and legs. Had I inherited his sickness, his dropsy? Was there no child in the womb? Had we all been deceived; all, save my sister? Sweet Christ, not that; not that! Again I prayed with all the passion of soul and body that, if I might not bring forth a living child, then a dead one. A dead child. Did ever woman, before, pray for a dead child?

The pains in arms and legs never lessened; rather they grew so agonising I could neither sit with comfort, nor stand, nor lie long in one place. I would crouch upon the floor, knees drawn to my chin, head bowed upon knees. And all the time the agony, and all the time the fear, and all the time the praying . . . the useless praying.

'Madam, do not sit so!' the midwives would admonish me. 'You will suffocate the child; it cannot breathe!' Then I would rise, my women supporting me; but the cramp in my swollen arms and legs pierced as though I were crucified. And all the time I knew how, throughout Christendom, yes, even in Catholic countries, laughter grew ever louder; the Christian world laughing at a barren old woman that thought herself young enough to bear a child!

I remember how once I cried out to Gardiner, the only man I could truly trust, 'In all this country I so love and that once loved me, what friend but you? My husband that cannot wait to get away from this land and from me . . . from me? The Cardinal that forever blames me that I do not deal sufficiently with heretics, though the fires never cease to burn? My Council forever at odds giving no true counsel but countenancing those that best stuff them with gold? My sister with her ruthless plotting? And Renard? Renard! Do you know what he wrote to the Cardinal . . . and both men my friends?'

He shifted his eyes.

'Then, my lord, I will tell you. Renard wrote thus: *If the Queen die without issue—as she will—then cast aside your red hat, marry Elizabeth, and make yourself King of England.* Does Renard, that I held my friend, doubt I am with child; does he, too, look to my death and take his stand with my sister?'

'Madam, he truly believes the Queen is with child; only today he wrote to his master *We all hope the child will be born at the end of this month.* As for his quip about the Cardinal—!' Gardiner permitted himself one of his rare, sour laughs, 'Madam, he jests, though it's not a jest to my taste. Renard knows full well that Pole is wed to the Church. Had he wanted a wife of flesh-and-blood, he had wedded you, Madam, when the people wished it—when you first came to the throne. Come now, take no huff with Renard, for certain it is that walk the world over, save for myself, you'll find no truer friend.'

These days I see-sawed, riding high to my glorious hope, dropping into the abyss of my fears, rising, dropping . . . *Today I shall hold my child in my arms.* Then I would look at those swollen arms all unfit to hold a pin let alone a babe and ask myself *Pregnancy? Dropsy?* And I would tell myself that a woman who is so little a woman that she knows not whether she be pregnant or no, must surely be an object for laughter. Such a one deserves her fate; for her there can be no pity—least of all from her husband.

I prayed still more fervently that I might, at the least, bear a dead child. Then, perhaps, Philip would a little pity me. Perhaps he would come again to my bed to give me, once more, my blessed hope. To such a strait I was come!

Little hope of that! Too long he had fretted to be gone. I could not blame him. Here in this ever-raining country he knew himself disliked; it pinched his pride. In Brussels his father was a sick man, tormented with gout and worn beyond his years. Aware of his sins—for his private life had not been virtuous—he longed to put into his son's hands the crown of Spain and all those temporal powers he so wearily held. He longed to retire into a monastery, to pray away his sins, to spend his last days in hope of God's mercy. It was Philip's clear duty to go; but for my condition I should have gone with him. I wanted, with all my heart, to comfort the old tired man; yet so selfish are we made that I could not endure that my husband should leave me. In my sick state I was sure that, let him stay, all would go well; let him go—and black disaster.

To hurry my business on, my own prayers were not enough. I was not worthy. I commanded alms for the poor; I commanded prayers and intercessions throughout the kingdom for my delivery—a safe delivery I no longer asked. A child alive or dead; I would accept God's will. To live with my husband as his wife, to know again the sweet burden of pregnancy—it was all I asked. From my window I would watch the priests walk in procession across the courtyard and into the church. And I would send my own prayers, all unworthy, up to God, praying with so intense a will that all strength drained from me and I would drop to the ground like a stone.

And still, *Courage, Madam, courage!* my women would exhort me. *When the Queen holds her prince in her arms she will laugh again.* And there would follow the oft-told tale of dates mistaken, of women gone far beyond their time; and always the happy outcome. And I would listen until pain dimmed my wits and in my world of pain I sat blind and dumb.

The little Dormer no longer joined in such talk and, at times, I would wonder why. But the love between us being like to that between mother and child, I thought a certain delicacy held her back. These days she would sit apart silent, and, as I thought, a little sad. Well, but she had the green sickness, she was in love. But why so sad? Her love was returned. Don Gomez, count of Feria, the Spanish ambassador-extraordinary, had asked permission to marry and it had been freely granted; we held it, my husband and I, a happy match. Betrothed she was; but marry she would not—nor would so much as hear of it—until my child was born. But for me, she might even now be a happy wife expecting her own child. She was not sleeping well, Clarencieux said. She wept and cried out in her sleep, *No! No! Not now! We must wait . . . we must wait the time!*

'I keep her from her happiness!' I said. 'If the time is long to me, to her it may be longer!'

I sent for the girl. I asked if she would care to leave my service. I did not add how much I should miss her sweet young face. 'No!' she cried out, 'No! I will never leave the Queen until she be over her trouble.'

Not *until her child is born;* but *until she be over her trouble.* What did she mean by that? I did not ask. She had a shining honesty, she would not lie to me . . . and I did not want to hear what my heart suspected.

And now it was August. Hard to believe it was high summer. Rain still fell from an overcast sky, so that days that should be bright were often winter-black. What we had feared had become certainty—a poor harvest and high prices. As for my own harvest, I had given up hope of even a dead child—and what a hope is that! Yet still those about me strove with their encouragements; one Spanish envoy, even now, wrote home,

> We still have hope that a child will be born to England by the end of this month. . . .

But I no longer hoped; nor did Philip.

My husband was heartsick of England. He was wild to leave this country of bitter disappointments—to leave an ageing, barren wife, a people that spent his gold and gave him nothing in return, not even thanks; a Parliament that, for all my pleading, refused to crown him, and a Council, that, for all his gifts, rapped him over the knuckles when, as Regent, during my retirement, he attempted to give advice. Why should he stay in this rain-sodden, unfriendly country? In the Netherlands the crown of Spain awaited him, together with all the princely and ducal crowns of his father's vast possessions. As for Spain, itself, that country clamoured for the sight of its new young King.

He would come from Whitehall or Westminster, now and again, to visit me. He was always the perfection of courtesy; but his fine manners unwarmed by any true affection did not cheat me into thinking he came for love of me. He did not stay above an hour at any time; my heart was the clock that ticked away the minutes. His barge had scarce been sighted when, so it seemed to me, I was at my window, straining for a last sight of him. I never asked him to stay—though I must bite upon my tongue to keep the words unsaid; but more than once my physicians advised him not to go. He knew as well as I, they meant him to stay until the child was born . . . or until they considered all hope was dead. It could not be a matter of more than a few days now; but he had no mind for such matters. Nor could I blame him—a young man caught in the net of women's affairs; had he loved me it had been different.

Yet, for all I understood his mind in the matter, I was half-mad with longing for him—the feel of his body for a little while next to my own, the touch of his mouth, of his hand, even. There is that plant we call the camomile; the more you tread it underfoot, the stronger it springs. My love—to my shame I say it—was like that plant. But the camomile though it has no beauty is yet fruitful. Its first attribute I share, but not the second!

Once a scandal begins there's no end to it. The tale of the substitute child spread into every corner of the land. There was even a woman swore I had sent, in secret, to bargain—a bag of gold against her new-born son.

'Madam, we must put an end to such villainous lies!' Gardiner spoke harsh as though I, myself, were the culprit. 'Prison for the wretch, but first a whipping at the cart's tail!'

'God has blessed her; it is not for me to punish!'

He said no more; but his face was a tell-tale that paid me no compliment.

The wretched autumn passed. In fields the corn lay beaten to the ground, diseased and useless, apples lay green and maggoty; in the Queen's private garden flowers lay broken, and folk walked the highroads mud to the very knees. Food prices, already risen, rose again sharply. There would be food—for those that could pay for it; but for the others . . .

And, in this picture of misery, God has set me fair and square.

I sent for my Comptroller. I commanded him to save all he could of money and food for those in need. He shook his head.

'I can save nothing, Madam, nothing. We are already in debt. It is those women that have left their own homes to fatten upon the Queen!'

'Send them away!'

'Madam, I dare not. I have spoken on the matter with the lord King. It is the custom at the Queen's lying in; it must be observed, he said. And, indeed, Madam, he is wise. Send them away and you spread the lying rumours yet further!'

So there they remained, eating of the food that cost good money and should have been better used elsewhere.

Dormer asked that she might speak with me in private. She looked pale; when she spoke her voice was low and shaken so that I could scarce catch her words. I thought, It is the matter of her missed marriage; and my heart sank at the notion of her going. Yet it was not of that she spoke but of me.

'Madam!' Suddenly she flung herself upon her knees. My fingers went under her chin. I lifted her wet face. 'What is it, my girl? Tell me. Whatever it is I will help you!'

'Madam, you can help me and all England; but most of all, yourself!' Tears choked her and she could not speak.

'Madam, once you asked us, Clarencieux and me, why we did not share your joy. Does the Queen remember my answer?'

'I remember.'

'Madam, I was wrong. There is no right time; there will be none . . . ever.'

I stared at her. Did she, this child, dare set at naught the experience of those that should know! The spirit of my father rose in me I lifted my hand to strike her down. Steady and sorrowful she looked at me; my hand dropped. A child; but honest and steadfast that dared the thing those others had not dared . . . the thing I knew in my own heart.

'Madam,' she said, 'the weeks go by; one week and another week; and one month and another month; and always they tell you the same thing . . . *The Queen became pregnant many days after that named in the first count.* But among the people there is no more hope. *There is no child nor never was,* they say. And, Madam, they say more. *The Queen is dead and no-one tells us so. They wait until inch by inch, the Spaniard*—forgive me, Madam, that I name him so, but I am sworn to report true, *steal the crown. We have a Queen no longer and it is time for a crowning.*'

'And whom do they propose to crown?' My voice was steady as a rock, cold as water.

'Madam, there's a man goes about in Sussex; he swears he is Courtenay new-come from abroad. He says the crown is his by right of royal blood and he means to have it. He will have it, he says, in his own right and that of his sweet bedfellow, his wedded wife.'

'And who is the fortunate lady that shall wear my crown and sleep in the royal bed?'

She said nothing; her cheeks that had been so white were scarlet now. I held her eyes; I beat her down with my will.

'It is, Madam, the lady Elizabeth,' she said at last.

'Who could believe such a nonsense? Courtenay is abroad, and there he will stay—if he knows what's good for him! And my sister; do you suppose she'd lend herself to so mad a farce?'

Again she said nothing and I answered myself. *She would . . . so long as it suit her purpose. Thereafter, death to the pretender and death to the Queen. There is no love in her, no pity, no loyalty. She fastens on my weakness and my grief to snatch at the crown.*

'Oh Dormer, little Dormer!' I cried out. 'I see it now! They flatter me with false hope to lend me courage—physicians, midwives women—all, all! None speaks the truth but you! And though my own heart knows the truth yet still I listen to them; I listen. And all the while I shut myself away from the people that think me dead—and maybe glad to think it; though some, I think, would weep for me!'

'You have more friends, Madam, than you know! There's many a lady weeps for you, and many a gentleman dead, avenging insult to the Queen! And all good Catholics pray for you, not only here but throughout Christendom . . .'

'I thank those that weep and those that protect my good name, and even more those that pray for me. But most of all, I thank you for your truth.'

I sent for my Chancellor; the words I must say were more bitter than death.

'It is time to make an end of false hopes; of this death-in-life. It is time to show myself to the people!'

'God will not forget you, Madam. He will remember you in His good time.'

I sent for my Comptroller and for my Chamberlain; I gave my orders for departure. I would leave this place of sorrows and I would leave in high procession. I would show all England whether I was alive or dead!

'Madam the Queen is wise,' my good Buttes said. 'Even the most careful of physicians may be mistaken in the matter of a first child. Pray you, forgive me, Madam!' I smiled upon him, thanking him in my heart that he took the blame upon himself. 'It shall not happen again,' he said, 'God is good!'

And what did he mean by that? That next time God would truly bless me with a child? Or that he and I, together, would see to it that I did not fool myself a second time; that I must give up all hope of a child?

I did not ask.

Chapter Five

I could not, as yet, face London and all the clamour of state business; nor was I certain how my people would receive me. I had disappointed their hope of an heir; I had been rumoured dead that was undoubtedly alive. I decided upon a few days at Oatlands that I might accustom myself, in some degree, to a public court after my late seclusion. For all I had commanded a high procession, I, myself, for very weakness, must ride in a litter; yet I kept the curtains drawn back that the people might see my face and know for a certainty that I lived. So I rode, all smiles, acknowledging the greetings, hiding my grief both at my ruined hopes and the ruined harvest. *We are alike in this, my country and I! My own harvest is ruined; also, my hopes are fallen fruit.* The thought was forever in my mind; the sad countryside drowned in rain and my heart in tears.

Yet, as I rode, I still had some comfort; for from every village and hamlet folk came out with greetings and with gifts to show their kindness. People in towns may laugh at a false pregnancy but countryfolk that need sons upon the land and daughters to play their part, know the tragedy of such false hopes.

I spent some few days at Oatlands to regain my strength, though strong again I was never to be. All movement in the womb had stopped, though not the pains. But to those pains I paid little heed; for now I must suffer anguish greater than any pain. Philip had written that he could delay no longer; affairs in the Netherlands called and must be obeyed.

In the second week of August I rode for London. I came to my city of Westminster in the twilight of a cold summer evening, the curtains of my litter drawn close. My courage had left me. I had no child for my people . . . and my husband was leaving me. Nor was my comfort the greater that Philip was not there to greet me; he had not expected me until the morrow.

Back again in my own familiar place to which I had expected to return with my child, sorrow overcame me with all the force of my first anguish. There is but one way to fight, though not always to conquer grief. On my knees I besought the blessed Mother of God that I might perform the one function any woman—even a gypsy in the ditch—may perform; and the prayer done, I knelt still, wordlessly praying.

How long I knelt I cannot say. I had risen to my knees when I heard footsteps in the room beyond. Though I lie in my grave yet my heart will leap to the fall of those feet—Philip's feet. Two men came in together; they were talking and I knew the voice of Renard. I guessed that, hearing of my arrival, they had come to greet me; finding me absent, they were whiling away time until I should appear. Renard must have been trying to persuade my husband to stay a little longer; for I heard Philip break in very sharp, 'By God *no*! I'll endure no more! I am for Flanders at once!'

My heart stood still. I wanted to cry out, to tell them I was there; but no sound came from my throat. I had, besides, the strangest feeling that Philip knew I was there, and meant me to hear what he might not say to my face; else why did two Spaniards talk together in English? Maybe he meant to be kind; but it was dire cruelty in him.

'Why do you think I came into England? Not to bed with a woman; there are women everywhere, younger, handsomer . . .'

'But not kinder,' Renard broke in.

'Kindness? I stand in no need of kindness from women! I am not here for such kindness but to win this heretic country for God!'

'Then, sir, will you not stay and fight?'

'Even in the press of battle a man must rest. And, as God hears me, I need rest; rest from enemies in this country that fret my spirit and seek my life. Look!'

He must have thrown open his doublet for I heard Renard take in his breath. 'Sir, you go armed?'

Armed and I had not known it!

'I eat nothing, my good Renard, but what my own cooks prepare. Is it pleasant, do you think, to go forever in fear of poison? A soldier's death a man may face; but death by poison—a rat's death! By God no! And hark this, also! If I need rest from my enemies, I need rest still more from my wife. Oh she is kind, she is gentle, she is well enough! But I'd not have a woman too eager; she wearies me with her love.'

Did he fault me then for my obedience? I had thought he liked his women submissive. And so he did—if submission came after a fight, and he the winner! But me he had won at a glance.

'I dare not look at a pretty petticoat lest tears come into those eyes of hers—such pale, peering eyes. By God she weeps too much!'

'Sir, she has cause!'

'The fault is in her, in her; not in me! If it were her sister now!' The words came in an outburst sudden as shocking. 'Why was it not her sister I wedded?'

'Madam Elizabeth does not wear the crown.'

'Not yet. But if the Queen is not quicker about her business, may well do! Elizabeth! I could beget lusty sons upon her. Never tell me she's a heretic! When a man's in bed with a woman her notions melt like snow in the sun. By God if it were Madam Elizabeth I had to wife, I'd stay in spite of everything—or take her with me!'

So! Elizabeth. Elizabeth again! And I such a fool I had not married her off to ship her abroad. I had bid her wear her best gown to honour my husband. All my life I had suffered on her account; yet, I think, I never hated her so much as in that moment.

'Well!' my husband's voice came again. 'Madam my wife is, it seems, not here! I'll wait no longer!'

I heard the closing of the door behind them.

I had thought myself sufficiently unhappy; now misery pierced me through and through with its most bitter pain. My husband was leaving, not so much because he wearied of England—but because he wearied of me. *If it had been Madam Elizabeth I'd stay in spite of everything—or else take her with me!* Jealousy was a rat to gnaw to the very bone.

Pride, no doubt, should have stiffened me. But where was my pride now, my woman's pride, my Tudor pride? For the sake of the child he and I, and all England needed, I could not, without a struggle, let him go.

That night, Philip, according to his courteous custom, came to wish me Goodnight in my bed.

If you go now how shall we get us a child? I bent the full force of my will upon him. I must, I confess it, have looked less than my poor best. I had been weeping—a habit I had fallen into since girlhood, and not without cause. I had tried, God knows, to rid myself of it, but when there are no words to fit my grief, then tears can, a little, ease my sorrow. This night, whether my reddened lids and my *pale peering* eyes disgusted him or whether the memory of my sister caused him to turn away with even more despatch than usual, I cannot say. His kiss was upon my cheek and he, already at the door, when, in spite of myself, the question cried itself aloud. 'If you go now, how shall we get us a son?'

'Madam, my first wife knew her business! I have a son!' he said, cruel; for all his courtesy he could be cruel as a cat.

'But I . . . I have not!'

'My son will inherit all I have; I am content!'

'But not England,' and I was desperate.

'That was never mine; nor never will be. You deny me even the shadow of a crown!'

'*I* deny you! I would give you the heart out of my breast!'

'What use of that?' He was angered in the matter of the crown and not without reason. He bore the name of *King*; he worked for the good of this country; in my seclusion he had taken my place upon the Council—and never the longed-for, the deserved reward. Yet still I felt the cruelty of his words, and the way he threw my love back in my face.

'I have my heir,' he said. 'You have your kingdom. And if no heir of your body present himself, God has arranged things well enough!'

'Do not put your going away upon God!' I cried out, 'and if you will not stay now, shall you return . . . ever? Come back you must! If not for love of me then for love of Christ. Or do you regard a heretic upon the throne of England as God's arrangement and good enough?'

'I shall come back. As for a heretic upon the throne we'll take that hurdle when we come to it!'

He came back to the bed, lifted my hand and kissed it; but I saw his eyes cold, indifferent. Cruel he could be but never ill-bred, his courtesy natural to him as breathing.

All that night I lay tossing in my cold bed.

When a man's in bed with a woman her notions melt like snow in the sun. Did he mean to take his hurdle that way? He did not know my sister!

I had done my part. I could do no more, nor I would not. Love him I did with every drop of my heart's blood; this husband of mine that, caring nothing for me, had awakened the woman within me. I said no more on the matter; but I could not keep my eyes from him, knowing how soon I was to lose him. So debonair, so elegant and so young. Sweet Christ, how young! And I would catch sight of myself in some mirror—pale, sickly and old . . . old. How could such a one as I hope to keep him?

In the last week of August I set out upon my calvary. We were to ride through London to Greenwich for Philip's embarkation. Of my anguish I must show no sign; I had my women paint me into some semblance of health, I wore my finest habit. I looked—at some little distance—not unlike myself when young. And, indeed, my improved looks lent me some spirit; I found I could smile, laugh, even jest a little. Let Philip carry with him a memory pleasing enough to bring him home again!

We had meant to part in Whitehall but, at the last moment, I could not bring myself to leave him before I must. So through London we went in high procession; before and behind us men-at-arms, trumpeters, knights, and bishops. And in the midst, since I was not yet strong enough to ride, in an open litter—myself.

It was long and long, indeed, since London had seen its Queen; now the city was full for St. Bartholomew's Fair; what fitter occasion to show them all I lived! Now the people pressed forward that they might see my face; and I blessed Jane Dormer for her truth to me. They had, indeed, thought me dead. Those in front cried out *It is the Queen; Our Queen. The Queen herself. God save Queen Mary!* and those behind hearing the news cried out also, so that the air was full of the sound of their gladness. But how long, I wondered, before—give them the chance—they would be shouting for my sister? Some few cried out *God save the King!* And it troubled me that his welcome was less warm than my own. But soon he would return; soon they would understand the good things he had given them—the true faith, increased prosperity. *In spite of the Council, in spite of Parliament and the people, in spite of everything, I'll have you crowned in Westminster with every ancient ceremony.* But withdrawn and proud, riding there, I doubt he caught my wordless promise.

The Cardinal all in scarlet, Cross and Hat borne before him upon cushions, raised his hand now and then solemnly to bless the people. I was deeply moved at the sight. God's faith was truly coming into its own. But Gardiner told me later, that some had turned aside to spit; and some had spat without troubling themselves with that courtesy. He had marked them that so blasphemously bore themselves and had sent to seek them out—if it might be done; if not the whole city must bear the fine in punishment.

For all my smiling upon the people I was ill-pleased at this stinting of welcome to the King; the more so since my heart and courage were down. Months of disappointment, months of sickness, my present weakness and now the loss of my husband, all but overthrew me. But a Queen must bear herself queenly; and the painting of my face playing its part, I sat within the litter smiling . . . smiling.

At the Tower wharf we took barge and so came to Greenwich.

And who should be waiting there to greet us? Who but my sister? I had not sent for her, I had not wanted her. And how did she know we should be there, and when? I had not known it myself. But . . . Philip had known; he had known time and place of his departure. And he had not expected me there; no, nor wanted me, neither. I saw the sly look pass between them and I knew at once that she, she also, had neither expected nor wanted me; I was to have stayed behind at Whitehall. She had arranged this meeting for their private conversations; and the matter of those conversations I could guess—what those two should do were I obliging enough to die. A Queen she meant to be; a virgin—never. I doubted she was one now!

'Madam and sister,' she rose from her curtsey and stood smoothing the folds of her green-and-white gown. 'I have come to bid my brother the King a safe journey and a swift return.' She turned to smile upon Philip.

I could not speak for anger; I turned my back upon her, but she, nothing daunted, continued there; the two handsome heads, the red and the gold, close together. Later, when the dark summer night was bright with torches, my Council arrived. At the sight of my sister I saw Gardiner's eyes gleam fierce beneath frowning brows.

'Well,' he told me later, 'I am not surprised. Some such trickery I had expected!' And it came to me that he was here less to bid his King Farewell than to protect his Queen. Then, 'Madam,' he said, 'that letter . . . do you believe me now?'

'I believe you!' I laid my hand upon his; his old, dry hand. So frail he looked, so aged; it came to me with sorrow and some fear, that soon I must lose this valued friend. Yet still he wore his eagle's look . . . but the eagle was sick, was old.

My husband was to sail on the twenty-ninth of August. Three of my lords, Pembroke, Arundel and Huntingdon, were to go with him to do him honour; and, being skilled upon all Council affairs, to advise him, and to watch his interests. Three days we had together and I counted upon three nights. For two nights I saw nothing of him save when he came to bid me Goodnight. Business pressed hard, he said, and time was short. Well so much was true! There was much, very much to be done.

The third night he came to lie with me, not like a lover but as a husband long sated with his duty. That duty performed, he rose and put his bedgown about his nakedness. 'I trust I leave you earnest of my return!' he said.

'God grant it!' And I did not know that he had been arranging for the most part of his household—servants, horses, dogs and hawks to be sent after him; clear sign of his intent.

The day that must come, comes. Like the Hebrews of old I had rather in my grief rend my garments and put ashes on my head than make myself fine. But once more I was high-painted and richly dressed, and he already cloaked, when Farewells said, we left the royal apartments. Through the endless chambers, through the long gallery that leads to the great staircase we went, hand-in-hand; and there the court waited—his courtiers and mine, massed either side, and standing to left and right in the great hall below.

He was going. I had long known it; yet my heart, despite my anguish, had never truly believed it. In my blood, I had felt some last-minute miracle must keep him with me. Now, as his Spaniards came to kiss my hand and he, himself, saluted my ladies, kissing each upon the lips, I understood at last, there would be no miracle.

I held myself stiff, fingers clenched into my palms, and gave no sign of grief; not even when he knelt before my sister and she bent to take his salute. I saw how his kiss lingered then, young mouth upon young mouth . . . and I did not care. He was leaving me; nothing mattered but that. He took my hand and placed it within that of my cousin the Cardinal. 'I leave Madam the Queen in your care,' he said. *Madam the Queen . . . not my wife; not my wife!*

Down the great staircase he went; and it was much as I could do to stand where I was, for longing to go after him, to take those last few steps with him. But we had arranged this manner of our parting and I stood stiff, unmoving—at what a cost God alone knows. I followed him with my eyes until the staircase took him from my sight; then I went hurrying down the long gallery to stand at a window that overlooks the river. And even now I must not weep, must not smear the clear mirrors of my eyes, diminish yet further my weak sight. I saw him turn towards a friend and he was laughing. Already he had forgotten me.

As the boat began to move he waved his bonnet towards my window. I did not see it for the shortness of my sight; it was Jane Dormer plucking at my gown told me so. But whether he waved a goodbye to the land he hated, or to the wife he did not love, who can say? He was always debonair. I stood looking, my eyes still further blurred with tears until the river's curve took him from my sight.

Chapter Six

Philip was gone; gone from me, but not from England. At Dover winds were contrary and he was forced to stay. I wished, heart and soul, I had ridden with him, taking those extra days a blessing to lighten my misfortunes. God knows how often I was tempted to ride after him; but who knows when a wind may change, who dare take a chance upon it? Yet for five whole days it remained hostile. But had I been certain of yet longer delay I had not dared follow him. We had made our public Farewell with all dignity and high ceremony; to repeat it was to spoil a great occasion, Philip would not easily forgive me; he had a great sense of fitness . . . but had he loved me a little, might he not have sacrificed fitness to love?

Yet I had some comfort; he was still upon English soil. I could send him gifts, ask his advice, send him messages of loving regard. My messengers were constant upon the Dover road.

But the wind changed and the ships sailed . . . and the Dover road was empty of my messengers.

Philip was gone and my life empty save of grief and fear. I feared for his very life; French pirates might take him upon the sea, French soldiers upon the land. That there was some sort of truce between France and Spain mattered nothing; Henri would not scruple to lay hands upon his enemy. In my very real fear for my husband I put—or tried to put—jealousy of my sister from my mind. She cared no more for him than ambition dictated; and as for him—he was faithful, he was chaste.

Pole, my Cardinal-archbishop, wrote a prayer for Philip's safety; a beautiful prayer. I said it when I awoke and before I slept; I think, even in sleep it was on my lips. And when Philip was safe-come to Brussels, I said it every day and every night until he should come home again. That prayer is writ upon my heart.

Lord Jesus, Thou who didst choose for me my spouse and consort a man who more than all others reproduces Thy Image; whom Thou didst send into the world in holiness and justice, I beseech Thee, by Thy most precious Blood, assuage my grief . . .

In spite of all my praying I was a sick woman, heart and body. My body, in spite of myself, must, at times, betray me. Pain puts its mark upon us, forces us against our will into such movements of unease that, though the tongue utter no word, the matter is clear. My grief, though I died of it, I must keep locked from sight. I knew how throughout Christendom, and even in this dear country of mine, folk jeered at the fool of a Queen that, wed to a young husband, thought with a little paint and many gifts to wipe out the years between them. And, bitterest of all, I could see, as in a picture, my sister and her friends laughing . . . laughing. And my own friends? Of how many could I be sure? Even Renard I had so trusted had not scrupled to advise my cousin the Cardinal to cast aside his red hat, to marry my sister and to rule with her—King and Queen. Earnest or jest—the words had been spoken! Sunk deep in melancholy, I tried yet to show a cheerful spirit.

'It is right and proper the King should leave us!' I said it again and again. 'The Emperor is a sick man; how shall the son stay away from his father? No! He must go where most he is needed! He will come back to us when he may; of that you may be sure!'

More than once I caught de Noailles' smile while I spoke; a half-smile, very hateful; a lifting of one brow, a quirking of the lips that was all but a sneer. And he had his quips and jests, some of them with sly prickings to draw blood. Oh they were not made to my face, so much he did not dare; but double-edged they came back to me, as they were meant—remarks I must not appear to resent, since, for my very dignity, I must ignore their double-edge. I let him go his way. As soon as might be, I would ask his recall.

But it was not only his sly smiling and jesting; he had been carrying himself very arrogant of late and I thought to take him down a peg or two. I was returning from chapel, prayer-book in hand and, folded within it, the Cardinal's prayer. De Noailles, meeting me in the way, bowed himself three times to the ground. I held out the paper saying, 'Mr. Ambassador, do you not think this is a beautiful prayer?'

'Why yes, Madam, very beautiful!' And once again—that smile. I knew I should ignore it, this subtle insult to my husband. But the lifted brow, the quirking mouth were too much for me. I rushed in upon the danger.

'Mr. Ambassador, why do you smile?'

'To liken any mortal man to our Saviour, does it not a little smack of . . . blasphemy?'

'This is not *any* man; it is the King!' I reminded him somewhat sharp. 'And, moreover, if any man strive with all his might to model himself upon Christ, is that not a laurel he might wear?'

'Why yes!' he said again and would have bowed himself away but that I caught him by the sleeve.

'Mr. Ambassador,' I said, 'will you please explain yourself?'

'But, Madam, there is nothing to explain. The thing is self-evident! Christ is the son of God; man the son of man!' And when still I held him fast he said, unwilling, 'If Madam the Queen would know more, she must ask her Chancellor.'

So seeing I could get no more from him I was forced to let him go. But *what* must I ask my Chancellor? Nothing; nothing at all. The man meant to be insolent; nothing more!

But, all the same, I sent for Gardiner. Though he liked neither my husband nor my marriage he was a man to speak truth; and the sourer the truth, the more his enjoyment! But now his fierce eyes showed no pleasure. He spread his hands, and for the first time I saw they trembled a little.

'No man is like Christ, nor Christ like any man that ever lived. The prayer is excessive; in that de Noailles is not far wrong.'

'For the most part you are right!' I told him. 'But surely God gives us credit for our endeavours. And for de Noailles and his sly smiling, bid him bear himself with better manners or I'll find the way to make him!'

'Madam, I will. A spiteful dog, de Noailles, that goes beyond his instructions.'

And so I put aside both insinuations and my Chancellor's evasive answers and forgot them both.

The long, cold summer passed unnoticed into cold, wet, autumn; One could scarce mark the difference. The corn had long mildewed, the green fruit fallen; cattle looked thin; they moved very slow, lacking all spirit. It would be a hard winter for the poor; already prices were beyond their scant means. Everywhere rivers, swollen with incessant rain, overflowed; boats sailed through Westminster Hall and out again.

And still the rain fell.

How could any country, though it had no other trouble, be aught but wretched? But other troubles we had; troubles aplenty. Still heretics went to the fire condemned thereto by the church; yet all the time greater severity in the matter was being urged upon me. *Dare you, Madam, for mere squeamishness condemn souls to the everlasting fire?* Thus my Cardinal, thus my Chancellor, thus Bonner my good bishop of London; and thus many another. And each time I would answer, 'This last seven months there have been more fires lit than ever before! They have been a cause of anger to Catholic and heretic alike; to the heretic bitter fear, bitter pain; to the Catholic distress, and disgust, too. Too much agony . . . too few souls saved!'

'Is not even one soul saved from eternal fire worth it all?' one or the other would ask.

'I do not hold the scales!' I would answer.

But each time my answer would come with lessening assurance. Who was I to set myself up against my church? Who was I to set myself against the voice of Rome? For Cardinal and bishops alike spoke with the voice of him that speaks for God!

As for my marriage, the people liked it as little as ever; they found it endurable only because my husband had left, taking the most part of his Spaniards with him. Their dislike, their fear, showed itself in constant small revolts. Revolts are like fireworks; they may set the kingdom ablaze, or fall harmless to the ground; one never knows. And, as a distempered body may show itself in an outbreak of boils, so this anger showed itself, also, in a constant outpouring of seditious papers, scurrilous, lying, filthy.

Nor did things go much better with my Council. Before his departure Philip had called a full meeting to inform them that I had chosen the Cardinal as my first councillor to act with them for the good of the realm; and, in view of my condition to act as Regent at need. This was not strict truth. It was Philip that had so chosen and in such affairs I never questioned his wisdom. This pleased none; especially Gardiner whom I, myself, reckoned the first.

Gardiner himself, as might have been expected, brought me news of the Council's unwillingness. 'Madam; the Cardinal is but new-come into this country and his fervour for the Faith smacks more of the Inquisition than of England. It is not pleasing to Englishmen, no, not even to the most faithful. Madam the Queen herself, has tried to temper his zeal—but in vain. How many there are that, good Catholics though they be, question this point of worship or that, trembling in their secret hearts lest their thoughts be known, and themselves hurried to the stake! I tell you, Madam, the Cardinal must not lead the Council; put him at the head and many a heart—yes, even true Catholic hearts—will harden against God. Madam, I am your Chancellor; yet first of all I am a bishop and I say to you choose someone less zealous for the Faith; it is expedient.'

'Yourself, my friend?'

He spread his hands; and again I noted their trembling.

'Not I, Madam; I am not well.'

'I will send you my own physicians.'

'Madam, old age is a sickness no physician can cure!'

'Oh Gardiner, Gardiner dear friend!' I held out my hands towards him. 'How shall I stand when you can no longer be my guide?'

'God will surely raise up someone at your need!' he said.

Well, there was little comfort in that!

So there I was, wretched mind and body, and weak with longing for my husband. I wanted my child; England's child. I knew that, as long as Philip had no child by me he did not regard me as truly his wife; that he would never come back to me. And, if he never came, how should I get me a child?

I wrote to him every day; sometimes two or three times in the same day. I sent him minutes of my Council asking his advice; first because I needed his wisdom, secondly because I meant to drive it home that he was the King—England's King. I sent him gifts of every kind, from the most costly to the simplest. My costly gifts must always be something I had by me; I was desperately short of money. I sent him in one day a great venison pasty such as he relished, together with the splendid jewel my father had always worn in his bonnet.

'You'll not tempt him with any gift, great or small!' Renard said. 'He'll be satisfied with nothing less than the crown. And that, Madam, is less a gift than a right! Crown him; or you will lose him; you and the country with you! It does not march with his dignity to be consort only. Madam, you must have him crowned—and not the consort's crown, neither.'

'Renard,' I told him, 'I will move heaven and earth in the matter.

He shall be crowned with all the ancient customs of English Kings.'

'Nothing less will suit him, Madam. I know of no other way to bring him back!'

Good advice? Maybe. It marched with my own desires; but I no longer trusted Renard as once. His jest concerning the Cardinal and my sister—if it was jest—had bitten deep. Was he not preparing a King true-crowned, to match my sister should I die?

For the truth is, in spite of all my resolution, I was eaten with jealousy of my sister, and, my distrust for her being no less, I sent for her to Greenwich that I might have her under my eye. I had no fear that she would catch the Cardinal within the net of her charms. I thought, rather, that he, courtly and scholarly, might bring her—for certainly none other could—into the Faith.

But he thought otherwise. 'Madam Elizabeth will never come into the Faith. Oh she will promise; and she will keep that promise where she can be seen and so long as it turn to her advantage. But when it shall no longer serve her turn—then God pity all poor Catholics!'

'Yet, Cousin, I implore you, speak with her on the matter. If we might truly bring her into the Faith how great a thing for her and for us all! Then there could be no cause to revolt; we should be a truly united country. And, if God see fit not to bless me with children—which Christ forfend—then with how good a heart could I make her my heir?'

'Madam you should know her by now. She's not to be trusted. No more than you, will she change her faith; but unlike you, she'll make a show of it. And behind that show? There'll be plotting and scheming and a marking down for punishment of all that stand by you and by God. Show her favour and you render her more dangerous.'

And so, also, said Gardiner. These days he was so sick a man I read death in his face and wondered how I should manage without his bitter wisdom.

'Madam, leave her where she is in the country—so long as she stay quiet. Already the people are sufficiently angry; heretics because we burn them, waverers because they, too, may burn; and true Catholics because we do not burn enough heretics. We are too slow, they say, to save this country for God! Bring her to London—or near London—and she could be the spark to set all ablaze. And it will be the easier because poor harvests swell discontent. Empty bellies sharpen anger whatever a man's faith. They say, also, the country is poor because of the Queen's marriage. They say . . .'

'They say! They say!' I heard my voice growl deep in my throat. 'They saw for themselves the wagons laden with bullion the King brought from Spain. And more; from his own pocket he has laid down two gold pieces for every one we ourselves have spent.'

'People forget. Now there go about rumours of war between France and Spain. Our people fear lest we be dragged into it. They fear, Madam, the waste both of life and gold that such a war must bring!'

'Spain is pledged by marriage contract not to drag us into her own wars. When the time comes that Spain wastes English lives and English gold, then let the people complain and I will listen! No, Gardiner; the King is faithful to his word and he is generous . . .'

'And he is a Spaniard; a *foreigner*. And for that the people will never forgive him! And to whom will they turn? To Madam Elizabeth! I tell you again, Madam, she is the spark to set the whole land afire!'

'All the more need to keep her under our eye. There, at least, she must make some show of loyalty.'

'Show, Madam. *Show!*' Suddenly he gave way, having no strength to stand out longer. 'Well, Madam, send for her if you must! Maybe the appearance of loyalty shall be of some service to us; God alone knows.'

So, riding quiet and discreet—which was wisdom in her—to Greenwich she came. She looked young, she looked innocent; that was always the first thing I marked with her. And she was clever. Never the slightest lack in respect towards me, nor yet exaggeration of the same. Her manner was perfect; respect from subject to Queen, obedient affection from young sister to older . . . so much older! That; and concern for my sick looks. And I would look at her and I would think, *If I die and you inherit, all the anguish of this country finding its God will come to nothing; to worse than nothing. You will bring all true believers to their death . . .*

It was in her mind, also; the thought ran to and fro between us.

During those days Elizabeth was at Greenwich, the Cardinal never so much as set eyes upon her. Though her apartments were near his own, he took care that he and she should never meet. She tried to make her opportunities that she might measure her strength, her wits against his. She set her spies to watch his comings and goings that they might—oh so innocently—meet; he set his spies for the opposite reason. 'I'll not make a mock of my faith to bandy words with antichrist!' he said. Yes, antichrist was the word he used—and he as courtly a gentleman as ever stepped!

If Pole would not so much as look at her, Gardiner continually followed her with his eyes, fierce still, for all their weakness; also, he planted spies amongst her own ladies to catch her every word. He was forever my good watch-dog. But, if to those two she was anathema, to the rest of the court she was all their joy. For she carried a spark within her that, let her but stand by the door, and all eyes turned to her; her praises were on every lip—Catholic or heretic. She knew how to be all things to all men.

Her false sweetness that could show so bitter an edge I could endure no longer. Within the week I had commanded her back to the country. Nor did it comfort me that, as she rode through London the people crowded the streets, perched themselves upon roof-tops and in trees to cheer her; to cast into her lap autumn posies and bright-berried garlands. She had hidden herself among her ladies, but she had not covered her face; and didn't they know that face, the Londoners? Didn't they know that flaming head of hers, and the grace with which she carried herself in the green-and-white gown, the Tudor colours? And she herself? Didn't she realise all that; and hadn't she counted upon it to the full?

Chapter Seven

The days dragged by; lonely and sad they were, yet full of business affairs. My health continued poor; I slept not more than three hours or four. I rose at dawn to kneel in silent prayer; then to early Mass and thereafter to break a fast with food I did not want nor my stomach tolerate. Breakfast being done I must study documents—home affairs, foreign policies and religious matters, until dinner. Often enough I could not eat but must sit, lips held tight, lest I vomit. Many an afternoon, and evening, too, I spent with my Council working far into the night. But still there were long hours to get through which I spent writing to my husband, telling him, as always, of my Council's discussions, asking his advice upon what we had done, and upon business to come. My letters finished, I would spend the rest of the night in prayer until, for weariness, I fell asleep. And that very weariness preventing restful sleep, filled my mind with troubled dreams, so that I would awake crying out for my husband to return.

In the matter of his crowning I could as yet do nothing. Parliament was not sitting and would not meet until November; then I should raise the matter again. And this time I meant to have my way. It was not fitting that the King of England go uncrowned.

But, before Parliament could meet, three notable heretics must come to trial.

Cranmer, Ridley and Latimer.

And notable, indeed. The first, archbishop of Canterbury, the second, bishop of London, the last bishop of Worcester. All three now deprived of their high office.

Already they had been tried and their guilt found. Now, their refusal to obey the new laws concerning worship, had enlarged the first charge against them; now they stood accused not of heresy alone—but of treason. So, seeing how grave the charge was become, my bishops thought that, in the name of justice, these men should be given a second trial—though all three had done more harm to the Faith than any that had gone before them. Thereafter let no man complain of injustice. For months they had lain in prison while good priests exhorted them to return to God. But it was all useless; the Devil had stiffened them. Yet I would have saved them if I could. They were old men; they had been priests, and in that office had stood in high estate. Should not such old men be let to die, either in their prisons; or if they would stay quiet, to return not to their high office but to their own homes?

But the Cardinal would have none of it! He silenced me with the old unanswerable question—*Would you save bodies that are born to perish at the expense of immortal souls?* And he would point out the value of making an example of such illustrious heretics. Gardiner would remind me of danger to God's whole orchard by reason of one rotten branch. And from my husband in Flanders I need not his frequent reminders that, unless I showed myself worthy before God, He would not see fit to send me a child.

In the second week of September—that sad September of rotted fruit and mildewed corn—Cranmer faced his judges; in the last week, Ridley and Latimer must face their own. The commission was headed by my lords and bishops of Lincoln, Bristol and Gloucester.

Of the guilt of all three there could be no question. They, that should lead men to Heaven and not to Hell, had, in the pulpit and out, exhorted their flock to cast away those hallowed rites they were pleased to call *Romish superstition*. The chief source of corruption was Cranmer; his influence was felt not in this country alone; for his words, like evil birds, winged across the sea to carry corruption to countless souls. And then, back they came, these words, strengthened by heretics abroad, set down in the most seditious writings—attacks of the most filthy sort upon me and my good bishops. And these writings were seized upon with joy by heretics in this, my own country, translated, added to and broadcast so that like ill seed they sprang up to spread corruption still further. It was such writings that lashed out against my good bishop of London, faithful servant of God. He was not only *bloody Bonner*, he was *antichrist*, he was *spawn of the devil*. It would not be long, I knew, before they named me so as well. So there it was! A continued corruption flowing outward from this country returning enhanced to make further mischief for us all.

When Cranmer appeared before the commission to answer charges of blasphemy, heresy and treason, he put off his cap and bowed himself to the ground. 'I bow, humble, not to the Pope of Rome, but to this court of the Queen's proctors, in humble respect to the Queen,' he told them.

Hardly an auspicious beginning!

Then my lord bishop of Glousceter said, 'You have fallen low, your candle is dim; let your light shine and be saved. God is merciful, and so is the Queen; for you might have suffered long ago!' And to that gentle speech Cranmer answered, 'I will never consent that the bishop of Rome have any jurisdiction within this realm.'

'Sir,' he was warned, 'that is treason!'

And he, 'Before God I protest I am no traitor!' And then, as of purpose to make the charge against himself blacker, added, 'I will never consent to the bishop of Rome, for then I sell myself to the Devil!' And then, 'The King is head of this realm, and so I have sworn!' And, being questioned, at last, as to that holiest of mysteries, the Sacrament, he cried out, 'If it be proved by any doctor that, a thousand years after his death, Christ's body is truly there, I will give over!' And there he stood, chopping his cheap logic against faith! Did he not know, he that had been Archbishop of England, that all knowledge, all philosophies must bow before faith; that always faith must bear away the palm?

And then, not content with what he had already said, he must go on, 'I believe that whoever eats and drinks that Sacrament, Christ is within him, whole Christ. But not corporeally, God says, *Confess me before all men and be not afraid. If you do so I will stand with you; if you shrink from me, I will shrink from you!* This a comfortable and terrible saying that makes me set all fear apart!'

So does the Devil use the Scriptures for his own purpose!

So backward and forward went the argument; and at last my lord bishop of Gloucester put an end to it.

'Master Cranmer—I am sorry I cannot otherwise name you—I am right sorry for your obstinacy. But who can save him that is obstinate to be lost? God would save you but you refuse it.' And Cranmer—how worthy a reply had his cause been worthy, 'If I have offended against the law of this land I will gladly suffer punishment.' And then injured his cause, 'But for obeying the Pope, what jurisdiction has a foreigner in this land?' For which my father must have applauded him; and for which my father's soul must be answerable.

'Master Cranmer', he was told, 'you must appear before the court of Rome to answer these charges. You shall have forty days in which to answer.'

So back to prison he went. And forty days being passed, and he showing no regard for the jurisdiction of the court of Rome, was adjudged heretic and condemned to death.

These days Cranmer was much in my thoughts. He was a man I had always hated—and hated is not a word I lightly use. I have never used it of my sister, nor of any other, save Anne Bullen. But with this priest and my father's harlot I had good cause; they had most bitterly wronged my mother. He it was, a young man fresh from the university, that had so cleverly advised my father in the so-called divorce that put my mother from her place and put the crown upon the head of the harlot. Him I might have come to forgive, as I had forgiven Gardiner; for though in that matter he had acted with Cranmer, he had done what he had thought to be right, never swerving from the course he held to be true. But Cranmer was a trimmer of sails; and it had angered me, those early months of my reign, that I must keep the man for my archbishop. Now he had spoken his own death sentence and so strangely are we made, I felt an unwillingness he should die.

When I confessed as much to Gardiner, those overhung eyes of his gleamed yellow; weak of body, his spirit was fierce as ever.

'The man's a heretic; *the* arch-heretic!' and his voice was unbelieving.

'An old man . . .'

'So was Hooper—and a better man, too!'

That I had wept over Hooper I did not tell him.

'He is no longer that same young man that stained my mother's honour, naming her incestuous and myself bastard!'

But for all that, I could not but remember how he had condemned me all through my growing years to fear, humiliation and hopeless grief.

'The leopard does not change his spots!' he said.

I said no more. But, *If he should recant; what then?* It was a question I must forever ask myself; a question I must, for my soul's sake, ask of my cousin the Cardinal.

'Do you wish him to recant?' And his tone was cold, judicial.

'Cousin . . . I think I do.'

'Why should you wish to save so infamous, so injurious a heretic?'

'I think because I hate him so much. I think I am afraid . . . afraid I might rejoice at his end.'

'In that case, Madam, you must cleanse your own heart. If the man be obstinate to burn—why then he must burn! The matter is not in the Queen's hands but in that of the church."

'Is it possible he may recant?'

He shrugged. 'He is a man to see several sides of the same question. He may come back to the Faith not so much in fear of the fire but because he sees the truth. But, if burn he must; then, Madam, search your own heart that there be not one grain of anger or bitterness left. Search your soul strictly lest you fall into mortal sin.'

A week later Ridley stood to his trial. My lord bishop of Lincoln came to tell me of the affair. I did not want to hear; I did not want to hear the sentence. But those things are done in the Queen's name; for if heresy be the church's affair, treason is the Queen's—and to those things she must listen.

'The man looked older than his years,' the bishop told me. 'Prison is not kind to any man! There he stood, weak and ill, in an old wool gown—he that had been my brother bishop high in authority, glorious in vestments. My heart, for the moment, turned over in my breast—a brother bishop to be brought so low! Yet what must one do to a bishop that abjures God? Five questions of heresy stand against him; no need to raise any but one. He denies the blessed miracle of the Sacrament.'

'Is there no end to the foolishness, the ingratitude of men? Christ offers us His own flesh-and-blood; and, because of His Grace that miracle has never been withdrawn, men are fools enough to forget it. Truly, my lord, I think it is the fools make more mischief than the wicked.'

'Ridley is no fool, Madam; he argues very strait. Were it otherwise we might confound him to his salvation. He says, very clear, *If you mean that the real flesh and blood is in the bread and wine we take into our mouth at the Sacrament, then I cannot subscribe to it. But the Sacrament does bring about a change. The bread that was common bread now represents Christ's body; the wine represents His blood. The change is in the spirit. For the true substance of the bread and the wine, remains that same substance that nourishes the flesh of man, as the grace and spirit of God nourishes the soul.* Those, Madam are his very words.'

'For all his learning a man's a fool if he cannot put by his little opinions and accept the miracle of God!' I cried out, passionate.

He said on a deep sigh, 'Madam, had you seen him, I doubt you could have forborne pity. He was cheerful; and that, had his cause not been the devil's, is a thing to admire. And he was witty, catching each shade of a word, and making play upon it, sending it back, as though he played at ball. And, Madam, never a sign a fear upon him. How could one help but pity him?'

'I pity him, indeed! That a man so near his end should play with his salvation as a game, setting no store by the eternal damnation of his soul!'

'The devil blinds him. Oh Madam, Madam, had you been there you had seen the pity of it. There he stood old and tired so that he could scarce keep his feet . . . and poor. Madam, so poor! As for myself, how could I forget that once he sat in my own chair in my own Cathedral. Then he was a prince of the church and, like a prince he had looked! His decent gown is threadbare now; tied to his waist by a string he carries his Bible. I think he does not see well for he peered at us as through a mist. He had an old felt hat that, for courtesy, he carried beneath his arm, he that had once been crowned with a mitre. Oh Madam, Madam, one must have a heart of stone not to pity him. One must keep remembering why he was there; it was the only way to keep my heart from crying out. *Let him go!'* And I, myself, must bite upon my lips remembering the man's gentleness to me when I had stood obstinate to my own faith, even in the shadow of death. None other had shown me true gentleness then, a gentleness without guile.

'Is there no way he may be saved?' And I held out my hands.

'None, Madam. He'll not abjure his heresies. You would think him eager for death. He went down upon one knee—he is perfect in courtesy; he said, and before God, heretic though he be, there's a sweetness in him. "My lords, if I must come before you, I pray you do not send for me until you be ready. I am an old man and it is great hurt to wait so long looking upon four walls." We told him we were sorry and that it should not occur again. Strange that a man should not fear the fire yet baulk at four harmless walls.'

'All men fear the fire; and those four walls are but ante-room to the stake!'

And I remembered how my father had shut me in my own room, walls and window darkened as in a prison cell, so that the four walls, unseen, enclosed me in that darkness like a grave. I know what it is to be alive and the fear of death upon me. I said, ashamed of the weakness that would have given the old man his life, 'He is, it seems, more concerned with his body than with his soul!'

'If that were so he must have recanted long ago. We besought him, Madam, to seek life both now and in the world to come; but he could scarce wait for us to finish. He asked leave to speak, and speak he did with such point, I think there was not one heart but was touched with pity; yet he spoke with such wit that, more than once, we were moved to laughter.'

'To jest in such a case?' I caught at the straw that might yet save him. 'Old and ill as he is, does he truly understand the business of the court?'

The straw broke in my hand.

'Madam, perfectly. It is the nature of the man. Old and ill, and, for all his brave show, I swear frightened, yet he turned all with a merry word. But all his wit cannot save him. For, hoping to the last for his salvation, question him as we would, still he said, *The bread is bread and the wine, wine. The change is not in the nature of these things but in their dignity*. Madam, him, too, we have put back to consider of his answer. But it is all one; he is obstinate to burn!'

That same day Latimer, too, came to his trial. And, my lord bishop came again to tell me how the matter had gone. The prisoner's garments were in worse case than before; now through the torn places one could see the wasted flesh. Someone had given him a cap with side-pieces, such as poor countrymen wear to shield their ears from cold. This he could not remove since, weak as he was, he must lean upon a staff; but with courtesy, he bowed himself before the court. To this he had come, Hugh Latimer, Anne Bullen's man. She had saved him from prison where, twenty-five years ago, he had been thrust for his heresies. She had implored my father to save him; she had made him her chaplain, through her he had been raised to the see of Worcester. Now, once again, he must answer for his heresies . . . and there was no Anne Bullen to save him. There was no-one but himself.

So there he stood, another old man, poor and broken in health; unlike Ridley's, his mind was enfeebled, unable to remember; but obstinate, obstinate still, standing strong upon his will in that unremembering mind of his. Christ, sweet Christ, must men run to destroy themselves? Save them, save them! Let them bend their stiff necks to your gentle yoke!

But still he stood by his appalling heresies, he, too, denying the blessed miracle, declaring *I have read my Bible seven times and I find in it no mention of bones and sinew!* But being brought into dispute, he could argue nothing; his memory had turned traitor.

'Madam, he was very faint; he asked that we should not keep him long. He was taken by a nausea and feared lest he vomit outright. He asked, Madam, as at his first trial, that he might be questioned and answer in English. He has forgotten his Latin, he that had been of all scholars the nonpareil! And then he desired us, his memory being gone, to be good to an old man, for to age and weakness we must all come.

'Madam, we had listened with patience and pity; but now our brother of Gloucester spoke, and spoke plain. "These be birds of one feather—all three! Latimer leans to Cranmer, Cranmer to Ridley, and Ridley upon his own wits!" So there it is, Madam; they must, all three, burn!'

I must speak no word against those that judged and rightly judged these heretic bishops; yet, for all that, my heart spoke a long sigh.

'Madam, your father and your brother set heretics in high places and sent many that held by the true faith to a traitor's death. You, Madam, have brought back the true faith. But how, if the one that comes after you shall bring back heresy to be the law of the land? What chance for the faithful then? None—unless the whole country be bound, and bound now, by a chain of unity; and that unity the blessed faith?'

But still my mind was on those three old men that must burn.

'When . . .?' I asked.

'Latimer and Ridley at once. Cranmer we judge it wise to keep awhile; we think he will recant. He was Primate of this country, its spiritual head . . . and many a heretic still holds him so. If only we might bring him to the truth! If he should recant, Madam—ah then! He would be the lock to secure the chain!'

I bowed my head in assent. I prayed with a true heart that Cranmer should not burn. I prayed he would open his heart to God, to worship as in his childhood he had been taught. I prayed with passion, not because I loved him but because I hated him. If *one spot of hatred remain in your heart then look to your own soul . . .*

The day before Latimer and Ridley suffered they underwent the wretched ordeal of degradation. It fills me with a sickness that they who have worn the vestments of a bishop, be stripped and have thrust upon them a travesty of those same vestments; that they should have their heads shaved so that no sign of tonsure remain, the very finger-nails scraped that no trace of holy oil linger. Essential it is, but none the less, my very soul must question it.

'They are to burn in the fire!' I cried out to Pole. 'Must we add degradation to their suffering?'

'It is laid down by Holy Church!' And he was clearly astonished at the question. 'Who shall question it? *You?*' And then, more gentle, 'Madam, steel yourself in this business; for it is God's business!'

Against that I could not argue. Indeed, in the days that were to follow, when grief and misfortune beat down upon me, I could not but wonder whether I, myself, was not being punished because my whole heart was not in the business; because I had put human bodies before human souls.

For Ridley and Latimer it was all over; again my lord bishop of Lincoln came to tell me of the event. And I must listen with a quiet face. But still I must remember that, but for their heresies, these had been good men. *But for their heresies.* There was the crux! Denying God's own miracle how might any man be called good? Their sentence had been carried out in the name of the church; and if my whole heart could not uphold it, then I must the more strengthen my spirit.

Ridley that resisted not the fire, calling it his marriage, resisted the degradation with all his poor strength. Nor would he take the blessed wafer in his hand preferring it should fall to the ground. But there came a priest that, taking him by the hand, fastened the wafer between his locked palms.

'The stakes, Madam, were set up in the town ditch; the mayor and sheriff were there together with a body of armed men. We feared lest the sight of the two old men would rouse anger in the heretics and pity in us all. Ridley had sent for his best gown, rich black velvet edged with fur; *a man goes in his best to his wedding*; he said. But Latimer, having no other, wore the old torn gown and over it a new shroud that fell to his feet.

'And as they went by, the folk wept and made no shift to hide their tears; so many, indeed, wept, it was hard to say who was heretic and who true believer. But those two, walking steady in the midst of the soldiers lest there be a last-minute attempt to save them, showed never a sign of faltering. Truly the Devil lent them courage!

'When they came to the ditch, those two kneeled down and each man kissed the stake. Then rising, Ridley said, *Be of good cheer, brother!* And the other, *God will give us strength to endure it.* Then, Madam, they were exhorted to a last-minute repentance, but it was useless.

'Then they were stripped for the fire. Ridley gave away everything —from the velvet gown to the truss about his wasted body. Latimer gave nothing—he had nothing to give; the poorest beggar must despise the rags he wore.

'Then came the smith to rivet the chains and Ridley said, *Drive the nails hard, for the flesh is weak.* Weak the flesh might be but his voice was high and clear. Then the fellow gave him a bag of gunpowder to hang about his neck and, *I thank you, friend, I take it as a gift from God,* Ridley said. *Have you one for my friend?*

' "Sir, I have!" the fellow said, himself weeping the while that, in such a strait, a man should think of another.'

'God!' and I smote my two hands together. 'Why are these heretics so obstinate to tear the heart within one's body!'

'Why, before God, are they obstinate to lose their souls? Well, Madam, they lit the faggots at Ridley's feet; and Latimer that had ever rated himself a coward to pain, cried out so that we all heard him, *Be of good comfort, brother, and play the man! This day we light such a candle as by God's Grace shall never be put out!*'

'I pray God it be not so!' Yet dying men oft-times turn prophet and their words echo down the ages!

'The flames began to spread upwards and Ridley cried from the fire, *Into Thy Hand, oh God I commend my spirit!* And Latimer, we heard, very clear, *Oh Father in Heaven receive my soul!*

'Would to God it may be so!' I said.

'Then, Madam, he stretched out his hands and dipped them in the flames and stroked his face as though he bathed it in cool water. He died very soon; a gentle death; more gentle than any I ever saw in the fire.'

'Pray God it was not the Devil gave him strength but God in His mercy!' For I was shaken lest the old man, at the last, strengthened by the Devil, had lost his soul. And I was shaken, too, by reason of those words of his. What had he meant by lighting a candle that should never be put out? It was, like the oracles of old, a saying to cut both ways. If he had meant a candle to light the way back to the true faith, then his soul was safe and the prophecy good. But if . . .

It was some moments before I understood that my good bishop was now talking about Ridley.

'A most cruel death. Madam, you had best not hear it.'

'Hear it I must! It is laid upon my soul. Shall the law condemn a man to suffer and the Queen not have courage to hear it?'

'The fire, Madam, was badly laid. It took time to come at him. How it must have been for him, Christ alone knows. But to us that watched—eternity! For who can endure to see a man die in torment, though it be for his own good? Hearts are not made of stone, Madam. Maybe God Himself ordained the long agony that the man's soul might, at the last, be snatched from the everlasting fire. He cried out, Madam, again and again, *Let the fire come at me*. For a while he endured his agony; then *I cannot burn . . . I cannot burn!* he cried and wept like a child. Madam, it was horrible! Then a fellow that stood by pulled out a faggot that smouldered at Ridley's feet and held it to the gunpowder at the neck. And it was the end.

'I tell you, Madam, my whole inside rose in vomit; I was wet through and through with my sweat. Did I not know we light our fires to save a man's soul for God, I could not do it. Madam, I asked myself this question. *If I might save a soul by burning my own flesh and not another's, should I do it?* I know my answer . . . and I am not proud of it.'

'We burn not to torment but to save from everlasting torment!' And then I heard my voice very deep as when I am moved beyond all tears, 'Seek out those that lit the fire so ill. See to it that they are punished!'

I sat alone in my room and I held my finger to the candle-flame. I bit upon my lips holding my finger steady. Time seemed eternal; the torment unendurable. Yet, when I looked upon the clock, the hand had not moved to the next minute. I lifted my finger from the flame, my blackened, reddened finger; and even as I lifted it into the air, the flesh rose in a great blister. I wept with the pain of it; and weeping still, I thought, To this pain, God alone knows how much magnified, we condemn others. Must we take this upon ourselves. Can we not leave it to God? And back came my answer. *We must not throw all upon God. Man must answer for the soul of his brother.*

I knelt in prayer and there remained until my whole body shook with the strain of it . . . and all the time the pain of my finger throbbed and swelled taking my mind from God.

Yet still I knelt, praying that the terrible burnings might stop; and the pain of my own burning overthrowing me, I prayed *Oh God, if you should say, Let my own body burn to save all heretic souls and clean heresy from this land, I would try to do it. Like Ridley I would command the chains be riveted that for all my crying I be left to burn; for cry out from the fire I must. God, I would essay the torment for you . . . but never ask it of me . . . never ask it!*

And, rising from my knees, I remembered the truss upon Ridley's wasted body, and it seemed to me that God Himself might have wept at the sight. All through the night I could not sleep for weeping over the poor, pitiful truss; nor, the blister having broken and the raw flesh catching upon the sheet, could I sleep for the pain in my finger.

Chapter Eight

The year of 'fifty-five that had begun in such hope, such happiness, was through months of increasing sorrow, to end at last in desolation. By the end of it, I had lost not only all hope of a child but all hope of a pregnancy; for my husband did not return—nor intend to return—until Parliament had agreed to a crowning; and not a consort's crown, neither! Equal sovereign with myself.

The whole of that year I did not recover my health. I was weak from my illness and sick with a hopeless hope for the sight of my husband. I was troubled by dissensions in my Council and worn by battles with my Parliament. Two things I most desperately needed. I needed money and I needed my husband crowned—and which need more desperate I cannot say. Without money I could not carry on the business of the state; without the crowning there would be no heir of my body to inherit not only England but the vast possessions provided for in my marriage contract. Of my own woman's need for husband and child I need not speak.

And all the time the terrible burnings. The church demanded it and my conscience assented; my conscience but not my heart. Where the heart would lead, I may often doubt; where conscience speaks—though it be to my own hurt—my way is always clear. I can no other way. To burn out heresy from the land is right. One must not look too close upon human agony; one must fix one's eyes upon God. Did I, in my weakness, appear to waver, then from the Netherlands Philip exhorted me, his father, the Emperor exhorted me; nor did my bishops leave their exhortations. Often enough I wept in the privacy of my closet that I was a Queen—a Queen with God upon my conscience to send human flesh to the fire. And because I was so constrained, I had lost the love of my people!

How often I wept as I prayed, remembering my mother; like her, my tears wet the very stones where I knelt.

In my despair I turned to Renard; though I was no longer sure of his faithfulness to myself, yet, if he kept faith with Philip, that of itself meant keeping faith with me.

'I have lost the love of my people. I think no Queen ever came to crown—nor no King, neither, with such love. Now it is gone . . . gone. My church saves souls for God—and I suffer thereby. I suffer not only in the loss of my people's love, but in my own soul. I have set my little mind against the mighty conscience of the Church and with my conscience I have come to terms. Not so with my heart; my heart cries out against the burnings. And between heart and conscience I am torn. I tell you, Renard, whether he that burns be high or low, I suffer with him; within myself I suffer. With every burning strength goes from me never to return.'

'I know it, Madam. The Queen's martyrdom is longer, slower than death in the fire! Madam, might it not be wise to halt the burnings; give the people time to recover?'

'My conscience is in the keeping of my church; that conscience must be my guide.'

'Expediency, Madam, may be a better guide! It is perhaps a cold word but it is the right word; yet, if you dislike it, then there's another—clemency.'

'You talk to me of mercy in such a case? What mercy to save a human soul from the eternal fire?'

'I said *clemency*, Madam. Mercy is a divine attribute, clemency a lesser, human one; in this case, a pause in which to gather strength. But call it what you will! Madam, stay the executions a little!'

'Renard, you are a voice crying in the wilderness. I cannot hear it for the great chorus that commands me. And if I could, I would not. When my church commands—I obey!'

I was to remember this talk with Renard, it was the last I had with him; for early in September he was recalled to Brussels and thence to Paris.

'Who shall take your place?' And I wrung my hands.

'No-one, Madam. The Emperor abdicates; all his possessions go to his son. That son is the King of England. There needs no ambassador.'

'Who shall stand my friend?'

'Every true Spaniard, Madam. And there is one, especially, you may trust. You may, Madam, trust him with your life!'

And, when I looked my question, 'It is de Figueroa,' he said. 'Don Gomez. He's in love, Madam.'

'But not with *me*!' And I made myself to smile.

'He loves all she loves. For the sake of Mistress Dormer, as well as for your own, he'll serve you to the last drop of his blood.'

'That would do my poor Dormer ill-service!' I said.

'They know their duty both of them; nor will it be hard. Don Gomez stays here for the present; ambassador extraordinary. As soon as the Emperor abdicates he will be recalled; yet he will return again—not as ambassador but as the Queen's friend. He will bring you messages from the King, both open and secret; he will be backwards and forwards until the King returns . . . nor will that be long. As soon as the abdication ceremonies are complete the King will be with you again.'

And the crowning? It was a question I did not ask.

'God is good!' he added. And what did he mean by that? That Parliament would relent? Or that God would send my husband back without a crowning? I did not ask. With that oracular saying I must make myself content.

I said Farewell to Renard with grief. He had been a most knowledgeable man and my good friend. My affection for him, it is true, had been somewhat diminished by his advice that, in the event of my death, Philip should marry my sister. This I should never have believed save that Gardiner, himself, had told it me. I had never questioned Renard upon this, for that had been the end of all kindliness between us. Yet I had tried to come to terms with it. If such a marriage were for the good of my country and for Philip, himself, must I not make myself content? But for all my efforts I could not believe it. Yet if Renard believed it must I not give him credit? Now he was going, all the old trust and kindliness swelled my heart; I should miss those talks in my closet, friend to friend. He was the only one to whom I could open my heart about Philip. His going must leave yet more emptiness in my all-but empty life.

What I had said to Renard was true. With every burning, strength flowed from me. My ill-health grew worse. I vomited often; at times the pains in my head were such that I must beat it against the wall that one pain drive out the other. Sometimes, not only hands and feet, but my entire body would swell into a dropsy such as my father had suffered. At these times I dared not look into a mirror lest I see a thin peaked face, a pinhead set upon a swollen body. 'It is not a true dropsy,

God be praised,’ Buttes, my physician, said. ‘It is a false dropsy that comes from anguish of the spirit.’

Then there was no cure for me, until my husband returned; none at all.

Adding to my grief. I never saw Gardiner but I read death in his face; read it grieving not for him that was old and tired and ready to lay down his burden, but for myself that must go missing his bitter wisdom. If I read death in his face, maybe he read the same in mine; for he advised me to send for my sister.

This advice from him, so entirely unexpected, so utterly out of character with this man that had never ceased urging me to be rid of her, astonished me. And he, seeing me all amazed, said, ‘Madam, it is no longer safe to keep her from you! You need her good will, you need her countenance. Madam, you must show her some favour!’

And when still I stared not knowing what to make of this turnabout, he said, ‘The Queen knows there’s discontent everywhere. Religion has split the country in two; but in all else the people are at one. They blame the Queen, believers and heretics alike, because the harvests are bad. The former say she is not sufficiently God’s friend; the latter that she is God’s enemy. Food is at famine prices; and taxes are high though the Queen has lightened them—and her own purse with it! Yet still they are more than folk can afford; and for this they blame the Queen’s marriage. It is all a great nonsense. The King has brought with him more gold than has ever been spent on him. But the people are ignorant . . .’

‘. . . and they hate foreigners.’ I finished for him. ‘Gardiner, you never wanted my marriage; you also do not like foreigners!’

‘I am an Englishman; and like an Englishman I speak. But, Madam, it is not me you must consider, but the people. Should they turn against you, to whom will they turn instead? The answer you know full well. And in this, too, the people are one—believer and heretic alike. Therefore I say, send for the lady Elizabeth, show her good countenance, buy her loyalty!’

‘There’s not enough treasure in all Christendom to buy that!’ I said, bitter.

‘Then pay what you have. Her strength is your strength!”

‘Your advice comes too late. I do not want her near me. I want not her company nor her bought loyalty. There’s no man can trust her word! No, nor God, neither! She professes herself of the true faith; so she thinks to win me. Simple I may be, but not such a fool! No need to scratch her to find a heretic! I do not want her associated in the minds of the people with me and my favour; I do not want her associated with the crown!'

And I do not want her cleverness, nor her youth; nor her eyes watchful upon me and my sorrows, calculating her chance of the crown . . .

'Until the Queen bears a child, Madam Elizabeth must forever be associated with the crown.'

'Am I not a woman like any other, a *woman*!' And I remembered how once, my father, desperate for a son, had cried out, *Am I not a man like any other! A man! A man!*

He said no more. He sighed very deep and left me.

I did not send for my sister.

October came in; Parliament re-assembled and I must strengthen myself to fight for Philip's crown. November came in and still I did not send for her. It was the first time I had turned a deaf ear to my Chancellor's advice. He was my loyal friend, my best, my shrewdest adviser. *Was? Had been* . . . once. Now he was old, he was sick, he was near his death. Now, it seemed, feebleness of body was clouding the clear mind. This last piece of advice I dared not take. To bring her near me, to countenance her, give her place next to myself; was this not, in all but words, to declare her my heir? I could not do it. For I doubted strongly as I doubt still—that she is my father's daughter. I read and re-read old documents and letters; I studied what witnesses had said about Anne Bullen—both her friends and her enemies. I weighed every word in the indictment against her, and especially the notes written thereon in my father's own hand. I scrutinised every word spoken at the trial.

And this, since I am sworn to the truth, I am bound to say. I believe that, though justice was done, the trial was in its essence unjust. The few things that were said in her favour had been omitted; or else a word added here and word there, to alter the whole meaning. I do not believe she lay with all the gallants named; she was too careful, too ambitious. But of one I am not at all sure—that there had not been incest between Anne Bullen and her brother. In that case, the child of that union might well be my sister. Between brother and sister there had been tremendous attraction, a more than ordinary affection. Incest, or anything approaching it, Anne Bullen had strenuously denied. Well that was natural enough! But her brother? He had never denied it;

neither in his examination, nor in the court-room, nor even upon the scaffold. Yet there had been no witness against them; none, save only his wife mad with jealousy against those two.

Over and over again, I would consider my sister, feature by feature; and then the whole aspect of her. I could find no trace in her of my father, save in manner, which, at one time, many had copied. Nor was that red head of hers any proof; more than one of her clan had just such hair. And, for overweight, she had not inherited my father's passion for music, that was a passion with me, also. That she was my father's daughter I might well doubt; that she was God's enemy I had no doubt at all. How dare I, then, declare this child of possible incest, my heir, lift God's enemy to the crown?

There was but one way out of this tangle. My husband must come back to me; he must get me with child. My body alone, my poor weak body was the rock against which the storm battered to overthrow Christ's kingdom. It was for this God had put me into the world; for this I had been strengthened to endure persecution and the fear of death.

I wrote to Philip. I implored him to return, were it but for one night; one night, only. He did not come. He sent his excuses—very reasonable excuses. One night in England, meant a journey of at least a week—or more if the winds were contrary. Such time could not be spared while important affairs were in train. 'And, indeed, Madam,' Don Gomez amplified these excuses, 'as the Queen knows, the process of complete abdication is no light thing. All earthly possessions, titles and so forth must be disposed of, documents drawn, loyalties transferred and accepted. It is not only the great ceremony of abdication itself; it must be followed by the equal ceremony of subject-princes swearing allegiance.

Yes, all reasonable enough; and I must possess my soul in what patience I might; but patience has never come easy to me. Now that my husband was to inherit his father's vast possessions, it was even more urgent to give him a son; a son to unite England and the Netherlands, and maybe Spain and every other kingship, princedom and dukedom besides. Don Carlos, son of Philip's first marriage, was a poor thing, feeble in mind and body alike. I wished him no harm; I pitied him that God had made him so . . . but in the name of the same God I prayed God Philip would come soon.

De Noailles sent requesting audience. I distrusted anything he might say but some little courtesy I must show. He came, his face grave; but his eyes gave him away.

'Madam, it is true that King Philip must tarry abroad for the great matter of abdication. The King as the Queen knows, has never neglected his duties be they pleasant or not . . .' His glance travelling me head to foot made it plain that a husband's duties towards me no man could perform with pleasure. 'But, Madam . . .' and he was careful, indeed, 'the King enjoys himself like any young man . . .'

Why should he not?' and I was a little sharp; for again his glance had made it clear that among those enjoyments I could not count.

'If Madam the Queen is content . . .'

'Why should I not be content? Nor, Mr. Ambassador, can I conceive it to be any business of yours!'

'The Queen's happiness is her friends' affair.'

'Among those friends I do not place you. Sir, I am not blind to certain intrigues among those that are my enemies. I will listen to you, sir, upon your own business and none other!'

Dismissed, he was yet not displeased with himself. My distrust of him was an old story and by it he set little store. He had pricked me with suspicion against my husband; for all my calmness, he, knowing my nature, was sure of some success. For where is the woman, deep in love with her husband, and he, far way, open to the flatteries of younger, more desirable women, but she must give ear to some suspicion, though it be against her will?

In my own presence I might shut de Noailles' mouth; but behind my back I could not shut it; nor could I stay the gossip that began now to cross the sea.

My husband was, indeed, making the most of his time before shouldering his new responsibilities—if the tales were true. He missed no festivity high or low, so the stories went. At every feast, every masquerade, and, above all, at every wedding, he led the rest; no jest too crude, too lewd, but he took his part therein. And he was drinking too much, my sober Philip! How could I believe such tales? Yet they kept coming—name and place and every detail.

At last I sent for de Figueroa. I questioned him, leading him with care; I thought I was being subtle but he came to the point at once.

'The King is wise. He builds up, as it were, to his responsibilities,' Don Gomez said. 'He is right to mingle freely with the people—all sorts and conditions of people. When first he went into Flanders they complained he was cold, formal and withdrawn. If now he attend festivities, if he drink with others in good fellowship—that is right; and they like him the better for it. As for his not being always sober—the Queen must forgive me that I repeat the slander—it is completely a lie. The King is one to take his drink well; no-one ever saw him but perfectly himself. Surely the Queen can find no fault there!'

It made good sense—so long as he were not too free of his mingling, nor intemperate in his drinking.

'Don Gomez,' I told him, 'my father danced and drank his way into the people's love. It is no bad way, so long as greater matters do not give way to such behaviour. You are soon for Flanders. Tell the King he must come back; let the time be never so short, nor duties long, he must come back!'

He looked at me with a pity more wounding than de Noailles' sneers. He said nothing but I knew his answer.

'In the matter of the crowning,' I told him, 'I would put him not equal with myself, but above, above! Tell him that! This is a stiff-necked Parliament; yet I work and will work for his crowning, his equal crowning, work with all the strength that is in me. Tell him so; I pray you, tell him! But let him not wait for that; let him delay no longer. He is needed here; most sorely needed. Let him but come—and the crown is his! His own self will more move Parliament than any word of mine!'

'Madam, I will do it. But, I must remind the Queen that, when he was here, the King could no more persuade your Parliament than could the Queen herself. Yet, Madam, I will truly urge it; for times do change and even Parliament may bend its stiff neck. For God watches over all!'

When he was gone I sent for Gardiner.

'Madam, leave the matter of the King's crowning, I beg you, with all my heart. To raise the question now would be fatal. We have first to press for a subsidy for the Queen; a much-needed subsidy. Madam, your household is sunk low, indeed! Your food poor, your servants threadbare and for the most part unpaid. As for your army—' and he threw up his hands. 'Of the navy, I need not speak! Our ships are few enough and in poor state! That Wardrobe and Treasury alike are empty—the Queen needs no telling. You have been too busy, Madam, paying your father's debts and your brother's also; you have returned to the church property that came into your own hands, property that by the Pope's good-will you were free to keep, is it any wonder . . .' Words failed again; he spread his empty hands.

'It is true; all true! My grandfather with patience and skill amassed a great fortune . . . and earned for himself the name of miser. Would God they might say the same of my father! No miser, he! He lived in splendour and left enormous debts. Nor were those that called themselves *Protector* more careful of the little that remained. To my father's debts they added my brother's. As you say, I have paid what debts I could. And if I returned to the church what was not mine to keep—it was no more than honest. Shall I cheat God? I have cut down my household expenses and every outgoing so that my grandfather's title descends to me . . . Miser!'

'True, Madam, but up to a point, only! Your marriage; no stinting there! The great fleet you sent to fetch the King home, the sailors new-clothed and ships fresh-painted and dressed over-all! It was right, it was proper; but it was not done for nothing! And the marriage, itself; the feasting, the pageants, the tournaments! And the gifts; Madam, the gifts! And the lodgings for the King and his train—how many in that train! Thousands rather than hundreds! And again, Madam, it was right and it was proper—and again it cost money we did not have. Even now the fleet waits at Calais until it shall please the King return. Again, very proper . . . if you can afford it. But if there's no money—what then? We borrow and we borrow; from foreign bankers, from such nobles and merchants as are willing—or unwilling —to lend; and all the gold the King brought with him, will not meet the demand. Madam, we *need* money; do not complicate matters with talk of a crowning, even the simplest, costs money, a great deal of money. Money, Madam, the Queen must have for her everyday expenses; and that money I will get if I die for it.'

For all he was a sick man his powers did not fail. Fierce and forthright; he reminded Parliament of the great debts I had inherited and how much I had paid from my own private purse. He did not ignore the cost of my marriage. No! But he reminded it of the wagons of Spanish bullion that had rolled in to the Mint. Never, he reminded them, had I asked for the great subsidies demanded by my father and my brother—subsidies that had been granted them. No, rather of my own free will, I had lightened taxes, paid back debts, returned to the church lands that I might have kept. Nay more; I had not kept for myself lands and treasures sequestered from traitors but had returned them to the widows and orphans. 'Must the Queen, her private purse so generously emptied to serve the needs of others, now go hat in hand, like a beggar imploring that which is her right?'

So careful a speech; so reasoned and so moving! Parliament gave me the money; a very large sum—a million in gold.

Gardiner had kept his word, spoken his own epitaph. That speech was his swansong. As he finished, he staggered and fell; they carried him from the Parliament chamber to Whitehall, it being nearer than his own Winchester House; and there he died.

On a November day, as cheerless as my own heart, he closed those fierce eyes of his in peace.

Chapter Nine

He was dead. Had I thought myself forlorn? Now I was forlorn, indeed! Since my girlhood he had been so great a figure in my life, first as enemy, then as friend. As a Chancellor he had been without equal; as a friend loyal and true, my only true friend, perhaps! Such a one I should not find again. I missed him intolerably. I missed his fierce glance, his sour laugh; I missed his sharp wisdom, his zeal for the Faith, and, equal with that zeal, his desire for the best good of this country. He had been swayed never by promise nor bribe. He had been the rock on which I leaned; without that shelter the sun must smite me by day and the moon by night.

And now I must find a new Chancellor. After much thought I chose Nicholas Heath, my archbishop of York. In this I reversed my father's policy, and my brother's also—if that unfortunate child could be said to have had one of his own. They had chosen statesmen rather than churchmen; I put my trust in men of God. Like Gardiner, Heath was one to strengthen me should I weaken in the punishing of heretics. And these days I needed strengthening. I believe that only the threat of God withholding a child should I weaken, kept me steady. And, even then, there were times when in my own heart I would say *Let men come to God, each in his own way. Let God look to His Own!* And, though I longed to rest upon that thought, I must forever listen to Heath reminding me, *There is but one way to God. If men must burn to light that way, then burn they must!*

My health, poor as it was, now took a turn for the worse, As with that Jewish King of old, a melancholy fell upon me. I despaired lest I die, childless, and the crown fall to my sister. It lay upon me, a black cloud, that, in this my England, Christ's kingdom must then be lost and the people, my sacred charge, forever damned.

In my despair I wrote again to Philip, urging his return.

He answered as before—with courteous refusal. He waited for the great matter of his father's abdication. Beneath his courtesies, one thing stood out clear. That he was still uncrowned was due to me—my own unwillingness. The fault was mine. I was the Queen. I had but to command.

That he should fault me that desired it with all my heart, cast me into yet deeper melancholy.

'I would give him the crown if I might!' I cried out to de Figueroa, as I had cried before, 'Did you not tell him so? Yes, and I would follow him as he chose—consort, wife, servant!'

'As to that last, I think not, Madam!' And he smiled. 'You are a Tudor; and, for extra weight, Spanish Tudor. Your pride, Madam, is as great as his own!'

'It is pride makes me humble.'

He gave me a long look. 'I believe it!' he said. 'But it would not serve you. He requires a wife to match himself in pride. Show yourself, humble, and, Madam—forgive me that I put it plain—you lose your game!'

The abdication was complete. Philip had succeeded to all his father's lands, to all his titles and honours—save one and to that I will return later. I had intended to see the great ceremony with my own eyes—this proudest moment in my husband's life. But he did not invite me; my ill-health and the pressure of our English affairs, his reasons. Without his invitation I could not got but must content myself seeing the affair through another's eyes—eyes of my ambassador, Mason.

'The Emperor had already left his palace and retired to a villa some few miles without Brussels. Now he came riding into the city upon a humble mule, led by a priest. He was clothed in a long, black gown of some plain stuff such as priests wear; and save for the Order of the Golden Fleece, he wore no jewel . . . and very strange it looked upon that poor gown! He was attended by priests, by priests only that chanted as they came.

'And thus humbly attended, he came into the great hall, his own great hall, where, in all their splendour they waited—princes of the church, subject princes, nobles from every land in Christendom and his own courtiers—all, all waiting for this man so humbly clad. By the throne stood King Philip. He was in black also; but it was black with a difference! It was costly stuff of great elegance and well set off with jewels. He was very pale, very grave. He stood head bared to hear his father speak.

'When the Emperor began, his voice though low was firm; then, suddenly overcome, for the occasion was both unusual and great, he was forced to lean upon a priest's arm. "I have lived a long life," he said when he was a little recovered, "and a hard one. I have fought in many lands for my faith and for my God; I have spared no effort for His Glory. Now age and sickness that come to all, Emperor and peasant alike, have come to me. It is time to lay down the burden. For, indeed, how shall a man guide great affairs that has not strength left to guide his own mule? And so I renounce all crowns, estates, titles, honours to my only son and heir; for I am assured that in all Christendom he is the man most fit to receive them."

'Then, Madam, he turned to King Philip, and it was a sight to move the heart—the old, sick father and the young strong son. "Do your duty well," he said, "lest men blame me that, too soon, I gave up my office. Fear God. Rule with justice. Respect the laws of those countries over which you shall bear rule. But, above all things, cherish our holy faith." And then, Madam, he said, "May God bless you with a son that, when you are old as I am, and feeble, you may resign your earthly kingdoms with the same good faith that I resign mine to you this day." '

'Amen to that!' I said. *God send my husband home that I may bear the son that is needful to all Christendom!*

'Then, Madam, the young man, weeping, knelt at the old man's feet and swore to be a worthy son of such a father!'

And let my husband prove as worthy a father of as worthy a son!

If I had been determined before to have my husband crowned, I vowed now I'd not rest until I saw it done. 'King of so vast an empire, how should he return to this little land an uncrowned King? There's no man can expect it!' I told my new Chancellor.

He spread his hands and said nothing. And I longed, for my old fierce, fighting Gardiner, as I was so often to long! A good archbishop this Heath; in all matters of the church firm and dedicated. But as a Chancellor—limited and weak. I began to see my father had been wise using statesmen in high places rather than churchmen. In Gardiner I had been fortunate; he had been more statesman than churchman. With Heath the church came first, the state second. He had not the cool, assured wisdom of Gardiner, the certainty that comes from long experience; still less the passion, the will to drive, to control Parliament.

Heath's advice was forever the same. *Patience. Patience.* And again, *Patience.*

Now I must set my own wits to work; and, so thinking, remembered a piece of advice Gardiner had once given me. *Wait until Parliament is finished. When the best part of the commons have ridden home, you may then try your luck with the lords. With promises and gifts you may get your way.*

More than ever the advice seemed good; Parliament out of the way, I might yet persuade my Council. I wrote asking Philip's advice in this matter. His answer was immediate.

Unless you are certain of success you are not to attempt it . . .

It was clear he feared lest he be made the laughing-stock of Europe. So, my Council, being, as usual, divided amongst itself, I decided to put by the project for the moment. Nothing for it, so it would seem, but to accept Heath's tedious advice.

But I am not a patient woman; nor was this a time for patience. Once more I set my wits to work and came to my answer roundabout. Both my father, and my brother young as he was, had been given the right to choose who should succeed to the crown. When Parliament assembled once more I asked for that same right.

I asked; and was refused. They had spied out the danger. So, my father's spirit descending upon me, I immediately and in high rage, dismissed this unyielding Parliament of mine.

'I blame Heath; and myself, also, for making him my Chancellor!' I told my cousin Cardinal Pole. 'He has neither the wit nor will to command these stiff-necked men that, calling themselves my government, hold it their duty to govern me, also!'

'Then, Madam, you are unjust! Gardiner's intellect was diamond-clear, his will steel, and his devotion to his Queen unbounded; yet he, could not—even in the first, full warmth of the people's love for you—carry Parliament with you in this matter. For to whom would you leave the crown had you your choice; to whom—failing your child—but your husband? And what is the bill you have just asked but the first hidden step to crowning him *now*? In this case Parliament is justified. And you, yourself? You show yourself a loving wife, true and kind, putting always her husband's dignity first. With that he should be satisfied!'

'Too loving, too true, too kind!' I cried out bitter. 'And he? How true? How kind? How loving?'

It was the first time I had spoken my bitterness aloud.

Silent I might be, nursing my injuries in my heart; but strange tales were reaching me from Flanders. He was, it seemed, taking his new honours lightly; in every wanton pleasure, his the foremost part. It was as though, released from me—and from his father maybe, also—he could not enough proclaim his freedom. That he gambled, that he danced and drank the night through, I knew. Disappointed, I could yet find excuses for him. He was young, from babyhood restrained to fit the pattern of the Spanish heir. What wonder if he allowed himself a little laxity now?

But now there came tales of ladies of easy virtue—which I take to mean no virtue at all; and to these rendezvous he would go masked. These last tales I did not believe. Philip was a chaste man—Renard had sworn it; and, for myself, I had no reason to disbelieve it. And, indeed, if he went masked, how should any man know *whose* face was concealed? It was jealousy and spite pinned those sordid tales upon him.

I did not believe them; yet I could not endure his fair name to be sullied; nor mine—nor mine, neither! For if the tales dishonoured him, they dishonoured me, also, that was his wife. There was but one way of putting an end to them. If for no other reason he must come home. I wrote to him; wrote again and again; and to his father now in his monastery at Yuste, I wrote also. I might have spared myself the humiliation; the result was—nothing!

Philip did not come. He was pressed with work! He was, besides, sick. At this last, myself unwell, I worked myself into a fever of concern for him. The nature of his illness I did not know; nor could I find out.

'I shall send my own physicians!' I told de Figueroa.

And he. 'The lord King is fatigued; so many duties! A little while, and he will be well again. Then he will come home.' Comfortable words; but I thought he did not look me in the face.

I sent my Chamberlain to Brussels to make enquiries; but for all the information I got he might have stayed at home. He reported almost exactly in de Figueroa's words. 'The King's duties are many; he is tired. He will come soon!'

'After too much pleasure sickness is not unusual,' de Noailles told me smooth and smiling,' and I was too ignorant, too fond, to come at his meaning.

So now I must content myself sending him any gift that might pleasure him—a fine horse, a hunting-dog of pedigree, a pair of gloves all worked with gold. And more than once I sent a great meat pasty rich yet light, gilded with lozenges of gold, such as he loved. With these gifts I sent never a reproach but loving messages only, together with my hopes for his speedy recovery and my longing for his return.

But in that last I must still hold myself into patience. And patience I needed. Philip meant what he said. Sick or well he would never return, without a crowning—and an equal crown. Always he had made that clear; now he made it clearer still. He was sending for the last of those possessions he had left behind—servants, hounds, horses, falcons, and books, ceremonial garments. Everything. He meant completely to withdraw himself. Now I understood the tale of that Queen of Carthage, who, by her lover deserted, threw herself upon her funeral pyre and burned to her death. Once I had thought her behaviour excessive; I thought so no longer. But she was a pagan; to a Christian self-destruction is a deadly sin.

I must go on living.

Chapter Ten

Christmas came and went. The year was ended; the bad year of 'fifty-five.

The new year came in. *God let this be a good year. Send us more men of true faith and let the burnings cease. Send us good harvests. Send back my husband; dear God give me a child.* These, my constant prayers sleeping and waking.

I tried to rouse myself from my grief, to shake off my ill-health, I must show myself more cheerful; my ladies should not be too much enclosed with a sick, sad woman. For God has given me one good gift that has never failed. Always I have been lovingly and faithfully served; even in my most desperate days of humiliation and danger I have always had true hearts to stand by me; yes, even in the hateful household Anne Bullen set up for the babe, my sister, at Hunsdon, ruled by her toadies and bullies, I yet found one heart to comfort me. It is a gift for which to thank God. But the love I need above all others, the love of one man—that is denied me.

I had my news of Philip, but little in his own hand, save when he desired a favour of me—grace to be shown to a servant of his, or some arrangement by which corn might be bought cheap at my east coast ports to be shipped with speed to the Netherlands; for harvests everywhere had been bad. And always, whether in my husband's own hand, or another's, the exhortation to burn, burn, burn to the greater glory of God; an exhortation that seemed to carry a note of threat. For, though he never said so, he gave me to understand that, even were he offered England's crown, he would never return until I showed myself more worthy of my faith. Never until then, should we come together again to make a child and found our line.

Cranmer lay still in prison. My bishops were more than ever anxious for his recantation. This man had been Primate of England; in a sense still was, since he had not, as yet, been degraded. If this arch-heretic should come back into the Faith, acknowledging the Pope to be God's Vicar here on earth, here was triumph, indeed! And, in that triumph, how many souls he had led astray might not be brought back to God?

In February a commission had sat to judge him, presided over by Bonner my good bishop of London that heretics called bloody; and Thurlby, my bishop of Ely. Thurlby, I myself, had chosen; for though heretics held Bonner to be bloody, there was no man could deny Thurlby was gentle. And more; between him and the prisoner there had been a bond of friendship. Cranmer had loved the younger man and advanced him; Thurlby was not one to forget a kindness. If any might prevail with Cranmer it was Thurlby.

I was passionate that this trial should be fair. Better men than Cranmer had burned, but I wanted no stain of vengeance on my soul. I was not only passionate for justice, I was importunate, also, that the trial should take place as soon as might be. For, though Cranmer should recant, there was no question of returning him to his see. I had, indeed, the perfect archbishop to hand; England needed a true lover of the Faith, a man steadfast and strong. The man I had long chosen was my cousin Pole, Cardinal and Legate; he speaks with the authority of the Pope who speaks with the authority of God. Already I had made known my wish to Rome and I expected assent any day. Then all England must bow to the authority of my lord archbishop of Canterbury, heretics must cast away their heresies; or, at very least, speak them no more. So it was that I could scarce wait for Cranmer to come to his trial.

We had not spoken on the matter, my cousin and I; he was not one for dead man's shoes, until the shoes be truly empty. He sensed, though, that I had no wish for Cranmer to recant.

'I pray he may abjure his heresies,' he said to me once, 'it would be a victory for God!'

'So you may think! But I know the man. Unstable as water! If he recant, be sure he'll renege. Like a dog, back he'll come to his vomit!'

'Then he must come to his just punishment!' He looked at me steadfast. 'You'd not weep!'

'I want justice for him. Neither more nor less! But, believe it, cousin! There's never a man burned but I have suffered, soul and body both!'

'I know it!' he said.

'I'd have no man come to the fire, if I had my way; not even this man, this *yea-and-nay*, as best suits his purpose. His finger stirred the pot of my father's affairs, and then of my brother's affairs; and always to my undoing, and injury to the Faith. Never once did he say *Nay* to any that commanded him. To say *Nay* to my father was not easy; yet you said it, Cousin!'

'And paid for it; and my family with me!' We were silent remembering the long years of his exile; and how my father had butchered his whole family—all, all save for young Courtenay. And we remembered how his mother had refused to lay her white head on the block, protesting she was no traitor, and how, she, struggling still, that head had been hacked from her body.

'To refuse my father was not easy!' I said again. 'But this archbishop that should have spoken for God, denied Him. He it was that worked to separate this country from Rome. When my father declared himself head of the English church, this archbishop said *Yea*! When my father declared his marriage incestuous and myself a bastard, this same archbishop said *Yea*. When my father declared himself true-wed to his harlot, this archbishop said *Yea*. And to her divorce and death-sentence said *Yea*, also; and would have prepared her for dying, too, but she refused the Sacrament at such hands. At my father's whim he set aside the blameless lady Anne of Cleves; and he played his liar's part in the death of Catherine Howard with no compassion for her youth and ignorance, inciting her to confess with promise of mercy he knew well would never be given.

'And for myself, he made my young life bitter and my womanhood, also, with his coaxing and his threatening and his bullying. He forever whipped up my father's anger against me, and thereafter my brother's, because I'd not abjure Rome, nor deny true Christ in bread and wine. No, Cousin! Because of that man's injuries against the innocent, God Himself will see to it that he goes to the fire. Then, at the last, it may be that God in His infinite mercy, will save his soul!'

He looked at me, his face white and stern as though carved in marble. 'Do not put it all upon God!' he said. 'Consent to burn a man with but the shadow of hatred in your heart—and you destroy your own soul. Must I tell you again?'

No need. No need! Every day before his trial and on the day of his dying, I prayed for his soul.

In mid-February when trees stood black against the sky, Cranmer was brought from the Bocardo prison to face his judges. The court received him with courtesy; and Thurlby, all gentleness, besought him to consider the mischief he did to his own soul, and to the souls of those once entrusted to him. But he, continuing obstinate, Bonner cried out, 'This is the man that has pulled down so many churches and is now come to be judged by his own church! This is the man that condemned the blessed Sacrament! This is the man that, like Lucifer, sat in the place of Christ upon an altar, to judge others! Now he is come to be judged himself!'

So being judged and condemned, Cranmer was carried back to prison; it was Thurlby told me what happened then. 'The most unseemly struggle . . . ugly and pitiful; the old man, I think, could not help himself, the strain upon him had been great. Being condemned, as himself knew, he might no longer carry the crozier; yet when they tried to take it from him, he clung fast. He could not let it go, the sacred symbol of what had once been his office, and was his no longer. Madam, they had to pull his fingers away one by one. And, that being done, he stood looking at his empty hand as though he could not believe the thing had happened. Then, shaking his head in melancholy fashion, he came to himself; for he pulled from his sleeve a paper and desired it might be delivered to the next general Council of the Church.'

'He has been twice tried and twice his guilt found. How shall that help him?'

'He claims, Madam, that at neither trial had he legal aid. I have a copy of his paper for the Queen!'

'Leave it with me!'

When he was gone I sat down to the paper.

> I intend to speak no ill against the holy Catholic church nor the authority thereof which I hold in great reverence, to whom my mind is in all things to obey. And, if my tongue has slipped or I am wrongly reported, I am most ready to amend it. . . .

It sounded to me much like recantation; I read on weighing each word.

> Although the bishop of Rome bears the place of Christ on earth and has authority of God, he has not become unsinnable. Therefore if he shall command me anything that is not right to be done, he ought to take it in good part that he be not therein obeyed. And if

he command anything against the precepts of God he must not be obeyed but rather, lawfully resisted. . . .

Oh Cranmer, Cranmer how you trim your sails! The Pope stands in the place of Christ—so you admit; yet man need not obey him! Man may lift his puny voice against him that speaks with the voice of God!

He goes on to say, If a man believe the Pope has commanded him against God, he may appear to the Church Council and the Council has power to hear him. It is impossible, he says, for him to admit the authority of the bishop of Rome in this country since he had sworn his solemn oath.

to King Henry VIII of glorious memory, according to the laws of England.

And then,

It has never been in my mind to write or speak anything against the holy Catholic church of Christ. I may err; but heretic I cannot be, inasmuch as I am ready in all things to follow the most sacred word of Christ. . . .

And finally he says he is at one with the most holy Catholic church, gladly using our form of prayer, the very words, save for one thing.

I cannot allow the words lately brought in of the Sacrament. I cannot consent to words not accustomed in Scripture and unknown to the ancient fathers, but new-invented to the destruction of souls and overthrow of the pure, old religion. . . .

Was there ever such a hotch-potch of nonsense? He believes and does not believe. He will submit and not submit. He is at one with the Catholic church yet regards the words of the blessed Sacrament new-invented for the destruction of souls. Maybe prison had dulled those once-clear wits of his!

The appeal was dismissed.

It was Thurlby that told me of the ceremony of degradation that followed.

'Madam, it was a sight to break the heart. He was good to me when

I needed help and I loved the man. Then, head shaved, nails scraped, in an old torn gown too short, too thin, he let them lead him back to prison . . . and never a struggle nor a look of anger. I think the man's heart is broken.'

'My lord bishop,' I said, 'I have thought much of this ceremony. If a man must burn, must we degrade him also? It is a question I have asked before . . . and must go on asking!'

'Madam, it is needful. When he is no longer a priest then we must take from him every sign of priesthood. And it serves another purpose, also. When we take from him every sign of priesthood, then we break his pride. And when pride is broken, it is easier to see the truth. And, Madam, one more thing. It is a warning more terrible than any word. It is a sight to fill the heart with terror. I have known it call back souls that have wandered, to shock them back to righteousness.'

Cranmer was no longer a priest, no longer himself; and I could pity him. It was now he wrote his first submission—if submission you could call the yea-and nay affair. He would obey the Queen's Majesty in all things, he said, because

> she has by Parliament's authority received the Pope's authority within the realm.

Was there ever such a piece of hair-splitting! Yet, even in this hair-splitting he was not content. As I had prophesied, having submitted, he reneged, and then submitted again. Thereafter he once more reneged, once more submitted; six times in all submitting, reneging. Well it is natural to endeavour to save one's body from the fire if one have not the upholding faith.

His last submission I have here, under my hand.

> I, Thomas Cranmer, late archbishop of Canterbury do renounce and detest all manner of heresies that are contrary to the lawful doctrines. I acknowledge in my heart, and confess one holy Catholic Church whereof I acknowledge the Bishop of Rome to be supreme head on earth as Christ's Vicar, to whom all people should be subject.
>
> I believe and worship in the Sacraments of the altar the very body and blood of Christ contained in the form of bread and wine;

and through the almighty power of God turned into the body of our Saviour Jesus Christ and the wine into his blood.

'Now we shall publish it throughout the land,' my cousin the Cardinal said.

'And now he must go free!' I told him.

'Go *free*? The arch-heretic!' He lifted an unbelieving face.

'He is no longer a heretic. He is a poor, old man broken in health and wits, without a penny to buy himself decent food in prison. We must give him a small sum on which he can live and leave him to what peace he may find!'

'Madam!' For the moment anger choked him. Then, 'You would do God and the country much mischief! The man was Primate of this country! More than any other heretic he must suffer! Through him countless souls have been lost. God and the country require it!'

'Not God nor the country will be the worse for the saving of one poor old man; rather the true faith will gain and men be the better for mercy shown!'

At the word *mercy* he made the same weary gesture I had seen before. 'Madam, you know full well the man is a weather-cock. Six times he has submitted and each time reneged. Burn him now while he is at one with God and we save his soul. Let him go free and back he'll come, once more, to his heresies. If then we burn him—as, indeed we must—his soul goes straight to the everlasting fire.'

Against that I could argue nothing.

The year had moved on to March; true March weather that bit sharp as a wolf. During Cranmer's time in prison the wolf had gentled to a lamb. Celandine was bright in new grass, willow golden by clear-running streams; the mildew and corruption of last year's evil harvest clean swept away. And still I did not stint my prayers. *May this seedtime be blessed that the people be fed and more content. And for my own seedtime and harvest, I beseech you God!* And for the old man in the Tower I did not forget to pray, also, *May this new spring clean corruption from his soul; and he himself come to the good harvest of his salvation.*

On the twenty-first day of March, when life runs quick in blood and sap, when the very day is a hymn to life, itself, Cranmer went to his death. Men-at-arms lined the streets, their captains mounted high, watchful lest there be a last-minute attempt at rescue; with a burning there is always that fear, and today the crowds were very great. The road being empty as yet of the prisoner and his procession, there was a great buzz; men were laying wagers, some believing in the prisoner's submission and glad for the saving of his soul; others swearing that, at the last, he would stand by his heresies.

And now, word coming that the procession had left the prison, the crowd fell to silence; and, indeed, as the man in the midst went his slow way—poor, old and broken in health, many wept. I doubt but that, had I been there I myself must have wept, even though this was for the saving of his soul; I am but human. Before him walked the chaplain, the mayor and aldermen of Oxford; at his either hand, a friar. Before and behind went armed men.

And so they came to St. Mary's church where the prisoner was to hear his funeral sermon; thereafter himself to address the crowd, publicly to renounce his heresies. To address the congregation was a privilege allowed to no heretic but to him, and him alone. He that had been Primate of all England should speak the words to bring home souls he had lost.

Inside the church was a low bench and upon this he must stand to hear his own funeral sermon. Dr. Coles, that preached it, told me what happened.

'He listened, Madam, with every show of grief, lifting his hands to heaven and the tears streaming down his cheeks. But whence came his grief—for past heresies or shame of his submission—we were not then to know. But, Madam, this I know now, to let him speak was a grave mistake.'

'It was to clear his soul and to save others.'

'His soul was never clean of heresy. Fear of death is one thing; certain death another. He would have saved his life if he could; in the face of death he had no hope and nothing more to fear.

'First he asked us all to pray for him. He had sinned much, he said; but among all his sins was one that grieved him most—and to that he would come later. He knelt then, praying aloud for mercy; and we, fools that we were, prayed with him. Then, rising to his feet he said, his voice low and weak yet withal clear

'*I believe in every article of the Catholic faith taught by our Saviour Jesus Christ and his apostles.* That, Madam, we had looked for. Then, mark you, Madam, he said, *I have offended greatly against Henry and Catherine in that divorce whereof I was the cause and author. . . .*'

'Said he so?' I could find no more word but for the very marvel of it, the tears poured down my cheeks.

'And then, Madam, he went further. For he said, *This divorce was the seed-plot of all the calamities of this realm. Hence the violent death of good men, hence the schism of the whole kingdom, hence heretics, hence the slaughter of many souls and bodies. I have sinned against heaven which, through me, stands empty of many souls. I have sinned against earth depriving men of their soul's food. Of them that perished for the lack of it, I am the sole slayer; and the souls of the dead I have defrauded of daily soul-saving sacrifice, I mean the Mass.*

'So far, Madam, it had gone better than we had expected.'

'Yes!' I cried out, 'Yes! God has saved him at the last and I rejoice!' For the words echoed and re-echoed in my heart, *I have offended greatly against Henry and Catherine in that divorce.*

'Had he stopped then, Madam, his soul had, indeed, been saved! But now the voice that had been so weak came out strong.

'And now I come to the great thing that so much troubles my conscience more than anything I ever did or said in my life.

'And then, Madam, out it came, the thing I tremble even to take upon my tongue,

'It is the writing and the publishing abroad of that which I knew to be untrue. I do here renounce and refuse them. Those things were written by my hand in fear of death and to save my life if it might be. All those things I have said and written since my degradation are untrue. And, forasmuch as my right hand offended writing contrary to my heart, this hand shall first be burned. . . .

'Then, Madam, there was a hubbub to the very roof; but above it all his voice could be plainly heard.

'As for the Pope I refuse him. He is God's enemy; anti-Christ. And for the Sacrament I believe that which I have written in my books and taught all my life; and it shall justify me at the last judgment. . . .

'So then, Madam, they pulled him from his place, and out of the church, he being roughly handled by good folk of the Faith, until we came to the ditch and the stake. And there, Madam, he kneeled to pray. Then they fastened him to the stake with an iron ring and they lit the fire. There was some smoke; but the wood did not catch; it had been raining and the wind blew damp. He stood very still and patiently endured. When the flame crept high enough he put forth his hand and held it in the fire that all might see he kept his vow.

'It was a hard death, Madam; and most patiently endured; and all the time his eyes were lifted towards heaven and his lips moved in prayer. I pray God that in the heat of the fire, light came to his soul!'

'Amen!' I said. 'Pray God that the slow burning saved his soul at the last!'

Cranmer was dead. Corrupter of souls, he had cleft the country in twain, he had opened wide the door of heresies; and through him many souls burned to eternity. Yes, he was rightly dead . . . but for nights, thereafter, I could not sleep. The words rang through my head, the great words, *I have offended against Henry and Catherine in the matter of the divorce, I have offended against Catherine, I have offended. . . .* And I remembered an old man steadfast in the fire; and I remembered how I had put my own finger to the candle and could not endure the pain of it, and how I had wept over my scorched and blistered hand. And still I told myself it was right for Cranmer, above all men, to die; he had called God's Vicar anti-Christ, he had denied the Sacrament. Yet in the long nights my heart could not be still. I saw the face I had hated and hated no longer. The fire had burned away all my bitterness against him.

But that fire had burned away yet more of my strength—strength of body and soul. I seemed never free from nausea that turned to vomiting; nor from the pain stabbed through and through my blinded eyes. I could not walk upon my swollen feet. I would have no time-piece now, in my closet; there needed no moving hands to remind me that, as they moved, men burned. The time-piece of my own heart was sufficient reminder.

Nor was my soul in better shape. The old question tormented me without respite. *Is it right to burn men's bodies that their souls be saved? Should we not leave the punishment to God?* Always the question came sharp and clear, as if for the first time; and always I was troubled at my own doubts. I am bound to obey my priests; bound, above all, to obey God's Voice speaking on earth. The burning of heretics is a command laid not only upon me but upon all true believers in Christendom. If I were not careful, I should, with my doubting and my pitying, lose my own soul.

Chapter Eleven

My Cardinal was now my archbishop of Canterbury. On the day Cranmer suffered, Pole took his full vows and, three days later, attended by god-fearing princes of church and state, amidst a vast concourse, he was consecrated to his great office. For the consecration I had chosen the Greyfriars church at Greenwich.

'Madam, a bishop should be consecrated in his own see,' Pole reminded me not best-pleased.

'We must bow to the times,' I told him. 'The country is full of unrest and anger. It is split in its faith, it is hungry on account of famine, it is sullen because of high prices. And my sister with her friends ferments the trouble. I'll not have you ride the countryside, not even with an armed escort. As for the Greyfriars church, I have chosen it because it is dear to me; there I was baptised. It is bound up with my whole life!'

So in this church he was consecrated. Once he might have been my husband and my King; now he was my father in God. Since his return he had watched over me like a tender, earthly father—a tenderer father than my own had ever been. But now he was more than any father ghostly or earthly. He was the voice of England's church; he was the voice of the Pope, he was God's Voice in the land. I prayed that, with his stern sense of duty together with his true gentleness, he would bind up the wounds of my people and bring all heretics into their safe harbour.

Surely now I had pleased God! Many heretics we had saved to Him; and with my new archbishop we should save yet more. Now he must remember me to send my husband home. The great matter of the abdication was over; already Philip had taken upon himself, and never a murmur of dissent, all his father's great titles—kingdoms, princedoms, dukedoms; all honours save one—the honour I coveted for him most.

It was my cardinal-archbishop that broke the news.

Philip had not been elected Emperor.

It was a thing I could not, at first, believe. I had taken it for granted he would succeed to this highest honour, also. No man could stand higher, nor better become it.

'Then . . . who?' I asked.

'One of his Hapsburg kin—an uncle or cousin, I fancy. So undistinguished a man I cannot recall him; a man of such small stature he must diminish the title. The glory of the Holy Roman Empire falls low!'

'And low, indeed!' I said, bitter. 'Well, it is not Henri of France! There's comfort in that, though the comfort be poor!'

'It could be that they considered King Philip too young!' he said, anxious to spare Philip's pride, to bring me some comfort.

'His father was younger when they elected him!' And I'd take no false comfort.

'He had been a King longer or maybe . . .' he spoke slow and uncertain, 'it is the tales that go about.'

'What tales?' Anger took me. 'Philip danced, Philip drank in good fellowship! A young man—why not? Nor was it for his own pleasure! It was to please those that had faulted him for his grave manners. Can he never do right? No! It is not just! His father's virtue was not so shining; yet they made him Emperor!'

'His father had greater discretion. They made him Emperor before his . . . lapses, were widely known.'

'I grieve for Philip. I grieve still more for Christendom! He was the right man, the only man! He is a true servant of God to fight for his Master. He would have worked to unite all Christendom—and he would have done it, too! As for his *lapses*, they are not so serious but that God will forgive him!'

Philip carried himself high and proud; but for all that his pride was down. Set aside as Emperor, and here, in England, uncrowned!

And now, even, his last request—ignored. He asked Parliament for help to drive the French from the Netherlands; he was refused—and in no uncertain terms! 'Not one man, not one bullet, not one penny! The war is none of our making,' they answered him. 'Your wars are not our concern; it is set down so in the marriage-treaty.'

My heart bled for his pride hurt every way. I must and should have him crowned; but until that time I must contrive some especial honour. I commanded new coins to be struck bearing his picture and title, *Philippus Rex Angliae*. Set against a crowning it was little enough; but, at the moment, all I could do. Let him but return and, God helping me, he should have his crown!

Parliament's refusal to help Philip in his French wars, though it had angered me, now stood me in good stead. His own resources being insufficient for him to meet the enemy in the field, he was forced to make a truce. Five years of peace.

'Five years of peace! This young King has done what the old man, his father, could not do!' Pole said. 'He has made peace between France and Spain!'

'A truce, a truce, only!' I said. 'And maybe the old man knew the French too well. Who can trust France?'

'Madam, if France break the truce then we English will want to know why! Meanwhile the King is free to come back. Madam, you should thank God for it!'

'I pray for it! But as for thanking God, it is full soon. What if the King return to Spain his true home, where he is well-loved? Why should he come back to England that has refused him both crown and help?'

'He will come because he knows this country's needs; its disorders and its distresses. He knows, too, the remedy; a remedy that, with God's good grace, the Queen shall supply. An heir. And, Madam, it may be, also, that in his heart, he is not sorry Parliament refused him help. He may be glad to be done with fighting a while. He would never admit it; but all the same it might be so!'

'Pray God you are right. For now—though I must not say so—I, too, am glad Parliament refused him. Come war—and men are wounded, or taken prisoner, if they be not killed outright. I had rather be wife than widow; I have had so short a time to be wife I am not yet practised in my new estate. But, before God, Cousin, whatever mood he bring home with him, I'll do my best to please him!'

I waited for news of my husband's return. I waited and waited. I put my pride in my pocket; I wrote to him that had been Emperor, once more, begging that he command Philip home. And much good that did me! From his monastery my father-in-law made it clear that he was no longer concerned with the world. It began to look as though my husband had no mind to return, much less live with me again.

Spring wore on; it was young summer, it was high summer, it was September. And all the time scarce a word from my husband save, as before, to ask a favour for one man or another that had rendered him good service, or a further despatch of corn at a low price; each request set within a well-turned compliment to *My Queen and well-loved wife*. And that was all.

As for my Cardinal-archbishop, he seemed to have fallen somewhat from favour. He had been left to take the King's place, to sit with me, co-Regent upon the Council. Now, with neither warning nor explanation, Philip appointed Don Juan de Figueroa, kinsman to Don Gomez, in Pole's place. A Spaniard to replace an Englishman in that highest of places! A Spaniard to sit upon an English Council! It was, as you may believe, not well received; my Council refused him place.

Blame my husband for neglect of our English affairs I could not. However he might amuse himself at night—and to that I could no longer blind myself, though then I did not know the whole of it—he was never a man to put aside duty for pleasure. He spent long hours in close work upon our affairs; he was in constant communication with Don Juan upon affairs of state: with Pole upon matters spiritual, being especially concerned with the matter of heretics. To me he addressed himself upon matters of state and religion, both. But it was a matter of compliment only; he held me too uncertain in my mind concerning the first, and too reluctant in the second. And who shall say he was wrong? In matters of policies it is often the last man to speak that has my voice; in the matter of punishment I was not then as constant as he—or I, myself—could wish.

Weary of overmuch waiting and hope, I sent for Don Gomez de Figueroa, now my lord duke of Feria, whom Philip had left as my own especial adviser and messenger.

'The lord King must return,' I told him again. 'He is free of the French wars, and it is his duty; he should be here. As long as he remains abroad our business of state drags on too long. All my Council's notes must be put into Latin and sent to Brussels; he considers them, makes his notes, gives his advice and states his wishes. We follow both advice and wishes as best we can but it is not always possible. We need his guiding hand.'

'You have it, Madam.'

'It is too far away. We waste time sending our despatches and waiting for his answers. Affairs move fast, sometimes his answers come too late. But, my lord, he has another duty, a more important duty to me and to England. Need I put it clearer?' And had he not been so kind a gentleman and his betrothed my little Dormer, I had been shamed at that last reminder.

'I understand, Madam the Queen!'

'Then, sir, you must put the matter plain. And if the answer be not to my taste, never spare me. I am a woman hear to the truth though it kill me. Better the one swift stroke than murder by a thousand poisoned pins.'

'Is it permitted to ask Madam the Queen a question? You talk of the King's duty to this country; *what* duty where the King wears no crown? *What* duty where obedience is given him only if it be not ill-convenient?'

'And a husband's duty?' I answered his question with another.

'How shall a man live with his wife when he is not her equal?'

'The matter is not of my offending!'

'Yet still the offence is there! Nor is it the only one. I doubt, Madam, even a crowning will bring him back. For here he is put to great expense. He does a King's work; yet he receives neither income nor subsidy. Yet he must pay for attendants here that he himself has not chosen—English attendants, mark you! And he must employ others abroad; and these are not all Spaniards or Netherlanders as one might expect. No, but your English lords of whom he has no need, but employs out of compliment to the Queen and this country. Madam, his pockets are not bottomless.'

'If he were more with us he'd need a smaller court abroad!' I said, somewhat nettled, though, indeed, I had asked for the truth. 'And to employ our English here in England—what else?'

'If he did not return to England, he'd need none of your English, Madam. And why should he return to this country of heretics?'

'There are heretics everywhere in Christendom, go where you will! Yes, even in Spain—or why your own Inquisition? With such heretics as we have here, we deal as the church requires. We shall, in time, be rid of them!'

'Not in your time, Madam; nor ever! In this country of yours heretics spring from the ashes as grass after a burning. And further; Madam—you ask for plain speech and he is your friend that gives it—there is continual revolt; revolt against *you*, Madam! Such revolts you put down; but with too gentle a hand! Madam, you do not sit easy on the throne, nor never will. I tell you, Madam, so long as you live, there will be trouble and very great trouble to the crown!'

'Then the King should be here to protect it!'

'The crown is not his!'

My anger flared; we were back again, full circle. I bit upon my tongue. At last I said, 'That there will be trouble so long as I live, I do not believe. But that you are my true friend, that I do believe. Therefore, I implore you, write; write to the King that he shall come home!'

'Madam, I will. Or, better still, with the Queen's permission I will go speak with him in person. But—' His hands spread empty, spoke for him.

'Go; go at once. And God go with you!'

When he was gone I gave myself to my grief. Disappointment, hurt pride and rejection curdled within me. I was sick, mind and body, yet upon my shoulders, and mine alone, lay responsibility for my country. The burden was too much. I needed my husband. I needed his wisdom and his help; if not for love of me, then for my very life and the life of this dear country, he must come home.

There began a new phase in my love for my husband; I think it had been coming upon me slowly. But whereas I had been content to name him in my prayers, to discuss his policies with my Council, and himself with my especial advisers like Pole or Don Gomez, I had never made complaint of him. It did not march with his dignity or mine. Now I could not keep his name from my tongue; for that name—though now it might be spoken in bitterness—was yet a bridge between us. When water flows between husband and wife any bridge is the only hope.

I longed, above all, to speak my griefs to a woman; there was but one I could trust to understand. The little Dormer. Like me she is born and bred English; like me she loves a gentleman of Spain. Her mother loved my mother; and Jane loves me that am old enough to be her own. And for myself, I love her as though she were my own child. When I am sick, I can bear no hand upon me but hers. She, and she alone, may change the wet bandages upon my eyes, sponge away the vomit. It is no life for so young a girl . . . and a girl in love. When I am well enough I remember it and I urge her to leave me, to take her happiness while she may. But she will not listen. She will never leave me to my griefs, she says.

'My griefs will end only with my death!' I tell her; and once I said, 'Some, like my sister, cannot wait for the day!'

'Madam, put away such thoughts. Now it is all dark night with the Queen; but joy comes in the morning.'

But for me there is no bright morning.

My grief, it seemed, could not contain itself within the narrow limits of my body. Like a rat it gnawed from within to destroy the brittle confines of my frame. Then speak I must, before the rat utterly destroy me. These days I spent hours alone with Jane Dormer, I, forever talking, she all loving patience, listening.

Was it for this I married? For this? Did I deceive myself that England needs a King? Or did the lust of the flesh drive me; and for that am I punished? And if it be so, am I not punished enough, enough? Am I not left to my unrest and my fears, to my pain and my sorrow, to bear them alone . . . alone? Where is the child that should inherit after me? And how shall I get me a child lacking a husband? And what shall the country do lacking that child? Shall my sister sit in my place? That may well be, God knows, soon, all too soon! And will she not put back the clock to burn the faithful? Or shall my husband lose no time returning when I am safe-dead, once more to wed an English Queen? Shall my sister sleep in his bed to bear his son?

How often I spoke thus, I do not know; nor how much I spoke at one time. The thing was always in my head and in my heart; it poured from my mouth like vomit, not to be stayed. And upon that last thought, I would beat with my fists upon my head that pain should drive out pain. Then gently Jane Dormer would take away those beating hands; she would put her young arms about me to comfort me as a loving child may comfort her mother—as I would have comforted my own had I been let to stay with her. And once I cried out, 'My mother and I, unhappy Queens both; each by a young husband deserted. But she, at least, bore a child to keep this country's faith with God. But I stand in worse case, having no child and this country will be lost for God. I have failed my country, failed my husband, failed my God. Failed, failed!' And I rocked myself backwards and forwards.

'Hush, Madam, dear Madam, you will hurt yourself with grieving. Leave your weeping, leave punishing yourself. You are blameless. Soon all will be well again; the King will return, I know it!'

'*What* do you know? And how? And wipe that smile from your lips—or your Spaniard will wipe it for you! They have no heart, these Spaniards, none at all!' And then knowing where her heart was set and rightly set, I cried out, 'Never heed me! A true man is a true man whatever his country. Hold fast to him and wed him while you may!' And on that last thought the tears ran down my cheeks; save for this girl I was desolate. Always there has been love between myself and those that serve me; but the years go by and some are wedded, and some, like Clarencieux that was once governess of my ladies, old age has taken, and some death—for sickness and misadventure hold no tenderness for the young. But if I have been served always with love, I have not always been served with discretion; one here and there has let fall a loving word to be picked up and used against me. So now I feared that, for very kindness, they should talk of me and my griefs. But this girl was discreet beyond her years. *Never leave me*, I wanted to cry out. But, God forbid I should grieve any young heart. I said, instead, 'Don Gomez is a good gentleman, wed him as soon as may be; and I will give you such a wedding as I should give my own daughter, had God so blessed me!'

She went down upon both knees and lifted my hand to her lips. 'I will never leave the Queen while she has need of me; not though she, herself, should send me away!'

'Never is a long time! Oh Jane—' and for the first time I called her by her baptismal name as though she were, indeed, the daughter I never had, 'I think I'll not be long setting you free.'

She pretended she did not understand. 'Madam, when we are sad, happiness seems long acoming!' And the tears spilled from those true eyes of hers. For she knew, as I knew, that my husband would never live with me again. A few nights he might spend to play his husband's part; but stay with me, live with me—never! If she remained with me till I was past my griefs, her freedom could come only with my death . . . and if my life must continue in this wise, that could not be long.

Now seeing her overwrought, and pitying her that so young must bear the heaviness of my grief, I began to talk to her of that land where she should one day live and I never see. I spoke of those things my mother had once told me; and the grey day turned warm and bright with sunshine and before our very eyes golden oranges swung against a deep blue sky.

Chapter Twelve

Shall my sister wear the crown? It was a question I might well ask. It lay at the heart of a plot now unravelling; a plot greater than any as yet conceived; greater than the Jane Grey revolt, greater even than Wyatt's rebellion; it spread its tentacles into France and into the Netherlands, itself.

And the plot? To murder me. To set my sister on the throne; she and her husband. And that husband? Once again—Courtenay... And let me say at once, whatever part my sister played in this monstrous affair, Courtenay played none. He'd have no more to do with treason; he wanted neither my sister nor the crown. He remained abroad and closed his ears to all temptation. Courtenay keeping faith at last.

This new plot, so vast, so intricate, must be unravelled inch by inch; it was several months before the pattern lay clear. Paget, to my astonished anger, was deep in the affair. Paget whom my father had cast into the Tower where he had languished the length of my brother's reign—Paget that I had set free, his honours and possessions restored; that, knowing his shrewd brain and trusting in his faithfulness to me, I had placed upon my Council, raising him to the high and trusted place of Privy Seal. He had been working with Philip's enemy and mine—de Noailles; and drawing huge sums from France. *Never trust him!* Gardiner had warned me more than once. I had thought it was enmity that spoke, for between those two had been bitterness and anger; I saw now my old friend had spoken not in enmity but in love for me. Now that Gardiner was dead, Paget had made himself supreme upon the Council—a man with a golden voice and a heart of baser metal. So it was that he had inveigled many of my councillors into the plot—Arundel, Pembroke, Cobham, Petre and Dudley traitor son of a traitor house, house of Northumberland.

I knew not now whom I might trust save my cousin Pole; and he, by his own desire, was not of the Council. But his influence was strong; always he was invited to sit with us; and so held in honour he was, that when he spoke they listened with a respect they did not always accord each other, often his was the final word.

The revolt had been carefully planned. Risings all over the country were to take place at one and the same time. From the west the rebels would march led by Sir Anthony Kingston.

This was another blow upon the heart. 'Is there no end to man's ingratitude?' I cried out to my cousin. 'Once this man was charged with sedition and his guilt found. Yet I pardoned him, holding him to be rash and thoughtless but a man of good will.'

'Madam, your clemency will forever rise to trouble you. He it was that had charge of Hooper in prison; since the old man's death Kingston has always been your enemy.'

'Even queens must bow to the church's will!' And I remembered how I had wept at Hooper's execution; for if you can separate a man from his heresies, Hooper had been a saintly man.

Dudley was to march on Portsmouth and, with French help, take it in the name of Elizabeth. He was another I had spared the axe! At the moment he was in France arranging the affair with its King; and receiving for reward a large pension. And this from Henri whose truce with England still held, and that had so lately made a five years' truce with Philip. Henri held his honour light, indeed!

In London, the work of the rebels was to be divided. Some were to march on the Tower, take it, man the guns and seize all the gold—gold brought from Spain—together with all the jewels. The other party was to fire the city, attack any palace where I might possibly be, and, in the confusion of fire and fighting, carry me away, either to the Tower or ship me to France, as was more convenient; and if that journey should be my last, no question would be asked nor any tear shed!

To lay hands upon a hallowed Queen! It was treason, and it was blasphemy. My anger forever burned at ingratitude, at trust betrayed. I was fearless and fearful by turns; now telling myself that God would not allow it, then that I had not been eager enough about His work. But fearful or fearless, I resolved always to fight for my crown and for my God. How we should meet this revolt I must leave to my captains—wondering the while how many were traitors; my own part I knew well. I must renew my vows to God and never cease from praying.

And God heard me; for he sent a star, a red star to blaze in the sky, its fiery tail burning directly above London. And it was this star, so fiery-bright, that brought from the darkness those parts of the plot not as yet uncovered. Such a star had never before been seen by living man; and all men, true and traitor alike, took it for warning. The rebels in fear cried out, *This star will make an end of us unless we first make an end of the Queen!* and cared not at all who might hear them. And true men, hearing this, cried out, *This star of fire is a warning to men of true faith to burn all heretics, they and everything they possess!* So it was, that the rebels, wildly talking, spread the news before the time appointed; and watch being kept, and letters being taken along with those that carried them, the whole devilish plot was laid clear. Thread by thread it was unravelled, and every thread led back to my sister, sitting quiet at Hatfield.

I had never trusted her, yet more than once I had saved her from a traitor's death. I had, at my husband's request, received her at court, shown her favour, given her her rightful place; and even then she had been deep in treason. Returned home to Hatfield, she had lived very quiet, wearing one face to please true believers, and another to please heretics. All things to all men! So she had gathered to herself the love of my people, stealing the loyalty that belonged to me. No wonder I had found their affection grown cold!

'Madam,' my Cardinal-archbishop told me, 'they have taken Kingston on his way to the west. So there's an end to that rebellion!'

'For which I thank God; and the country must thank Him, also!'

Kingston had reason to thank Him too; he was a sick man and died on his way to prison.

Meanwhile I had sent my good lord Clinton to France to demand the return of Dudley and others of my traitors.

Henri refused; and refused with laughter. 'My country is free to all! Besides, it is so large, how should I know who comes and goes?' And then, not concealing his satisfaction, 'I am sorry to hear of the trouble in England. But, indeed, your discontents are so many they fill this land of mine and overflow into Italy. If the tales be true, I cannot wonder at it! For myself, I do not listen to tittle-tattle; but this I do know—you English are not to be trusted.'

Fine talk from Henri, that breaker of promises!

And then, final blow to me that longed for my husband, and longed with some hope since he had written he would be home soon! Henri was heard to say—not to Clinton direct, but where Clinton must hear—'It is my opinion that the King of England means to dissolve his marriage with the Queen!'

Cruel words. They were meant to weaken me, to strengthen my enemies; to strengthen that arch-enemy my sister. I would not, could not believe them . . . but were they not all of a piece with Philip's behaviour to me? I thrust that fear deep down in my heart. My people must be convinced that all was well between the King and Queen. I sent Paget to Brussels to implore my husband's return. Yes, Paget; a man with a golden tongue. A traitor, not from conviction but from hope of reward. He was one to turn his coat for him that paid him best. I was not, you may believe it, scant with ready gold; nor with promise of more on his return.

But it was all one. 'I'll not return,' Philip told him very plain, 'until the Queen crown me. She has the authority and must use it.' And then, for all to hear, 'The Queen my wife has no love for me; she has shown none, ever!' And this of me that loved him next to Christ Himself!

'He must be crowned and at once!' I cried out, when Paget had delivered Philip's cruel message. 'Stay you here. Yourself shall hear my mind on the matter!' And I sent for my cousin.

'Madam,' Pole said when I had opened the business to him, 'it will not do! There is too much discontent, too much disaffection. It is not the time!'

And so said Paget. 'Madam, I did my uttermost for the King's return; but return he will not without a crowning. Nor is he anxious to come! To be crowned now is to put himself in some danger. He could be assassinated—the people are so bitter. Yes, Madam, *murder!* Leave it for the present, I pray you.'

When true friend and false urge the same thing, it is wise to consider their advice.

By June every bit of information concerning the revolt was in our hands. And not only did every thread lead to my sister; from her each thread emanated. She was, indeed, the very spider in the web. We had clearest proof in a letter written to de Noailles from the Constable of France.

> . . . above all you must prevent Madam Elizabeth from making any sort of move to undertake what you have written to me; for it would spoil everything and lose the advantage which the rebels may expect from their plans. . . .

Why should the Constable of France concern himself with any move my sister might make? And why should such a move ruin any advantage she might have? And *what* advantage? And how was it that he who commanded the armies of France knew so much of her affairs; and, again, *Why was he concerned in the matter*?

The answers are clear enough, but could she not wait a little . . . a little for the crown? I was weak from sickness, childless, and unable to name my successor. She was the people's sweetheart and their choice. Did she fear, perhaps, that God would show His kindness to send my husband home to give me a child? Surely she knew I was liker to die first.

And all the time the rumours. *The Queen's Spanish husband is coming with his armies to punish the traitors . . . but God knows how many innocent folk will suffer also. . . .* Sweet Christ let him come! If he love me or not, let him come! For, always, everywhere the spiteful tongues. *The King will break his marriage with the Queen, the barren Queen. He will marry the Princess Elizabeth and they will reign together. . . .* I knew whence came that last wicked rumour—the tongue of de Noailles repeating his master's words.

Now that de Noailles was so clearly implicated, some of my Council, fearful lest their own loyalty be called into question, urged that he be tried as a traitor to the crown. But my cousin advised otherwise. 'He has broken his ambassador's conditions and could well be tried. Yet it is wiser to know nothing. Try him—and you must find him guilty and his punishment must follow. It cannot be otherwise. But that would make trouble and very grave trouble. You would be in the right of it; yet France, and not France, alone, but every other country, would withdraw its ambassadors.'

While we considered, de Noailles acted. He begged leave to be recalled and did not wait for his answer; nor would he have been refused. Henri had no wish for the disgrace of an ambassador punished. De Noailles' brother François, already here as special envoy, remained as resident ambassador until yet a third brother could arrive. Was there never an end to that family?

And still there remained the question of my sister.

'Madam, you have shilly-shallied too long,' my cousin Pole advised me. 'Gardiner, your truest friend, warned you to make an end of her. You had cause enough, God knows, yet you refused. Now He gives you another chance—a last chance. She is a traitor proved. So long as she lives you shall have no peace!'

But my husband thought otherwise. While I hesitated over this matter of gravest import, wondering whether truth and justice would stand against her subtle lying, weighing the temper of the people should she be brought to trial, Philip wrote urging once more the old plan of marrying her to Philibert of Savoy. Marry her to a foreigner, get her out of the country. Then the people would forget her; there would be no question of her succession, ever! It was the only way. Certain and safe! But even then I could not be sure of him. Was this a feint to cover his real desire. Or did he mean it in earnest?'

Either way he had reckoned without my sister! I knew what would happen were any attempt made to marry and carry her out of the country. And, besides, I, myself, had sworn never to force her.

'And that is just as well!' Pole advised me. 'Her head taken for treason is one thing; a forced marriage another! The Princess of England, the people's own Princess, the heir-apparent to the crown, forced into marriage with an obscure foreigner—the people would not allow it; nor Parliament, neither. Parliament would stand by her; and you, Madam, and the King would lose face!'

Parliament would stand by her. Why? Because she had won all hearts with her posturing and pretending? Or because I was a sick woman and they meant to keep my successor close at hand? And Philip? He was no fool! Didn't he know such a marriage would never be allowed? Again and again, Renard's words came back to me; did Philip mean, if I should die to marry her himself? A pleasant thought for a sick woman. A thought to corrode the heart.

And still Philip did not come. Nor did he any more urge my sister's marriage. Why? Had he been informed of the consequences of so useless an attempt? Of the people's certain anger and their refusal? And was he well-pleased in his secret heart? He wrote no more, neither, of a crowning. Had he given up all hope; and discarding it, discarded me, also?

So there I was, the most wretched woman in Christendom—my husband no longer to be looked for, the love of my people lost and showered upon that traitorous sister of mine, my Council divided in its loyalties, Parliament intransigent, and France filling my traitors' pockets with gold and, brazenly giving them shelter. And all the time I must cope, as best I might, with the betrayal of my own sick body.

Yet still the work of the state must go on. My foremost, unhappy business was to consider with my Council, the late rebellion. Each man we considered with the utmost care. The leaders must die a traitor's death; all men, whatever their faith, declared it just—we could do no other. But others that should have come to their death, traitors all, though in a lesser degree, we cast into prison. It was I, that in face of my Council's disapproval, had yet commanded it. 'We may yet save their souls,' I said. *And their bodies, too,* but that last I kept in my own heart.

Traitors I might save; but in the burning of avowed heretics I had no choice. To such burnings I should have become accustomed; it is the church's punishment throughout Christendom. Yet it became more and more repugnant to me. As truly as heretics were chained for the fire, so was I chained in my body's sickness; and by my own inward fire, wasted. Grief of spirit weakened flesh, weakness of flesh weakened spirit, so that my cousin Pole must forever seek to encourage me with his own strength, his own faith; and, sometimes, with sharp words he must recall me to my duty.

Me, he could command; but against my people's ever-growing anger he could do nothing. Before, when heretics had gone to their death, they had been kept from attempts at rescue by armed men. Now, since Cranmer's death, mounted soldiers kept back the mob with halberds. And it was always so, whether the heretic be of great account like Cranmer, or some poor wretch, unknown and worthless, save in the sight of God.

Chapter Thirteen

Philip did not come; and now I knew that, save for a miracle, he never would. There were days when, in weakness and utter despair, I lay upon the floor without strength to rise. Then it seemed to me I had but to let go, to sink into the darkness never to wake. Once, my cousin the Cardinal found me thus. 'Rouse yourself!' and his gentle voice was cold, was sharp. 'You are about God's business. Who shall do it if not you?'

'Yes, yes!' I told him and wept. But when he was gone I cried into the empty air, *The one that should help me is not come!* And I remembered de Noailles' sly words—his hints of a young man's pleasures. That Philip tarried for some light of love, I did not believe; it was not in his nature. But the sneers of the King of France concerning me and my marriage, his loud assurances that my husband meant to put me aside to wed my sister, maddened me; and maddened me, indeed! I fell upon Philip's picture that stood over by my bed, my hands uplifted to tear at it with my finger-nails.

I felt hands upon my own; hands gentle but strong, that took my own wild hands and held them fast. Someone brought me to a stool, and there I sat rocking backwards and forwards, and Philip's undamaged face smiling still. Jane Dormer knelt by me, sponging away my tears with cool, scented vinegar; yet still tears dropped into the bowl she held, and her own joined them.

'I have done my best!' I cried out, 'my best for an ungrateful country, an ungrateful husband! If he'll not return, then let him stay away! I'll make myself content as before I married!' But even as I spoke I knew it was not true. How could I content myself, having known a man's authority in this troubled country; having known a Queen's need for a child; having known a woman's need of a man for the comfort of her body. I am, God forgive me, a Tudor; I know their lusts.

Yet if he had failed me as a man, had I not failed him not only as a woman but every way? He had done a husband's duty by me but I was, as yet, barren. In the matter of his crowning I had done nothing. I had been forced to deny him aid in his wars with France. In the punishment of heretics I had shown myself neither forward nor faithful enough. For all these things he blamed me—and with some justice.

I wrote to him again putting down my pride, imploring him to return that he might see for himself my willingness to please him every way.

I have the letter by me as I write, all blotted with my tears and scratched about with alterations; the fair copy went to him. I said if he distrusted me, it might be that I, in my turn, might come to distrust him—and that to me would be worse than death. The bitterness of such distrust I had already tasted.

> . . . with as humble wise as is possible for me, being your very loyal and obedient wife, which to be, I confess myself more fortunate than other women, having such a husband as your Highness, I entreat you that we both pray God that we may meet and live together. And that same God whose hand is in the direction of the heart of Kings, will I hope, enlighten us in such a manner that all shall tend to your glory and satisfaction. . . .

To this, no answer. He had a heart hard to turn from his desires—and a pride to match it.

In all that long and bitter year of 'fifty-six, one thing, alone, consoled me—my faith; and the observance of those old, religious rites the Queen performs for the poor and the sick. To me, most blessed, because most Christlike, are the Easter rites of Maundy and the Blessing of the Rings. Of all rites, the most holy, the most deeply symbolical that any sovereign can perform, is the washing of the feet of the poor. And, because I was so unhappy, I carried out the Maundy rites with greater care than ever before.

I was at Greenwich for the Holy Week; upon the Thursday I came into the Great Hall together with my ladies, and all of us covered with long white aprons. Each lady carried a towel about her neck while, some bore a silver basin, others a silver jug; and all of them a posy of spring flowers. Next came my Cardinal-archbishop leading the princes of the church, all in their finest vestments, behind them walked my Council together with other of my great lords; and, leading the procession, went young choristers all in white and singing like angels.

The old women, my honoured guests, sat upon benches by the wall, forty-one of them—the number of my years. The ceremony began by my lord bishop of Chichester, humbly kneeling, while I went to each old woman, my ladies following. On both knees I knelt before those feet worn with age and toil. Tenderly, as though I washed the feet of the Lord Jesus himself, I washed the right foot and gently dried it with the towel held out to me. I signed the foot with the cross and kissed it with reverence; then into the old hand, a lady put a spring posy. I did not rise, but upon my knees moved to the next old woman and so I did with all forty-one, nor scanted any service, nor rose from my knees until that rite was finished.

When I stood again upon my feet my whole body trembled for weariness. I was far from well, and the hall large; I had been upon my knees nigh upon two hours. Nor was I by any means finished. In the great doorway stood my lord Cardinal and behind him a table spread with platters, forty-one in all; and each platter piled high with salted fish and two loaves in memory of Christ's miracle. He passed me platter after platter and, with my own hands, I carried them to the old women; now each held upon her lap a platter and a spring posy. Each must receive also a cup of wine; my ladies would have carried this for me but I was fain to do all myself, for the glory of God, and so for the third time I made my round.

Nor even now was my task by any means finished. A fourth time I made my journey giving to each old woman a length of fine wool sufficient for cloak and gown; on my fifth journey I carried shoes and stockings, on my sixth, a leather purse for each, containing forty-one silver pennies, new and of full weight. And so I came to my last journey, giving to each one the fine apron my ladies wore and the soft towel they carried.

And all the time the little choristers sang and the great hall was filled with mercy and with kindness so that you might have thought yourself in heaven.

I reached my closet scarce able to stand yet unable to end this day without further offering, so filled I was with holy joy. Something more I must give for the love of God. I was wearing a gown of fine velvet lined all with marten—the best I had, as befits one that serves God. I bade my ladies put upon me a plainer gown; and, carrying the rich one upon my arm, I came again into the hall. There I went about to see which of them all appeared the neediest and on her lap I laid my gown.

It had been a day of pure joy, all griefs laid aside. It was not so much the giving, though I love to give; it was the deep inner meaning of the rite; the joy of doing it for the love of God. Eight times I had gone about the hall and once upon my knees. My spirit was lifted up, but my body brought low; by the end of the day the old, painful swellings began in hands and feet. But God gives strength to those that have will to do His work. I was able, the next day, to bless the rings.

To bless the cramp rings may be done only by the Queen of England and no other. While Anne Bullen lived, and long after, I had been angered, remembering the harlot that, my mother still living, had taken upon herself that holy rite. Since my crowning I had twice performed this ceremony with deepest joy; now, again, it was spoiled for me, remembering that woman's daughter. How long before my sister, I, being dead, or even living still, would take upon herself this same ceremony?

This act of devotion I carry out in the Grey Friars chapel in Greenwich Palace; that same chapel where I had knelt in grief and humiliation when they baptised my sister; and where I had carried the infant, my brother, to his own baptism.

The blessing of the cramp rings is always performed after the Adoration of the Cross. Four benches enclose a square before the high altar; and, in the centre, a stool holds two basins of silver, each with its cover. Both basins contain rings of gold and silver; the one holds rings belonging to those that are sick and would be cured, and each bears the owner's name. The other basin holds rings belonging to the Queen; they are for the poor sick that have none of their own.

Before these basins the Queen must kneel in prayer; then she takes the rings dropping them from one hand to the other, all the while praying God to sanctify them to their use; and to show again His miracle in the healing of the sick.

Thereafter comes the blessing of the scrofulous. This is done in a small closed gallery that the sick may be private. This, I confess, I dread; for the stench of their affliction is such that it is hard not to vomit. Before the ceremony the Queen must receive absolution and this my lord Cardinal gave me. Then the priest prays aloud saying, but in the Latin tongue, *She places her hand upon the sick and he shall be well.*

I beckon to the first, sick creature, and kneeling still, my hands held like a cross. I press upon the sick spot, while the priest repeats, *She shall place her hand upon the sick and he shall be well.* And all the time I kneel, hands clasped in a cross; and now I forget the stink and I forget the weariness, for I am filled with the spirit of God.

Now the priest brings me a basin filled with gold angels, new-minted and each pierced to take a cord. Again the sick folk come, one by one, and kneel while I touch the ulcer with the coin, and sign it with the cross. Then, with my own hands, I pass a riband through the hole and hang it about the neck of the sick. They, for their part, vow never to part with this hallowed coin, save in their direst need. The ceremony being done, my cousin the Cardinal presents me with a basin that I may wash my hands and return again to the oratory.

I am strong upon my knees for the rest of the service; I am strong upon my feet. But, when at last, I reach my closet, then so weak is the flesh, I vomit.

Later my lord Cardinal sends his secretary to enquire of me.

'Madam,' he says, 'I have never seen such Christian devotion, such true humility, such perfect love.' And he looks at me as though I were a saint.

And he meant it, too. For he wrote the same to his friend in Italy. No letter leaves the Legate's office but the Cardinal sees it first; and this letter he showed me for my strength and comfort.

> It was a great and rare example of goodness. Her Majesty performed all those acts with such humility and love of religion, offering her prayers to God with a great devotion and affection; and enduring for so long a time and so patiently, so much fatigue. I dare swear there was never a Queen in Christendom of greater goodness than this one. I pray God long to save and prosper her for the glory of His divine honour and for the exaltation of God's holy church, not less than for the consolation and elevation of the people of this land.

It was a great comfort, this letter; for the more my spirit is exalted, the more my body is brought low. The swellings that had begun in my hands and feet spread to my entire body. For several days I could not walk, nor stand, nor lie down, nor hold any weight in my hand. But I bore it all with joy; Christ had suffered for me, could I not, a little, suffer in His sweet service?

But now I must put by my joy in sacred rites and come back to my painful duties. What must I do with my sister? When I might have had her head or kept her in perpetual prison, or married her out of

England, I had, for lack of proof, taken no step against her. Now, some upon my Council—and not a few, neither—advised me to take her by the hand and make much of her. I am a plain woman and such a piece of hypocrisy is not to my taste.

I wrote to Philip; I laid the matter clear before him and asked his advice. Meanwhile I did nothing; but I had Hatfield watched. My sister was keeping open house and a merry one. There was dancing and singing, there were masques and hunting-parties . . . and more questionable diversions. Reports showed her to be the centre of sedition in her neighbourhood; the plague-spot whence infection spread ever outwards. For still she meant to try for the crown and many of her neighbours she entangled in her treason. Some she won through flattery, some through admiration of her person, some because they hoped to mend their own fortune thereby. My lord Braye, speaking, no doubt, for others of his feather, said, *If my neighbour at Hatfield come to the throne I hope to pay my debts and be my own man again!* She had a name for being generous and gay, gracious and buxom*—though as to that last, I never saw her bow her will to any—save when she must, to me her Queen. And, for my lord Braye's hope, he might as well forget it! Generous she could be . . . when it suited her purpose; but how quickly the picture could change! I knew her to be miserly, suspicious and utterly unyielding.

Not only did I set a watch upon Hatfield. Any house where she had lived I had ransacked. The search brought to light evidence aplenty. Seditious writings enough to hang any man or woman—gentle or simple. But as usual she'd been clever! In her own hand—not a word; nothing to incriminate her! Make use of it, and she might claim—and would claim—they had been put there by an enemy hand. So there she sat, very pretty at Hatfield, both eyes upon my crown!

I, longing only to serve my people had lost their love. She, play-acting open-handed, open-hearted—she that watched always her own interests—had their love. *King Harry's lass* they called her.

It was June when Philip's answer came at last. He advised me not to break up the Hatfield household, as I had intended; nor, any way accuse my sister. The last thing we must do was to make her a popular martyr. I must see to it that, though accusation might be made of her friends and servants, it must fall short of herself. But by no means

* Original meaning obedient, compliant.

must I leave her free to her plotting. I must make a show of friendship and keep her under my own eye; or, if I could not stomach her presence, under the eye of those I could trust. That I show her favour, he made abundantly clear. The people loved her; me they did not love.

His advice, his commands, indeed, were not easy for me to obey. She was a traitor. But my husband commanded and I was sworn to obey.

Keep her under your own eye or under the eye of those you can trust. I did not want her at court; with the alternative I hastened to comply.

I sent to warn her of my intentions. I must remove certain of her household, and specially Ashley that ruled it—a foolish woman with a wagging tongue. I asked her not to take it amiss since I did it, not only for her good name, but to save herself from danger of their treason; also there were others whose loose behaviour shed little credit upon her household.

To pretend love where none lies, I find distasteful. But Philip had commanded it and I, myself, could see the sense of it. So I assured her of my regard—though the words stuck in my throat—and sent her a valuable ring in token thereof.

Thus purging her household, I sent for her two chief servants, her Comptroller and the fool Ashley, dabbling both of them in the affairs of their betters. I sent also for the Italian tutor; we strongly suspected, my Council and I, that he was a spy to send his news into France.

Innocent, all three! They had learned their lesson well from their mistress. From the Comptroller and the tutor we could get nothing, so I was forced to send them both back to Hatfield, advising my sister to be rid of them. Ashley fared less well. A fool she might be; but on this occasion clever enough to hold her tongue. I sent her to cool her heels in the Tower and took some satisfaction therefrom. Nor did I wait to see whether my sister obeyed me in the matter of her Comptroller—I sent in his place Sir Thomas Pope—a gentleman of parts and great integrity. I promised that she, herself, would, at once, feel the benefit of the change. And, indeed she did; for Sir Thomas was an excellent choice, as she afterwards came to admit.

These purges gave her to think . . . as I had meant. She answered at once protesting her entire innocence. It was a letter unendurably long and bedevilled with outlandish conceits, so that it was well-nigh unreadable, even to me that knew her style. I came at last upon some plainer word

. . . It vexes me so much that the devil owes me such a hate as to put me in any part of his mischievous instigations and I wish he had found some other way to spite me . . .

She wishes there were surgeons

. . . for making anatomies of hearts that might show my thoughts to your Majesty, as there are expert physicians of the body, for then, I doubt not that whatsoever any should suggest by malice, yet your Majesty should be sure by knowledge, so that the more such misty clouds obfuscate the clear light of my truth, the more my tried thoughts should glister to the dimming of their hid malice.

There is a good deal more of such flowery exposition before she finally beseeches God to preserve me against wicked people that would end my life, though I note, there is no good wish for my health. She signs herself

Your Majesty's most obedient subject and humble sister.

She adds date and place: 2nd August, from Hatfield.

What could I say to these too-plenteous protestations? And what could I do in face of my husband's command to show her favour and friendship?

I did what I could. I accepted her explanations and let the matter rest . . . for the present. Have her at court I would not; at Hatfield she was safe enough in honourable custody; honourable—but still custody. And there she should stay!

Chapter Fourteen

And now, as though I had not enough grief upon my heart nor trouble upon my head, came a new one. So far from returning, my husband stood upon the brink of war. War with France. Within so few months of its making, the five-year truce was broken; broken by France.

But it was more than war with France; much more. It was war with the Pope. His most Catholic Majesty against his most Catholic Holiness! It was a thing I could never, even in my most hateful nightmares, have imagined. Yet my husband was innocent in the matter, as every true person must admit; must, indeed, share in his horror at finding himself at war with God's Vicar. To express my own horror, my own distress and fear, is impossible; there are no words.

It came about in this way. Pope Julian, the good old man, had recently died. Cardinal Caraffa, together with my cousin Pole, had been named for the triple crown. My cousin—too liberal in his views—had just missed that highest honour and Cardinal Caraffa, taking the name of Paul IV sat in the seat of God's representative on earth.

'Now we may expect trouble!' my cousin had said at once.

And trouble there was; and not long in coming, neither!

No need to send for my cousin, this new war a-brewing. Himself sought me out and his face showed deepest concern.

'Disaster!' I cried out, and wrung my hands. 'Disaster to England, disaster in Spain—if it come to war!'

'It will come!' he said. 'This Pope is a hard man; fierce and vengeful. And he is old; too old. Above eighty. Like a child he is wayward and knows not what he does. God forgive me, if I speak ill of him; but his character is known throughout Christendom.'

'How does such a man come to be elected?'

'It is one of God's mysteries. This new Pope has little understanding of men, still less of those policies a Pope must use to keep unity in the Catholic church. To me, myself, he can bring little good. He hates me; he hates me with a personal hatred. In the College of Cardinals I have, at times, spoken against him; I am a man of more liberal view—and that he is not likely to forget!'

'Then we must keep you here safe!' I said. 'Clearly this Pope is a quarrelsome man and cares not at all whether his quarrel is just. Never would I dare to speak so of God's Vicar, save that all Christendom—even France herself—must know this quarrel with Spain to be unjust. He hates Spain because of the Italian cities that are in Spanish hands—where they belong. He complains that the King of Spain calls himself King of Sicily, King of Naples and duke of Milan.'

My cousin nodded. 'He was plotting with France even while France was negotiating peace with Spain. If the French turn the Spaniards out of Italy, the Pope will give Naples to one of Henri's sons, and Milan to another!'

'Philip's Naples! Philip's Milan!'

He nodded. 'And there are other inducements. The Pope promises to create so many French cardinals that the interests of France will always carry the day in Rome, and so throughout Christendom. Two great cities and God's Vicar forever on his side! What King, save he have great moral worth, could refuse the offer? Certainly not the King of France!'

Now the Pope harassed Philip every way. He excommunicated my husband's friends, the powerful Colonna, so that no man dare follow them or any way offer help. He imprisoned Philip's officials for no fault but that they did their duty, and insulted Spanish ambassadors. And finally, he declared Naples and Milan forfeit.

Thus, Philip, greatly reluctant though justly incensed, was forced into war. Even I, that am the Pope's most humble servant, could see no way out. For the Pope's supremacy in England I had risked first my life and then my crown. Anguish and terror filled me head-to-foot. I wrote to His Holiness that Philip was the truest Catholic in the world. I besought him not to force my husband into a war that must make a schism between those of the true faith; for, the breach being made, who should take advantage thereof but the heretics? I besought him in the name of Christ.

I received a letter in answer; an utterly useless letter. I copy from it now.

> . . . We love the Queen for her own sake, and for the sake of her mother who was good to us; and for the sake of her grandfather the most Catholic King of Spain. We could never have believed that his descendants could have deteriorated as much as Charles V and Philip II. We would willingly separate the Queen's cause from that of her—we know not what to call him—husband, cousin or nephew. . . .

Husband, cousin or nephew, we know not what to call him! It was a studied insult, as wrong as insulting. From Rome had come authority for our marriage. Pope he was; but God forgive me, my Tudor spirit rising, I walked about my closet uttering bitter words against him.

Nor did he stick at that; for worse followed.

> . . . We leave her as our dearest daughter, bidding her attend to the government of her own kingdom and not let herself be induced to do anything to our detriment or to any of our confederates, as for instance the King of France. For we would spare nothing, neither relations nor friends, in our maledictions and anathema against all who shall desert the cause of God. . . .

In other words mind my own business and separate myself from my husband. How might this last be done! Husband and wife are one flesh—so the Scriptures tell us. Philip had done no wrong; himself had been wronged!

No hope for it then but war.

On the first day of September, Spain's general, the great soldier, the duke of Alba, marched with twelve thousand men. And it was victory, victory all the way. Rome lay undefended; at Spain's mercy. Now, in fear and trembling the Pope begged a forty-day truce; and Alba granted the request. Many good Catholics thought him a fool; even the old Emperor in his monastery thought so. *When you have the advantage in war—take it take it and press it*, was ever his motto.

'It is man's wisdom to refuse; but God's wisdom comes first!' Pole said; and, in that, he spoke my own mind. But we were wrong, he and I. Who could trust this revengeful old man? And who trust France? Needless to say the truce was broken; and not by Philip.

Now it was war; total war. And war costs money. My private purse was empty. The million in gold late-granted by Parliament, I had laid out upon such inherited debts as were not yet paid; nor were like to be, unless I paid them while I had the means.

Parliament would not grant a fresh subsidy. Less than ever was it minded to pay for *the Spanish King's foreign wars.* And, indeed, they said, were they themselves so minded, the country could not carry the burden. And in this my Council agreed; Heath, my Chancellor, indeed, could find nothing to say but *We have no money! We have no money!* How I longed for Gardiner, the fierce old man that had browbeat Parliament and got his way.

I sent for Don Gomez. 'You are my especial adviser and the King's friend!' I reminded him. 'You must help me; me and the King! I have failed him in the matter of the crown—though I am not done with that by any means! But in the matter of raising money I'll not fail him!' *Dare not fail him lest I lose him altogether.* This last I did not say; but he knew it as well as I. 'Parliament refuses me; yet money he must and shall have!'

'Madam,' he said, 'I have already considered the matter. If the money be not given, why then it must be lent!'

'Parliament will refuse. . . .'

'Not Parliament, Madam; the country!'

'The *country*? How may it be done?'

'The Queen must ask it; from her lords, from her merchants, from other men of substance.'

'And if they refuse? I owe much to my merchants already, and more to foreign bankers; the interest on these debts mount daily.'

'It is the Queen that asks.'

'A forced loan, my lord?'

He nodded.

'That savours more of command than asking. I do not like it!'

'Do you like better to refuse the King?'

'I would not, for all the world, refuse him.'

I pondered the matter, prayed in the matter but could find no answer. I was desperate when I sent for my Chancellor.

'This money,' I told him, 'I must have! If it be not given, then it must be lent!'

He looked at me, jaw-dropped in dismay. 'Madam, consider the effects this shall have upon the people already!' he stopped. *You have lost their love.* I finished the sentence in my own mind. He began again, 'To force a loan; it was a measure used in your grandfather's time and much hated though it was, used to build up the country's wealth, not to waste in foreign wars.'

'Waste, my lord? Did you say . . . *waste*?'

'Madam, it was my word,' that mildest of men answered very firm.

To him I would not listen; my mind was set.

My Council and my Parliament heard me in amazement and great anger. I listened to them no more than to my Chancellor. With my own hand I drafted the letters. Each man, I said, must lend to his uttermost; but the least sum must be forty pounds.

Heath threw up his hands in dismay. 'On that, Madam, many a man keeps his family, pays his taxes and all his dues.'

'Then many will have plenty to spare,' I said. 'I will take nothing from those that have not. The money I need and I must have it!'

'On the Queen's head be it!'

And upon my head it was! There was anger in Parliament that I had set their wishes at naught, there was equal anger in the Council; and, among those that must pay, not only anger but alarm that spread down to the poorest. Who knew where the Queen's demands would stop? *No money for the Spaniard's wars!* They swore it! But in the end they paid.

And I paid, too; paid with insult from my people, in lewd ballad, in filthy lampoons and even filthier cartoons. Of this last there was one that even now sickens me with disgust; I can forget no detail. Some kind friend—one of the de Noailles' brothers, I fancy—saw that it found its way into my closet. It shows a naked woman, lean, ugly and old, the bones showing like those of a skeleton. The features are mine, though greatly exaggerated, they are clearly mine; and, that there should be no mistake in the matter, a crown sits upon the creature's hideous head. At her sagging breasts a thing that is clearly Philip, disgustingly suckles. Underneath the loathsome drawing is written *Maria, ruina Angliae.*

I commanded the filthy thing be torn down wherever it appeared; but as fast as this was done, there it was again! In the end I was forced to let them be; and there they stayed until wind and weather made an end of them.

Yes, I got the money; but I paid . . . I paid.

The days wore on; but there was no sweetness in them for me. I made no progresses, paid no visits, offered no public prayers. I never went abroad save when I must; and then never but in a closed litter. It was not that I was afraid; my father's daughter can have no fear of the people, but I could not endure to see hatred where once there had been love.

And still the burnings, the burnings! All through the late summer and autumn the burnings! I would ask myself, *What good? What good?* For heretics seemed no less in the land, rather they seemed to increase and were unafraid to declare their heresies; and I would wonder as I had wondered before whether from the ashes fresh heretics sprang. For, as they went to their last chance of salvation, crowds gathered to pray, and to weep. We feared, at times, the crowd would break through the cordon of men-at-arms to rescue the condemned men; to snatch them for this world's little span of life at the price of life eternal. And as they went the crowds wept and blessed them; and the condemned men themselves walked steadfast and sang as they went. That singing and steadfast they threw away salvation is enough to make Christ himself weep.

I could endure London no longer. I must leave for a while, the anger of my Parliament, the quarrels of my Council, and the false faces about my court. I must forget, if I could, the seditious papers, the lewd songs and the filthy drawings. I must forget above all—if forgetfulness were possible—the stench of burning flesh. For, that I die as truly though more slowly from these same fires, let my wasted body testify.

These late summer months I spent at Croyden. The house had belonged to my mother. We had never been there together, but she had loved it; and now, for her sake, I love it too, seeing her hand upon everything I touched, her feet walking the gardens where now I walked, my feet, maybe, treading in her very steps. Here and there about the house and village I would see an old face that had once looked into her own; and everywhere, in the village and beyond, memory of her goodness lingered. Even the young ones would speak of her care for the poor and the sick; for their parents had passed on the stories and her memory lingered; and not in the village alone, but in the house itself, so that we all felt it, myself down to the meanest servant, and lived the happier thereby.

Here, if not forget, I might for a little put aside the cares of state and the sorrows of my lot. With two or three of my ladies, of whom *my Jane* was one, we would—as my mother had done—visit the cottagers. We dressed very plain, I no better than any other, so that none knew, nor even suspected who I might be. I would sit by the hearth and the poor folk would talk of their joys which were few enough, and of their troubles, alas, only too many.

So I would listen to many things Queens do not often hear, of the injustices the poor must carry—the fines undeserved or too heavy; small enough maybe, but to them, their lives so poor, so hard, enough to darken their whole world. I would hear how my bailiff had taken a horse to draw a cart at ploughing-time when every man's horse is needed on his own strip of land; or how this same bailiff had exacted labour due or, not due, and had paid less than the fair price, or none at all. I would hear how this child lay sick—and no money to buy physic, or that man lay unburied for lack of a few pence. And all these things I made right, wishing the while that things might, as easily, be made right for me.

But what pleased me most was to play godmother to the children. I would send a bright lad to be apprenticed that he might have a good trade in his hand; or if his wits warranted it, I would send him to school. All about the countryside they called me *the good lady* and more than one whispered to me of *the bloody Queen* and prayed that one, merciful like myself, might sit in her place. Everywhere in the countryside about Croyden, folk said it was as though the good Queen from Spain had come again and that pleased me most. In this house where once she had lived, I must remember her Christian gentleness to all, a gentleness that had reached out even to Anne Bullen. That same gentleness I tried, and do try, to feel for all and especially for Anne Bullen's daughter . . . but I am not the saint my mother was!

A peasant's life is poor and hard; sometimes he is but one step from starvation; yet, whenever I saw a woman heavy with child, another little one, maybe, about her skirts, I would think, She is blessed, indeed. Her day is long and hard but she carries her husband's child and at nights sleeps warm by his side. And I would think, as still I think, that to be mistress of a house, so it be great enough for dignity, and to have my children rosy-cheeked and merry about the place, would be blessed, indeed! For I am a simple woman and content with simple things; but, being called to the crown, must do that duty for which God has chosen me.

The pleasant days passed; I had rejoiced in the hot sun, now I saw with foreboding, how early the leaves were falling, how in orchards withered fruit lay rotting in the grass, and in the fields the corn stood thin and brittle. There would be another ruined harvest; last year it had been ruined by too much rain, this year by too little. I knew the bitter need this second spoiled harvest must bring; but how dire that need nor how bitter the outcome I could not foresee.

One cannot put by the burden for ever. In the second week of September back I must go; back to a bitter, sullen London, back to an obstinate Parliament and a disaffected Council; back to the fires and the stink of burning; back to no hope of Philip—that last a worm to feed upon my heart.

On my homeward way news was brought me that lowered my spirits still further. Courtenay was dead.

He had died in Venice, a poor exile, died of a consumption of the lungs due to a neglected wetting; and, poor young man, never a friend nor servant to care for him. Rumour that is never still, whispered he was dead of poison—and the Queen of England not innocent!

Maybe I should have been glad of another danger removed; but I grieved for him. Royal and debonair and all set for glory—a glory his own foolishness had denied him. How sad that life, how tragic! From childhood to young manhood imprisoned—and no fault of his own. Released by my own hands, he had expected a Queen for wife and the consort's crown. Why not? All England had desired it; but I, I had not desired it. Disappointed, he had sunk to treason, conspiracy, and death in poverty. Death of the last White Rose, its flower scarce unfolded. I ordered masses for his soul, I doubt not God will show him mercy.

I was glad to stop at Lambeth Palace to eat my dinner with my cousin Pole. If I had thought to take cheer from his company, I was disappointed; clearly he was a much-harassed man.

'You are not much better for the country air!' he said.

'Your own looks are not much better!' I told him.

'No,' he said. 'I foresee trouble and great trouble! Last year food was scarce and prices high; this year . . .' He let fall his empty hands. 'Worse; far worse! And the people will blame you; they blame you for everything! Already they are saying that you rob the country to send not only gold overseas, but with it the people's food. That it is not true matters nothing; hungry folk will say anything! Parliament will grant you no more money. For, Madam, it does not forgive you your forced loans; nor will those that lent their money. Yet nobody will tell you the plain truth but me. Madam, I warn you, step with care! Parliament itself hard-pressed for gold, does not love you, no, nor the people that go hungry!'

'I would go hungry myself; I would go barefoot rather than rob the widow and the orphan!'

'That would help nobody, Madam!'

'So much misery! Some we cannot help, but some—' and, to my horror, I heard myself speaking of that I had meant to speak no more. 'Cousin, could we not, for a little, halt the burning? I cannot see that the fires destroy heresy; rather it springs stronger than before ever!'

Even as I spoke I knew it was useless. The tenderness was wiped from his face. 'Madam, we have argued this matter before!' And I heard the weariness in his voice. 'If heresy grow stronger, the fires must burn longer. I speak for the church. I am, pray God, a merciful man; but, Madam, consider! There's no man so dangerous as your heretic; for he would overthrow the foundations of religion in a Christian land. Never has there been so much revolt, so much treason, so much sin, so much evil of every kind since the door was opened to heresy in this land!'

'You are, indeed, a merciful man, as all Christendom knows. Had you been less merciful, less open to reason, you would even now be Pope. But you chose, instead, to consider the true nature of mercy; and having found it, to stand by it. Cousin you are, as you always have been, God's faithful soldier!' And I was ashamed of my weakness before the long experience of this gentle and merciful man.

So now, again, I must strengthen my spirit to the burden.

Chapter Fifteen

London, I found worse, even, than I had expected. I found more than anger, more than rebellion. I found hatred; hatred of me and my forced loans; hatred even more bitter on account of the never-ending burnings. The whole city seethed with hatred.

I understand very well that, save one believes the fire to be, in the last resource, the way to God, the sight of a man—and save for his heresies a good man—going to such a death is horrible. And the sight of such a man praising God amidst the flames is enough to shake the stoutest heart; that, also I knew for myself. How long, I wondered, before those that watched left their praying and their weeping to set upon the soldiers and free the prisoners?

From the ashes of every burning new heretics spring. Once I had told my cousin Pole. But now something worse was happening. The steadfast spirit of those that burned was shaking the weaker members of the true faith. They said—and did not care who heard them—*Burning is a hateful thing. We must ask ourselves if it be truly God's Will.* That is, indeed, a question to trouble the faint heart. Myself had asked it again and again; but it was a question my church had answered and that answer I must accept.

In the midst of my sorrows came joy; joy, unbelievable, overwhelming.

Philip was coming home.

'Why in the midst of warfare should he return?' my Chancellor asked, anxious. 'For whether he come or whether he stay where he is, it's all one. There's no money for his wars.'

'The reason makes no matter!' And I was all impatience. 'He is coming! And if it is money he needs, why then, money he shall have!'

'And how, Madam, do you propose to get it?'

'That is for you to find out, my lord Chancellor!' And away I went to thank my God. My church had been right. In our steady putting-down of heretics, God, at last, showed His pleasure. Philip was coming home; and with him my hope of a child.

He is coming home! In spite of the gloom all about me—in Parliament, in the Council and in the people, I carried joy in my spirit and in my flesh.

He is coming home.. Day after day I waited; it might have been myself of whom the old song sang,

> And long she waited and longer still in muckle
> grief and pain,
> And long she waited and waited still, but he came
> not home again.

For now we were into November; but there was no more word from Philip. In the dark cold days that must soon be darker, colder still, the miseries brought upon us by bad harvests, high prices and the diminished value of money, things were worse, even, than I had imagined possible. As winter closed in, people died in the streets of cold and hunger. And, in Christian England—how shall I tell·such abomination? Good, honest folk that hitherto had cherished their children, abandoned them upon doorsteps, hoping, most desperately, that others more fortunate, might pity these little ones. For now, like that other woman in the Scriptures, a mother must run, finger in ear, that she might not see the death of the child. It was a thing to break my heart that some should have children too many; and I, not one to bless me and my people.

Against such abandonment we were forced to make laws; yet still the practice continued; and then—last abomination of all—the hungry ate the flesh of the dead. And this, God help us, in a Christian country!

Once the good monks and nuns would have succoured the poor, but there were few such holy folk left. My father and brother between them, had driven them away and pulled down their houses. I had done what I could to bring them back. I had not only returned such of their property as had come into my hands, but, from my own lean purse, helped to rebuild a few religious houses. Some holy men and women had returned to their order, but they were all too few. What takes so short a time to destroy, takes long and long to build again; and it takes not only time but money too. My own means were not sufficient, but there were many that, having the means, and professing the Faith had rather part with life itself than with the least part of their gold.

As both my cousin Pole and my Chancellor had warned me, there was ever-growing resentment because of the empty exchequer. But more money I must have; money for the business of the state, for the relief of the poor, and for the King's affairs. Once more I opened the matter to Heath; it was clearer than ever that he was no Gardiner! He knew not where nor how to lay hands upon money, nor how to make money breed money, nor—even were he willing which he was not—how to force Parliament in the matter. With Parliament as with the Council, he carried no weight.

Instead of giving his mind to the matter he began to complain once more of the gold I had already sent to the Netherlands. I made short work of that! 'I have sent only that gold which the King himself brought into this country—and little enough of that!—together with that raised by loans; loans raised by me, myself, and by myself to be paid. Loans, my lord Chancellor, not gifts and it is I that suffered for it, I myself! I cut down expenses where I may; and even when I may not. I am one that likes to live well; yet I keep my table so poor, I earn for myself the name of *miser*; more than one foreign envoy has called me so, and that you know for yourself! I am one to give freely and love the giving; but what I give is unworthy of a prince, and on myself I spend nothing; I have nothing to spend!'

And when he would have reminded me that, but for the property I had given back to their rightful owners I should have done well enough, I dealt with him smartly. 'That comes ill from you, my lord bishop!'

'It comes well from your Chancellor. I beg you, Madam, do not let your too-merciful heart forever mislead you!'

'Leave my merciful heart out of the question. What's done, is done! Money we must have; how are we to get it?'

'I know but one way. Debase the currency.' He spoke as though he had long considered and found no fault in the monstrous suggestion. But for all that he could not meet my eye.

'No!' I said at once. 'Such a piece of dishonesty I'll not countenance!'

'Madam, your father allowed it and your brother, also!'

'They did as they must! For myself—' Suddenly my temper flared. 'By God no!' I cried out. 'I'll have none of that!'

'Madam, I beseech you, think again! I speak for your Council; and, indeed, Parliament will ask it of you!'

And while I tood stiff and obstinate, he said, 'Madam, if you stand against the people's anger, deny your Council and oppose your Parliament, then, Madam—and I say it in all reverence—God help you!'

'I pray He will; always!'

And still Philip did not come. But now I could see for myself that to come was impossible.

Victorious, he had made a truce with the Pope—and the Pope was not to be trusted. He had made a truce with France—and France was not to be trusted. Henri was moving his troops too near Calais—English Calais, my Calais. *Changing garrison*, their excuse to my ambassador. I'd not have the French menacing Calais. I had been crowned not only Queen of England, but also Queen of France. From childhood I had been taught to believe in my French right. Yet in all France I possessed Calais only, and the Calais Pale, together with the little harbour of Dunkirk. Over my dead body the French should take Calais!

I sent Pembroke with a sizable force. The French marched home again! But Philip must remain forever on the watch.

Towards the third week of November, my sister came riding from Hatfield to Somerset Place, her house in London. I had not sent for her; but I had not forbidden her, neither. She had, these past months, behaved well enough in the country; I had no excuse to forbid her her own house; and, moreover, my husband had advised me to show friendship for her.

'She comes, Madam, with a splendid retinue,' Jane Dormer said. 'A great train of servants all in white and green; her ladies and gentlemen in scarlet and miniver!'

'And she, herself!'

'The Princess . . . ' She spread her hands. 'Madam the Queen knows her tricks; none better!'

'Even I do not know them all! What of this one?'

'All in white, her hair flowing free; very virginal. And smiling and gracious, and gentle and modest. Butter wouldn't melt in her mouth!'

Yes, I knew her tricks; this was an old one that never failed!

'And the people?'

'There were bonnets cast into the air and flowers flung; there were tears and there were cheers, there were prayers and blessings.'

All those things I, myself, once had known and knew no more!

'She steals the people's heart from me! Who can trust her—Anne Bullen's daughter!' And then, as though some other spoke with my tongue, God Himself, perhaps, 'Anne Bullen's child; but not my father's. Born of incest—that woman and her brother!'

'Madam!' And she was paper-white with the shock of my words, so young she was she had not heard that long-ago scandal; so innocent, her mind could not conceive of it. 'It is not possible!' And then, again, *'Not possible!'*

'Only too possible. It stands in the indictment against them both. She denied it; but he? Never; not even when he stood on the scaffold.'

'But, Madam; brother and sister!'

'It has been known. No sense of rightness in either of those two; and like calling to like.'

'But, Madam, consider! The Princess has those same swellings of body and limb from which the Queen suffers; the Queen's father had them also.'

'My father had the dropsy from which he died. For myself—it could be that same thing, which God forbid! The dropsy is not a pretty thing. But as for her—I cannot say what those swellings may be; the dropsy is common enough! Besides, Buttes tells me such things may be produced at will.'

'*Witchcraft*, Madam?'

'Not always. Buttes tells me that the troubled mind working upon the body may produce such signs . . . and produce them when it is most convenient.'

'But, Madam, the lord King, your father, acknowledged her his child!'

'At the beginning only. He had more than one thought on the subject. First he declared her true-born, then a bastard of his own begetting, but, at the last, a bastard begotten upon the harlot by her own brother. As for me—I know not what to think! But, were I certain she would uphold the true faith in this land, I would be content to accept her my father's child—though a bastard still!'

For all her splendid show and all the blessings of London, not one of my Council nor any of the court had ridden out to bring her into

London, as is usual when one of the royal house enters the city; nor in my hearing was she mentioned. But all the same, first by ones and twos, and then in company, they went to pay their respects; and she, so I heard, received them with a modesty that was both gracious and royal. Yet still I did not send for her nor make any sign I knew of her presence.

My cousin Pole came from Lambeth to advise me.

'Madam, you do yourself no good! You should send for the Princess—for you cannot fault her. She behaves perfectly, continually enquiring of the Queen's health, sending messages of humble obedience, sending gifts. . . .'

'I fear the Greeks when they come bearing gifts.'

'Madam, if you give no sign of friendship, you will anger the people.'

'I can lose no more than their love—and that I have lost!'

'One can always be worse off than one is; and love may be won again. Madam, it is well, at least, to take the measure of the enemy.'

'I took that measure long ago.'

'Then make sure the measure be correct.'

At that my temper flared. 'She is not my enemy, alone, she is also the enemy of the Church; *your* enemy, Cousin! Yet you have never set eyes on her to take her measure—though you had chances enough! When she came to me at Greenwich, you kept your distance. Can it be possible, my lord archbishop, that you have changed your mind? Are you, also, curious to set eyes upon the fascinating creature?'

'I was wrong then. Yes, I must see her—though I am not like to be taken by her charms. I must judge for myself how dangerous she may be! You are right, Madam; she is, indeed, an enemy to our faith; and, so I say again, it is well to measure one's enemy!'

Well, he was right there! But I was obstinate and I was hurt. 'I will not send for her!' I told him.

'The lord King, your husband, wishes it!'

I sent for my sister.

She came to Whitehall; and, in my presence, those two met, that had never met before. She had not bargained for what she was to see—a handsome man that carried himself as royal as she did herself. He was, after all, of blood more royal than her own. She saw the beautiful thin face; a face worn by the spirit and the passion for his faith. She saw the gentleness of eye and mouth, but was not one to be misled thereby. She would read the warning in the chin; for all his gentleness, he'd not allow himself to give way to unrighteous pity for himself or for any other. She would know that, in him, she had met her match.

And he? He saw the tall young woman, very proud in her carriage; comely, with a high bosom and a trim waist. He saw that red hair of hers flowing free as a maiden's should, daring him to question her virginity, her doubtful virginity; again the old trick that never failed. He saw the black eyes set above an aquiline nose in the long sallow face; and would know her—Anne Bullen's daughter. And, for all she kept those proud eyes low, he would not miss their hardness and their pride. She had, in that first instant, known she could win him only with a show of humility.

I saw him make her a deep reverence, rendering fully unto Caesar those things that are Caesar's. I saw her sink, very humble, to her knees as though she rendered to God those things that belong to God. She asked his blessing and he gave it, she holding those lovely hands of hers folded in prayer rather higher than was need. She rose and they talked together in the Latin tongue; in that she outshone him, he having the scholar's precise turn of phrase, she, my father's charming fluency in that tongue. So gentle she was, so submissive, so *humble*! It was as Jane Dormer had said, You'd think butter wouldn't melt in her mouth!

I sat between them at supper, the two handsome creatures. There I was, little and thin and tired, my face more lined than should be, the hair that showed beneath the coif streaked all of grey, my short-sighted eyes peering from one to another; between those two, insignificant and . . . old; older even than he, that was by fifteen years my senior.

I tried to show myself gracious; but I could do no more than sit there hostile to my sister, hard as she herself and as cold.

When, supper being over, and she, with my permission having curtseyed herself away, my cousin said, 'There goes an enemy to you and to God. Gardiner was right. You should have made an end of her long ago. Now it is too late. By so much as you have lost the people's love, she has gained it. Now you must make the best of it. Show yourself friendly; and whatever you do, never slight her. It is a serpent to bite . . . and will bite. Madam, send her home with fair words. And for the rest, wait until the King return!'

Chapter Sixteen

Until the King return. And then? Youth calls to youth. And what of me with my faded looks; and what of my sister the young blood running in her veins like springtime sap? I could not put my sister's bright young image from my mind. How could I forget the joyous tumult her mere appearance had caused in London—*King Harry's lass*? How could I forget that my court, first in secret, and then in open numbers had flocked to pay her homage? How could I forget Pole's warning, *There goes an enemy to you and to God*? And, above all, how could I forget my husband's command to show friendship for her. Did he wait for the death of one Queen to marry the next? Or—and my heart dissolved in terror on the thought—did he mean not to wait? Did he mean to dissolve our marriage? Why not? My own father had shown him the way. Did my husband mean to set me aside, to breed upon my sister the sons he had not begotten upon me? At the thought hatred rose again in me; hatred bitter and destructive as poison. I could no longer endure the sight of her; for her own sake I must send her away.

On the last day of November I sent for her. I would not have her about me at Christmas-tide; I did not want my dislike, my distrust to curdle the holy season.

'Sister,' I said, 'I see that you join in our devotions, attending Mass and partaking of the Sacrament according to the true faith. But, do you worship with the inward heart as truly as with outward show?'

'Madam, I have said so!'

'Then, Sister, say it again.'

'I am of the Catholic faith,' she said, 'in which faith I truly believe.

'Will you swear by Christ that you acknowledge the miracle of the Sacrament; that the bread most truly becomes the flesh of our Lord and the wine His blood?'

'I believe it,' she said—and never a flicker of those hard eyes.

'Do you acknowledge the supremacy of the Pope as God's Vicar on earth?'

'I do acknowledge it!'

'Sister,' I told her, 'I ask you this very earnest, not to press you, nor any way to punish, but for the sake of this country.'

'It is right that sisters should be in accord,' she said.

'You have not always thought it! Sister, you make me speak plain what you already know!' And it was the first time I, myself, had raised with her the thing for which she so longed and had so often plotted. 'If you cannot truly believe in the blessed Catholic faith, never perjure your soul. Such perjury may bring you the crown of this land; but it would lose you your crown in Heaven.'

'God forbid!' she said, very quick.

'Amen to that!' I said; but whether she meant God forbid she should perjure herself; or God forbid we should reckon upon my death, I could not know! I suspect she meant nothing at all save a willingness to deceive me.

'Listen, Sister, listen well and answer with truth. If God should call you to be Queen, will you uphold the true faith in this land?'

'I will uphold it!' And it was as though she spoke the coronation oath. But what did she mean by *the true faith*? What reservation did she hide in that secret heart of hers?

'Sister,' I said, 'it has been the King's wish you should marry Savoy; whether it be still his wish I do not know. But you must not marry Savoy or any other foreign prince. Your place is here!' And it was as though I spoke my own death sentence; for were she wed to Savoy or any other, Philip was lost to her for ever.

'I shall never marry!' She looked at me very steady. 'I shall live and die a virgin!'

Are you a virgin? And I remembered again that rough-and-tumble with Tom Seymour in her bedchamber, in her very bed. Her own devoted Ashley had sworn it to the Council. And I remembered how, the tale going about that she was with child, she had out-faced the Council with her demand to show herself to them all, so that they could not quickly enough run to apologise. And she but fifteen!

She may well have guessed my thoughts; she was sharp as a bodkin. The colour flushed crimson into her sallow face.

'A Queen cannot remain a virgin,' I told her. 'A Queen must marry for the good of the state!'

'Why, Madam? Married or not—it is all one!'

And did she twit me that I had no child. Was she saying as plain as she dared, *A virgin Queen is better than a barren Queen. A virgin, by her own will is childless. So she preserves her pride and her dignity.* And, suddenly, it flashed upon me that, young as she was, she already suspected herself to be barren—maybe her games with Tom Seymour had whispered a warning. I knew her pride; was she already, with this same pride, covering her fear, hiding the truth about herself to herself?

To get any truth from her which she did not mean to reveal was hopeless. I left the subject. I said, 'Sister, I know well how you long for your home and for your friends. You are free to go whenever you choose.'

'I am at the Queen's command.' Her eyes betrayed nothing; yet I knew she was wondering what this dismissal might portend.

'They say of you that you are a buxom, liberal dame. Buxom you are not; you never bowed your will to another in your life. But liberal? Take care, sister, that you be not too liberal of your promises; so you shall keep your friends from their plotting.'

'If Madam the Queen misdoubts me . . .' and now that sallow skin of hers had gone a little green.

'Heed my warning and there'll be no room for doubt!' And let her make of that what she could!

Two days later she was gone; she, with her host of servants in green-and-white; her ladies and gentlemen all in scarlet and miniver. She was gone—bright as the red star that had flamed, and as menacing; gone to make Christmas merry, no doubt, with her well-wishers, the buxom, liberal dame! I went to Greenwich to spend the season of joy, all joyless.

In London the people tried, for a little, to forget their troubles and their angers. They drew in their belts yet tighter, and made what cheer they could; they welcomed St. Nicholas into their houses with the old carols and dances.

Alone in Greenwich I shut my door fast against the sound of merrymaking; because I, myself, was sick at heart, God forbid I should cause grief in the hearts of others. I could not, even at this time, forget that the fires, extinguished to grace our Saviour's birth, must flame once more in His honour. I prayed continually that God would allow my poor country, and me, some further respite, that I might win heretics by fair promises. Let them but make a show of returning to the true faith and I asked no more; for that faith must, in the end, win them. So low I was sunk! Philip's absence, the incessant burnings and my own body's weakness together had broken my courage.

My joyless Christmas passed. Pole came to visit me at Greenwich. He did not seem to be himself. Melancholy sat in his eye, and those eyes sunk deep in his head. The last gold had gone from his hair; head and beard were, alike, grey; nor did he jest, nor any way lighten our meeting with his accustomed wit. A grey old man.

I guessed what lay upon his mind but dared not speak of it. For several days he said nothing. At last he spoke.

'Madam, we scant our duty to God and man, you and I; you because of compassion, I because I am a coward. We do not save this country from corruption that spreads like a leprosy. We do not sufficiently harden our hearts to make an end of heresy!'

I had prayed for a slackening of the fires; now it seemed there was to be a quickening!

'When I was a child,' I said, 'I learned a little in the Greek. There was a passage in the psalms, as I remember, that proclaimed the wicked should be wiped from the face of the earth. It was a wrong translation my tutor told me. In the original Hebrew it reads that wickedness be wiped from the earth. *Wickedness*; not the wicked!'

'It is a splitting of hairs,' he said, very stern. 'For who shall do wickedness but wicked men? If it please you, Madam, pray that heresy be wiped from this world!'

'I do pray. But, Cousin, my tutor was Dr. Fetherstone that suffered for the Faith, *our* faith—an early martyr. His death I have never forgotten; nor the things he taught me; for he was a gentle teacher. He counselled me always to mercy, for he was a merciful man! As for these burnings—what scanting of duty? They stopped only for Christmas-tide. Christ Himself could not fault that!'

'Madam, you are—forgive me—too glib with the name of Christ. *Christ*!' he cried out in sudden passion, 'knew the heart of pity; pity for a man's soul that it go not to the everlasting fire!'

'Is there no other way to save a man's soul but by burning his body?' I held out my hands and they were shaking.

'You cannot save a man's soul by offering him sweetmeats. We must burn and burn and burn, till the last spot of corruption is burnt away!'

'Cousin,' and I tried another tack, 'martyrs beget martyrs—or so it would appear; of martyrs there's never a lack! Shall you win yet more martyrs for the false church?'

'Martyrs are led by God; heretics misled by the devil. Yet there's some wisdom in what you say. Too long we have allowed the crowd to walk with those that go to the fire; to comfort them with hymns, and with prayers beseeching God for them. This is devil's work; for the heretics go exalted to the stake and scarce feel the fire.'

'All flesh feels the fire.' And I remembered my scorched finger. 'But if you should be right—does it hurt God, if they, exalted by the devil, feel not the full pain?'

'It hurts God that they are not saved in the end. Daughter—' and now he spoke not as my cousin but as my archbishop, 'do as your church bids you. I tell you again that to comfort the heretic is devil's work.'

'My lord archbishop and Cardinal,' I said, in my turn calling him not Cousin, but by his great titles to obedience, 'you are not only the Primate of this land to direct all souls, to save them—if you can; you are also the voice of the Pope that is God's voice. What you command, no man may dispute; and what you order I shall obey!'

A few days later he showed me his pastoral letter addressed to the citizens of London; copies were, also, to be sent into every town and village throughout the land. It began by accusing all those that had shown undue gentleness to heretics; this was offence against God. Had such gentleness won, it had been good; a work of mercy. But gentleness had not won and there must be a change in behaviour. For to suffer heretics or any way to favour them

> . . . there cannot be a work of greater cruelty against the commonwealth. For be assured there is no kind of man so pernicious as these heretics be; there are no thieves, no murderers, no adulterers, nor no kind of treason to be compared with theirs who undermine the foundations of all commonwealth which is religion, and make an entry into all kind of vices. Whereever then does it come that when a heretic shall go to his execution he shall lack no comforting by you, lack no encouragement to die in his perverse opinions?
>
> This must not be suffered. For their boldness in their death is small argument of grace in them. Christ Himself showed more heaviness and dolour than did the thieves that hung beside him, especially one of them showing no fear. So like the blasphemer do all heretics go to their death. . . .

He went on to threaten all that offered prayers or showed pity for heretics obstinate in their dying, should themselves be punished. The net to catch all—those that suffered and those that falsely comforted—should be cast wider, drawn tighter.

I made no objection. I had given my conscience into his hands. He was a holy man, gentle where he might be, harsh where he must. Yet a question troubled me. *Is it right to give one's conscience to any other, though he speak with the voice of God?* A heretic's question. Had that corruption spread to me, to me, myself?

I put the question from me with horror.

Chapter Seventeen

Celebrating the birth of the Infant, I felt more desolate my own childlessness. The new year of 'fifty-seven came in. It began for me, as the old year had ended, in pain and grief, my world lit still by the fires; darkened still by the people's hatred for me and their open love of my sister.

This year the fires were to burn more fierce than ever—my cousin had warned me; but I was not prepared for the hideous events it was to bring forth.

The whole of that first month my Council—my bishops very eager in the matter—concerned itself with heretics. Not one of these meetings did I attend. I was too sick a woman and sickness clouds the mind. When one is concerned with dealing out death in the Name of God, the mind must be clear as glass.

Heath, since he was both Chancellor and archbishop of York, brought to my closet the findings of the Council. 'Madam; heresy, we have seen it for ourselves, means not only the overthrow of God's church in this land, but of the very kingdom itself. Until heresy is burnt out of the land, no true servant of God may rest upon duty done.'

My cousin Pole might well content himself with saying little in Council; I recognised his very voice.

'Since my Council has the matter in hand, it must ask itself what must be done further!' I told him.

But what it might do—and did do—never entered my head.

He must have reported my lack of response, for later that same day, my cousin asked for an audience.

'Madam, consider! In every Christian country—be it Catholic or heretic—offenders against that country's faith are punished by death. But these Protestants! Not only do they wound the body of holy church, they are eaten by their own dissensions. So many sects—and each stiff with hatred of the others! They'd burn each other if they could!'

'Then we have nothing to fear; they do our work for us!'

'Shall God's enemies do His work? Never think it! It is the devil's work they do! It is not only their anger, one sect with another; it is what that anger brings forth. Blasphemy; nothing less. And not in words alone. They spit in the very face of God!'

I took in my breath at that.

'Madam, I speak not in metaphor but in plain words. Men spit in the face of His image; I have seen it for myself!'

'They . . . *dare*?'

'A man spits—and no fire comes down from heaven; so he spits again and others follow him. And, Madam . . . ' he was clearly unwilling his tongue should even utter the words, 'there are some to deny the divinity of Christ, others that He ever existed.'

'Poor fools that run to lose their souls!'

'Poor country, indeed—if we waste our pity upon such fools! It is not pity we need, Madam, but stronger measures. For when men lose their fear of God, they give themselves to every licence. They are the rats that gnaw in the cellar of the house to bring it down altogether. If we do not make an end of them, they will make an end of Christianity!'

'Then, Cousin, the Council shall do as it must; but what more it may do, I cannot think!'

'Will the Queen allow the Council to think and then to proceed? It will act with conscience and with care . . . but the proceedings may not be pleasant.'

I said nothing to that; for what can be worse than gangs of chained men sent to their burning? He saw my reluctance to assent and was determined for my approval.

'Madam, believers and heretics alike know it is a Christian duty to destroy false gods. Madam, even Calvin, anti-christ says, *It is the duty of the Christian to destroy false gods. We must spare no man, nor his kin, nor blood nor life. We must forget our humanity when we fight for God's glory.*'

'So you, my lord archbishop, quote anti-Christ to me?'

'If the devil may quote the Scriptures to lose souls, may we not quote the devil to save them?'

And to that I could find no answer. For when Catholics and heretics, alike, agree that God's enemies must be destroyed out of the land, how should I, alone, disagree? And, moreover, I was divided in my own heart; for there went with me always the certain knowledge that, so long as I withheld heretics from their chance of salvation, so long would God withhold a child from me.

My Council and my bishops, wasting no time, went to work most thoroughly in the matter. Commissioners were appointed to search out every corner of the land; freedom was given to judges and to magistrates, even, to punish heretics at once with death. In every town great and small, suspect houses could be entered without warrant, books and papers examined. Into the fire went every book that smacked of heresy and into the fire went their owners. So far the universities had suffered little; now they were to suffer greatly. Every suspect, teacher or student was to be rigorously questioned, their rooms ransacked, every page of every book examined. But who has time to examine every page? God knows how many noble works perished! And into the fire followed their owners. And since books and scholars are more plentiful at universities than elsewhere, in those cities the holy fires were never still.

Yet I could not quarrel with that, even if I would! I am a lover of books and accounted something of a scholar. But better a book should burn than a human soul; for one word may spread more corruption than a hundred men. 'To burn a doubtful work is right; to burn one doubtful soul—God will require it of us!' I told my cousin.

'Of me; of me, especially that am archbishop and Cardinal. And I am willing. Yet still the Pope rebukes me that I am not forward enough in God's business . . . and maybe he is right!'

These days he wore a white and fragile look; the fire that burned human flesh, burned him also, as it did me. Yet he was upheld by some inner strength—as I am not; he looked as though the thin envelope of his flesh was sustained upon a frame of steel. 'We have not done enough; we have not gone deep enough!' he said.

'Heretics and their writings go to the fire. What more may be done?'

'There are certain dead heretics,' he said very slow, troubled yet certain. 'We have to finish our enquiries about them!'

Then seeing I did not understand—as, indeed, how should I?—he said, 'Dead heretics are more corrupting than those that live. Dead lips speak from the grave; their words pass from mouth to mouth of the living, strengthened by the mere fact of death. Those heretics that died before they could be tried, or, being tried, died not in the fire but a traitor's death on the gallows; or more needful, those heretics honoured in your brother's reign. We must take up their bodies . . .'

'. . . from the *grave?*'

He nodded. 'We shall burn them in the fire. And we shall enquire into the heresy not of the dead, alone, but also into his whole family—wife and children, father, mother, sister, brother; whether they laid information as was their duty, or whether they kept silent. And those that supported them, or any way concurred, even though by silence, must pay.'

'You would burn women . . . and children?'

'If it were my needful; but it will not, I think, come to that! There are other ways of paying. Every last inch of land, every last penny in a stocking shall be stripped from them. Let them wander the land . . .'

I looked out upon the winter Thames hard and bitter; as steel, at the cold rain falling and turning to ice as it fell; I saw the iron trees that could give no shelter. I thought of women and children wandering homeless, husbandless, fatherless, penniless . . . and no-one daring to help them.

'No!' I cried out. 'No! Take the bodies from the grave if you must, but do not harm the innocent!'

'Heretics, Madam! There are none innocent. Having burnt the tree shall we leave the roots? Oh!' and he was taken again by the sudden impatiences that had grown upon him these days, 'do you think I *want* this inquisition of the dead? Do you think I have not knelt in agony praying that this sort of judgment pass from me?' And he beat his lean body with long, thin hands.

And even then I would have urged him further against so dreadful a proceeding, but he said, calm and cold, and himself once more, 'Madam, you have no voice in this! Queen of England you are; but, by your own desire, in obedience to Rome. It is scarce a year since this country returned to the blessed fold. Do *you* rebel, now, Madam?'

The new and dreadful work began in Cambridge. By the will of the whole university, two heretic priests were taken from their graves. Inquisition was to be made upon their bodies—*carcasses* was the word used; but why strain at a word? Notices nailed upon every church door, and upon the cross in the market-place, invited any that would defend the doctrines held by the carcasses while in life, to appear before the commission at St. Mary's church, the eighteenth day of January.

It was an invitation no man accepted. So the bodies—what was left of them—were degraded from their priesthood. Holy oil was scraped from nails obscenely grown; heads upon which in death hair had grown, were completely shaved to obliterate even the memory of the tonsure. In the market-place they lay naked—a most dreadful warning; then, the curious having looked their full, the bodies were chained either side of the stake and burned.

The thought of the dead bodies burning, the helpless, dead bodies, brought the vomit up into my throat. It was more dreadful to me than burning the living. For the living, by their denial of God, consent to their punishment and go to their death exalted. But the dead have no will in the matter, nor can they benefit thereby since they are already damned. Now there fell upon me, with even greater severity than ever before, the old blinding pains in the head, skewering me from eyeball to eyeball. Yet it was a pain I learned to welcome; for the body may endure so much—and no more. After the agony of the body's pain comes oblivion; but from the agony in the soul there is no rest.

I tried to make my cousin understand my horror, my repulsion against bodies dragged from the grave for burning.

'It is but a prejudice in you!' he said. 'The dead body feels no pain!'

'It is *because* they are dead and because such punishment is useless! The living may repent; yes, even on a dying breath repent, and the soul be saved. But the dead are defenceless. . . .'

'They are already damned and no defence can save them. Nor, the man being dead, can we further torment him. We do it not for revenge, Christ save us! But for a symbol. If by use of a dead body that can no longer suffer hurt, we save souls from damnation then it is justified and it is right!'

The words made sense; but they brought no comfort.

The flames kindled at Cambridge for the burning of the dead, lit the way to other such burnings. When I heard what the commissioners had done at Oxford, I cried out in horror; and the cries rising ever louder, my horror grew with them. And the horror, reinforced my crying out; I screamed and could by no means be stopped, until the sense left my body and I went down into the darkness. And, even then, there was no forgetting, for I awoke in my bed the tears running down my face.

They had taken from her quiet grave a woman; a *woman*, her naked body defenceless to the public gaze. A good woman, if report spoke true. Catherine, wife to Peter Martyr that had burned for his heresies. Nor could the commission, for all its rigour, draw from any they examined, aught but that she had been honest and kind, good to the poor; and to those in trouble, a comfort and a shelter. Nor was there a word, neither, to prove her heretic; or, save for her husband, consorting with heretics. Burn her body they could not; there was no evidence. Return it to its quiet grave—having still some suspicion or fearing, maybe, public anger—they would not. So they cast it upon a dunghill; and there it lay while the dogs had had their way with it, and what was left lay buried under filth until it was lost to sight.

Now, not even the voice of my Cardinal-archbishop, for all he was armed with the authority of Rome, could quiet me.

'I am a true Catholic!' I cried out. 'I would give my body to the fire, if need be, praying that, if the flesh cry out, some godly hand might thrust me further into the flame. But to degrade a woman, a good woman, because her husband was a heretic and for that fault died—that is not work to please my gentle Christ!'

'You strain at the gnat!' he said as he had said before.

'Great pain deadens us; but the gnat stings the heart alive!'

'Good Christians bear both for the love of God!'

'And what of the people; how shall this seem in their eyes, yes, even to those most eager in the Faith? And what of my sister; what profit shall she make of this?'

'What people shall say in this matter, the church shall answer them. It is not the Queen's concern.'

'What my people think is the Queen's concern.'

'As for the lady Elizabeth—' he went on, as though he had not heard me, 'it were best for her to keep quiet; Madam, you would do well to warn her! She is a professed Catholic; if she renege we'll not stay the penalties against heretics for her!'

And what did he mean by that? Was it a demand for obedience . . . or a threat? And against whom? Her; or me?

From my sister no word.

But if she wrote none to me, there were words aplenty at Hatfield—spoken very quiet; and in the right quarter. Her subtle speech forever whipped up anger against me that permitted such obscenities against the dead, though she knew, none better, I had little power and less will in the matter. Her words did not stop at Hatfield; they spread throughout the country. How right the old Greek poet to call words winged! My sister's words went about the country on soft and secret wings—bats' wings in the darkness. When I had asked my cousin what might be said concerning the burning of the dead, he had told me the church would answer it. Well he was wrong! Like my sister—and partly through my sister—upon my shoulders fell the blame. I was the Queen! Yet, as always, her words could never be traced back to their source; she was too clever for that, the buxom, liberal dame!

But I knew more than she thought! My good friend, Sir Thomas Pope, the Comptroller I had put about her, sent me information. Yet I did nothing. In the matter of desecrating the dead, we were of like mind, she and I; I had no desire, for all her malice, she should suffer for it. As for punishing her for sedition, that time was long past—those that advised me so were right! But heavier than that advice, my husband's wish lay upon me like a command.

And still it went on, the burning both of the living and the dead. From their quiet grave heretics were dragged forth, their bodies enquired upon and cast into the fire or upon the dunghill. Yet still heretics sprang thicker than weeds. In time one grows used to everything. We go on accepting since we can do no other. And so I found myself creeping back towards health. The swellings subsided, the nausea lessened, the head pains were intermittent; sometimes I could see clear, think clear for days on end. I walked a little in my private garden, I began to attend Council meetings. Though still far from strong I received visitors and spoke with them—both my own people and foreigners alike—trying to take the pulse of the times. I even held a review at Greenwich . . . but I did not ride through London, not even in a closed litter.

Chapter Eighteen

Philip was coming home. My fears about insult to the dead, my shrinking from the never-ceasing fires had proved groundless. I had obeyed my church and God showed His pleasure by sending my husband home to me.

At Calais my ships waited. At Dover the royal lodgings stood fresh-furnished; and there, too, waited my most noble lords to ride with their King to Canterbury and bring him post-haste to London. Day after day I waited, sending messenger after messenger bearing both gifts and loving welcome. So long I had waited for this, planned for this! But now there was a difference in my waiting; now there was joy.

February passed; Philip did not come.

'Yet he will come!' I told my cousin Pole, reassuring myself rather than him.

'Yes, he will come because he must. The war in Italy spreads to France. Already his general D'Alba is on the march. The King comes himself to ask Parliament for money.'

So! Philip came not for love of me but to ask for money! I did not relish my answer.

'And, Madam, Parliament will refuse!'

That Parliament should refuse its King I relished even less.

'It is bound to refuse, Madam. We are not to fight in Spain's wars. It is written into the Queen's marriage contract!'

Oh that contract forever hedging Philip about with its wretched prohibitions!

'But France is forever our enemy, our trouble-maker. Fighting France he fights for us!'

'It is not sufficient reason. We are sworn to a five-year truce.'

'Truce!' I cried out goaded. 'A fig for your truce! France has broken it again and again!'

'Still, Madam, it is not enough. A quarrel here and there, a little piracy on the narrow seas, a man held to ransom! Can you prove the French King had a hand in that; or that it was even done with his knowledge? Complain—and he will send his apologies; and with that you will have to make yourself content. No! We must wait for an open act of aggression from the French King himself. And, Madam—a little patience—and it will come! Madam, it is the only wise policy!'

'Policy! Policy! I am a woman to speak plain and plain I mean to speak. The King must have money and he must have it now! You talk of an open act of aggression. Suppose Henri is too clever for us? Suppose he stop short of the direct act until Philip's resources are wasted and he be defeated? Then, Cousin, the French King will turn his attentions upon us; and Philip that can help us now will be powerless then. For our own sake as well as his he must have the money now! And so I shall tell my Parliament.'

To me it made good sense; but, since I am bound to the truth I must add I meant him to have the money for my sake, my own sake, also. For what, after all, had he got from me? Neither crown, nor child, nor my people's goodwill. The love of me, an ageing woman that would, if she might, put the whole world into his two hands, he counted not at all. And who could blame him, the strong and virile young man? Well, let him come for what reason he would, I should see his face again, and, God willing, get me a child. He should have the money he needed though I died for it. Empty treasury, empty Wardrobe! I swept them from my thoughts. *By God's Face!* My father's old oath was sudden in my mind, I would not be browbeat. All Philip needed he should have!

I besought my Council; they would have none of it. To my Parliament I spoke passionate and plain.

'France plays pirate in the narrow seas; she plunders our ships, she takes innocent men to set a high ransom upon them, or else to murder them. She harbours our traitors, she encourages our rebels with gold. She makes trouble for us in Ireland and in Scotland; and especially in Scotland. And will make more, I promise you! I beseech you watch Scotland. Have you forgot my cousin the little Queen of Scots, that she has been bred from infancy in France? Have you forgot her claim to succeed to this throne of ours—a better claim than that of the Princess Elizabeth? Mary Stuart descends through the elder daughter of our house and she is true-born. Have you forgot that this same little Stuart is betrothed to the Dauphin? What then of this country, if, God forfend, I leave no issue of my body? I will tell you. France and Scotland united will march to seize the crown. Witness how already the border raids grow ever more cruel, more constant. But now it will not be the back door only. Through the front door the enemy will come also. From front door and back door the enemy marching; from north and south the enemy pouring. Then there will be war for you! Then you must fight for our English customs, our English ways, our very right to be English. And then it will be too late! Then Spain will not nor cannot help us. Shall we free English become vassals of France—France which is ours by right, our own vassal? Do not, I beseech you, wait for that! Tread upon the adder now, while you may. Fight now in France to save disaster later!'

As with my Council, so with my Parliament. It would not listen. No-one would listen.

There is no money! I had heard it from my childhood, even when my father had been most lavish in his spending. It had not been true when first he came to the throne; his own father had left a vast treasure. But it was true of me. I had found an all-but empty treasury and a vast load of debts. From my personal fortune—little enough—I had paid what debts I might, returned that I considered not rightly mine, all tithes refused. To force a loan for Philip I had been driven to use my own private seal; I dared not do it again. Nothing for it but to sell some lands that still remained to me. When one is forced to sell, prices are low; and so I found. Yet still I sold what I could. Philip should find some gold on his return; he would know I had been busy in his affairs. But the gold I received was not enough; it was not enough.

In mid-March, when the willows hang green hair into the water and every hedge is bright with scarlet tassels of hazel; when primroses, small heralds of spring tell that the long winter is over, that now is ploughing time, seed-time, season for harvest-hopes, young Robert Dudley—son to traitor Northumberland and by me forgiven—knelt to tell me that Philip was home again, his feet actually upon English soil. A splendid young man to look upon, this Dudley; but had he been a hunchbacked cripple his news had made him beautiful in my eyes.

'Madam, the lord King landed at Dover last night; it was ten o' the clock and he went to his lodgings. He sends the Queen his thanks that all was so splendidly prepared, he need waste no moment in coming to the Queen.'

'Is he well? Is he weary?'

'He is well, Madam, and he is not weary. This morning, at sun-up, he rode to Canterbury to pray and to make offerings. Now, Madam, he rides all haste for Greenwich and will arrive tomorrow; he prays the Queen, of her kindness, to join him there.'

Of my kindness—and my heart bursting with joy! I was glad I had spared this beautiful young man to bring me my beautiful news. I bent and, as though he were my own son, kissed him; and feeling the fresh young mouth beneath my own, it was as though I kissed Philip himself.

I longed to ride out to meet him on his way; but his word was my law and I must wait. I sent at once for my cousin. 'My lord archbishop,' I said, 'tomorrow I ride for Greenwich; will you come with me?'

'Madam, I must not. I long to set eyes upon the King, God knows. But I am Cardinal and Pope's Legate; and the King's truce with his Holiness is over. The lord King is still the Pope's enemy!'

It was a faithfulness that, for all my disappointment, I could not fault. I had longed to ride with him through London in state, he in his scarlet, the great Cross and the Hat borne before him; but he could do no other and I must make myself content.

I sat alone in my closet searching my face in the mirror. What I saw could not fail to diminish my joy; tears running down my cheeks did not add to the looks of an old tired woman.

Jane Dormer found me at this sad occupation. She knew, without telling, what ailed. She said, 'Come, Madam! Joy is the greatest beautifier in the world!'

'We are best not to leave it all to joy!' I wiped away my tears, noting with sorrow how my mouth had sunk a little at the corners. It was long since I had searched my face so close.

Now there was a hustling and a bustling; my ladies laughing and chattering, my women running hither and thither with unguents, with pastes, with paints, with brushes and combs.

'They say the Queen's cousin, the little Queen of Scots, bathes daily in wine to preserve the beauty of her skin!' Jane Dormer said, laughing at such fantastic behaviour.

'It may preserve beauty, if beauty be already there—though I doubt it,' I told her. 'But even so, it is wilful waste. I could not countenance it; no, nor afford it neither!' Yet countenance it I should have done and afforded it, too, had I thought it might help me even a little!

'Madam the Queen is well enough!' said my dear Anne of Cleves come to offer congratulations on this glad occasion. 'The Queen has a waist a young girl might envy. The same cannot be said of me!' And she laughed.

And, indeed, it could not. Good living had thickened that neat figure of hers. Upon her, too, the years had set their mark but a mark how different from mine; she had a happy, contented look. Life was ever merry in her house with music and dancing and kindliness and good cheer; and no poor man ever turned empty away. Strange that my father should have put away this comely, kind woman for the foolish, babyfaced Howard.

'The waist is well enough!' I said, 'but what of these?' And I held out my hands thin and fallen into wrinkles from many swellings; already patches of brown heralded the coming of age.

She said nothing. She stretched out her own plump white hand, lifted my own and kissed first one and then the other.

All that day I was restless with my joy; I went pacing backwards and forwards. I found it hard, God forgive me, to pray. For though I thanked God with a full heart, my thoughts, when I knelt, winged back to Philip and my happiness. That night I could not sleep. Sometimes I lay my hand upon the pillow where his head should lie; sometimes I brought it back to lie upon my breast where his head had never lain. My body was no longer my own. It lay open, vulnerable, soft, as on my wedding-night; this time I could not fail of getting me a child. I would put away for ever the fear of my sister that she would send to the gallows all those of the true faith; that she would sit in my place, wear my crown, lie, maybe, in this very bed with my same bed-fellow.

Dawn was blue against the windows when I came from my sleepless bed. Jane Dormer found me rising from my knees. 'Why, Madam,' she cried out, 'have you knelt the night through?'

'No!' I told her. 'But I have not slept the night through, neither.'

And now came my women to brush and to curl, to powder and to paint; to bring gowns and jewels. I chose a gown of green taffetas upon a petticoat of gold tissue having raised roses of gold; for green is always kind to my hair that keeps still somewhat its colour. And, being dressed at last, my eyes bright with joy, and my cheeks with paint, I thought Philip would not find me entirely unworthy to stand beside his comely youth.

And so by water to Greenwich; for if I might not show my cousin in all his Cardinal's glory to London, I had liefer the river than the stinking streets. The royal barge all hung with garlands bore the King's colours as well as my own—the scarlet and yellow well fitted to Spain, the green-and-white like this English spring. And so gay was the sight that folk upon the river, for all their gloom and the turning of their heart from me, could not forbear to wave. And I, waving back, vowed to win them again so that, for my sake they would accept Philip with love—their crowned King. And all the time within me, shone very steady, my hope of a child.

And so, in the March sunshine, a smart breeze bearing us forward, we came to Greenwich. The last hours of long waiting, I find always the worst; the length of time that has gone before, seems as nothing to these. When I could no longer endure the laughter and the chatter and the musicians at their instruments, I betook myself to my closet there, in quiet and prayer to find what patience I might.

I must have fallen asleep worn out with my sleepless night; it would be like me, over-anxious, to miss the longed-for moment. For, suddenly I started to the roll of cannon; they were firing salvoes. Philip, then, must be in sight! I tried to rise, but for a little, the trembling of my limbs stayed me. I called to Jane that had been waiting in the ante-room, it being her gentle way to wait upon my comfort though it was not her duty-time. 'The King will be here in ten minutes, Madam! The Queen's household stands ready, each one in his place!' She gave me her arm and, for a moment, I leant upon it; then, since I must show no sign of weakness, I let it go. And so, my ladies following, I came to the head of the great staircase to greet him in that place I had bidden him Farewell; and there my ladies withdrew to take their place with those others that waited. Lining the broad stairs, my court stood, each in his degree—upon the highest stairs my Council, my bishops and my high nobles; descending thence to lesser officers of state, lesser lords and gentlemen each with his lady down to the great hall where the palace guard stood to attention.

I stood alone on the topmost stair and gave no sign that I was ravaged with my joy, trembling within myself like a virgin bride awaiting her lord. But when the sound of cheering told me he was come, it was all I could do not to gather my skirts in both hands, and like any girl to her lover, run to meet him. I stood quiet; his sense of decorum is very great.

He was here, my heart's love. Beneath the black jewelled bonnet, the fair hair shone; and he, suited in black velvet, standing out elegant and distinguished from his gay-coloured followers. Alone he came, slow and proud, up the stair-case—and there was no-one else in the whole world. He knelt and kissed my hand; and then I felt his kiss upon my lips. The kiss was cold. Far warmer were the tears upon my mouth; my own tears.

Philip had brought with him his cousin Christina of Denmark, duchess of Milan and Lorraine. She was bewitching, and she was clever too, they said; beneath those dimpled charms, a statesman, cool and ruthless. She had come to negotiate the marriage of my sister with Philibert of Savoy; a marriage for which my husband appeared still eager—an eagerness I could not entirely trust. I longed for Madam the duchess to perform her mission and begone—and my sister with her. For though I knew my sister would not and must not marry out of the country while yet I had no child, I hoped soon to put that last matter right. Then she would understand how hopeless her case, she was, after all, nothing but a possible claimant; a child born of my body, the undoubted heir. Surely she would take what offered! I thought, too, that, in joy of my news, the people would let her go! Dear God let it be soon, was my constant prayer.

The truth is, I was jealous of them both—the lady from Lorraine and my sister. A court is a hot-bed of gossip; and now some said—and not too softly neither—that my husband was in love with his cousin and meant to marry her; others that it was my sister he intended to take to wife. But all gossip agreed that he meant to divorce me.

I took my trouble to Lambeth since my cousin could not come to me.

'Put it from your mind!' he advised me. 'The King is here for one thing only—money for his French wars. Any talk of divorce, at this time, would put an end to that hope; and he knows it!'

I found little comfort in this advice. The words *at this time* were ominous. I thought it possible—should I show no sign of pregnancy—my husband, the money safe in his hands, might well press for divorce. Meanwhile, might he not be a little glad of the gossip, hoping, maybe, that fear would spur me on to press Parliament on his account. *Oh my love, I need no fear to spur me on. I would spill my heart's blood to give you all your heart desires, save one only thing—never put me away. . . .*

Gossip there was; his friends might encourage it and he, himself, not deplore it, but his behaviour to me gave such gossip the lie. In public he behaved with perfect courtesy and gentleness; in private, though always courteous, he was somewhat cold. He came to my bed to perform his marital duties; and, if there was no passion in him, there was no unkindness, neither. So, though jealousy forever fed upon my heart, I tried to put it by. I commanded thanksgivings for the King's return, to be offered in every church; and in every town village and hamlet, salvoes and joybells. To London, where soon we should be returning, I sent my especial commands. I could, at least, cover the city's indifference—if, indeed, it were nothing worse—with an appearance of joy.

We spent that first week at Greenwich; and Philip's courtesy was such that, never once did he mention the money he so urgently needed. I could not, however, blind myself to the fact that, all too soon, the question must rear a troublesome head. But in his continued kindness to me, gossip somewhat lessened, and with it my own fear. If he were enamoured of my sister or of his cousin, he gave no sign. He asked me once why I had not invited the former to court. Was it English decorum that she should not be present until her match was made?

Or until it be refused—as refused it will be! That last piece of information I kept to myself. I had had from Sir Thomas Pope the certain information that there was no hope of her leaving the country; to think it, was delusion, merely. Not for this foreign match or any other would she put her barque to sea; as long as life was to her, her feet would stand firm upon English soil.

I let Philip think what he would. It was enough for me to have the pretty lady from Lorraine at my court, without my sister further enhancing my faded looks with her young comeliness.

The week being passed, we took the river for London and so came to the water-gate of the Tower; and there waited my lord Mayor and his aldermen, and all of them in scarlet, furred; and with them, in their holiday livery, the master of every gild, to ride with us into London. The city had put on a good show! The streets were crowded to left and right, and behind them rose scaffolding with seats for such as could pay for them; and every seat filled! So we rode in high procession, while the guns boomed and bells rang amidst a fluttering of kerchiefs and a throwing up of caps and the cheers of the people.

Then, in the sight of all, my lord Mayor dismounted and, in a fine speech, welcomed us in the name of the city; thereafter kneeling, he presented, first to Philip and then to me—as I had privily commanded—the keys and the sword of London. Whereat the 'prentice boys set up such a cheering, and the people joining in, I thought the basin of the sky must crack with the noise of it.

It was all very fine; Philip, I could see, was well-pleased. He removed his bonnet—which omission had caused such heart-burnings at his first coming into England. I saw him bow and bow again . . . and his beloved face was smiling.

So we rode through London, my husband and I, in the joyful noise and the ribands and the garlands and the gild-banners waving in the March wind; and I was all humble in my joy. I had done God's work, though at times I had fainted by the way. Now He smiled again. That work I would continue, nor ever any more question. This welcome was a promise; a sign that He would turn His Face to grant us a child.

And I forgot, in that moment, that it was a welcome I had bought and paid for!

Chapter Nineteen

The bells stopped ringing; the *laudes* and *te deums* died away. One cannot put on a show forever. In spite of Philip's gracious courtesy my people could not like him—*the foreigner.* And certainly no-one wanted to spend money on war—*the Spaniard's War* they called it, slighting him and his just cause; yet God knows we had suffered sufficient injuries from France!

At my first Council meeting since Philip's return, I asked again for help—money, men and arms.

Again the blank, forbidding faces. Again the old, tired arguments. *The Queen's marriage-treaty forbids.... Insult from France we shall continue to endure until we ourselves are minded to end them; we need no Spaniard to avenge our wrongs.* They were not to be moved.

Philip was gravely displeased; I knew the signs. He showed me an even finer gallantry in public; I might have been a visiting Queen. In private, he was more than ever cold, his courtesy more formal, more careful. Save that he visited me in my bed, we might have been strangers. Yet still he said nothing; he knew very well that, saying nothing, he said all. He referred to the matter once and once only. 'This country of yours will be forced to fight—and fight soon. I have my certain news from France. It will be war for you whether you will or not. It is a thousand pities not to use me while you may! Well, since my time here is short, let us make the most of it!' So in spite of his displeasure, he showed a gracious face everywhere—save in the privacy of the Queen's rooms. It was natural, his disappointment; but the fault was none of mine. I had done what I could, both in the matter of loans and the sale of lands. Yet blame me he did; but as it were, obliquely. *A ruler should rule;* the phrase was often on his lips. Yes he could be cruel!

I knew he was making presents to such upon my Council as he deemed useful; again there were gifts of gold, of jewels; again there were promises of positions, honours and pensions. To bribe is not my way; perhaps I had done better to make it my way. But it was Philip's way; and though time pressed and inwardly he chafed, he knew how to wait. So we rode on progress, we offered public prayers; we received all visitors distinguished and humble. We had masques, we had hunting-parties, we had other diversions. But though he took part in all, he never lost sight of this purpose nor yet of that other purpose—to have my sister at the court. I suspected, even then, and I am certain now, that it was this he desired and not at all her marriage to his friend.

'She'll not come!' I told him very plain. 'She has no mind for a marriage with Savoy!'

'I take it, Madam, you are her Queen!'

'Sir, I have told you, I'll not force her, nor any maid into marriage. Marriage is a sacrament. Force it—either party unwilling—and it is sacrilege.' And I wanted to cry out, *I know the meaning of marriage because, my love, I love you!*

But now in the short time before he must depart, he did not urge me in the matter of my sister; unable to deny him anything, I sent for her at last. It was as I had known. She was sick and could not come. She sent her deep regrets—the swellings of hand and feet forbade all travel.

It set my thoughts again upon the old track. These swellings; were they a legacy from my father, and was she truly his daughter? Or did she bring them upon herself at will? If a witch may bring sickness upon another, might not my sister by her own will and for her own purpose bring sickness upon herself? My father, and many another, myself included, had held Anne Bullen a witch—and she was every inch Anne Bullen's daughter!

It was clear to me that the swellings would not subside until the fair Christina was gone. So, in the end, our visitor must depart, having, for the first time in her life, failed of her mission. By merely staying where she was and doing nothing, my sister had had her way. It seemed to me that this formidable young woman grew ever more formidable with every danger that threatened. It was as though danger hardened about her like armour for her protection.

My life was now somewhat pleasanter. The fair Christina was gone, Elizabeth remained at Hatfield . . . and my husband was more content; his bribes were beginning to work—or so he thought. For myself, I believe that those who pocketed his gold would have done nothing.

But now the thing both my husband and my cousin had foreseen, came about.

France had over-reached herself. She had made it impossible for us to keep from war.

In the first week of April, Wotton, our ambassador in France, sounded a warning. He had learned of a revolt planned to take place shortly in the north, aided by invasion from Scotland; and all to be paid for with French gold. I could, he wrote, trust the bearer of the letter to tell me all.

'Madam, I am to say that the French King himself is in this matter up to the neck. He encourages our malcontents, furthers our rebels and traitors; and especially he encourages Stafford.'

'Stafford!' And I took in my breath.

'Madam, he is the very heart of the revolt!'

Thomas Stafford. I could have staked my life on him—grandson to her that had been my dearest friend and my mother's before me. Lady Salisbury would turn in her grave if she knew! Stafford, nephew to my cousin the Cardinal! But Pole had cast him off—Stafford had betrayed the true faith. He had betrayed God. Did I expect greater faithfulness to his Queen?

'Madam, Sir Thomas goes backwards and forwards between England and France. He is to lead the revolt, King Henri furnishing the means—ships, gold, men, arms; everything! In the north the rebels are gathering—near Scarborough as far as we can tell. Stafford has friends there; and men, also, bound in service to his house. He is to march south to take London by surprise; he is to make you and the King prisoner. Thereafter he is to marry the lady Elizabeth.'

My sister. My sister once more! With her will or without, at the heart of every treason!

'He is to make her Queen and himself King, no doubt!' It was the old story all over again.

'Yes, Madam. But I am bound to tell the Queen that the lady Elizabeth knows nothing of the affair.'

'How can anyone know that?' I heard my voice deep and disturbed.

'If she show herself unwilling she's to be taken by force.'

There'll not need much force to persuade her to the crown!

'Does he think, the young fool, my people would accept him?'

'Madam, he does. But nothing is left to chance. He is to carry not only gold and men and engines of war; but letters and bills and pamphlets to arouse the people. He carries his banners also. . . .'

He stopped.

'You may speak!' I said. 'Or I may imagine worse than the truth.'

'There can be nothing worse, Madam! Each banner—let the Queen forgive me that I repeat it—is lettered large, *Up Elizabeth, Down, Mary unrightful, unworthy Queen!*'

'Unworthy, maybe;' and I made my lips to smile. 'But unrightful—never! When may we expect our . . . friends?'

'Any moment, Madam. Dr. Wotton will keep the Queen informed.'

Up Elizabeth. Down Mary!

Was my sister truly innocent? Who can say; who penetrate that devious mind? Not those she called her friends, nor those that would make her Queen; least of all Stafford that would bed her to raise himself to the crown. As well think to handle a scorpion! Ruthless she would rid herself of him and every helper that could help no more. Once more I tormented myself with the old question. Why had I not made an end of her long ago? Again and again fate had given her into my hand; again and again I had opened my hand and let her go.

With every tide Wotton sent his information. When in the third week of April, Stafford eventually arrived, we were ready. Westmorland, best of captains, picked men behind him, was waiting.

Poor, foolish Stafford, poor, foolish young man! Had his plans gone awry, his French master deceiving him or betraying him at the last? Or, with the magic name *Elizabeth* had he thought to raise an army as he marched? He landed at Scarborough with a couple of ships and forty men all told. He managed to drum up as many again but no more, and they took the castle by surprise.

They did not keep it long. As soon as Westmorland appeared the poor wretch submitted. Those rebels we could, we spared, the others we hanged. Stafford, himself, with more mercy than he had dared hope, came to an honourable end; he had fully expected a traitor's death. For the sake of his grandam I spared him that!

There were many upon my Council, and others, others, too, believed my sister deep in the plot; and especially Don Gomez. He had his own intelligence and sent me warning through his betrothed Jane Dormer. But Philip would have none of it; it did not suit his purpose to believe it.

'This time, at the least, she is innocent. Even under torment Stafford could say no other!' he reminded me. 'Imprison her—and the people will have her out, even if it means storming the Tower itself! Sign her death warrant—and you'll not find one to obey you! And she? She has but to speak—and you will find yourself in prison. You will certainly lose your crown, and very like your head with it! No, Madam. You must send for her again; and take no excuse. She must be recovered in health by now! I think, Madam, you need her countenance now more than she needs yours.'

Plain speaking; I should have welcomed it, I that pride myself upon plain speech; but I wondered whether his desire to set eyes on my sister again, was not the cause of it.

'Now, Madam, this Parliament of yours must move!' It was his way to change a subject when he considered it finished. 'It can, with honour, no longer sit still and do nothing! With this last treachery France has broken the peace finally and for ever. You must take up arms. And now the country will stand by you—if you do not set it further against you by accusing the lady Elizabeth. Leave your suspicions until another time; soon or late she will make a slip!'

'Not she!' I said, bitter.

Philip was right in one thing! Now all England—Council and Parliament, and, most of all, the people, were a tip-toe for war with France. Stafford's attempt at revolt had given me the right to declare war. Had Stafford succeeded, five thousand Scots, all fed with French gold, stood ready to pour across the border. Thanks to God, and my good Wotton, we had escaped bloody civil war.

On Mayday my Council met. I remember the day because everywhere folk were bringing in green branches. Many had been out in the woods all night, it is an old heathenish custom; and what else they did, less innocent than gathering branches, it is not hard to guess. I sat at the head of my Council and of it I asked nothing. No need. *The Spaniard's war* had become *England's war*!

War. War with France! The whole nation was blithe. We'd not have Frenchmen interfering, stirring up trouble. No! We'd teach them the lesson they'd been asking for—and one they'd not soon forget.

No money? We should send our forces at once—eight thousand foot soldiers; five to fight in the field, three to guard Calais; and another five thousand to man the fleet. All along the coast beacons must stand ready to give their warning.

No money? For a just war there is always money! Subsidies were immediately granted; and I myself sold yet more lands, more jewels . . . but honours and places I did not sell.

I was happy to be at war with France; and not for Philip's sake alone. Peace I love; but justice I love better. France, I have always held, to be mine. I had been taught from the time I was old enough to understand anything that France belonged to the English crown, and the entitlement, clear. I had been shown upon a map how this piece of France, and then that, had come to us through dowry, or inheritance, until we owned more than the French King himself. For that inheritance the fifth Henry had fought and won. And, as in a *conte de fée*, had received his reward—the French princess and the whole of France, a free gift, when the French King should die. My arms are quartered with the lilies of France, my title at my crowning had proclaimed me her Queen.

Right and title I had, but little else—Calais and the Calais Pale together with the little port of Dunkirk. Well, now we should win all again, God helping. And since He aye helps the right, I should become the Queen of France in fact as well as in name.

The first day of June, in the year of grace fifteen hundred and fifty-seven, I sent Norroy Herald to declare war. It was not until a whole week later that he tracked down his majesty, disporting himself at the hunt near Rheims.

Henri expressed extreme amazement—and maybe he was truly amazed; we had endured his insolence overlong. Had he expected this declaration, I doubt not he had been in Paris.

My herald told me of his reception. The King had kept him waiting while he changed his hunting-gear for a dress more formal. 'There he sat, Madam, beneath the cloth of Estate, and the whole court about him. His brows were drawn together so that they met above that great nose of his, his mouth was a thin line in his beard. Clearly he was in no good mood. I was suited, as is proper to the occasion, all in black; and so that he should know my errand at once, I carried my tabard spread upon my left arm. But even without that he knew; he knew well enough! His face was a tell-tale.

'When he saw my tabard—the fleur-de-lis and leopards quartered, the blood rushed into his face; I thought he had been taken of an apoplexy. He did not give me leave to speak. But, "Who sent you?" he asked harsh and angry.

' "My mistress the Queen of England!"

' "But not of France!" he burst out, his eyes still upon my tabard. "Well, where is your patent? Let us hear it!" And still his eyes could not leave the tabard with the royal lilies of France!

'I handed the warrant to his officer. It begins, Madam, as you know, with a list of our injuries at the hands of France. The man had scarce begun to read when the King stopped him. Henri had no mind to have those ill-doings published, still less to answer them.

' "So! A woman defies me in arms; and Philip, that brave warrior, shelters beneath her petticoats!" and he laughed aloud; but he was not, it was well seen, amused. "I have no fear," he said, "but that God will stand for the right!"

' "Sir, no Christian can doubt it!" I told him.

'He turned on me a black look. "I mean," he said, "God will stand with us to answer your mistress to our satisfaction!" To that, Madam, I made no answer. I made the correct salutation and left at once!'

So it was war! For the moment I was taken of a foreboding. Finished the tournament and the joust! Now men must fight to kill or be killed . . . and among them my husband. Numbered the days I spent with him, numbered the nights; numbered, perhaps, for ever! I shook off my melancholy. Philip had got what he wanted; and what he wanted, I wanted, also. I am no lover of war, nor yet bred to be a soldier's wife; but I knew our cause to be just; and not only just. It was inevitable. When I had cried out to my Parliament, *If not now, then later! And it will be harder,* I had spoken the truth from my heart.

English Calais was all set to her defence. Calais, we doubted not, must be first object of French attack. At home, Pembroke, his forces gathered, was ready to leave for France; Philip, too, was making ready for departure. Now that things were moving in his direction, warmth had taken the chill off his courtesy. He showed me both consideration and kindliness; it was his way of saying Thank you. I should have been happy, making the most of these days; maybe, even then, I had lost the gift of happiness. The thought forever nagged at me, *Soon he will be gone . . . will he ever come back? What should bring him back to a country that does not love him and a woman he does not love?* And always the one answer, the only answer. *A child.* If God should grant me to do my woman's part, Philip must return. Then I should put our child in his arms, and with it the entire rule of the country. I had done my best for England; and that best was not good enough. I was sick; I was weary of bearing rules—I was weary to death.

Chapter Twenty

Philip was not to sail for several weeks; he must collect his forces, be provided with money and with arms. Meanwhile news from France was good. Pembroke had chased the French from Calais. He had made nonsense of the French boast that they would take it and restore it—a jewel to the French crown. Calais, my Calais was safe. In Calais my English made a rhyme; it was sung everywhere in England. The 'prentice boys whistled it in the streets and little ones, scarce able to speak, and not knowing the meaning, sang it also. Everywhere it was whistled and sung, the doggerel, sweeter to me than fine poetry.

When Frenchman shall our Calais win,
Then iron and lead like cork shall swim.

God, I believed, would never let English Calais fall into French hands, so long as we played our part.

In these days before Philip's departure, my sister's hand was sought once more in marriage. Gustavus, King of Sweden, proposed her as bride for his eldest son. He approached her direct which was discourtesy—and useless; without my consent she could not marry. It was a marriage good enough for her, bastard as she was, or indeed for any princess however royal—for it held a crown. I prayed she would favour the offer and rid me of not the least of my troubles. If only I might be free of her; her constant plotting and my fear for the true faith in my country! But not she! For what is the crown of Sweden beside the crown of England?

Her answer was, as I might have expected, a model of discretion; she sent it to me for my approval.

It is not for me to dispose of myself. You do discourtesy to Madam the Queen. It is to her you must make offer for me. . . .

And to me, myself, she wrote,

I like so well my present state of virginity that I persuade myself there is not any kind of life comparable with it.

Again this harping upon virginity—why?

'So young and so discreet!' Philip was all admiration.

'So clever and so sly!' I told him. 'It is not the state of virginity—if she be, indeed, a virgin—but the crown of England that is incomparable.'

'You doubt her virginity?'

'I am not the only doubter!' And I did not add that I was swayed this way and that, whether she was truly a virgin; and must be—her body not her will at fault—forever a virgin. The secrets of my sister's body I could discuss with no-one; not even with herself.

'Then send for her, Madam! Let us judge for ourselves whether she be a paragon of virtue or a deceitful hussy!'

But always I put him off with excuses. He had not been able to hide his pleasure that she had refused Sweden; nor did he, I noticed, ever again press the claim of his friend of Savoy.

But still he urged me. 'Madam, I should see our sister before I leave. And that must be soon. There may be no other chance!'

And what did he mean by that last? Did he threaten me with his death in battle? Or with his no return? Or—the thought ran poison in my veins—was there some unspoken pact between them? And I remembered the day of his first departure, the way their eyes had slid together; and my doubts came crowding back. Why was he pleased that she had refused the Swedish marriage? Why did he no longer press the claims of Savoy?

I bit upon my jealousy and the taste was bitter.

Preparations for Philip's journey were complete. With every passing hour my passion for him grew; and with it jealousy of my sister. I remember the day when he, still urgent in the matter, my bitterness broke from me.

'She is not my father's daughter; she is a bastard born of incest.'

I heard myself appalled; I had not meant so to speak, but my bitterness was greater than my strength.

He said, 'You would do well not to think it; certainly not to speak it. Your father recognised her as his child.'

'But still a bastard—except at the first. Afterwards, not only that!

Child of incest, brother with sister; incest; it was charged in the indictment against her mother.'

'That indictment is best forgotten. Your father was an old man! It does not stand to his credit. Nor do I care such a thought to sully the mind of the purest of women!' And he took my hand. 'A bastard she must be in the eyes of all Catholics and other right-minded people. But, alas, all Christendom is not of our faith; and remember, Madam, at the end, he did acknowledge her his child and named her in the succession. And more than that; those that love Spain are not liked in this land. You, Madam, have married Spain; but she is dearly loved. Whether she will or no, she must always be the hope of all disaffection. So, Madam, you must keep her loving towards us; you must show yourself loving. It is not a question whether you will or no; it is a question of *must*; of need.'

'And if I should bear a child; will there then be need?'

'When that miracle happens we shall see!'

Yes, he could be cruel, my sweet Philip!

I sent for my sister. I could no longer stand out against my husband; I had never denied him anything I might give. And, moreover, a thing was forever in my mind. Suppose I should die childless? It was not impossible. And I remembered what Renard had once said; in that case Philip's life might be in danger; his very safety must depend upon my sister. He might, of course, seek to marry her; Renard had once said that too—but not to me. I had no illusions on that score; but I did not, for all my jealousy, think it likely. She might admire Philip—what woman did not? But she had an intense dislike of Spain . . . and she had sung aloud the praises of virginity. The mere chance that Philip's life—and certainly his dignity which he held as dear—might depend upon my sister, was enough. He and I, alike, must show her favour.

It was midsummer day when she came, like sweet summer itself, all in green and gold. She came, as always, surrounded with every sign of royalty—as I, at her age, knowing my father's anger against me, had never dared. She had brought with her a full court—high officials, ladies and gentlemen, knights, men-at-arms and servants—and every one in her own livery. Philip and I were at Richmond when she entered London and rode in full procession to Somerset House—her London home. Wherever she rode the people stood thick, leaving shop or bench to cheer; and, having rested a little, down the Thames she came, the river lined thick with waving folk on either hand.

They say I showed her all the courtesy of a visiting Queen. They say I sent the royal barge with musicians for her; they talk about a pavilion prepared for her, all hung with gold tissue. It is not true. I sent no royal barge; she came in her own barge all hung with her own colours, her own standard flying. And in that barge she sat alone save for four of her ladies. But one barge was not enough for her! There followed a second and a third, filled with her best gentlemen and all of them in green damask with bonnets of silver tissue set off with green feathers. She could always put on a better show than I. She was, as I must always recognise, a pageant in herself.

I thought it sufficient to meet her at the great door, but Philip would not have it so. It was discourtesy, he said, not to meet her at the water-gate. And when I deemed it more than sufficient that I, alone, should go, he would not have that neither. So the water-gate it must be; and the two of us together. And, though I felt we paid her too much of honour, he had his way.

Always her carriage was royal; but now, as she stepped from the barge she moved as though she were already Queen . . . not such a Queen as I, but a Queen from Avalon, that magic country where no-one grows old. Kingly, Philip greeted her—equal to equal. He bent to kiss her cheek; and down she went in her curtsey, the green-and-gold gown spread about her on the grass, her jewelled head like a flower that bends before the wind He took her hand and raised her; and back we went into the house. I watched close for any sign of understanding between them; I could find nothing. Her manner to him was grave; no sign of that biting wit of hers, nor sound of the too-high laughter. She was thoughtful, slow to speak, attentive; his every word weighed and stored within that clever head of hers. As for him; for all my watching I saw nothing but correct courtesy.

We supped beneath a great tree while music played; and later, when lanterns lit the twilight, I watched them still. And still I saw nothing but what might not be seen between well-bred folk whose acquaintance is slight; yet, all the time, I was aware of a hidden understanding; a calculating each upon the other; and a secret admiration.

At last, night having fallen, Philip and I went with her to the barge, the servants standing either hand with flaming torches. At the water's edge she curtseyed very low to me, speaking her thanks for kindness shown. Yet during the past hours I had said no friendly word; nothing beyond that demanded by merest courtesy, she knew it as well as I; she was too proud, too shrewd to show it. To Philip she curtseyed, also, though not so deep; he lifted her from the ground and kissed her full upon the lips. A common enough greeting at his court . . . maybe. But this was no common kiss. Was it a pledge? The memory of that kiss forever pricked me.

Philip said, as we went across the dew-wet grass, 'She is formidable. I have watched and taken her measure.' And then he said, 'She carries herself like the world's beauty; but for all that a beauty she is not! A few years, and that skin of hers will darken and wrinkle; it is too fine. That red hair of hers will fade; I know the sort!' And did his glance rest upon me? 'As for those eyes! They are not young eyes; not even now. They are old eyes, watchful, hard!' And then, in spite of himself, admiration burst from him. 'But that grace! She'll lose it, never!'

On the third day of July, I said Farewell to my love, that was never my lover. I had ridden to Dover with him, remembering how, at his last going, wind and tide had kept him ashore three days; precious days I might have spent with him. And, as we rode, I showed myself cheerful; I knew, if I wanted him back, I must send him off with a cheerful face. But for all that my heart was low and low, indeed!

Last night, being made ready for bed within the castle, I had shut my eyes before the looking-glass. I did not want to see the tired face in the mirror; and, over my shoulder, as it were, the young face of my sister laughing out of those hard, beautiful eyes . . . Anne Bullen's eyes.

Philip had been late in coming; when he came to me at last, I turned to him with passion. This night I would get me a child. He took me kindly but without love—a duty to be done. Well, let it be duty with him so long as he gave me the thing I craved. I would thank both him and God, nor ever question whether I had conceived in love or no; nor even whether bearing this child I should die.

The moment of parting had come. I stood in the still-falling rain upon the rain-wet beach. Behind me grey cliffs reached up to the low grey sky; before me, tall ships towered upon a grey sea. What had happened to high summer? Well, it was already winter in my heart!

I watched the small boat row out to take Philip from me; I bit upon my lips lest I cry out with the pain of it. I tasted blood salt within my mouth. He bowed with all his courtier's grace, Spanish grace, royal grace . . . but never with a lover's grace; and my heart was bitter with loss, bitter as the sea.

And goodbye, my love, goodbye! my heart cried like a child within me.

I saw the boat grow less upon the grey sea; I saw it reach the flagship; saw the small distant figure go up the ladder nimble as a boy.

Goodbye; my love, goodbye!

Chapter Twenty-One

In my grief I was a little comforted by my cousin. Once more Philip had left me in his care; for though those two might not meet in public—Pope's enemy and Pope's cardinal—they had, with the Pope's knowledge, though scarce with his approval, met in private. As ever my cousin played the part of a kind father to me; of all men save Philip, he is most dear to me.

But I was not to have this comfort long.

In June the blow fell. Quite suddenly my cousin was accused of heresy. We should, I suppose, have been prepared for some sign of enmity on the part of the Pope. But we were not prepared; and certainly of such an accusation no man could have dreamed. In May, my cousin, without his knowledge or my own, had been deprived of his legateship. It is the Pope's custom to command all his legates to Rome every year for re-appointment; this year he had not summoned Pole. Being much concerned with Stafford's rebellion, with the return of the King and preparations for the French wars, we had given the matter little thought. Since he had not deprived the Cardinal of the Hat nor of his see, we considered it an oversight and went our blind way.

But now! *Heresy!* Such a charge against him, the most single-minded, the most zealous, the most devoted Catholic in Christendom; against him that my Parliament had thanked for delivering the country from heresy; that had kept the purifying fires constant to burn out corruption from the land; that had commanded that the dead taken from their graves to enquire whether corruption still spread from their remains!

'This Pope!' I cried out shocked to the very heart. 'His quarrel is with me because I carried war into France. Yet me he cannot fault; my cause is just. But you! Upon you he takes his revenge; on your innocent head falls the fire of his anger!'

'There's no truth in the accusation; none! Yet it will be brought against me that, before I came into England, I invited many scholars into my house; it is a scholar's duty! There were those amongst them that leaned towards heresy; and with these I would argue, to turn them from such dangerous opinions. But before I was let to come into England I was questioned on the matter and cleared. Do you think any Pope would have sent me into this land of heretics did I lean ever so slightly towards heresy? But now; not only does he rake up that for which I was questioned and cleared, but also he remembers that, in my green days, I was not whole-hearted in the burning of heretics—though since those days I have never faltered.'

'Cousin, I have seen for myself your zeal for the Faith. Since this is revenge against me, I must deal with the matter.'

I commanded a special envoy to Rome. 'Tell His Holiness that the Cardinal is innocent of the charges against him. Were he guilty of heresy in the slightest degree, I, myself, must be his greatest enemy. As for the exact charges, I have not seen them. I pray the Pope to set them out in detail that I may consider them. Meanwhile I must hold the Cardinal faultless in the Faith. He is a man of God that has brought my country into the true Catholic worship; what he has accomplished here could have been done by no other man.'

My protest was worse than useless; it had but served to feed the Pope's anger. My ambassador sent me urgent, secret news that Pole was to be summoned to Rome to answer the charges and that he stood in danger of his life. During my cousin's absence—and if he went I doubted his return—the priest Peto was to take his place as archbishop. I am forever the Pope's obedient servant; but this Peto was an old man, very frail. He had been my mother's confessor and, when I was small, my own. He was saintly, he was good; I loved and esteemed him. But to put so old and feeble a man that could not frighten a mouse, in place of Pole not only saintly but strong, was as little to Rome's benefit as to my own.

Send my cousin to Rome I would not. This Pope would have him burnt. Of my own will I had put my country and myself in obedience to Rome; and for that obedience was paying with my country's dislike and anger. Obedience to the Pope lies at the root of my faith; but I am a Tudor. Though I died beneath the Pope's displeasure, I'd not allow my cousin, innocent as he was, to leave for Rome. *I* would not allow; but what of the Cardinal himself? If he received that summons, that summons he must obey.

Very well then; that summons he should never receive. I sent my commands to Calais. Not the Papal legate, alone, but every messenger whose post-bag might contain the summons must be searched and detained. Not one was to be allowed to cross into England.

My cousin, of course, knew nothing of all this! From time to time, he would express wonder that no news had come from Rome.

'Let well alone!' I warned him. 'It is a sorry sight to see God's Pope accusing his own cardinal.'

'I was chosen before ever he came to be Pope. I had never been cardinal by his will!'

'The Pope, himself, which God forfend, shall yet make schism within the Catholic church itself!'

'Heretics could ask nothing better!' he said; his face these days wore a stricken look. 'I have written to His Holiness setting out my defence. It is here, under my hand. I wrote him a letter, also.' And he read aloud,

> '... as you are without example in what you have done against me, so I am without example how I ought to behave to your Holiness....

'Well I must not widen the rift nor show the Pope's injustice to the world!' he sighed deeply and tore both letter and justification across.

'At least he has not put you from your place as archbishop!' I said affecting a cheerfulness I did not feel. For how long until one of the Pope's messengers slipped through the net—and the summons received, obeyed?

So the matter dragged on. In Rome the Pope wondered that he received no reply. At home the old man Peto refused the honour—he was not fit, he said; he asked nothing but to end his days in prayer and meditation. In Calais my commands were obeyed and my cousin did not receive his summons. That last sounds simple enough; but I would wake in the night taken with horror that I had dared to thwart and deceive the Pope; had made it possible for a cardinal to ignore Rome's summons.

This could hardly be the end of the matter. Yet—who could say? The Pope was an old man; God might see fit to take him to Himself! Meanwhile the days went by and I kept by me my truest friend. And, in my loneliness, knowing the increasing dislike of my people, and my Council scarce to be trusted, it was a comfort I can never express. Though he never openly advised me in my affairs nor yet accepted a seat upon my Council, he did, in truth, direct affairs of state. I remember my Chancellor, Heath, that middling man, crying out in some anger, 'This Cardinal is our uncrowned King!'

'There is but one uncrowned King!' I said very quick. 'But crowned he shall as soon as he comes home again!'

He answered nothing but bowed himself low and took himself away.

Things took their usual way. Heretics went to the stake, my Council quarrelled, my Parliament was intransigent; and I was once more a sick woman. There was, however, some promise that this year might be better than the last. Harvests looked to be good; the long misery of near-famine no longer threatened. And for me, myself, the greatest hope of all. It was too early as yet to know; but the hope was there.

Save for the defence of Calais, news from France could not be definite. But though, as yet, there had been no decisive victory, what we did hear was good enough. Calais remained safe in our hands, we more than held our own on land; and, in the narrow seas, our fleet punished every ship that had no business there. We were, at the least, free of pirates.

From my sister, no news. She remained quiet at Hatfield . . . quiet but not harmless. Sir Thomas Pope sent to warn me more than once that her unseen hand stirred the pot of unrest. Yet I could do nothing. I could make no accusation—as ever, she was discreet. Nor could I fly in the face of my husband's constant injunction, *Show open friendship with Madam Elizabeth;* and my cousin Pole who disliked and distrusted her, was constant, also, with that same advice.

As for myself, I was the more unwilling to send for her, since, sick as I was, it must savour too much of naming my successor.

'My own dislike I could put by!' I told Pole. 'But not my fear. I am afraid, Cousin, afraid of the evil she will bring down upon the true faith—give her but the power! I am afraid she will make martyrs of those that stand by God!'

'Send for her, Madam. See to it that she openly pledge herself to the true faith. She'll not say *No* when she understands that the crown will come with *Yes*.'

'*May* come, Cousin, *may* come . . . or may not.' I saw his eyes enquiring upon me; but it was over-early to speak my trembling hope. 'As for her *Yes* or *No*—shall you trust her longer than it suits her advantage?'

July was golden in the land; but for me, sick in body and low in spirit, it was a sad month. For that month my dear Anne of Cleves died. She died at Chelsea, easily, happily, as she had lived. A sudden end with no fear nor pain, nor wasting of her strength. Save that for me her death must ever be untimely, it was a good death.

I had seen her little of late. We had exchanged letters, gifts and greetings. I envied her, sometimes, her trouble-free life surrounded by affection; friends, servants, the very stranger within the house, all alike, speaking her praises. And well she deserved them—a free-hearted mistress and a faithful friend. Dying, her kind heart remembered everyone—from me, down to the humblest servant. When I heard the terms of her will I was deeply touched, for she desired . . . *my most dearest and entirely beloved sovereign and lady, Queen Mary, to be overseer to my Will.* And in that will she bequeathed to me . . . *as a token of my especial trust and friendship my best jewel. To the lady Elizabeth's grace, my second-best jewel.*

It was, I think, the first time in my life that anyone—save my mother—had given me, from love alone, the best. It was, perhaps, the first time in her life, any had put my sister second to me!

I sent for her that she might hear for herself, the will; I ordered mourning for the court. Yet my sister came all in white, with a knot or two of black riband; black did not become her and she knew it. And I remembered how Anne had loved her, saying she had rather be mother to the little Elizabeth than Queen of England! Yet for this love my sister could not sacrifice any diminishing of her looks.

Certainly she did not relish the will. She had expected to be left the best part of Anne's wealth. But, indeed, so open-handed my father's fourth wife, so generous in her charities, so liberal of her living, there was not a great deal left. I saw my sister's black eyes harden; saw a dusky red mount into those sallow cheeks of hers. That; and nothing else! No sign of regret at a dear friend's death; nor thanks for having been remembered. The second-best jewel was valuable enough; I think there was little difference between first and second; but my sister's jewel had been labelled *second* and I never saw her wear it.

I thought much of Anne these days, remembering how she had come—a young woman that had just missed beauty; and how my father had taken against her because she was taller than he fancied in a woman, and because he was already taken in the toils of the little Howard's bright hair. And I remembered her loyal heart and her kindness; and I thought had he held fast to that marriage he had been a happier man and I, perhaps, a happier woman. For then I had not come to the throne; she had been young and lusty and knew her duty. I appointed her burial in Westminster Abbey and a funeral of great splendour such as she would have loved. But it could not comfort me for the neglect that, in my own troubles, I had shown; nor for the way I missed her, she being dead. She had brought loving kindness into a life where there had been little enough, and now it was too late.

August came in and I dared to believe in my sweet hope. My monthly cycle could never furnish me with certainty; nor could daily nausea prove me pregnant, nausea being my daily portion. But I was growing fuller in body though my face as thin as ever. Yet I was reluctant to speak too soon. Once already I had disappointed my husband beyond all enduring, I had disappointed my people; and I had made myself the laughing-stock of Christendom. This time I would wait until the increase of my belly put the matter beyond all doubt. Then I should proclaim my blessed news; then Philip would come to see his child. And when he did come, be his stay here long or short, he should be crowned though I died for it.

Meanwhile I must content myself that he was in France; for the news was excellent and so continued. At the end of this same month the two armies met before the walls of St. Quentin—and the French sent packing with great loss of men, arms and engines of war; and best of all, Montmorenci, that great soldier, taken prisoner. Montmorenci, himself, Constable of France!

The way to Paris lay open.

God was on our side. Throughout the country, and especially in London, where I could see and hear for myself, there were bells, there were bonfires, there was dancing in the streets; there was, also, alas, more than usual drunkenness and a great picking of quarrels therefrom. But in all our churches *laudes* went up to God and *te deums* and prayers of thanks.

God had shown himself on our side. Now Philip would march at once on Paris; now Philip would make an end!

But Philip did not march; and I, and all Christendom wondered.

Assionleville, one of my husband's captains, came from France to explain the matter.

'The lord King himself was not at St. Quentin, he was besieging Cambrai; and Cambrai was about to fall. When our messengers brought us news that the way to Paris lay open the lord King did not believe it. He consulted with us, his captains, and all of us agreed it was unlikely; the news was a trick to lead us onto the Paris road and take us and our armies in a trap. The lord King is not one to gamble on such a chance; the risk was too great. And, moreover, Madam, Cambrai, remember, was about to fall. There's a saying in your country about the bird in one's hand!'

Cambrai did fall. A second feather in our cap; but not the topmost plume. And now Paris was, indeed, ours for the taking.

'Madam,' Assionleville, come for the second time, told me, 'joybells rang out here and in Spain and in the Spanish Netherlands. But in France the bells tolled. The French King took the news like a stricken man. He goes now with his full court in procession, together with statesmen, priests and judges, to pray for victory. They are to go all in black and in sackcloth, yes, even the finest lady of them all, Madam the Queen herself; she and the King together leading the procession. They are taking the holy relics from la Salute Chapelle to Nôtre Dame!'

'Do they think thus to cozen God?' I asked. 'We have our own relics, we know how to pray, too! Our cause is just and God looks to His Own.' And I gave commands for public prayers and thanksgiving.

Maybe the relics within Nôtre Dame were more efficacious than in la Salute; maybe the prayers of fear are more intense than those of joy. But to many the fault lay with my husband and his captains that were too prudent to take the chance God had clearly offered. With the road to Paris open and Paris herself panic-stricken, he did not press on. *The King's courage does not equal his caution. A soldier must take his chances!* They said it everywhere and cared nothing that it must come to the Queen's ears, his wife's ears.

'The King is in the right of it!' Assionleville told me in full court and did not hide his anger at the talk. 'Here, in England, it is easy enough to say this and that; but over there it is different! The King dared not venture it; he is short of money, short of men, short of arms. His own Spaniards will follow him anywhere; but the mercenaries! Mercenaries fight not for a cause but for money! Unpaid, they desert; and more, they take with them whatever they can lay hands upon—arms, ammunition, food—everything! You cannot blame them; they must reimburse themselves or starve. And, Madam, your own English. . . .'

'I know! I know!' I interrupted him. I did not want to hear the shameful truth—that many of our own English had deserted, also. 'Sir,' I told him that all might hear me, 'the lord King does wisely and well. Go back and tell him that, in the matter of money, I will do what I may. God knows how little it may be, but be assured I will scrape the barrel!'

But the scraping yielded little. Parliament was not in a giving mood; as for myself, already I had sold what I could but even now, with little else to sell, I never sold honours and I never sold places. Short of money, my husband must now content himself with garrisoning St. Quentin and Cambrai; and himself retired to Brussels.

A man can do only what he considers best. To him it was the wisest thing; but it was a mistake—a mistake that cost me dear. Distant in time and place from the actual fighting, we can look back and see the whole thing clear before us; those in the thick of it are not so fortunate.

France began to pluck up her courage. Why not? The enemy had withdrawn to home ground. Henri recalled the de Guise from Italy; and who gladder than that great captain to shake the thankless soil of Italy from his boots! For the Pope, that unjust, passionate man—God forgive me that I say it!—had cried out *Go and ill luck go with you! You have done little for your King, less for your church, and nothing at all for your honour!* True it was, on the face of it; but luck had been against the de Guise. And if he had not won outstanding victories for the Pope, he had kept Spain at bay—and that was more than any other captain could have done. The wisdom of his delaying tactics was beyond so hasty a man as this Pope. The de Guise was a very great captain—as we were to find to our cost!

Now the Pope, telling himself that he had no obligation to France—France that he had dragged into his war—sought another ally. And who should that be—but Spain!

Peace between Spain and the Pope! Christ be praised! I took in my breath very deep; it came out again on a long sigh—as though I relieved me of an intolerable burden. The quarrel, in which I, myself, had played my unwilling part, had shaken me to the very soul; nor had it left Philip unscathed. Whatever the Pope's shortcomings as a man, in his great office he was sanctified. To be reconciled with him was to be reconciled with God. Yet, even while the bells rang out the great tidings, I knew that, for all the reconciliation, Philip and I still bore the scar; but, as for my cousin, the accusation of heresy was a wound that never healed. And though, as if to seal the peace, the good old man the Pope had named as legate, died, and though no other legate had been named and nothing more ever said about heresy, the charge still stood. My cousin continued with his accustomed work; but it was as though he bled inwardly.

I, myself, felt the wound of my own disobedience—though before God I could have done no other. I am my father's daughter to have my way; but unlike my father I have great reverence for the Pope. I had stood with my husband defying the Pope's demands; I had made it impossible for the Pope's cardinal to obey the summons to Rome. Guilt sat heavy upon me.

I knew but one way to purge my sins—to be more zealous for my faith. Not one heretic, were it in my power, should escape salvation. Fine words these and true; but put it plain and just as true—my atonement must work itself out in the pain of others; in harsher measures against the enemies of God. The total burning of human flesh, forever repugnant to me, must be my goal until the land was purged of heretics.

I suffered that others must suffer because of my disobedience. I suffered because I knew, with foreboding, that, in my own person, I should be called upon to pay my debt in full. I prayed that, whatever my punishment, it should not rob my husband and my country of the much longed-for, much needed child.

Peace with Pope. But not peace with France. War must go on until we had the victory. In our success lay peace for my country and safety for the crown. For our victory I had no fear. The Pope was now our friend and France's enemy. Whatever evil might befall me, myself, we should win this war. God would see to it!

Chapter Twenty-Two

Autumn was come; and with the ripening of the year came my own ripening. I was with child. It was certain; my physicians had set a date. In April I should hold my baby in my arms. But still I sent no word to Philip. Little more than three months pregnant, I dared not risk his second disappointment; the more so that his mind was anxiously occupied with the French wars.

Things had taken a grave turn. When the Pope had quarrelled with the de Guise and sent him packing, I had thanked God, for from that quarrel had come our own peace with Rome. But now the quarrel began to look something less than a blessing. And soon we were to see it as clear disaster—though how great a disaster, how unimaginable, we were yet to learn. Little by little we began to understand. With the arrival of the de Guise in France the tide began to turn against us. As he advanced, our forces retreated. We took this, at the first, for fortune of war. We had had our victories, we must look for set-backs; soon there would be victories again.

So still I said nothing of my tremendous hope. Save for my cousin the Cardinal, and my own women—sworn all of them to secrecy until I, myself, should speak—no word was breathed of the matter. Until Philip was told it must remain secret. I was sick; I was weak as though water not blood filled my veins. But this, my usual wretched condition, filled me now with rapture. These were not useless miseries; I suffered them gladly, they had become a condition of pregnancy, they served my cause. Some women, I know, carry a child in the full bloom of health; I am not one of them. But give me my child and I'd be content to suffer now, and for the rest of my life. So I put off sorrow and I sent for my virginals and lute; I surprised myself, sometimes, by the sound of my own laughter.

Pregnancy, I thought, became me. Though my face remained thin, the rounding of arms and bosom gifted me with something of my youthful comeliness, the more so that there was not, as yet, any swelling of the belly to mar the neatness of my shape and tell a tale. That autumn of 'fifty-seven everyone remarked upon my renewed looks; the word *handsome* I do not use—though others did; and often. The new ambassador from Venice had expected to find an elderly dame and was pleasantly surprised. He told Jane Dormer that he found me a very handsome lady.

'Flattery, my girl, flattery!' But for all that I was pleased. 'Is he blind that he cannot see the lines? They called me *the Pearl of England* once; yes, and *the Flower of Christendom,* also. God forgive me my vanity to remember such a thing. Well, the pearl's lustre is dimmed, the flower withered.'

'By no means, Madam. Troubles have played their part; and the Queen spares herself no work. If the Queen would allow herself some rest, she would show herself as handsome as ever!'

'Rest? How shall I rest?' And again fear struck at me; for in the weakness of my body and the fullness of my joy, I would, had I been let, have closed my eyes to spare them that were God's enemies. But I was not let; thus I was forever torn that, though men must rightly burn, my whole heart could not assent thereto. To stop the burnings I had no power; my church commanded it. Maybe it was as well; how many souls now gone to their salvation had then been lost!

'Madam,' she said, 'conscience drives the Queen too far; one has but to look in her face to read her mind. Why waste your strength upon those matters she must leave to her bishops and her judges? *The Queen does her duty well.* So said the Signor Ambassador Michiel before he left this country, and so he wrote to Venice—for he told Don Gomez so. *When this country went into the darkness of heresy, she remained a light . . . !*'

'A very feeble light.'

'But still a light. *A light so buffeted by the wind*—these, Madam, are his very words, *that true worshippers feared it must be put out altogether. But always she kept it burning that it might shine as now it shines.*'

'The Cardinal Pole said that once; almost the very words. I fancy that now he thinks me less shining in the matter.'

'Madam, the light is safe. Be content to leave the tending of it to others.'

'But if my whole heart does not consent thereto, do I not break faith with God?'

'By no means, Madam; for still heretics are given the chance to save their souls. Madam, you press too hard upon yourself. Michiel cannot stint his praises not in this alone but every way; and he speaks them where it can gain him no favour. He says you are one never to break your word. He says you are a better scholar and quicker of understanding than any women and most men.'

'There he flatters me indeed! For though I am the better scholar, I cannot match my sister for quickness of understanding. But has he no kinder word for me; no word more womanly?' And it was not vanity, I swear it. It was reassurance of womanly charm I desperately needed; some charm to win my husband back to me.

'Madam, he admires you as a woman. He admires your grace in the dance, he admires your excellent music-making. He told me so himself; he said—and I have his words by heart that I may repeat them to you—*the Queen excels the best performers by the speed of her hands and the style of her playing*. But, above all things, he admires your courage and your compassionate heart. *She is very valiant*—again, Madam, I speak his very words, *one never to flinch in the face of danger, but rather to show more than ever a grandeur and a dignity*.'

'Without a fault, it would seem!' I laughed but the words were balm upon my heart.

She looked at me; she said nothing. But those eyes of hers betrayed her.

'Come now,' I said, brisk, 'tell me what's amiss that I may study to amend me.'

'He says, Madam . . .' She stopped, somewhat troubled. 'He says you are—forgive me, Madam—more miserly than becomes so bounteous and generous a Queen!'

That was a shaft to strike home.

'If I were not what he chooses to call *miserly*, I should have nothing with which to be generous. Oh Jane, Jane; all my life I have struggled against poverty! I might have had great wealth, but I could not take that which is God's. I have been so poor; I had never a new gown, not even for my crowning, not even for my marriage. No, but I had the tailors make over for me what I found in the Wardrobe. Oh I have gone fine enough; but always another woman has stood within that gown; nothing new—ever! Some land and jewels I had; but I sold the best part for my husband's war. I have given to the poor; I have helped rebuild some few monasteries here and there; I have paid what debts I might—debts none of my making . . .'

'We that are near the Queen, know it well. But others hear only of her fine gowns, her jewels, and the gifts she receives . . . they hear also of the Queen's careful table. All this I have told the Signor Michiel; I have, Madam, corrected his opinion.'

'Then I am still without fault?'

'Not even the Queen is without fault. But you have those faults, he says, that are virtue in a woman. You are all woman, he says—sudden and passionate; spice to your goodness!'

'Well I trust his successor shall think likewise. I can afford to lose no jot of any man's good opinion.'

Michiel's praises of my virtues pricked my conscience with regard to my sister. Since her childhood I had shown her little kindness; that I had good reason makes no matter, compassion has little to do with reason. And to her I had once broken my word. I had given her a ring in token of good faith and with it had pledged my countenance and favour, let her fault be what it might! I had sent her to the Tower; that she deserved it and more, is nothing to the point. She had returned my ring and I had refused my countenance. Traitor she might be . . . and was; and is! But I had broken my word.

So conscience pricking and, in the full of my joy fearing her no longer, I summoned her to court; and was the more happy doing so that I obeyed my husband.

She came, as ever, royally attended. I found no pleasure in her company—nor no fault, neither. To me she never spoke from the heart but from the head; as always there was a constant watchfulness about her. I kept her with me at Greenwich and at Richmond; and all the time we never talked together as sisters should, nor ever uttered a single word of import. Now and again I would catch those calculating eyes upon my fuller shape, but my belly, as yet, was no tell-tale. And still I said no word. Let her guess what she would! But she was never one for guessing; no doubt she had wheedled my news from some unsuspecting woman of mine; nor would she hesitate to question my laundrywoman. Well, my periods being always irregular, she'd get little good there!

Winter was on us; in France things began to look somewhat anxious. In December we heard that the de Guise was on the march for Calais. March in the bitter weather, march upon Calais! So incredible the news, we did not believe it. *Calais can never be taken and the French know it!* and *March in winter and the roads already freezing! Campaign in winter—who ever heard of such a thing. None but a madman would attempt it. It is all a piece of bluff!* So we believed, even the wiseheads upon my Council.

But soon we were forced to bite upon our words. From every road in France the enemy was converging upon Calais.

I summoned my Council.

Calais cannot be taken. Again they echoed the general opinion.

'Why not?' It was Heath, my Chancellor, that spoke, that mild man, startling us all with the suddenness, the unexpectedness of his question. 'It can be taken. It may be taken already! And I will tell you why! Because the walls have not been repaired this fifty years or more; there has never been enough money. The town has never been sufficiently garrisoned; and now there are not enough men to hold it!'

'It is sufficiently garrisoned!' Paget shouted, actually shouted in the presence of his Queen.

'My lord, your clock is stopped!' Paulet, my Treasurer, cried out, glad to make him sing small, for there was hatred between those two. 'Pembroke, having secured the city—as he thought, carried his forces further into France. I doubt there are five hundred men left within the city! Men should stick to their last! Money is not your affair, my lord Privy Seal; and of warfare you know nothing. As for you, my lord Chancellor, if you knew the walls to be unsound, why did you not speak before?'

'There has never been the money . . .' Heath spread his hands.

'What excuse is that? My lord Treasurer, answer, you!' And now it was Paget fierce to attack; but before Paulet could open his mouth, Paget had turned again upon Heath. 'You, my lord Chancellor-archbishop, are more priest, it seems, than statesman. Why did your lordship that knows so much, not share your knowledge with the rest of us?'

'I followed the advice of our captains,' Heath said, all confused. 'Pembroke thought the number sufficient. Besides, we did not expect, not one of us, this attack. The Council has said repeatedly, *The French will not campaign in winter!* The frozen roads will not allow it!'

'Then the captains were wrong, and the Council was wrong! All, all of us wrong!' Paget broke in, impatient. 'Frozen roads are easier for marching than spring mud or summer dust! So here's the enemy within the Calais Pale and fortress after fortress in their hands. How long before they sit down before Calais itself?'

'Let us not fight among ourselves!' My voice came out deep with authority. 'We have fighting enough on our hands. As to the defence of Calais—there are, it seems, two opinions. We must put it to the vote!'

'Voting will not help us, Madam!' Paulet said, lips drawn to a thin line. 'Calais must look to herself! There's no money for her defence; I am your Treasurer and you may believe me! *I* stick to my last!' And he sent a look of hatred at Paget. 'With her five hundred men, her great fortress, and the sea to protect her on the north, she'll do well enough till spring. By then, with God's help, I shall have found the money!'

So the matter being thrown open for discussion, the greater part of my Council were solid behind Paulet. Calais would do very well for a while yet. The French on the march? A show; a show merely. They'd be mad to attack before spring—by then, were help needed, help we should send. So the vote being taken it was decided that Calais would do well enough until the spring.

Well we were wrong. Heath that could see no further than his own nose and Paget that could see a good deal further, were right; both of them right! In the third week of December, Wentworth, governor of Calais, and Grey, governor of nearby Guisnes, sent urgent messages for help. *We have not enough men, not enough guns, not enough food, nor any medical supplies. Our walls are in desperate condition. Without immediate help we cannot stand.*

'Wentworth is one to run before his own shadow!' Paulet said, contemptuous. 'I do assure Madam the Queen the French will take no step against Calais until the spring—if at all!'

'Wentworth and Grey are brave men, both! They'd not ask for help unless it were needed. Why wait for spring?' Paget demanded, sharp and anxious.

'Because we have neither men nor money! How many times must you be told? By spring we can send the help we cannot send now; all the help they need!' Paulet told him contemptuous still.

'By spring it will be too late!' Paget said with the quiet that comes from despair.

What Paulet had said and those that stood by him, made sense—or appeared to, Calais had been safe for two hundred years. I believed, even then, she could never be taken. Nothing, neither in my father's time nor in my brother's, had been said about the condition of her walls. I believed she must always remain ours. But Heath still urging the town's immediate need, and Paget supporting him, Paulet forever contemptuous, went about saying that men of their sort, having but one idea in their head at a time, were obstinate to maintain it. And the most part of the Council knowing the state of the Exchequer followed him. As for myself, I must be content with what my Council judged best. I am no captain of men nor versed in the stratagems of war.

January came in with sleet, the bitter winds freezing the rain as it fell so that ice lay glassy upon snow. A new year is forever a time of hope. This year of 'fifty-eight I felt to be a year of grace, indeed! And now, so certain was I that all was well with the child I carried, that I bade my cousin—my own hands being too swollen for the pen—to acquaint my husband with our joyful news.

There being no more secret in the matter, we brought in the new year with festival . . . but before the walls of Calais, Englishmen were uselessly, miserably dying. The de Guise had not waited for spring—he was not such a fool! The French had not yet taken the town itself, but they had the harbour. Our men were cut off from the sea by which any help must come. And Wentworth had spoken no more than truth. Winter is, at best, a bitter time for campaigning—especially in a foreign land; but at worst! Cut off from help of any kind and in desperate need for everything—even for shoes upon their feet—God help all Englishmen in Calais!

Asking help of God is not enough; the whole country must do its part—Parliament and Council, the church and the common people and myself—especially myself. I could not wait upon Paulet's prudence. I must keep Calais for my unborn son.

Money, money for Calais.

From my Parliament I demanded immediate subsidies. Some money it gave; but, influenced, maybe, by my Council, not enough; not near enough.

Money, money for Calais.

I sent into every town, hamlet and village to beg money—give or lend—as much as a man could spare; and more, more! And not money alone! Men, and arms; we were desperate for both. But money came first; mercenaries will not remain unpaid. But for my condition, I had gone myself, to beg. That it is unusual and unseemly for a Queen of England, big with child, to ride abroad, weighed nothing with me. But my health being poor, I feared to lose my child. And, since without God, armies be they never so great must fail, I commanded that, in every church prayers be constant. I commanded, also, religious processions; they had served the King of France well. And every man rich or poor, I called upon to give to those poorer than himself.

If Calais should fall? If the unspeakable should happen! It was a question I must forever ask; ask of my Council, ask of my Parliament, ask of my cousin Pole, ask of any man that might answer me. And always the same answer. *Calais will never fall!*

But if . . . if?

Lord Grey, my governor of Guisnes, answered the question for me

> . . . I am now clean cut off from relief which I looked for out of England and from Calais. I know not how to have help either of men or victuals. There rests none other way for the succour of Calais and the rest of your Highness's places on this side, but a power of men out of England, or from the King's Majesty, or from both without delay by sea as well as by land. . . .

But once again help must have been delayed by long argument within my Council, but that I, myself, driven beyond endurance in this extremity, spoke out with passion. There are times, I believe, when at need, the spirit of my father speaks through me. My cousin Pole wrote to my husband of the affair.

> . . . The most serene Queen has shown her usual firmness, which has comforted us the more, as I was, at first, anxious lest such unexpected news must seriously agitate her Majesty, especially as she is pregnant. . . .

He said also that I was not cast down nor dismayed but had set about getting help, both human and divine; but since he, too, believes that men that ask help from God must first help themselves he added,

> . . . I deemed it my duty to give notice of this to your Majesty that you may put forth your vigorous arm and aid, which we are certain you will do with such speed as present need requires. . . .

My cousin had written that I showed firmness and courage; the truth is quite otherwise. I was much cast-down, much dismayed. I was a sick woman; when I spoke to my Council and to my Parliament upon the urgency of sending help to Calais. It was not firmness; rather it was passion, an anger I could not control.

The joys of pregnancy are great. But next month would see my forty-second birthday, and I was pregnant for the first time; nor has my health ever been good. So, in spite of my joy, the misery of my body had its way with me. This, together with distress on account of Calais, anxiety concerning the help my husband could furnish, and above all my longing to see him, brought me low, indeed! Yet still I listened; and half-believed those that said, *Calais is ours and we shall keep it*; though my heart warned otherwise.

Hour by hour we waited upon the news; my Council, my Parliament, the country and most of all, myself. It must be several days before we should hear from Philip; and I was anxious upon two counts—the help he should send to Calais, and his reception of the news of my pregnancy. To me, my city and my child were, in some curious way, bound up one with the other.

Here in England we wasted no moment. Parliament voted the money we needed and there were volunteers now a-plenty; though how to get men or gold into Calais was another matter. If we attacked the harbour from the sea, under cover of night, taking the enemy by surprise we might manage it. And if, at the same time, Philip should fall upon the city, then our victory was certain.

If . . . if. . . .

Chapter Twenty-Three

On the fifth day of January, the French attacked Calais castle, last protection to the town. It was but two days since I had sent Philip my great news, together with the request for immediate help for Calais. I could not, as yet, expect an answer; I could only believe and pray that he was moving with the greatest possible despatch.

But even now, we, at home, did not know the half of it. Help was needed more bitterly than any of us suspected. Heath had told us of the unfitness of the city's walls but the Council had pooh-poohed it away. There had been no mention that the castle fortress was itself in parlous condition—its walls, rotten with age, great gaps where stone had fallen and left to lie. We did not know, either, how insufficient our men for so great a task. That there were few enough we knew; but any moment Philip must come marching and for so short a time we could keep the enemy at bay.

Secure at home, we could not begin to understand the heroic task those few men were set to do. We did not understand they dared not rest by day or night. When darkness fell and the firing ceased, weary, and many of them wounded, they must labour the night through, patching up the breaches with whatever came to hand—stones, branches wedged into place with old rags, broken bits from weapons, anything, anything! Throughout the long, cold winter night working; and then, with first morning-light, into the battle once more. God knows how they managed as they did!

Day after day the French guns pounding; day after day waiting for help—help from us in England, help from Philip in Brussels; help that never came. And day after day Wentworth that held the town, swearing that, come hell or high water, he should never yield.

On the tenth day of January we heard the news. The fortress had fallen. The only hope for Calais lay in Calais herself. Across the wooden bridge that led from the castle to the town the French came swarming.

It was the end. Wentworth that had sworn never to yield must eat his words. It was a truce he asked; a truce only, for surely help must come from sea or land.

It was a truce to end in the firing and sacking of Calais, my Calais; to end in the raping of women and the carrying away of such treasure as the city possessed. Coward Wentworth they called him; and, in my bitterness, I called him so too. Here, at home, it was easy enough to blame him. Yet he had done his uttermost—and more than many another in his position. He had even flooded part of the town from the sea. From the beginning my Council had grossly misled him, both as to the condition of the walls and the belief that the enemy would not march in winter. The men inside Calais had been totally insufficient, even had they not lacked every need; and of these few, some were in the French King's pay. I wondered, sometimes, if Paulet himself and some others of my Council had not been seduced by French gold! Be that as it may, these few, tired, ill-equipped men must bear the brunt of the French armies, well-supplied with every need. Help from the sea we had hoped to send; but we had not enough ships; and the French fleet blocked the harbour mouth. Nor from the land, neither, did help come. Philip did not appear before Calais, not even near it. If Wentworth had failed us, we had failed him. If Calais were lost, we in England had lost it. But my people blamed Philip and Philip alone—the Spaniard that had dragged us into his wars!

All England mourned; the wound to English pride went deep. But Henri, when he heard the news, had himself clad in white satin and went dancing to a wedding. And well might he dance! But I sat in my darkened closet in a black gown. *When I am dead,* I cried out, and cared not a whit that my words be carried across the sea to Paris, *when they open my body to embalm it they shall find writ across my naked heart, the one word Calais.* I mourned not only in the physical darkness of my black-curtained room but in darkness of the soul. With Calais, I had lost the last of my people's love. I knew it. Grief lay heavy upon my heart as a still-born child.

Nor could I be roused from my despair by those that reminded me of the precious hope I carried—the child to be born in April.

Only when the long-desired, long awaited letter arrived from my husband did I bid them draw the dark curtains that I might see his beloved hand and comfort me, a little, with my husband's joy in my news.

The letter was writ not to me but to my cousin Pole and dated January twenty-one; my cousin, himself, brought it and left it with me.

> . . . I have received your letter dated January 4th in which you send me news of the pregnancy of my beloved wife, which has given me greater joy than I can express to you. It is the one thing in the world which I have most desired and which is of the greatest importance for the cause of our religion and the welfare of our realm. I offer thanks to God for his great mercy which has gone far to soften the loss of Calais. . . .

My beloved wife. . . . In the pale sunshine sliding between the drawn curtains, the words blazed in letters of light. Yet soon enough my spirits were down. *My beloved wife*. Why had he not written them to me, myself? Well, but they had been written, and with that I must be content. I kept this letter by me, though it was not writ to me—the one reminder of my husband's kindness. But soon even this comfort was dimmed. I knew well what they said of him and me—the whisper at court is no whisper. *If the King do as little to comfort the Queen as he did for Calais, then she is lost, also!*

I sent for Don Gomez, new-arrived from the Netherlands; he had not yet had time to seek audience but I could not wait. I asked him blunt and plain why Philip had left Calais to her fate.

'It is not so, Madam; the lord King tried the march from Brussels but the roads were worse than they had ever been; snow had frozen the ice, ice upon snow; and always the blinding driving sleet defeated him. . . .'

Yet the French could march. I said nothing; I waited.

'The French marched on home ground, every man their friend, the very peasant running from his house to offer help. King Philip must march in hostile country . . . and not only along icy roads but in the fog, also. He might easily have been taken. . . .'

But he did not try again. . . .

'Madam, we are in God's hand, from the meanest soldier to the King himself!'

I see now that Philip is not, nor never was a dedicated fighter. His talent lies in his head rather than in his sword. He serves his cause best by planning and preparing for his captains; should fate set his plans awry, he needs time to think and plan again. He is a slow, deliberate and subtle thinker. He knows the success of his campaign depends upon himself and he is not one lightly to throw away a victory. He is no coward; God forbid men should think it! He is a likely man with a sword, as every tournament must prove. But he is best employed to conduct a war rather than to fight in the field; and, without stratagem, no war can be won. I could not expect my people to understand this which came so late to my own understanding, and they continued to vilify the King.

Calais fallen, the de Guise lost no time. By the thirteenth day of January his forces lay before Guisnes, my second city in the Calais Pale. And it was not only those armies that had sacked Calais, but the whole strength of France, from every road converging upon the town; nor did they find the bitter weather a hindrance, for when courage is high, bad weather makes little odds.

But for our few men shut within the town, it was as with Calais. No help! There could be none. From despairing England, all-but emptied of men and gold, none; from Philip in Brussels, none. If he had not dared the treacherous roads before, still less would he dare them now, filled as they were with enemy troops. Every day more French arrived before Guisnes; more and more. To defend the town against such odds was useless slaughter of such men we had. Eight furious assaults Grey its governor withstood; at long last he fired the town and retired into the castle; that, at least, he might hope to hold.

For a week he did hold out. Himself, grievously wounded, yet forever in the forefront, he urged on his men. Once, by incredible luck he all-but had his hands on the de Guise, the de Guise himself; by incredible bad luck, lost him, the de Guise twisting himself away leaving his cloak in Grey's blood-slippery hand. It was borne in upon me that God had closed his eyes against our distress; I had not endeavoured to the full for His glory.

It was Calais all over again; a handful of men fighting by day and mending the breaches by night; some falling asleep at their task, others working while they slept. And, as always, the wounded must be carried away and the dead buried.

Always the news was bad. Always, always.

'Madam, the French are building a bridge to the castle; a bridge of barrels and planks, strong enough for their armies to cross. The lord Governor implores help; he *beseeches* you, Madam! Help and at once! But, Madam, I fear, I fear greatly it is too late!'

Guisnes fell. Young Arthur Grey, his father's lieutenant, came to tell me of the surrender.

'My father stood firm to the defence, though he bled greatly from his wounds. He would not have his men see how desperate his condition and had himself carried from the field. But when he heard that the enemy had taken the fort that guards the castle and the ditch between, and were attacking the bastions within the very walls, then, Madam, bitterly wounded as he was, and faint from bleeding, he bade them tie him to a chair—for of himself he could not sit upright—and carry him back to the fighting. So, seeing him lifted high, our men took courage and fought with yet grimmer will than before, so that, at one time, it seemed that the enemy must turn and run.'

'A heroic deed worthy of a heroic man. I shall not forget it!' And I pitied the young man white, even at the telling of it, and glistening with sweat at the memory.

'But, Madam, flesh-and-blood, however brave, cannot stand against guns. When the cannon speaks, flesh will bleed and hearts stop their beating. And guns the French have aplenty; enough, Madam, to storm all our bastions at one and the same time; a ring of death-dealing shells and ourselves at the centre. And their men outnumbered ours, Madam, ten to one at the least; and some of our men, by reason of their wounds, fighting upon their bleeding stumps! Madam, our men were *brave*!'

I nodded. I could not speak for the choking up of my throat nor see clear for the running of my tears.

'All day long the great guns booming, and the sky red with flame and black and smoke . . . and still my father, tied upright in the chair, encouraged the men. Madam, more than once, he escaped death by a hair's breadth, for he was *the* mark—as the Queen may well understand. But, God be praised, each time the bullet passed him by. It was as though God stretched out His hand as a shield.

'All that day and the next and the next—the unequal fighting, the terrible fighting! And all that night and the next, our death-weary men struggling to make good the damage. And always more and more French troops arriving fresh and rested, good shoes on their feet. *Good shoes*. That might sound little enough in so great an issue. . . .'

'I know, I know.' And I pictured our few men in their worn boots or with no boots . . . and some without feet, bleeding into the mud.

'Then, Madam, the Mary Bulwark fell, the great strong tower, there were not enough to hold it; and those few weary and most of them wounded, and all of them hungry. Hunger, Madam, bites sharp as any sword; they had neither heart nor strength left—and who could blame them? To stay within—so few there were—would be massacre. Even before the Mary Bulwark fell my father knew—as we all knew—it was the end.

'So, seeing nothing for it, my father agreed to parley. The French demanded two hostages, and I, Madam, was one—I asked it. So we were put outside; and, as we went, our feet slipped and slithered beneath us. For it was not earth we walked on but bodies; and some were frozen and stiff and some were warm still; and all alike were beslimed with blood.'

He turned away his face as though he would have retched; he choked down his vomit and took up his tale.

'My father and the de Guise discussed the truce, my father bound still to his chair upon the fortress walls, for he would not descend to parley; the de Guise standing below, shouting upwards, all stiff and proud with victory.

'The de Guise stated his terms. They were dishonourable; after so heroic a defence—an insult. We must march out, standards furled and pointed to the ground; and furled and lowered in disgrace, we must hand them over to the enemy. My father would have none of it. But our men, some maddened by wounds already gangrenous, others scarce able to stand upright for weakness, clamoured, *A truce. A truce at any price!* And, mad indeed, they were! There were some to lay hands upon my father, to cast him, all wounded as he was, from the walls. So they forced him to agree to the terms. Such men one must forgive; they were not, Madam, in their right mind.

'But the de Guise knows a fine soldier and an honourable man when he sees one! Our men marched out standards flying; and, as they marched, the de Guise bared his head and all his captains did likewise; and all the men followed that same example. It was a sight, Madam, terrible and glorious. . . .'

His voice faltered and again he turned his head, this time lest I should see his tears. He was, after all, a young man, and weak still from his wounds . . . and he had been a hostage.

'Madam,' and it was as though he pleaded with me, 'it was an honourable surrender!'

'Your father is the bravest of men and of unstained honour. Where he should have looked for help he was ill-served. He deserves well of us; we shall not forget it!' Which words cost my lord Grey dear!

For they raised his ransom from seven thousand to twenty thousand crowns; nor would he let me, any way, help in the matter—he knew my poverty. *The kindness of my Queen is worth any cost!* he told the de Guise.

Calais, Guisnes; and then Hamme, last town in the Calais Pale. Nothing left now of my English inheritance in France; nothing save little Dunkirk.

'Yet still I am Queen of France,' I told my Council. 'And still I quarter my arms with the lilies and leopards; and shall do till I die! And so shall my son after me; and after him, his son's sons. Every inch of English ground in France shall come back to us!'

'Madam,' Paget said very firm, yet with a gentleness strange in him, 'it is no longer a question of winning back what we have lost. A greater task is to hand. We must look for invasion!'

I had not thought so far; I had not thought that Henri would so dare! Anger shook me head-to-foot. My voice came out deep and strong. 'They shall find us ready and waiting. Our navy shall nip at them so that they run as from a mad dog!'

So we lit our beacons and we held our runners in readiness; we drummed up every able man from every town and village. There were few enough—and our very hearths and homes threatened! We set out fighting ships to their best advantage—in the narrow seas and also along the full length of our eastern coast and to the south also; watch-dogs, teeth bared.

All along our coast the beacons flared, the ships stood ready. But the sea is not the only way into England. Across the border the Scots waited; their grudge not as yet full-fed, their morale strengthened by the marriage of their little Queen to the heir of France—that last, an added inducement to invade along with the French.

'If I do not name Anne Bullen's daughter next in succession,' I told my cousin Pole, and to name her my father's child stuck in my throat, 'or even if I do, the Scots will, I think, press the rights of this same little Queen of theirs. And before God, why not? She stands nearest to our throne. And a good Catholic to boot!'

'Madam,' he said, 'do you forget the child you carry? A little patience, and the country will see its undoubted heir.' For we were come into the month of February.

'I have not forgotten. But still I'll not count upon my chick till it be hatched.' For my first, false pregnancy I had by no means forgot; nor could not, ever.

Early in February I went into retirement; for my physicians had advised me that my child would be born not in April but in March; and early in the month rather than late. And, indeed, my whole shape confirmed this advice; I was stout, somewhat puffed about hands and feet and the breasts were full.

'You may tell Don Gomez to inform his Majesty that the Queen will be brought to bed next month!' I told Jane Dormer; for Don Gomez had been sent with enquiries from my husband.

She looked at me; she said nothing.

'Aye, my girl, you may tell him!' I was a little put out that she gave no sign of pleasure. And then I saw the look in her eyes and thought I knew the reason.

'Never look so sad!' I said and I was smiling. 'Well, you have been patient enough! Next month shall bring us both our heart's desire—myself safe-delivered, and you wedded and bedded.'

She knelt to kiss my hand; but there the sorrow in her eyes did not lighten.

'Have no fear for me!' I told her. 'I shall bear my child. And, if I should die in that business, what better way to die that a child may live? As for you, come what may, my child's christening shall see your wedding-feast!'

March came in; my belly had risen somewhat higher; from my breasts the midwife expressed some droplets of milk. I felt increasingly unwell; and within the womb I doubted I felt movement. Or, if movement there was, could so slight a flutter be that of a living child? But the midwives assured me all was well. Mine were the natural doubts of a mother carrying her first child; and so I was assured, also, by those matrons that were experienced in such matters. Day after day passed, and I could not thrust down my doubts; this savoured overmuch of that first time. Yet, surely they must be right, those that were knowledgeable in such affairs, matrons and midwives, both. Maybe the child had moved while I slept; but so heart-shaking an event must surely have awakened me to joy. These days I would hold myself very still, my whole being bent to attention; was there not a flutter, the slightest, faintest flutter? I must not, dare not let myself doubt.

But others, too, had their doubt and showed it. As the month drew on, my Parliament pressed me to name my successor. *The Queen must give assurance to the country lest, God forbid, she die without issue.* To hear my own dark fear brought thus into daylight was terror and anguish.

Name my successor. If it were not to be the fruit of my body—who then? *Who?* Elizabeth I could not bring myself to name. I was, as I am, more than ever certain she is not my father's child. I desired, with all my heart, that Parliament would declare her bastard; yet I feared to raise the question. My second Parliament had refused me in the matter. I dared not face denial now. 'I had liefer name Mary Stuart my heir. She is legitimate, she is royal, she is of the true faith. She is everything the lady Elizabeth is not!' I told my Council, watching the while to see how they took the matter. They let it pass; their faces betrayed nothing. Yet I felt anger strong in the air. Let me press the matter now, and they would fight me to the uttermost. I said no more.

I let the days pass and named no-one; and all the time I prayed God for a quick and safe delivery. And all the time, bearing the burden of my own great fear, I still must bear the burden of the nation's fear—invasion by sea and land; we were ill-equipped to meet either, our losses in France had brought us low. My Council could see but one way in the matter. They sent, myself unwilling, to my husband demanding help. He had, they told him, a two-fold duty. We had aided him to the uttermost in his French wars and, through him now found ourselves involved with France to our grievous hurt and present fears. But, had he no other responsibility at all, there still remained the greatest of all—he was King of England!

'King of England!' And all Christendom heard how he laughed. 'A King without a crown; what King is that? And English help in France; *what* help?' And then, all laughter wiped from his face, 'The English are not soldiers; neither their captains nor their men. Cowards and turn-tails all!'

'And this after Calais! This after Guisnes! Lost, both lost because of help he promised and never sent! No, but he sat safe in Brussels while our men fought his battles, and lacking his help, died!' Paget cried out leaping from his place at the Council table. 'By God, this is too much! *What King?* he asks. No King of ours!'

My cousin Pole came to my closet to report of this meeting since none other dared. I was that day in worse state than usual and had not attended. Well, maybe it was as well! For God knows what epithets learned of my father and by me till now forgot, might not have gone flying to bespatter Paget blacker than his own black words.

'And, Madam, by all the faces about the table, the nods and the mutterings, the whole Council seemed to agree with him; yes, even Paulet! The whole Council, for the first time, at one!'

'What shall the King say to such insult? What must I do? How punish?'

'There must be no punishment, Madam. You must put that out of your head. And with it all thought of a crowning now; or ever. The King has angered not the Council alone. His words are already common property; anger in the people burns against him deeper, fiercer than ever before!'

It was an anger that, in spite of myself, I must understand. When Philip's words had first been reported to me, I had felt that same anger hot against the man I worshipped next to Christ, himself. He had smeared our English courage, had slighted our losses, had left us to bear the whole burden in France. Yet, in the matter of the crowning, Philip himself had been slighted; it was a thing I must bear in mind.

'Punishment there must be!' I told my cousin. 'If I allow Paget's insult to go unchecked, the King will never return to a country and a Queen that holds him so low!'

'Madam, the King's to blame!'

'Two wrongs never made one right!'

'Shall you punish Paget because he speaks the truth?'

'I would punish him for an unwise councillor that goes about to make his mischief.'

'No, Madam! You would punish him to bring the King home again! Oh Madam, Madam, it is useless! The mischief was done before ever Paget opened his mouth. Behind the King's words lie all the Spanish contempt of England; behind Paget's all the English hatred of Spain.' He stopped; he said, slow and unwilling, 'Madam, I fail in my duty if I fail of the truth. The King might have mended matters but chose to make them worse. The King has not done well by you! He has deepened the people's anger not against himself, alone, but against you, against *you,* Madam! There have been differences between the Queen and the people, as the Queen well knows. But the hope of a child brought joy to us all; a grandson to great Henry, and to Catherine of Spain whom they loved. They were ready, Madam, to make a fresh start. But now? The insult has been spoken to poison goodwill.

How shall the people take joy in a child born of unloved Queen and a hated King? Better, Madam, that the King stay away!'

'How long, Cousin, how long?'

'Till the air be somewhat sweeter.'

'And when shall that be?'

'When God works His miracle!'

I made him no answer. After the long anguish of disappointment to bear a child my people did not want! How might I endure that?

I buried my face in my hands; and, in the darkness of my own making, saw my sister's face, the hard eyes, the thin mouth, all a smiling triumph.

Chapter Twenty-Four

This year of Grace fifteen fifty-eight! It began badly enough with loss of my cities in France; and how shall it end? Will it ever? It goes so slow I think it never will! For still Philip does not come. Wretched days these must be for me and for us all, save for the great promise I carry within me. For now I do fully believe that God will send us the blessing that shall comfort all our losses and turn all griefs to joy. For, in spite of my cousin the Cardinal, I know that my people shall have great joy of my child; and that Philip will come again, for what father can forego the sight of his new-born babe? And I know, too, that he and the child together, shall win back all hearts to himself and to me.

And this hope I sorely need; for I see trouble all around and more to come!

First and foremost, we must reckon with the French. But it is not for them, only, that we watch; we cast anxious eyes upon Scotland, upon Wales and upon Ireland; for in these parts the French never cease their mischief. We have too few ships for our need; my father, for all his magnificence, did scarce enough for the Fleet. Some new ships he did build, but too many he lost in war, in storm, or, like the *Mary Rose*, by accident; though he, himself, once sailed to do battle in France like a hero in an old song, *His sails were all of taffety, his masts of beaten gold.* And that was true enough; for the masts of his flagship were all gilded and the sails were strong-woven silk. Well, I have done what I may, though gold and silk come not into the matter. I have managed in spite of a lean purse to build a few ships and to repair some old ones. But still the east and south-east coast is not well defended as should be. Yet my fleet does more than watch! Like hornets our ships dart into French harbours to sting them well. So far we have kept the narrow seas more or less free; but it is a constant strain upon our resources. The patched-up ships are like old dogs that, teeth missing, cannot bite as they should. But still they can bark and bark they do!

For the rest there is misery enough; discontent everywhere. The people blame the King for the loss of Calais, Guisnes and Cambrai; for the death of Englishmen in France. And me, that brought him to this country, they blame still more, though I weep tears of blood for my cities taken, my people dead. Food is still scarce, one good harvest cannot cure all; and once prices go up are not like to come down again. And the burnings increase; and with them, so it seems, the number of heretics. These go, for the most part, joyful to their death, as it might be to a wedding. 'I think the fire breeds heretics!' I told my cousin the Cardinal.

'It is not the fire that breeds heretics but the Devil!' he answered. 'When the fire does not burn away a man's heresies, be sure that man is truly of the Devil! Were it not for the holy fires, the country would be over-run like a field of good corn by tares!'

'It is a hard saying but a true one!' I told him, 'For here, in my own England, heretic priests preach against me with a cruel tongue. And in Geneva, the man Knox does not cease to spew out his gall against me!'

'Madam, you should have closed his mouth when he preached his heresies and seditions here in England. Now you may see what comes of undue clemency! Now he mocks at the Queen's mercy! Now he publishes his filthy writings . . .'

'. . . against *the monstrous regiment* of women—of which I am head and chief offender.'

'Naturally, Madam, since you would destroy all heretics in this land over which you rule. *Regimen!* A pedant's word and spelt in the new-fangled way for extra conceit. Why doesn't he say *rule* or *reign*; use plain English and be done with it!'

'Oh he uses less pedantic words; he speaks the plainest English, I promise you! He descends from the pedant to the peasant—the common abuse of the common people!'

Someone had seen to it that the filthy writing find its way into my closet. I did not want to touch it, still less to read it; but there it lay beneath my eyes, drawing me like a lodestar. I found myself reading and re-reading the thing. Yet even now, though I have the thing by heart, I cannot quite believe such things should be said of me, so that still I cast upon it an eye unwilling yet hatefully drawn.

> How abominable before God is the empire or rule of a wicked woman, yes of a traitoress and bastard....

Bastard. Out it comes again the old rod with which I must be beaten; and, for all I am Queen, the pain of that beating is no less than when I was a girl.

He declares it contrary to the will of God that women should bear the regimen over men; he attacks us all as inconstant, impatient, feeble and foolish; we are cruel, we lack counsel, we lack the power to rule. Woman is made to serve man and to obey him. Not only am I castigated with the rest of my sex, I am singled out for his especial spite; he refers to the

> indecent joy, and the bonfires and banqueting, which were in London and elsewhere when that cursed Jezebel was proclaimed Queen....

Cursed Jezebel! What have I done to deserve so foul a name? This Jezebel was, as I remember, a most cruel and lustful whore. Yet the pain of that insult is less than the pain that I have lost my people's love. I think of those glorious days but five years ago—and how distant they seem!—when my people, setting at nought the might of Northumberland the Protector, his peers and his bishops, his armies and his ships and his great wealth, gathered to my cause and brought me, in love, into my capital. It is not the glory of those days I remember so much as the love I have lost.

And still I cannot put by the obscene paper. The writing goes on to prophesy God's swift judgment upon

> the inordinate appetites of that cruel monster Mary, unworthy by reason of her bloody tyranny of the name of woman. Cursed Jezebel of England....

Again Jezebel! Again! He goes on to name those who have enterprised against their Queen. *Martyrs* he calls them—Wyatt and Cranmer and a host of others; heretics and traitor every one! But above them all he sets Jane Grey. *Innocent Jane Grey* he calls her. Does he think then, I must sit still and let heretics betray God, and traitors rob me of my crown? *Innocent Jane Grey* that but for God's mercy had drowned the country in a sea of blood. Yet I spared her once;

and her kindred with her! And I would have spared her a second time has I been let; but I was not let. And those that prevented me were right; for when it comes to sparing one life rather than many, what shall one do?

But God, the man Knox says, has given open testimony against me.

> . . . Man and woman, learned and unlearned, nobles and men of baser sort, aged fathers and tender damsels, and finally the bones of the dead, as well women as men have tasted of her cruelty. . . .
>
> . . . The day of Vengeance which shall apprehend that horrible monster. Jezebel of England, and such as maintain her monstrous cruelty, is already appointed in the Council of the Eternal. . . . It is so nigh that she shall not reign in tyranny as long as hitherto she has done; but God Himself shall declare her His enemy when he shall put contempt upon her according to her cruelty and shall kindle the hearts of such as did sometime favour her, that he may execute His judgments. . . .

Jane Dormer found me white as the paper that shook in my hand.

'Madam, dearest Madam, burn this thing!' she implored me.

'This copy I may burn; what then? Can I burn every copy of this accursed thing that finds its way into every house, into the Queen's own closet? See what the man says of me; see! *Bastard, cruel monster, cursed Jezebel. . . .*' And I thrust the paper into her hand.

She let it fall.

'Such words should have no power to touch God's anointed,' she said.

'They should not; but they do! They touch me to the quick of my soul.'

'God will punish him!'

'Why should He do my work for me? I should have punished him myself when I had him under my hand! No! But I must leave him free for his filthy writings. Now all that can, read his words and repeat them to those that cannot of themselves read. Yet in all these lies there is one grain of truth. I came to my crowning secure in the people's love—*indecent joy*, he calls it. Well, he need have no more fear of that! Love is turned to hatred; and his writings, as they must, deepen that hatred. It is not love that is indecent; it is hatred; hatred that runs like poison in the blood—that is the indecentest thing of all!'

'Madam,' and she was kneeling, her face all tender with love, turned upwards to me. 'People are fickle. Yesterday they loved the Queen, today their love wanes, tomorrow it will wax again. You will see!'

'Yes,' I said, 'when my son is born they will turn to me again!'

She said nothing to that; maybe she did not hear.

I am not well. Hands and feet are swollen. At times I cannot bear shoe upon foot nor carry a cup in my hand. But my belly swells and I am content. Though all eyes turn now to Anne Bullen's daughter that sits in her house sly and smiling, when my son is born, it will be a different story. Then those eyes will turn to their true lodestar and rest there content.

Everything is ready for my blessed delivery; and delivery, indeed! Delivery of this people from the sin of heresy, delivery that shall continue when I, myself, am gone; for there shall come after me a true Catholic prince born of my body. The crib stands ready, the swaddling-clothes folded about the warming-pans, for the weather is still sharp. In the chest lies the precious shawl my mother brought from Spain. I bade Jane Dormer bring it to me.

'My mother brought it to England for the christening of her son.' And I touched it gently as I had seen her do more than once when, big with child, she dreamed, like me, of a son.

'It was used but once, once only, for a little boy that lived a few days. She'd not allow it for my own christening though I was her only living child and she loved me deeply. It was for her *son*. I think it will pleasure her now in heaven to know it will be used once more.'

She said nothing; nor could I see her face as she bent upon the shawl folding it with careful fingers to return it to the chest.

Everything is ready and waiting; horses bridled and saddled, messengers a tip-toe to ride into Canterbury to fetch the silver font in which I myself was christened, and my sister and brother likewise; in which royal children for generations have been christened. Other messengers wait, letters already prepared, to carry the news to Philip in the Netherlands. The names and order of those to serve in the christening service are all set down.

'Even now I must smile to think of old Norfolk and some half-dozen high peers in England, all clad in their great robes, with aprons tied about them and towel in hand, to take their part in those last two christenings. No, I mistake, a little! When my brother was christened, Norfolk lay in the Tower. What a quarrelling, what a to-do over the honours and order of precedence!' I told Jane Dormer, laughing; and then, overcome by memories, 'Oh but I wish my old friend Gardiner were alive today! I would he might see my happiness! For in spite of everything I am happy. No need now to fear for the succession. My son shall wear the crown!'

'Pray God!' she said.

March has been a long, long month. The winds are bitter; and, in spite of great fires and braziers forever burning at my elbow, I am always cold. Often there is a cruel pain shooting through breast and belly; and there are days I am so weak I dare not lie in my bed lest I fall, but must have a mattress spread upon the floor. Sometimes I think I am very ill; but most times I know these to be but the pains of pregnancy biting hard because I am old to be about this business, and have never been strong. I am glad, then, to endure my pains not only with patience but with joy; for if these be truly the pains of pregnancy how light they weigh against the joy of bearing a child! There are, beside, days when I am well enough; but good days or bad, it will not be long before I hold my child in my arms. I pray for a son; but a daughter will be very dear to my heart. I shall look to my babe's well-being as my mother looked to mine; I shall show him that same tender care she showed me. I long for the pains of childbirth; never mind how bitter, they shall be sweet to me.

I have nothing left to wish for, save that God send my husband back to me. Send him back, dear God! I weary soul and body for the sight of him, the touch of him. But if God says *No!* then I must make myself content, for Kings and Queens have each their duties; and, if I should die in mine, well it is a good way to die. No long and wasting sickness but a time set; as the old, tired soul departs purified and in peace, a new, pure soul is born into the world.

The end of the month is come; because I feel so ill, and because I must face the possibility of death, I have made my will. It is signed, sealed and witnessed; and I have laid it by in case, God sparing me, I should need to alter or to add to it. There are many pages; it took several days awriting. It is writ, for the most part, in my secretary's hand, but where my desire is most earnest, I have writ the passage myself; it was not easy because of my swollen fingers. I think I have set down everything clear. I have not named my successor; I carry my successor beneath my heart. Now my will is made, I feel myself at peace.

It is April. Parliament has risen but all members must hold themselves in readiness for the birth of my child. Spain's child, England's child. This is the month of my physicians' promise and the midwives agree. Any day, now, before cold spring give way to early summer, the joybells will ring out and, in every church, prayers will rise in thanks to God. There are some I know, that wish for my death and the child's death, also; but these are heretics . . . and God watches over all!

The month draws on. I look at my physicians and at my midwives. I ask no questions. I dare not. And, *Patience!* they say. *With a first child one cannot tell to the day!* It is a tale I have heard before! This morning I asked Jane Dormer to lay her hand upon my belly to feel for movement. She said she has no knowledge in such matters. I shall not ask her again. Her answer troubles my conscience. But for me she would be married having that knowledge she now lacks. Once again she has sent her lover away; he came from Brussels with my husband's greetings and wishes for a speedy and joyous ending to my affair. Don Gomez begged that they be married forthwith; they are deep in love . . . yet for all that she sent him away. Sometimes I look at her and I think, When she is wed she will leave me and go home to Spain. I say *home* because Spain is my mother's country and it is my husband's country and it will be, also, my son's country. Perhaps, one day we shall go together, all of us—Philip, the child and I.

Chapter Twenty-Five

Written in the hand of Jane Dormer.
Hampton Court, March 15th, 1558
These are sad days for England; sadder still for us that love the Queen. Sick, troubled and lonely, she yet lives them in joy; it is a joyfulness to break the heart. She thinks, within a few days to bear her child. We that serve her know that hope is false. Once she asked me to feel for movement of the child but I put the matter off. I was ignorant in such affairs, I said. Her physician, old Dr. Buttes, has told me of the tumour she carries within her body. With the dropsy she might haved lived to a fair age; from the tumour she must die and die soon. She carries within her not life but death. This she does not know; what will happen when she understands at last? Can even her courage stand then?

March 31st
Yesterday she made her will. In full confidence of bearing a child the will was made. Today she said to me, 'Bring me my will and read it aloud. I must be certain there is no error nor anything not perfectly clear. My wits these days are not always bright!' So I took it from its place and brought it to her. It is very long; many pages. A Queen's will. It is writ, for the most part, by her secretary, though some passages are writ in her own hand. These last are not, alas, in her beautiful Italianate style, but marred; the letters drunk by reason of her dropsy.

At the head of the first page stands the sign of the cross; and it begins, *In the name of God, Amen*. She never sets out upon any business great or small, but she invokes the name of God. There follow, as is proper, her high-sounding titles.

I, Mary, by grace of God, Queen of England, Spain, France. . . .

She nodded. 'Yes, France, also! It is still mine and my son shall win it back, every inch! Go on reading.'

> ... both Sicilies, Jerusalem, and Ireland, Defender of the Faith, Arch-duchess of Austria, Duchess of Burgundy, Milan and Brabant, Countess of Hapsburg, Flanders and Tyrol; and lawful wife to the most noble and virtuous Philip. King of the said realms and dominions of England....

She looked at me, a little smile on the tucked-in corners of her mouth. 'I am a poor thing,' she said, 'to bear the weight of so many titles!' She nodded to me to go on.

> ... thinking myself to be with child in lawful marriage with my dearly beloved husband ...

She said on a deep sigh, 'Lawful marriage! You'd think marriage between a King and a Queen, blessed by the Pope and contracted by every rite of the true Christian church, would need no word as to lawfulness. But it is not always so....' She sighed again, remembering, I think, her mother of whom these days she often speaks.

> First I do commend my soul to the mercy of Almighty God, the Maker and the Redeemer, thereof; and to the good prayers and help of the most pure and blessed Virgin, the lady St. Mary and of all the Company of Heaven....

'The next lines,' she said, 'you need not read, I leave this poor body of mine to be buried in such time and place and with such prayers as those that oversee my will shall deem right and proper. But the words that follow; read them, my child, that we may judge together if the matter be clear. For, if it be faithfully followed, I shall sleep the sounder.'

> ... I will that the body of the virtuous lady my most dear and well-beloved mother of happy memory, Queen Catherine, that lies now buried at Peterborough shall, within as short a time as conveniently may be after my burial, be removed and laid in the place of my own sepulture, in which place I will my executors to cause honourable tombs for a decent memory of us....

She said, 'I am a woman grown; yet it is comfort to know that, at the last, I shall lie by her side. I lost her too soon; not by death but by the cruelty of man. Yet, even now, there are times I miss her as though I were still the child from whom she was so cruelly torn.' And, indeed, so small the Queen is, so innocent her eyes that, for all she is worn with grief and pain she has the look of a child; a forlorn child.

'Read on, my Jane!' she said.

> . . . It is also my will that, within one month after my death, there may be distributed the sum of one thousand pounds, to be given in relief of poor prisoners. . . .

I looked at her then. What other than she, her life so pure, would remember sinners in their prison? Not King nor Queen nor lord nor great priest has done that ever!

She said, 'I have writ the amount in my own hand lest my executors misread and make the sum not pounds but marks!'

Well, I should not wonder if they did. The sum is great and she so poor!

'I wish it were more,' she said, 'much, much more! When I was a girl, my tutor . . .' She wrinkled that short nose of hers recalling the name. 'Fetherstone . . . as I think. So good a man! Himself imprisoned for no crime but truth to his faith, commended to me the care of all prisoners rotting in our cruel gaols—guilty as well as innocent. And the greater their crime, he said, the more their need. Read on; there must be no mistake!'

So I read on. Bequests to religious houses she has restored, or hoped to restore—the Observant friars at Greenwich, the Black friars of St. Bartholomew, the nuns of Langley and the monks of Westminster—with the request that they pray for her soul and the soul of her dear husband both now and when he shall come to his death. There are legacies, also, to the University of Oxford, to help poor scholars that would be priests; and from these, she begs prayers for the soul of her father that, to my mind [illegible]y needs them.

Legacies for religious houses, for churches, for schools—these things I had expected; though not with such generosity. But the next bequest! This, like that for the prisoners, is something new again, something I think no King nor prince of church or state, ever thought to do. She is the first; and, as I read, tears come to my eyes. She has not forgotten those that, being of no more use, no man cares for.

> . . . and especially and forasmuch as there is presently no house or hospital ordained and provided for the relief and help of poor old soldiers such as have been hurt or maimed in the service of the realm. . . .

She said, 'I cannot put them from my mind, these men that come wounded from our wars to drag themselves about the country. They have served us, they have protected us to their own hurt; and what do they get for thanks? A beggarly crust, if they be lucky! But, more like, the dogs set upon them. Honour, conscience and charity, alike, cry out that they shall be honourably provided for. All this I have set down; and with it, where the hospital shall stand and how it shall be managed; what wages shall be paid to the Master and to his assistants; and what moneys shall be at their disposal. It was not easy; but God be thanked, it is done!'

A very sick woman—though how sick she knows not; one that has suffered more than her share of griefs; yet still she drives that compassionate heart of hers to the service of others.

There is no stilling the voice of her conscience. If she has injured any—though she cannot recall such—she asks the overseers of her will to make the wrong good; and, in the matter of debts she forgets nothing. She asks that all moneys owing—and especially the loans granted by her loving subjects—be paid as soon as may be after her death.

'Oh my debts, my debts!' She lifted her hands and let them fall. 'I have lived frugal all my life; like my grandfather I have earned me the name of miser. I have curbed, and with what difficulty, God alone knows, the desire, the natural desire, to give and give again! Only to my dear lord and husband did I indulge myself to give freely; and then it was more honest exchange than giving; for he brought great wealth with him.'

They weigh heavy upon her, these debts incurred by war, and by the country's needs; and those other debts left by her father and her brother, not yet entirely met. Again and again she returns to them—she has a spirit fastidious and just. She remembers her servants, all of them, great and small; whether still in her service or no, they shall be paid according to the length and manner of their employment, and the amount is clearly set down.

And so she comes, at last, to the greatest matter of all—the crown of England. And in her mind there is no doubt. Her child will inherit.

And when I look at her drawn face and her poor swollen body there is no doubt in my mind, neither; but my certainty, alas, how different from hers!

The crown of England and Ireland, together with her titles in France and all other kingdoms of which she, by the providence of God, is the lawful inheritor and Queen, together with all castles, fortresses and honours shall wholly and entirely descend to

> the heirs and fruits of my body, according to the laws of this realm.

And, as I read, she, knowing the words off by heart, repeated them in her low, deep voice.

> . . . and the government, order and rule of the said heir and issue, I recommend unto my most dear lord and husband, during the minority of the said heir according to the laws of this realm. . . .

Above all she remembers Philip's dignity and glory. She wills and requires obedience to this by the duty her subjects owe her as Lady and Queen. For it has pleased God

> to show me the greatest favour in the world as to appoint me so noble, so virtuous and worthy a prince to be my most dear and noble husband . . .

She looked at me and smiled. 'The prayer my cousin the Cardinal made for him is right and proper, for all de Noailles mocked at it. The King is as near the perfection of Jesus as mortal man can be.'

Could she, I wondered, be entirely sincere? I looked into her candid face. She was speaking the truth from her heart. May God preserve me from such a husband! I thought; and then, God preserve her from knowing the truth about her own!

And so she goes on in her true, blunt way to say what is best left unsaid.

> . . . It has ever been his endeavour to reduce this realm into the unity of Christ's church and to conserve the same.

She uses the word *reduce* regardless of its fatal other-meaning, as when a general, victorious, turns his attention to the beaten enemy.

And then, incredibly, she presents Philip, as of right, to the love and duty of her subjects.

> I have no legacy nor jewel that I covet more to leave his Highness to requite the nobility of his heart towards me and this realm; nor he, more desirous to have, than the love of my subjects. I do especially recommend this same duty and love unto his Highness that they naturally owe to me. . . .

I could not look at her. She appears clear in her mind, her wishes proper and set down plain. But has illness begun to affect her that she no longer knows she has lost the love of the most part of her people, whatever their faith? And has she forgotten it is through this same Philip she has lost it? Has she forgotten the country is torn by its worship; that though good Catholics rejoice that she has tried to bring unity into the church, she has, in spite of all laws passed by Parliament, failed? Doesn't she *know* that the burnings are the deepest cause of hatred against her and her husband? And, above all, doesn't she understand that, in its secret heart, the greater part of this land is heretic; that let her name what heir she will, even though it be the child of her body, the country will take Elizabeth for Queen; Elizabeth and none other? I think she does not. I think that, at times, false hope and grievous sickness have clouded the clear mind. The love of her people new-sprung at the birth of her child is just such a dream and a delusion as the child itself.

Being the woman she is, loving and generous, she cannot leave her husband with nothing more tangible than love of her people. Maybe because of her poverty, maybe because she chooses the things that have given her the deepest joy, she leaves him the ring of her betrothal together with his other gifts to her. These words are writ, also, in her own hand. I can guess at the slow difficult writing, her face twisted with the pain of her effort.

> . . . I do most humbly beseech my most dearest lord and husband to accept of my bequest and to keep for a memory of me, one jewel, being a table diamond which the Emperor's Majesty sent me by the count of Egmont, as an assurance, at the betrothal of my said lord and husband. And also one other table diamond which his Majesty sent to me by the marquis de las Navas; and the collar of gold set with nine diamonds which his Majesty gave me the

Epiphany after our marriage; also, the ruby now set in a gold ring which his Majesty sent me by the count of Feria . . .

'Such joy I had of them,' she said, 'I trust they shall go back to him the dearer for my sake!'

The ring of her betrothal he had not, of himself, sent! The gifts sent in his absence, himself uncaring! Yet, because they had come from him, beyond all words precious. She is giving them back enriched by all her love, all her longing. These, and the love of her people, are the most precious things in all her world! And he? The enrichment he will not even perceive.

She must have seen the shadow cross my face, for she said, 'Is there some fault in the writing? Some error?'

'Neither fault nor error, Madam!' *Nothing but the errors of a too-loving heart.* For this last testament reveals in little the whole shape and pattern of her life—her mercy and her honesty; an honesty so forthright, it has done more damage than good. It reveals, also, her loneliness; it shows clear her belief in the true faith, her love of God, her husband, and her people. Yet all save God have deserted her; and heretics believe God, too, has turned His back.

It is not cheerful reading, the will of one you love that is shortly to die and does not know it!

'I am not going to die!' she said, catching in that strange way of hers, one's thoughts. 'Not yet, so never look so sad! Nor do I want to die; for God He knows the joy I have now of my life! I long to see the face of my child, I long and long! Yet, it is God's Will that some women die in childbirth. If it be His Will for me, I am content.'

It was hard not to turn my look from the deep happiness in her sunken eyes, the smile upon her bloodless lips—the whole woman looking confident into the future . . . and the poor, swollen belly telling its lying tale.

April 20th

The willow flowers are dusted all of gold; the air is sweet still with violets but the primroses are gone; the year moves on.

Day by day the Queen grows more pinched, more anxious. Yet still she hopes . . . she hopes. She dare do no other. But I think fear shakes her in the deep places of the soul. Her longing, her need for her husband is very great. She sends message after message imploring him to return in the name of God. A ship stands by at Calais to bring him home. I pray daily, *Dear God let him come!*

May 3rd

Mayday came in. There were some rejoicings; people brought in great branches, but save for the boys and girls, it is all half-hearted. It rains continually; the hawthorn flowers hang sodden, brown and beaten. There will be no good harvest this year and for my poor Queen, none at all.

May 30th

Now the Queen must face the truth. She can count up to nine as well as another. She knows to the hour her husband left her; she knows, too, by bitter experience, the utmost limit to which nine months may stretch. There can be no child. Then what does she make of the thing that swells within her, seeming to grow with a life of its own? She does not ask. She does not want to know . . . she knows only too well.

Once she spoke to me on the matter; once and only once.

'I thought to have embraced the pains of labour and was glad because they are blessed pains to set free new life; and, because the work being accomplished, the pains are ended. Now I must endure a useless, ugly agony—and to that there's no ending, save in death. My father endured it, lived with it for years. And so might I have done; but God in His mercy has planted within me that which shall make a quick end.' And her hand went to her belly. 'Well, of such mercy I must not complain. God will give me courage; and I have my faith to sustain me if courage fail. He has given me a husband steadfast in kindness; surely He will give me time, a little time to win my people again.' And the tears poured down her wasted cheeks.

June 7th

The midwives have gone home, the cradle and shawl put by. I think the Queen bleeds inwardly to her death. But the question of the succession cannot be put by. Now she must decide; and the decision must be final. She knows it; and the King knows it. He has sent my betrothed Don Gomez to enquire of the Queen's health; but that is not the true reason.

'I am to visit Madam Elizabeth,' he told me. 'I am to assure her of my master's desire she shall have the crown. I am to promise support and friendship.'

Friendship. No more? My eyes alone, asked my question; and he, understanding, answered it.

'The King . . .' he was hesitant, 'bids me express his wish that Madam Elizabeth be betrothed . . .'

'To Sweden? To Savoy?'

'To either. It is a feint to blind this country to the truth—Queen and people alike. He means her for himself.'

'The Queen is not dead!' I cried out.

'Not yet! And he would still husband the Queen of England.'

So Madam Slyboots is to have all—her sister's crown and her sister's bed!

'Thank God I am not to wed a King!' I said and my tears overflowed. He lifted my chin in his hand. 'I thank God, also!' he said.

July 20th

The Queen grows daily worse. She is weak and melancholy. These days blackness falls upon her, as it were a curtain of darkness. And, in that darkness, she lies still as stone and as senseless. It lasts a very short time; a minute, perhaps, but to me, the time seems endless. These periods will become more frequent, last longer, so her physicians say. At first she will come from her darkness with a clear mind; but, little by little, the clear mind will cloud. There is always someone to watch by her when the darkness falls, to stay until light comes again. Usually by her wish and by my own, it is I that watch.

Still the King does not come. The French war drags itself on. Now the enemy win a victory by a sudden attack on Dunkirk; now we make a sudden attack and send them flying; then again they attack—and so it goes. To whom Dunkirk belongs we do not know.

We have just had news to settle that last question and set all our bells aringing. We made our sudden attack, the Flemings fighting alongside us, and took Dunkirk. Now it is well-fortified, well guarded and—ours! The Queen came from her short darkness to the sound of bells. She asked the reason and her thin face lit up. 'Calais next!' she said. 'We shall win Calais back!' And who should cloud her short joy with doubt? But she, I think, will never see that day; nor I doubt, will any Englishman, ever! It is too rich a city, too great a port to be lost to France again. But still our ships make sudden, darting raids upon the French coast towns, and still our beacons redden the night sky . . . but we have neither men enough nor ships enough to defend our own coast.

July 30th

Joy for Dunkirk does not last long. It is ours, for the present, but there's no more news of victory. And still the war! Always the war and never a word of peace! To add to our troubles bad summer has followed bad spring. It is cold and very wet, and our spirits are damped along with the weather. The Queen continues melancholy; her hope for Calais died a quick death and other hope she has none. She has put by for ever her hope of a child; and from her husband comes no word of return. She struggles against despair wasting her poor strength. She does not sleep; I know it. I have a pallet by her bed. She rises four or five times the night to pray. I hear her desperate weeping, her piteous prayers for guidance. I lie still. It is all I can do for her. Did she know I hear her weeping and her entreaties, her pride would suffer; the edifice of her courage crumble.

No rest for her by day or night. All the troubles of the country lie upon her already burdened heart. It is not only the great and pressing concerns, but those, also, that are always with us; she talks often of the poor and the sick, of those that lie in prison and of old soldiers, wishing she had more to leave for their comfort. But, above all, she is eaten with grief for the absence of her husband. She speaks little about it but her mind is constant upon him; she speaks, obliquely as it were, talking of the happiness of wives with their husbands and children, contrasting it, I am sure, with her own bleak lot, as for instance, when she speaks of her godchildren.

'I was a godmother at four years old; what could I know of a godmother's duties? Now I have so many children in God, I cannot count them but upon my fingers. Yet I know and remember them all. Many of them have children of their own and some have grandchildren; and these, too, I remember, for my children in God are all the children I am like to have!'

Yet she never speaks one word against the husband that could so easily return; and it would be a brave man or woman that dare breathe criticism against him. Sometimes I think she will die not from the thing that grows within her, but of hunger for the sight of her husband.

The fits of blackness begin to fall more often and, as her physicians warned us, they last longer. She drops into darkness as a stone into the sea; and each time she takes a little longer to return into light. Will the time come when her mind forever lies like a pebble on the dark ocean bed, never to see daylight again? I pray not. I pray her mind be clear and joyful when she goes to meet her God. Maybe God sends her this time of not-knowing that body and spirit may alike rest. 'It is like a little death,' she says. 'If death be so gentle I shall not fear it!'

August 1st

Today a fearful thing happened. The Queen went to rest upon her daybed; when I brought my stool to sit beside her, she shook her head. 'You are losing your roses,' she said. 'And what will Don Gomez say then? Go walk in the garden and bring your roses back with you!' And when I hesitated, she said, 'I am well enough; and the others are in the next room. You may leave the door ajar.' So away I went, glad to catch a breath of sweet summer; but all the time my mind was with her in the darkened room. I turned my back upon the bright garden and, as I came up towards the Queen's rooms, I heard the stir of alarum; I picked up my skirts and ran as I have not run since a child. One of the Queen's ladies, Mary Strelley it was, came running to meet me. 'Come quick!' she called as she ran. I did not stay to ask what was amiss but ran the faster.

In the Queen's closet I found my lady Bacon and the two Seymour sisters looking scared; and the Queen, bolt upright upon the daybed. 'I'll hear no more from unkind mouths!' she was crying out. 'Get you gone, all of you! All save my Jane. Jane, stay you!'

When they had taken themselves off, she bade me close the door.

'I died one of my little deaths,' she said, 'and I would I had died forever; I was coming back into the light, my body still as death, my spirit struggling to be free—you know how it is, you have seen it! Through the open door there came a murmur of voices that, at first, made no sense. But soon it made sense and sense enough! They were talking of the King and of my sister; the names linked fast . . . linked in *marriage*! My wits were back again; I understood more than I wanted!'

She stopped. She said, 'Jane, you are bound to obey your Queen, are you not?'

'But of course, Madam!' and I was somewhat puzzled.

'Then you must answer my question; and you must swear by Christ not to lie to me!'

I began to understand.

'If you love me, swear!' And she held out the cross that had been her mother's; these days she wears it always about her neck.

I hesitated; and she, holding out the cross, I touched it with my finger.

'Is it true, what those women said; is there an understanding between the King and my sister?'

'He admires her. He shows her the courtesy due from the King to the Queen's sister.'

'No more than that? Does he not plan to wed her . . . when I am dead?'

'She'll be too old for that, God willing!' And I tried to turn a jest.

'And . . . if she be not too old?'

'Madam, the lady Elizabeth loves France and hates Spain.'

'That is no answer. Spain she may hate; but the King of Spain—that's another matter! A fine man like the King may make her change her mind . . . were he willing. *Is* he willing?' And her voice was suddenly sharp.

'Madam; how can he be? He is wed; and she vowed to a virgin life. He has not seen her above twice or thrice. His mind, besides, is set all upon war. The war being over, back he will come and the Queen shall see for herself. . . .'

'*What* shall the Queen see? Her eyes will be closed in death!?'

And when I made no answer she said, 'Oh Jane, Jane! Should my sister wear the crown, which God forbid, might she not reverse her loves and her hates? Might she not for the King's sake come to hate France and love Spain? They said so, my women at their gossip . . . they said other things, also!' She was silent. Then, 'I am a sick woman; play me no tricks. You tell me no lies; but you do not tell the truth, neither. You hedge this way and that! Now, answer me one thing plain. Was the King faithless to my bed; did he play me false here, in my own house?'

'No, Madam. Nor could not. There's not one of us all but loves you too well to play the harlot in the King's bed.'

'You answer too quick, my girl! You give your game away! *They* might be too loving; but what of the King? What of *him*? Come now, you are sworn to the truth?'

'Under the Queen's favour, I am sworn to tell no lie! Madam, forgive me; I can say no more!'

'If I am not to hear the truth from you that love me, I must hear it from one that does not. She, at least, will spare me nothing!'

August 2nd

The lady Elizabeth has come. And gone.

Those two talked together and talked alone. She is a quick and clever liar that young woman, but this time it suited her to tell the truth! I saw her as she came from the Queen and through the room where we sat. She was very pale, her face a mask. She nodded to us, red head high and haughty; and, as we went down upon our curtseys, she said, careless, 'Which of you is Dormer?' though she knows me full well. 'Dormer is to go to the Queen!'

I found my mistress pacing the room and more distressed than I have ever seen her. Her face was grey, her eyes peering as though she could not well see, her hands restless and shaking upon her gown. She said, 'God has taken from me the last of His gifts and my heart is broken. And, when the heart is broken, courage and pride break too!'

She stopped; her hands went up to her throat as though to thrust back sickness.

'My husband is unfaithful,' she said. 'He has never been faithful. Never! Here, in my own court, he made me a laughing-stock and throughout the courts of Christendom. But I think you know it, for you would not speak lest you lied; and against lying you were forsworn! He takes strange women to his bed and cares not at all whether they be clean or no! Now he casts his lustful eye upon my sister. *The King cannot love; he can only lust!* She said that, my sister. And she says true. Her you cannot deceive; she has knowedge in such affairs. But I? I am the fool, the ignorant fool! Yet, before I agreed to this marriage I questioned Renard; Renard that I thought my friend. He swore my prince was chaste. Well, the man sought his country's good and I must not blame him! All these years I have lived ignorant, the fool that knows nothing!'

And now, it seemed, she could not stay her talking. All these months so silent! And now the words poured from her like a flood that cannot be stopped.

'The King has a mistress in Spain, did you know that? But of course you knew it! Everyone in Christendom knows it, everyone save me, save me alone! He is more faithful to his mistress than to his wife; and more fortunate!' She gave a thin and bitter laugh. 'He has several children by her; little girls and he loves them dearly. A good father!' And still she laughed, the tears running down her face.

'He always ran after petticoats—here, there and everywhere; Spain, England, Flanders, it made no matter! No wonder de Noailles laughed at Pole's prayer—the prayer that likened the King to Christ! No wonder! Once he tried to tell me the truth but I would not listen . . . I would not listen! No, but I thought him a spiteful fool. Spiteful he was; but never a fool. I was the fool, the loving fool. Sweet Christ!' And I think she had forgotten me. 'I had rather be a loving fool than bitter with the truth. . . .

'That he was gay in Flanders, I knew; laughing, dancing, drinking, at every wedding feast, at every masque the foremost. I knew and was glad for him, my grave Philip so hard-pressed he had no time to write to me, his wife! My poor Philip, I thought; soon he must shoulder his father's burdens, let him laugh while he may!

'But of his wenching I knew nothing. There was conspiracy amongst you all, loving maybe, to fool me. And you, yourself, Jane Dormer, have not been guiltless; no, not even yesterday, when I questioned you close. Oh you told me no lie; but you did not tell the truth, neither!

'And the truth is this! My husband would have played me false in my own house, yes, even within days of our marriage, but that my ladies were faithful. Things come back to my mind, things I did not understand then, I understand now. Dacre; why did she leave the court in such a hurry; why did she not return until the King was safe across the sea? I'll tell you why! She was a pretty woman and *young*. And I, so poor a thing! He lusted for her; he spied upon her both at her dressing and her undressing. By bribes and treachery he came into her bedchamber and she, all naked for her bed! He tried to force her; she fought for her honour—like a wild cat, says Madam Elizabeth that has the story pat and took some joy in the telling; yet I cannot doubt the truth. When Dacre asked leave to go, she had scratches upon her—face and neck; she had also, a swollen lip.

I remember asking her about them; an accident she said, a stumble in the dark. I guessed at some love-play and said no more. But *who* partnered her in that game, I did not know.'

She stopped. She took in a long breath, she began again.

'So when he could not get one of my ladies, he went further afield. He took tradesmen's daughters; an honest tradesmen is apt to lock up daughters, so the girls were, for the most part, clean. He was careful, my wise Philip, until he went into Flanders. They used to sing a ditty about him and me. I had that, too, of my sister. No doubt you've heard it.'

She began to sing, her voice low and deep, as when she is moved.

> 'Baker's daughter in russet gown,
> Is better than Queen without her crown . . .
> And Queen with her crown so long as she live,
> Than baker's daughter has less to give!

'A pretty song, is it not?'

She put out her hand in a blind way, as though she must fall. I took it and led her to a chair, she talking the while.

'In England he was careful what women he took to his bed. In Flanders, not so careful. There was a woman, D'Aler; you see I have her name. A full-blown beauty; her virtue less than her looks. He could not keep from her, though she is a common harlot. But it was not only that woman! There were others, others. Oh!' she cried out, in an agony, 'wasting his precious seed upon the making of bastards, seed that should make royal princes!' She put her hands before her face the while she rocked backwards and forwards.

She took her hands from her face, she stopped her rocking.

She said, and now she was curiously quiet, 'The King was sick a while ago; is still sick for all I know! I sent him gifts—a jewel for his hat, a fine sword, and dishes to tempt his appetite. I wept for him, prayed for him . . . and all the time Christendom laughed; and it was right to laugh! I could laugh myself. *It was the Pox; the great Pox!*' She began to laugh, while the tears poured down her cheeks and into her mouth.

'*The Pox!*' she cried out again. 'And I tried to cure it with a venison pasty! Oh my prince, my chaste and virtuous prince! Now I know why he was not made Holy Roman Emperor in his father's place. Now I know!'

'The Emperor himself was not always virtuous . . .'

'No!' she cried, 'but he was discreet! But the King! He had all Christendom laughing at him . . . and at me; at me!'

Her laughter stopped suddenly, as one turns off wine with a spigot.

'God sends His own punishments,' she said, 'oh my poor Philip! He received from his father his full inheritance—lands, titles; every honour save one—one he could not inherit but must, of himself, be judged worthy. He is not the Holy Roman Emperor—the most coveted title in Christendom; not he, but some obscure kinsman. And I didn't know why. . . . I didn't *know*! Now, now I understand! God could not take so blemished a man for such service. Oh—' and her voice was pitiful, 'my poor, flawed love!'

There was a long silence. Then she said, and in her voice there was neither anger nor pity, 'Well now I have the truth at last! The truth; the truth was ever my bane. I was bred to speak truth; to make a true question, expect a true answer. Why then, when at last, I have it, do I cry out against it? Did I think the truth could not hurt? It hurts, it *hurts*. It is a sharp knife to cut into the flesh. Well, I must not complain if with the flesh it cut away the disease. These tears of mine, I take for a new baptism. There is nothing can hurt me ever again.

August 7th

Since the Queen learned the truth she has gone back into silence. Her melancholy has increased; she prays so long I wonder she can sustain herself upon her knees. And as she prays, she weeps. They said of her mother that, being deserted by her husband and bereft of child, the ground where she prayed was wet with her tears. Like mother, like daughter! Poor sad ladies, marrying each a husband younger than herself, and by that husband deserted, left to weep her heart away.

August 10th

After three days of silence the Queen has spoken to me. Today, after long praying, she said, 'I see God's plan clear. The King's unfaithfulness is my punishment, and his sins I must take upon myself. I have not been forward enough in God's business. I was ever more concerned with the suffering of the flesh in the fire, forgetting the suffering of the soul in the eternal fire. Twice God warned me; twice He withheld the promised child. It is my just punishment. Now I ask nothing but that my sin be visited upon me, upon me, alone; now I expect nothing but to do His work. And that work I will urge on without respite, making up for time lost. All heretics shall burn. And since God is debonair, maybe he will forgive me!'

'Madam, always you have done God's work; and have suffered for it, sometimes at the risk of your life. I think He has little to forgive!'

'I wish I might believe you!' she said.

The Queen has sent for the Cardinal; not this time as cousin and adviser, but as Primate of England. She has sent, also, for her Council, and her commands to Parliament. Every priest and judge, every sheriff and officer—and, indeed, every man whatsoever, though he hold no office—must be forward in God's business. He must act, not in spite, but in duty to God and his fellow-men. Every heretic to the stake. No more playing at mercy; for with God, alone, is mercy.

August 11th

The weather continues wet and cold. Last summer brought good harvest. One good harvest in three! Prices rise yet higher, and the people are more bitter than ever. It is not the dear food, alone, that is responsible; but it plays its part. The people have gone hungry before and have tightened their belts, without undue bitterness. In the past, the bad harvests were considered the will of God; they are still considered the will of God—His judgment upon the Queen. It is the burning; the continual, the terrible burning. I am, I hope, a good Catholic. I know it is right to burn out heresies; but to burn out heresies and to burn heretics, are two different things. To burn human flesh I find, God forgive me, hateful and horrible. Maybe I have lived too long with a merciful Queen; yet it is this same Queen commands all.

Every day she asks for news of God's Work by which alone, she lives. How many have gone to the fire? How many saved for God? How many lost to the Devil? She scans the daily lists, she nods, she smiles, she seems well-satisfied. '*Fire burns corruption from the heart. False mercy is cruelty!* Gardiner said that long ago! It is a lesson hard to learn; I think I have mastered it at last. I think God will forgive me and send me a child!' She tells me this over and over again, speaking as though she has said it never before. I wonder, at times, whether sorrow has not stolen from her wits; ever since she talked with Madam Elizabeth I have wondered. For in every other thing she is gentle and loving; in this, alone, she cannot be moved.

August 12th

Today the Queen sent for me. I found her, as usual, at her restless pacing. I am used to her sick looks, yet I found myself profoundly shocked at her face, grey as ash, the skin no more than a thin covering upon the bones; she was, even more than usual distressed. She said, thin hands pressed upon thin bosom, 'There's a fellow in Hampshire, as arrant a heretic as ever breathed. He had a fair trial—God will not forgive those that sentence without just cause! They did, indeed, strive to the uttermost to save him; I think my sheriffs grow weary in God's business! But the man was obstinate to burn. Now! The very wood lit, the fellow cries out he is of the true faith; he believes in the real Presence, he recognises obedience to the Pope! So, out goes the fire and the sheriff returns him to prison unscathed.'

'The sheriff can do no other,' I reminded her. 'Madam, it is the custom.'

'But not the *law*. Nor shall it any longer be the custom. Already too many heretics have slipped through our hands. This fellow lied in the face of God Himself. How shall this poor country suffer if we allow Him to be mocked by such fellows! Sit down, my girl, and write!'

So down I sat and she, still wandering the room, dictated.

'Address it to *Sir Richard Pearsall, Sheriff of the county of Hampshire.* Are you ready?

> The Queen's Majesty cannot but find it very strange that the sheriff has stayed one, Bembridge, from execution, the man being condemned for heresy. Therefore, Sir Richard is straitly commanded to cause him to be executed out of hand. And, if he still continues in the Catholic faith, as he outwardly pretends, then suffer some such learned and discreet man as the Bishop of Winchester shall appoint, to have access unto him for the better confirmation of the Catholic faith; and to be present, also, with him at his death for the better aiding of him to die God's servant. The said sheriff is commanded to repair hither immediately after the execution to answer the doings therein. . . .'

I looked at her appalled. The man had confessed his sin, had come back into the Faith. She said—and she was smiling the curious, rather frightening smile I have seen more than once of late—'There has been overmuch lying when the fire begins to bite; men forget that other fire which bites more cruel and lasts to all eternity. I make provision for his soul. I send him a good priest. Is that not true mercy?'

She crossed to the table, she took up the pen, wincing with the pain of her swollen hand; she looked up from her laborious signing. 'Leave me, my girl!' she said.

I sent to beg audience of the lord Cardinal; in other circumstances I had not dared. But I would not have the repentant sinner suffer; nor, since the man had recanted, dare I let the Queen, sick in mind as in body, take his death upon her soul.

The lord Cardinal has just come from the Queen; he looks a frail and troubled man. To my mind it is a question which of those two shall first come to his death. He said, as he came through the ante-room where I sat alone, 'You did right to send for me, my child. The Queen is ill; we have driven her too far, the Church and I . . . too far, too far!'

'And the condemned man!' I dared to ask.

He smiled that rare smile of his. 'Rest assured no wrong shall be done!'

I knelt to kiss his ring; he laid his hand upon my head in blessing. 'You have put aside your own happiness to serve the Queen. God shall reward you!'

Since she dictated that letter the Queen has been more herself. She has done what she believes to be right; and the Cardinal has assured her she need trouble herself no further in the matter. She may safely leave it to her church; he, himself, will answer for it. It is as though an intolerable burden has been lifted from her heart.

Although she is calmer, she is still bitterly unhappy; no place can hold happiness for her now, least of all Hampton Court. Here she suffered her most grievous losses, twice bereft of the hope of a child. Here, driven still by that same hope, she whipped herself beyond her strength to please God; whipped herself almost into a madness but that, the Cardinal, absolving her, gave her some peace. God grant it may continue.

August 28th

This day we removed to Whitehall. The longing was on her to see London again, her London; and, last flicker of her dying powers, to busy herself once more in matters of state. Yesterday I was, myself, indisposed; it was nothing but woman's sickness. I must have looked poorly for the Queen would not suffer me to go by water but sent her own litter, with her own physician for my comfort. Being arrived at Whitehall, she asked, as soon as she had set foot on land, whether I had arrived and how I did. And I, having hastened to the water-stairs to greet her, was able to assure her, from my own lips, that, owing to her kindness, I was recovered and well.

'So am not I!' she said, and I could have wept for the pitiful, shrunken look of her.

September 12th

The Queen continues low in mind and body. Alas for riding through London in state, alas for transacting business! She keeps her chamber; the fits of darkness fall more often, last longer; yet recovering, her wits are clear enough.

We heard today that the King is negotiating a peace with France. God send good may come of it! The war has dragged on too long. The Council waited upon the Queen to inform her of the matter, for she is not well enough to leave her chamber.

'No!' she says. 'No peace, unless they give back Calais!'

'Madam, that they will never do! There had been peace long ere this but for Calais. Calais is the stumbling-block!'

'Then we must go on stumbling!' she says.

'Madam,' Heath informs her, 'the Pope has written to you and to the King, and to the King of France. He demands the war shall end. He asks, *What are true Christians doing fighting each other? They should be fighting heretics*. The Queen has seen the letter for herself!'

'Yes,' she says. 'I think so . . . or, perhaps . . . no. I do not remember. The Pope demands peace? Then we are bound to obey. But Calais is a high price to pay. We must haggle a bit, first.'

The Council bow themselves away; she turns to me her worn face radiant. 'When the peace is made, the King will come home!' she says. 'I had given up hope; but now I do my duty by God and my faith, He has remembered me!' I think she has forgotten about Calais.

September 14th

Three days ago the Emperor died in his monastery at Yuste. He died peacefully, in an odour of sanctity he had not, for all his great title, attained to in life. We feared for the Queen, how she would take the news; we need not have feared. It was the Cardinal broke it to her. 'She took it very quiet,' he told us. 'It was as though God had already whispered in her ear. We knelt and prayed together for his soul.'

A little later she sent for me. She was smiling a little, her own good smile.

'The leaves fall,' she said. 'The last of those I knew in my childhood is gone. I was betrothed to him once; I was four years old. The Emperor—he was that even then—was twenty-four. Full young to bear so much glory! So old he seemed to me then so *old*! Yet a few days ago it seemed we were old together. Now he will grow old no more. . . .'

She went on; but now she spoke not to me, but to her own heart.

'A tall young man he was, fair of colouring; an Englishman you might have thought him. He was kind. He would talk with me, play at draughts with me, listen to my music, which was kind indeed! For though they reckoned me an accomplished musician, I was but four years old! And I could never sing. I loved him as a good child loves a kind father!

'I remember the day lady Salisbury—the Cardinal's mother you know; she was my lady governor—told me he had married Portugal. I was nine years old—and nothing hurt but pride; and that did smart, I do assure you! And then, a year later, Philip was born . . . and I did not know the blessing that birth should bring to me.

'The Emperor; from the time I was four years old, I never saw him again. But he has been my life-long friend. He watched over me, he saved me from the worst of my father's punishments, he sent me good advice; he bade his ambassadors, before all things, stand my friend. Twice, when my life was in danger because I'd not forswear my faith, he planned my escape—though it might have involved all Christendom in war; but I was a coward and would not leave. Now he is dead and I am his son's wife.' She paused; she said with a small smile, 'My father never meant I should marry. I was thrust in and out of betrothals—so many you cannot think! I was the pawn upon his chessboard; but that his pawn should become a Queen! Nothing was further from his purpose. And so I must wait for my marriage; I pray God it has not come too late.'

September 30th

Peace. Peace at last! On the Somme, the King of England and the King of France have come to terms. There has been much haggling, much acrimony; and how long the peace will last God alone knows! The Queen cannot speak her joy. She lies back in the great chair smiling. *Soon!* she says. *Soon he will be home!* And, for myself, I do pray it, also. We, too, have waited long, my betrothed and I.

All this time Madam Elizabeth remains quiet at Hatfield. She sends no congratulations upon the peace, nor hope for the King's return. She sends no word, neither, of greeting nor enquiry as to the Queen's health—though she knows full well the Queen's condition. She knows, too, that she, herself, has aggravated it by the anguish she caused at their last meeting. Maybe it is lack of heart; maybe, discretion. Madam Elizabeth must not appear too anxious. She knows well this is the Queen's last illness. She knows she has but to sit still and the crown will fall into her lap. She knows with absolute certainty that, should the Queen name Mary Stuart—or any other—Parliament will still give the crown to Anne Bullen's daughter. Even a blind man may see which way the wind blows! Every day there's a trooping to Hatfield; it is not only every least courtier on the make, but peers and high officers of State—the Queen's own Council together with members of Parliament, both Houses. Already they pay her the respect due to a reigning Queen; and, like a reigning Queen, she accepts it.

October 15th

There is no news of the King's return; he is in Brussels, enjoying himself, no doubt, after his labours. The Queen says nothing on the matter; I think she no longer looks for his return. She keeps her room; the dark fits of not-knowing fall upon her so often, and last so long, there are days when she is scarce recovered from one before she falls into another. Sometimes whole days pass and she lies blind, unhearing, speechless. Other days she crouches upon the floor and weeps; weeps for the days lost in darkness. There are, however, some days when she is herself; but always she is in a fever, hot to the touch and shaking a little with cold, though the room is warm. She sleeps little and eats less; she will take, perhaps, a sip of wine or a morsel of bread. She is burning herself away with longing for the husband that could come and does not come.

Once she said to me, 'I should have heeded my mother's warning. *Never wed a man younger than yourself, never mind how little the difference. For every day the difference widens. You do not notice it; but he, he does. And then—one day, there's a chasm neither of you can cross.* But the difference between my husband and me is not little. Eleven years. Too much . . . too much. . . .' And once she said, 'I was a pretty girl, so pretty! *The desire of all eyes* they called me. And two men truly loved me; the King of Scots and the Duke of Bavaria. Both offered for me—and no dowry! But my father would not let me wed, ever. . . .'

She sends for Philip, sends and sends again; but there are affairs, it seems, of more weight than a dying wife.

The succession troubles her still. It keeps her from her rest. 'If I could believe Anne Bullen's daughter my father's daughter, also, I should learn to make myself content. That she is a bastard, born of an infamous woman, would weigh less against that! So long as she was my father's child, so long as she uphold the true faith in this land, I am content she should have the crown.'

October 28th

This day the Queen has added a codicil to her will. She sent for her secretary and bade me stay that he might read it aloud so we might judge, all three, that there's no misunderstanding nor other fault therein.

Slow and clear he began.

The codicil made by me, Mary, Queen of England. . . .

. . . I then thought myself to be with child and did devise and dispose of the Imperial crown of the Realm of England and the crown of Ireland, with my title to France and all the dependencies thereof; and all other honours, castles, fortresses and perogatives belonging to the Crown, unto the heirs, issue and fruit of my body begot.

Forasmuch as God has hitherto sent me no heir of my body, it is yet only in His most divine Providence whether I shall have any or no. . . .

Does she not know she is mortally sick? Does she, even at this last, wait for some divine assurance?

She asks that the law of this land and the true faith be observed. From her successor she turns to her husband. She knows well that, in default of heirs of her body, her most dear husband can have no further governance in this country. Yet she beseeches him, by the great love she bears him and the humble duty she has always given him, to show friendship for England.

> . . . as God shall reward him, I pray it may please his Highness to show himself as a father in his care, or as a brother, or member of this realm, in his love and favour; and that he show himself as a most assured friend in his power and strength to my successor and to my Country and the subjects of this realm. . . .

Throughout the long codicil she does not once name *who*—failing the heirs of her body—that successor shall be; she gives no hint, neither, whether it be man or woman. She cannot, it seems, bring herself to write the detested name; not because of old hatred—all bitterness is dead within her—but because she so greatly fears for the persecution of the Faith.

November 9th

Still the Queen waits and still the King does not come. Again he sends my betrothed in his stead. Don Gomez lifts my chin in his hand—a trick I love in him—and says I look tired. I tell him I am well enough. 'And though your coming gives me great joy, God be my witness, I had rather the King came instead!'

'The King has sent his own physicians,' he says.

'What then?' I cry out, passionate in my grief for her. 'We have good physicians enough! Does the King not understand she is *dying*? The only thing she needs now is the sight of his face, the touch of his hand. And these I fear she'll know never again!'

I look into his face and there I see no hope.

'Have you not, at the least, a letter?' and my voice beseeches him.

'I have a letter; but it is not for the Queen; it is for the Council. It contains his pleasure that Madam Elizabeth shall succeed; and that she marry a husband of her own choosing.'

'I fancy I know the husband she has in mind . . . and it is not Savoy!'

He says nothing to that. Instead, 'I have also a commission to Madam Elizabeth herself. I am to say that the King is on his knees before her and prays her wait a little in her marriage.'

'I see now why he does not come!' I say. 'He cannot face the Queen. Her true eyes would pierce to his secret heart.'

'It is in my mind also. I think husband and sister wait, both of them, the day when the cry goes out *La Reine est morte, vive la Reine!* I fancy nothing will stay him then hurrying back to the Queen of England!

'It is in *my* mind,' I tell him, 'that he'll get little from that! She'll not keep to any understanding between them—if understanding there be! She'll not wed with a foreigner, least of all with Spain. She sees what it is when a Queen loses the love of her people. That love she has now and means to keep it. Yet, for all that it may suit her to encourage the King; she has, I believe, a perverse desire to triumph over the Queen; a pleasure in the Queen's pain—for the Queen knows, in her heart, where the King's eyes stray. Whenever the lady Elizabeth was present, he could not keep his eyes from her! I saw it for myself when all three said Farewell at Greenwich. And she? Her glance, too, I caught. There is, I know not how to put it—a sort of love-hate between them.'

'You put it perfectly,' he says.

'But whatever there may be between them, she'll never have him!' I tell Don Gomez. 'And if she does not take him for husband, then she'll take him for enemy! I know her! He'll rue the day he commended her succession. Then he'll remember the woman that loved him utterly, that laid heart and will, crown, and all England beneath his feet.'

November 10th

The Queen has given way at last. Madam Elizabeth has come to my lord Clinton's house without the city; to be in at the death I must suppose.

Don Gomez, on his master's instructions, has visited her; he had never set eyes on her before. She received him with a cool courtesy. He finds her clever; too clever. He finds her royal and commanding, vain and proud; he finds her subtle and untruthful. 'Never were sisters so unlike,' he says. 'Of any understanding between her and the King, she is all bland ignorance. She thanked him for his kindness concerning her marriage and assured me she had no desire to change her present state. She observed, by the way as it seemed, how much favour the Queen had lost by marriage with a foreigner—even so illustrious a foreigner as the King of Spain. The message—that he is on his knees before her—she received smiling and made no comment. I asked her, roundabout, what faith she professed, and she answered as roundabout, *The true faith naturally*; and fixed those bold eyes upon me daring me to make further question, and I swear there was mockery in them. She will bring all England back to its heresies. She will make this a completely heretic country.'

'Then God pity poor Catholics! She will punish, and not for the sake of conscience; no, but to even the score!'

'Certainly this will become a heretic country; but its God will be a woman. She will punish and reward for one faith only—that which serves its goddess-Queen best!'

November 12th

There is death in the Queen's face. She knows it is time to name her successor. Today she sent several gentlemen of the Council to bid Madam Elizabeth declare her faith. This time there was no evasion. *I will uphold and maintain the Catholic faith according to my promise.* The lie direct; or else a forswearing of her friends. Well, what's a lie to her, or a breaking of faith, if it bring the crown? But if it bring peace to my dying mistress I'll not quarrel with it.

'Then I name her my successor, praying God she keep her word,' the Queen said and summoned a full Council. Rising from her bed, she had herself dressed that she might herself inform them as to her decision.

'Pray God I have done right!' she said to me when once more she lay exhausted in her bed. 'But, if I have not—it is all one! They will make her Queen in spite of me! She always knew how to be first with everyone, even with my dear lady Anne of Cleves. She said once—the lady Anne—*I had rather be mother to the little Elizabeth than Queen of England*. But for all that she left me her best jewel, to my sister, the second-best.' And she smiled a little.

I think that last memory stirred some fancy within her, for late in the afternoon, she sent me to Somerset House, Madam Elizabeth having removed into London itself. An omen that!

'Take this casket,' the Queen told me. She lifted the lid and I saw it held her own personal jewels. 'Give it to her—a token of good faith between us. Tell her to keep her promise to uphold the Faith, in this dear land; tell her to be good to my servants, tell her to pay my debts!'

It was not a happy errand. I cannot like the lady; nor, I think, can the most part of women. More even than the deceit and treachery with which she has troubled my mistress, I hate the coldness she has shown. Never once has she enquired of the Queen's health nor sent a loving word in her most bitter disappointment.

Madam Elizabeth received me with the coldness I had expected. She was the hard, bright, calculating creature I have always known; nor did she seem young to me that have four years less than she. Always she carried herself most royal; now there was about her an air of majesty triumphant. She received the casket with seeming indifference and bade her woman put it by. But the gleam in her eye told me that, the moment I was gone, her fingers would be among the jewels weighing up the value of this piece and that.

She bade me thank my mistress and take back with me assurance of her faith, 'which the Queen will prize above any jewel'. She is not one, the lady Elizabeth, to give freely, save words; which she uses as counterfeit instead of true coin. There was, as she spoke, a faint smile touching her mouth, as though to ask *Can even the Queen be so simple as to believe this promise of mine?*

I am grieved to the heart's core for my Queen. All those things for which she has suffered, all she believes, all she desires—to be swept away; so much rubbish! I was glad to leave that bright, relentless presence. When all is over I shall be happy to leave England, if only never to see that face again.

My mistress cannot die in peace. She is greatly troubled that Madam Elizabeth will not keep her word. *Have I betrayed God?* she asks again and again. She has sent for her cousin, the Cardinal. For, the first time he must fail her; he lies sick in his bed, his death-bed, some say. Whose soul shall seek God first?

November 13th

The Queen is too weak to rise. She lies in her bed, quiet and peaceful. The priest recites the Mass, and she listens, her lips moving in prayer. There is no more darkness in her mind, nor any confusion. She speaks little and knows perfectly what she says. But, for the most part, she lies silent, thinking, as she tells me, of those friends that are faithful still. How few they are, she does not, God be thanked, know. For the court does not stint its daily worship at Somerset House, so that the Queen dying, Madam Elizabeth untimely holds full court. My mistress is loving and grateful to us all. Today she said, 'Oh Jane, my dear, I should have hastened your marriage. Happiness is not to be wasted; not a single day, a single hour, a single minute!'

'So much is true,' I told her. 'And my happiness is to be with the Queen!'

I think she did not hear, for she went on, 'It was not only for my own sake that I kept you here—though what I should have done without you, I do not know! It was for your sake, too. I thought the King would come home. I thought we would give you the wedding you deserve; the wedding I would have given my own daughter had God so blessed me!' And it was pitiful, the longing in her face for the child she will never have and the husband she will never see.

November 14th

We are moving towards the end. There is a change in the Queen's face; the features are sharpened, even the nose, the small, short nose, standing out high. She lies, for the most part, still; whether she lies insensible, whether she sleeps, whether her mind is clear, it is not always possible to say. Now and again she opens her eyes but I think she does not see this world. When she speaks her voice is very low, scarce to be heard. Once I heard her whisper *It is a child to gladden any father's heart* and her hand moved across the sheet as though she were writing. I thought, at first, it was to her husband she wrote, of the child she has never borne. Then I understood she was back in her girlhood and it was Elizabeth of whom she spoke; for she said, shaking her head the while, *No caps nor kerchiefs nor petticoats nor smocks. Write, write to* . . . But she has forgotten Mr. Secretary's name; Cromwell that shadowed her whole young life.

This afternoon she awoke; her eyes were clear and she perfectly in her right mind; but still that mind dwelt upon the past.

'He was a loving child, my brother. When he was small he would pull at my skirts and lift his little arms to come to me. But they took him from the hands of the women—and he but four, or five perhaps . . . too young, too young! And the Council shaped him to their own ends; and especially those two that called themselves *Protectors*, but all they protected was themselves, certainly not the child that, between them, they brought to his death; nor yet the country they delivered up to heresy! That poor child! He must not move, so it seemed, without leave of Protector Somerset, his *dearest* uncle. He dared not breathe save by Protector Northumberland's favour; nor, in the end, save that man gave the nod, dared the sick child die in peace. Between them Somerset and Northumberland flawed the pure jewel and brought all England into danger of damnation.'

She lay silent. Then, 'Poor child,' she said, 'poor lost child! There's not a day or night but I pray for his soul! I think God will be merciful to a child over-young to understand his heresies, one that suffered much in his short life.'

November 16th

The Queen sleeps much and her dreams are happy. 'The happiness stays with me all day,' she says. 'In my dreams little children come and play and it is always summer. They pull at my skirts and lift their laughing faces to me where I sit, a child at my breast; and I am young and well and pretty. The children are mine, my own. And everywhere there's music and angel-voices praising God; and sweeter still, the laughter of children at play. I think that, sinner though I be, since I have shown myself obedient to save souls, God shows a kind face. He gives me a foretaste of Paradise.'

The dreaming hours are long, the waking hours short; the dreams will last longer, the waking shorter, until it is granted her to fall asleep. And since her dreams are filled with the laughter of children, her own children, God in His own way, grants her her heart's desire.

This evening she said to me, 'My life has been, as it were, a long, dark tunnel. When I was a child I played in the sunshine. Then the tunnel closed in on me, and there was no way but through it. Long and dark, cold and lonely . . . dear God, how lonely! And now I see daylight at the other end. Soon, God willing, I shall come out into the sunshine again.'

November 17th

This day at six o'clock in the morning, my Queen rendered her spirit unto God. She was forty-two years old.

Every day the Mass has been recited in her bedchamber; and, though sick unto death, she listened with devotion; and always made the responses with him that served the priest; never once did she fail though the words came slower. The Mass that nourished her childhood did not fail her now.

It was still the dark of the morning when she heard the Mass for the last time. When the priest recited *Agnus Dei qui tollis peccati mundi,* she answered weak but clear, *Misere nobis, misere nobis, misere nobis, dona nobis pacem.* When he lifted the sacred Host she adored it with her failing sight. Then her eyelids fell, gently, without so much as a sigh, she that had known so much sorrow, so much pain, slipped from this life into life eternal.

With the coming of full day, a pale gleam of winter sun lay like a blessing upon her dead face. I take it as a sign. Her purgatory was here on earth; and I doubt not that, as her dying eyes closed upon the sacred Host and opened upon life eternal, she saw her Saviour in all His glory. And I like to believe, also, that there came to meet her the souls of little children to bid her welcome and bring her into Heaven.

This same day, towards evening, died the Cardinal, her cousin. When the new Queen heard the news, with never a decent show of grief, she cried out in the Latin tongue and her voice was a trumpet, *This is the Lord's doing and it is marvellous in our eyes!* Marvellous indeed for her that had gained a crown and lost two adversaries in the same day! But for those two, more marvellous still. For he, also, having suffered his purgatory on earth, I doubt not their pure souls met before the footstool of God, wearing each his eternal crown.

December 12th

My Queen's body lay in state at St. James's until today, when it was carried in funeral procession to Westminster. Leading the great procession walked a company of mourners, bearing the banner of her device—the falcon and the hart; thereafter followed her husband's gentlemen clad all in black, walking two by two, and carrying the joint device of King and Queen—the falcon and the lion. There followed our own English knights, all in mourning, the esquires carrying their masters' banners of arms. Now came my lord marquis of Winchester, Paulet, high upon a black horse, carrying aloft the royal arms of England. Behind him, also high upon black steeds rode

Chester, Norroy and Clarence Heralds, the first bearing the Helm, Crest and Mantle, the second the Garter and Crown, the third the Sword. A little space, and there came slow-walking the great lords of the realm led by Somerset, Lancaster and Windsor Heralds, bearing all three, a white banner worked with saints all of gold.

Now came that for which all waited; the funeral carriage. On the black-covered coffin lay an image of the dead Queen clad in crimson and crowned. Beneath the royal robes the image wore—as of late she herself had worn—the robes of a religious. And there you have the whole character of the woman! Royal to the outward eye; but in her heart, the humblest of God's creatures. From the waist, downwards, flowed a quilt of cloth-of-gold worked with a great cross of silver. And, at the sight of the dead Queen, all angers forgotten, a great sigh arose like the moving of wind in the trees.

Immediately behind the dead Queen came the living Queen; she led a bevy of ladies and all of us in black gowns that flowed from saddle to ground. And I, riding slow with the rest, spoke to the new Queen in my thoughts, *You make a show of grief now because it is proper, but who can forget how you received the news of her death?*

Behind me, Heath, archbishop of York, led his bishops, priests and monks, in his degree and all of them chanting. And so we came, very slow, to the Abbey; and there waited my lords of the Council to take the Queen's coffin and carry it within. And with them waited four bishops to cense the body. All, all come to pay her the last honours, from the highest walking in procession, to those that waited, patient, in the winter cold; all save him that should be chiefest mourner of us all.

Nightlong she lay before the high altar where her noblest peers together with a hundred poor, good men in new gowns of black, kept their watch. High peers and humble men keeping watch together; it was what she would have wished.

December 13th

Today a Requiem Mass was held and the lord bishop of Winchester preached the funeral sermon.

'She was a King's daughter, she was a King's sister, she was a King's wife. She was a Queen; and by that same title, a King, also. What she suffered in each of these three degrees, I will now chronicle.'

And so he held before the eyes of men her patience, her compassion, her truth to the given word, and, above all, her steadfast love of God—a love that never doubted, never faltered however desperate and dangerous her condition.

'... She was never unmindful of her promise to this realm. She used singular mercy towards offenders, she used much pity and compassion towards the poor and oppressed, she used clemency towards her nobles. She restored more holy houses than ever did any prince of this realm; she restored to the Church property and such ornaments as were taken away and spoiled.

'She found this realm poisoned with heresy and purged it. Such was her knowledge and virtue there was never a prince on earth that had more of both....'

This and a great deal more; and all, all of it true. Never a prince like her for mercy, for compassion, for love of God and man.

December 14th

The new Queen loses no time in showing her true colours. The good bishop's speech displeasing her, she sent this day bidding him keep his house until her further pleasure be known. How long she will keep him there, or in some worse place, who can say? But of this one thing I am certain; though he spoke no more than truth, for praising the dead Queen she will forgive him never.

January 1559

Madam Queen Elizabeth has already broken the sworn oath made to the dying Queen—the oath that won my Queen's consent to the crown. She openly turns her back upon the true faith, she favours none that showed kindness to her sister. The good bishop she kept imprisoned a full month and then sent back to his see under her sovereign displeasure. Certain it is that her displeasure will last until she have need of him; and, if she have none, he shall lie beneath her anger all the days of his life.

Durham House. February 18th

I write this in the house leased by the Queen to the Spanish embassy; and I write it remembering the day of my Queen's birth. Whoever dare remember it openly shall surely be punished.

As soon as might be after her death we were married, Don Gomez and I; not with the high ceremony my Queen had wished, but very quiet, lest we bring upon ourselves yet more the anger of this new Queen. She shows herself passionate against all those that loved her sister—even those that are too weak to help themselves—old Clarencieux, and my own grandmother whom she never saw. All, all bear the weight of her anger—and especially my husband and I; he because my Queen trusted him, myself because she loved me. Madam the Queen slights and humiliates him in private audience and in public. He is minded to endure these insults no longer; nor allow me to remain at a court where I can, at best, expect no good and where at worst . . .

May 30th

My husband has left England and is now in Brussels where I am soon to join him. I remain behind to see that this house is in fitting order for the new ambassador; then my husband's kinsman, Don Juan de Ayala, will escort me to Brussels; for, thanks be to God, I am expecting a child. We are trying for a licence for my grandmother and for old Clarencieux; if not, we shall somehow smuggle them out of the country, that they may live out their few years in peace.

I shall be glad to leave England. I could not, for all my love of this country, be happy here again. For now Madam Elizabeth has all—her sister's crown and all that to it appertains; and, if she will, her sister's husband, also. Less than a month after my Queen's death, he was paying court to the new Queen; as still he does. He is in love as far as his nature allows, which is not much. And he is very much aware of every advantage a young, lusty wife may bring—especially if she be a Queen in her own right. And she? She is both drawn and repelled. She'll not have him; so she says and so she means. The sooner he understands this the better; for she will always be his enemy—an enemy quicker and cleverer than he. She knows how many beans make five; he will always try to make them six or seven. She is also completely unprincipled; she will, when it suits her, deny the broken promise with a smooth tongue. Let Philip look to himself!

Brussels. September 20th

Philip has, indeed, looked to himself. He no longer sues for Madam

Queen Elizabeth; he is to wed another Elizabeth, daughter to the King of France. The Queen is piqued. She swears it is a trick with a double edge—to blind France as to Philip's real intent—herself; and, at the same time, to make her jealous. She may have him, she says, any time she will. But she knows, as all Christendom knows, that time is passed; she lies to hide her humiliation. Philip is well rid ofher . . . and England has lost the chance of a great alliance, great riches and a great empire.

October 14th
Ten days ago, praise God and the blessed Virgin, I gave birth to a fine boy that shall, please God, inherit his father's virtues, his high looks, his honours, and his titles. My Queen would have loved this little one for she loved children, always. As soon as I am strong we leave for Spain; Clarencieux and my grandmother go with us—we managed to smuggle them out of England.

Aboard the Sancta Maria. *February 18th, 1560*
I write this once again on the day of my Queen's birth, being wishful to remember the day she was born, rather than the day she died. The winter months have been rough, the seas high; not fit to set out to sea with so young a child as mine. Now the weather is calm and we have ventured the journey. Soon I shall set foot upon the land my Queen so longed to see. Now England is no longer my country; but shall I ever forget England, her sharp springs and her gentle summers; forget kinsfolk and friends and the happy places of childhood . . . and the bitter-sweet days when I served my Queen?

Now my faith is brought low and my Queen execrated, all her goodness, her kindness, forgotten. Even her last wishes, so clearly set out in her will, are ignored; even her heart's desire that she should lie beside her beloved mother. My Queen lies alone in her grave; in Peterborough, Madam Queen Catherine lies in hers. Every day we hear of this one or that who, speaking good of the late Queen, comes to his punishment, who, speaking ill of her, creeps into the new Queen's favour. There is none dare speak of the good Queen a good word. But of ill words there are plenty. She that was merciful bears the name *bloody*. Then let me lift my voice that one day, when we now living are dust, I may be heard speaking clear.

She was passionate in her love of God; she was compassionate to men and women, loving especially the poor and the humble; and most of all, the children. The constant burnings wasted her—body and spirit, and all-but broke her heart. It was not individual souls, alone, she must save, but the whole land to her entrusted. So her church told her; and so obedient, into her church's hand, she put her will and conscience. And this obedience was her greatest sacrifice.

My Queen had a sad life; but always she accepted her sorrows as from God. And I believe that dying, her spirit was straight-way accepted of God. Though every heretic in Christendom blacken her memory, let my words stand to do her justice. And, since in the end, truth must prevail, I believe that some day, good men and women, howsoever they may worship, will add their voices to my own.

Some books consulted

BURNET, G. *A History of the Reformation of the Church of England.* Vol. I (1679).

CAUSTON, H. K. S. *The Howard Papers* (1862).

CLIFFORD, H. *The Life of Jane Dormer, Duchess of Feria* . . . transcribed from the ancient manuscript in the possession of the Lord Dormer by E. E. Estcourt and edited by J. Stevenson (Burns & Oates, 1886).

FRIEDMANN, P. *Ann Boleyn.* 2 vols. (Macmillan, 1884).

FROUDE, J. A. *History of England.* 10 vols. (1910–13).

FULLER, T. *History of the worthies of England* (1668).

HOWELL, T. B. (ed.). Cobbett's complete collection of *State Trials.* Vol. I (1816).

MACKIE, J. D. *The earlier Tudors* (Clarendon Press, 1952).

MANNING, C. R. (ed.) *Bedingfield Papers.* Norfolk & Norwich Archaeological Society Transactions. Vol 4 (1885).

NEALE, J. E. *Queen Elizabeth* (Cape, 1934).

NICHOLS, J. G. (ed.) *The Chronicle of Queen Jane.* Camden Society. O.S. 48 (1850).

NICHOLS, J. G. (ed.) *Literary remains of Edward VI.* 2 vols. (Roxburghe, 1857).

NICHOLS, J. G. (ed.) *Narratives of the days of the Reformation.* Camden Society. O.S. 77 (1859). Includes the narrative of Edward Underhill and the life and death of Thomas Cranmer.

POLLARD, A. F. *Henry VIII* (Longmans Green, 1951).

PRESCOTT, H. F. M. *Mary Tudor* (Eyre & Spottiswoode, 1962).

PROCTOR, J. *History of Wyatt's rebellion.* Antiquarian Repertory. Vol. 3, pp. 72–73 (1807–9).

STONE, J. M. *History of Mary I, Queen of England* (Sands & Co., 1901).

STOW, J. *Annales* begun by John Stow and continued by Edmund Howes (1631).

STRICKLAND, A. *Lives of the Queens of England.* 8 vols. (1851).

STRYPE, J. *Memorials of . . . Thomas Cranmer.* 2 vols. (1840).

WARE, SIR J. *Rerum Hibernicarum Annales* (1664).

WHITE, B. M. I. *Mary Tudor* (Macmillan, 1935).
WRIOTHESLEY, C. *A Chronicle of England* by Charles Wriothesley, Windsor Herald. Vol. I. Camden Society. N.S. 11 (1875).

State papers

Calendar of State papers. Spanish. 1553–58, 1558–60. Vol. 12 (1949).
Calendar of State papers. Venetian. 1553–58, 1558–60.
State papers during the reign of Henry VIII. Vol. I. (1830).
Acts of the Privy Council. 1558.
Dictionary of National Biography.
Encyclopaedia Britannica.

Author's note

The 'extracts from the diary' of Jane Dormer are fictitious but never imagined; although I have drawn far less on the diary than on the Spanish Calendar 1557–60, the content is historically correct. For example, the treatment of Don Gomez and Jane by Elizabeth; the smuggling of old Clarencieux and Jane's grandmother out of England; the departure of Don Gomez himself from England in a rage at Elizabeth's rudeness, while Jane had to stay behind to prepare the embassy for his successor; the birth of Jane's child and her setting out for Spain in the *Sancta Maria* are all to be found in the Spanish Calendar. The device has been designed to be true in fact and character.

If you would like a complete list of Arrow books please send a postcard to P.O. Box 29, Douglas, Isle of Man, Great Britain.